Rock Creek

Rock Creek

Kevin Flynn

Kilimanjaro Press
Richmond, Virginia

The content associated with this book is the sole work and responsibility of the author.

Rock Creek

Published by Kilimanjaro Press
Richmond, VA
kilimanjaro-press.com

Excerpts from lyrics to "No Other Love" are printed herein with the kind permission of Hanover Music Corp.

Cover art and design by Leah Meddaoui

Library of Congress Control Number: 2024933682

ISBN (paperback): 9781662950186
ISBN (hardcover): 9781662950179
ISBN (ebook): 9781662950193

To my wife Patrice, and my children Connor and Megan: my world

In memory of my cousin Jack Reges: the first and best critic of this book

1947

With patience born of adversity, she sat motionless on the edge of her bed for over an hour, waiting for life in the rest of the house to settle into the night.

One by one lights were extinguished, doors closed, foot shuffle slowed to a stop and bedsprings groaned. She waited still longer to make sure it was safe to rise. Then she fumbled under the bed for a flashlight and trained the beam on everything she'd be taking from this place: a small suitcase, the clothes she'd be wearing on her back, a roadmap and a piece of cardboard that she'd inscribed with the words "Washington DC."

She put on the trousers, shirt and jacket that she'd secretly taken the day before from her uncle's closet, and felt the hard object in the right pants pocket. She drew eyeliner from the suitcase and traced a mustache on her upper lip, then tied her hair into a bun and topped it with one of her uncle's hats. She moved to a wall mirror, sized up the mustache in the flashlight's glare, and smudged it to give it some thickness. It'll do for the night, she decided. She finished packing the bag, with the last item being a locket with a photo of her sister, who'd finally gone to sleep in the room next to hers. She buckled the bag shut, wincing as the snap! snap! broke the silence.

She moved to the bedroom door and quietly closed it behind her.

"What are you doing in here! I'm calling the police!"

Her aunt was in the hallway, wide-eyed, backing away.

"It's me, auntie." She came closer to her aunt, who was shaking. "Don't worry, auntie, it's just me," she said, and embraced her until the shaking stopped.

"Why are you looking like that? And – what's in the bag?"

"I'm leaving, auntie. I need to go. I didn't want to wake you. I left you both a note – one for Leah too."

She drew her aunt to a living room chair and sat her down.

"Where are you going?"

"Far away, auntie."

"How are you getting there? Are you taking a train?"

"No."

"Why are you dressed like that?"

"Because I'm not taking a train. Or a bus either."

Her aunt reached for her purse on the living room table.

"And I'm not taking any money. I have to make my own way."

Her aunt started to cry. "Please don't, auntie. There's nothing more that you could've done. You gave us a home and that was everything."

"Is it the community here?"

She put her hands on her aunt's shoulders. "It's not what's been outside of me. It's what's been inside. But I'll see you again, for sure." Even as she said the words she knew they were a lie.

"Can I wake Leah?"

"No, this is difficult enough. Please tell her I'll be writing soon. And that I love her." Her eyes were burning and she brushed her uncle's jacket sleeve across them.

Outside, with everything she'd ever known at her back, she strode across Williamsburg Bridge and the world opened before her.

In Manhattan she took the subway to the west side and a ferry to New Jersey. From the boat the Statue of Liberty could be seen to the south, but she was focused on her wristwatch and her map and didn't raise her eyes to glance at it. It's barely past midnight, *she said to herself.* Get to a road called Route 1, take it for 225 miles, maybe get there by daybreak.

She disembarked at Hoboken Terminal. After the subway and ferry, her budget didn't allow for more travel expenses.

She came to a road with traffic and found an open stretch. She took position on the shoulder, pulled her hat down lower, and held up her "Washington DC" cardboard. Cars went by without even slowing and she started to despair. She began counting them as they passed and got up to 30, but the 31st slowed to a stop and then backed up to where she was.

"Hop in," the man said.

She thought, I haven't been inside an automobile in four years. At least this time I have some say in the matter.

"So I take it you're going to Washington, my man?"

My man, she thought. So far, at least, it's working.

She motioned to her mouth, shook her head, held up the cardboard and pointed to it.

"Can't talk?"

She pointed again to the cardboard.

"But you can definitely hear."

Another nod.

"Well, if you don't know it already, the best way is by Route 1."

Another nod, more vigorous.

"But this road ain't it. It's a ways from here. Good thing for you, I'm heading over that way. Bad thing, I can only take you as far as New Brunswick."

She took her map from her pocket. New Brunswick would leave her about as far away from where she wanted to go as she was right then, but she shrugged her shoulders and mouthed the word yes.

That's how her night flight went – a pick-up followed by a drop-off followed by a pick-up and then another drop-off, one town's sign ("Welcome to Princeton") soon followed by another ("Now Leaving Princeton, Now Entering Ewing"), over and over. For one 80-mile stretch her ride was with a boy, he couldn't have been more than 17, in a low-slung, fire engine-red coupe that made the trip in less than an hour. In the heedless, careening rush on open road there wasn't a moment when she felt fear. All she knew was that she was making up time.

Somewhere south of Philadelphia she kept company with five crates of poultry, live but not for long, in the back of a truck. There, surrounded by oblivious chickens, she had an impulse to take off her hat and let her hair loose *to the wind, but she didn't want to risk even for a minute exposing herself as a girl alone on a dark highway fraught with the potential for joy but also danger.*

Every place that she passed through raised more questions in her head. She stored them all away, to be returned to later, in all the time that was now opening out before her.

The poultry truck let her out in a town called Halethorpe, just below Baltimore. It'd gotten colder and was starting to snow lightly. She wished that she'd brought a heavier jacket and cursed herself for thinking it would be warmer as she went further south. She walked to a gas station that was closed, but its flashing "Esso" sign would illuminate her as she stood waiting. Out of the gauzy whiteness a car emerged, with headlights that looked like bulging eyes.

"Hey pardner, throw the bag in the back." The man's voice sounded kind.

She went through her now-practiced gestures feigning muteness and he was accepting, as all but one of her other pick-ups had been. (That one hadn't let her past the footboard, he'd just said something like, Ain't about to give transport to no dummy.) "It's a long road to Atlanta," this man said, "and I like to talk to myself to keep awake, and nobody's ever talking back to me, so it'll be fine."

He didn't have a jacket on, just a sleeveless undershirt, and his right arm was muscled and bore a tattoo of the U.S. flag. When he reached down to move the stick shift she could see that his right middle finger had a tattoo of a small cross. She passed her fingers across her right forearm.

"Gonna put on some music, OK?"

He turned on the radio and the dial magically lighted. He moved the knob back-and-forth, getting nothing other than squawks and squeaks, until a resonant voice filled the car.

In the Williamsburg community where she'd lived for a year, the place that had circumscribed her entire American existence, this kind of music wasn't common. She leaned into the lighted dial as if it were a flickering amber about to give rise to a flame.

She turned to the man, pointed at the dial, and shrugged her shoulders.

"Where you been, pardner? It's Frank's latest. Called 'What'll I Do?'"

It was the most beautiful song she'd ever heard. It was about someone who was missing a girl who'd gone away, and for a few moments it made her think of Leah, whether she'd gotten up yet, whether she'd read the note – and whether it had really come as much of a surprise. That thought was displaced by another: Who is this Frank, and how can I hear more of him?

"Nice song, huh?" the man said.

She didn't react, just stared at the radio dial. An announcer came on: "Next after commercial, another Sinatra great, this one from '43, you know it as 'Put Your Dreams Away.'"

"You know pardner," the man went on, "I've been reading that Frank's about to make another movie soon and he might be growing himself a mustache for it. And you and I just met, and just take this the right way of course. But I'm thinking you kind of have Sinatra's features, but if he had that mustache. Funny."

She wasn't paying attention.

The song started. It was about someone telling a woman she didn't have to dream anymore, they were there to love her.

The man broke in: "Don't know about you, but I put my dreams away a long time ago."

A slow-moving truck loomed ahead and the man reached to downshift, and his hand passed across her left knee, and she flinched.

"Sorry, pardner, this stick is finicky sometimes."

She moved further to the right, closer to the car door, and tried to listen to the song. The man coughed twice, looked in the rearview mirror, reached out again for the stick shift, then took his hand back.

"I wanna listen to something else now," he said. "And if you don't know Frank's latest songs you probably don't know this fella. But what you're gonna hear has a whole lot more truth to it than any fruity love ballad."

He worked his way through the dial, to a grainy snippet of a voice or a song, until he got to pure sounds.

"We're a country of immigrants," the radio voice was saying. "Your parents and grandparents and great-grandparents came here to live the American dream. We weren't the first ones here, and we all know that."

Outside the snow had picked up and wind was swirling loudly. She had to strain to hear. Then the wind died down.

"But we also know that everything's different now, don't we? When countries send us their people now, they're not sending their best, are they? We're getting people who aren't like you or me, we're getting people who have lots of problems. We're getting people who are criminals, petty thieves, rapists, murderers."

The radio voice faded and the man quickly fiddled with the knob to bring it back. "This fella's a minister with his own church," he said, "and every Sunday he has a service and they make a recording of it, and they play it on the radio at night. Far as I'm concerned, pardner, it's God's mouth to his ear and back out to us."

The radio voice came in stronger. "And let's talk next about the so-called displaced persons, the so-called refugees. Let's talk about the Jews who are trying to come into this country from all over the world."

Snow was piling up on the windshield and the small space to see through the glass was narrowing. The driver put his foot to the gas. "The part coming up's gonna be good."

"Let's talk," the radio voice said, "about the Jews who weren't in any camps, and don't you believe everything you read, because the newspapers lie. The Jews we're getting, they weren't in any camps, and now they're being sent here to destroy us from within. Do you want them here?"

In the background a swelling crescendo of churchgoers saying "NO" could be heard.

"And why don't we want them?"

"THEY'RE OUR ENEMIES!"

There were many things that she wanted to say – scream – at that moment, but all she could do was endure forced silence in the face of madness.

"Maybe I should've had these things on," the man said. He flipped the switch for the windshield wipers, eased back into his seat. But another swell from the crowd caught his attention.

"I see by the way you're acting," he said to her, "that maybe you're not listening close." He turned up the radio volume.

"And what will the Jews be taking from us?"

"OUR JOBS!"

The man started rocking back-and-forth, squeezing the steering wheel with both hands. "A fucking Jew is gonna take my job."

In the distance she saw a sign, "Riverdale Rest Stop." She remembered from her map that Riverdale, Maryland wasn't far from Washington – this could be a place where she could get out, move on.

The man started slowing the car down, as if he had the same idea. "Pardner, I know you can't talk, but I can tell from your face that you don't agree with any of this." He switched off the radio. "When we first started off on this drive I figured you were a wop, like Sinatra. But all the wops I know hate the Jews, just like the micks and the krauts and everybody else hates 'em. And you don't seem to. So now I know what you are. Which means this is where we part ways."

She welcomed the impersonal winter chill that she was about to return to.

As the man pulled into the rest stop she pointed to the backseat, at her suitcase.

The man lurched the car into a dark space that he seemed to know well. "Before I let you out, Jewboy, you've got to show some gratitude for the trip." He took her by the neck and forced her across the console, and the stick shift stabbed into her rib. She heard the sound of a zipper and her hat fell over her eyes, so at least she was spared from seeing what he brought out from his pants.

"Get on it, Jewboy. Get right on it or you don't get out."

He pressed her on top of it and she felt its slime against her face. The man's hand tightened against her neck, she started to gasp, but she didn't want to open her mouth to get breath.

Her right hand was caught up in her uncle's jacket but she got it free, searched around in the pocket.

She felt herself starting to suffocate. I'll die first, she thought. The man gripped harder and moved her head around in circles.

She got her hand on the hard object in her uncle's jacket, yanked it out and put it to the man's crotch.

Even with her face muffled she got the words out loudly: "I've fired one of these before."

Actually, she never had.

"I've fired one of these before and I will now, if you don't let me go." She thrust the gun deep into the man's groin and worked it around, relishing his groans of pain.

He slowly backed up against the driver side door and his elbow tripped the handle, which turned on the overhead light. He stared at her: hat off, hair undone, with a gun pressed against all he needed to spawn offspring that would carry his hatred into the future.

"Don't shoot," he stammered, "whoever you are."

She moved him out of the car, keeping steady aim at her target.

"Bring my bag around," she told him, "and then leave. Pardner. *"*

For long minutes after his car had passed over the horizon she stayed in shooting position, training the gun in his wake. Finally she felt safe enough to put herself back together, seize her bag, and finish her trip on foot.

It was just past daybreak when she came to a sign: "Welcome to Washington, D.C." It was small, surprisingly nondescript, with a couple of the letters chipped, no more impressive than the 20 or more that she'd come upon on her journey. Nothing of the city that she'd read about, nothing that had fired her strivings, was anywhere in view. Her road companion, Route 1, right here, was just another two-lane, lined by foliage. None of that mattered to her. She'd reached the city limits.

She rubbed off her fake mustache, took off her hat and tossed it into the shrubs near the sign, tossed her hairband behind it, and started to walk.

Then she stopped, brought out the gun and stared at it.

She threw the gun into the shrubs and went on into town.

May 1952

1

Not far to the west of the Calvert Street Bridge stand some of Washington's most lavish mansions, not far to the east sit some of its most squalid slums. Under the bridge at sunrise on this late spring morning, just off a dirt footpath running hard by a creek, lies a skull.

The span runs some 150 feet over the southern end of Rock Creek Park, an untamed urban jungle, a vast expanse of unruly wilderness in the middle of the tidy garden that the capital city has always wanted to be. At its base the bridge is an imposing limestone structure with three graceful arches. At its summit it offers a majestic view high above the Park. Each year four or five desperate souls mount its cold railing and fling themselves from it.

Shane Kinnock parks his take-home Plymouth by a bluff in the bridge's shadow near the creek that winds through the Park and gives it its name. In the glare of his headlights are three uniformed cops standing in a circle, hunched over something.

Their breath smoke mixes with dew mist rising from the grass.

Shane's been called here from headquarters to follow up on what his sergeant called "a skull report," but he's taken his time getting here. On the way he's passed the few early risers, awake to greet the Saturday sunrise. There was a time when he'd go by people like them on mornings like this and he'd think to himself, today I'm going to protect you and everyone you know, you're all safe with me on the job.

He hasn't thought that way in a while.

He keeps the car idling for a few seconds. The uniforms are oblivious to him, oblivious to everything. He gets out of the car but doesn't go over to them. Instead he walks to the passenger side, opens the door, and takes from the front seat the two things that matter most to him in the world right now: a pack of Camels and a bottle of mouthwash. He swigs from the bottle and shoves it under the car seat, pops a cigarette from the pack and lights it. He puts his foot on the running board and his head against the door frame, closes his eyes and thinks. *Pay attention. Pay attention.*

The creek is wide enough here to count as a small river. This morning it's still and silent, as if something has backed it up. A breeze kicks up and carries the voices of the three uniforms. Beckley, O'Dell and Ackerman.

"Hey Beckley, the Nats win last night?" The voice is squeaky high, unmistakably O'Dell's.

"Rained out. I was out there doing security, you know? Two hours in a downpour before the umps would call it." Beckley turns and spits, snapping his neck like a copperhead. There's even a sizzle in his follow-through. "Not that I was out there all that long. Spent most of the night undercover and warm. Hot even."

"And miles away."

"You got it."

Shane hears a gurgle from the creek, which is starting to loosen.

O'Dell: "Jesus Christ, Beckley, you work security for the Nats, too? How many outside jobs you got?"

"What's it to ya? The Chief don't know, so why should you care."

"I thought Kaufman might care. You taking another job and not being around when he wants you to be on the door at one of his places. That Kaufman, there's a guy you gotta worry about."

"And why would that be?"

"Don't play dumb, Beckley. You've heard the story."

Beckley has to have heard the story. It seems everyone in Washington knows it, even though it's never been in any newspaper.

It's about the mobster Jake Kaufman.

About how when he was just 16 Jake Kaufman killed another boy, someone in the neighborhood who used to torment him, beat him up, call him "Jewboy Jake." About how a garbage man ended up finding the kid dumped head-first in a big rubbish can. About how the kid had been stabbed in the heart, with both eyes gouged out and shoved in his mouth. About the note that was pinned to the kid's school uniform. "Watch your mouth."

It's about how Jake Kaufman got everything he wanted from then on, without killing anyone else – didn't have to, after the story got around. And it's about how because of all that, a fair number of people say that Harry Truman, the man who runs the country, doesn't even run the city where he lays his head each night.

Beckley brushes off the Jake Kaufman story. He smiles tightly. "Listen, I watch the hebe's joints and I take his money, but he don't run my life, you understand? I don't care who somebody says he's killed." He shivers and crosses his arms briskly. "Christ, it's cold out here for goddam May, isn't it? You know, goddam *May*."

****

Beckley, O'Dell and Ackerman, three cops on assignment. Shane knows more than he wants to about all three of them – went through police training with all of them, worked side-by-side with two of them, knows the third from the bars and the track. When the war started ten years ago the three of them all somehow managed to find a cushy place where they could sleep through it. After it ended they crawled into the department along with hundreds of others and burrowed themselves in the woodwork, rotting the structure from within.

Of the three, only O'Dell is well known throughout the ranks of the force, but just for one thing. For years, every time the new sergeants' list was posted at headquarters, O'Dell looked in vain for his name and then said the same thing: "O'Dell gets fucked again." The phrase entered department folklore, to the point where that's the name by which hundreds of officers know him even if they've never met him. "O'Dell-Gets-Fucked-Again."

Shane lights another Camel off the first one and turns to confront the uniforms. They don't see him coming and his foot-fall is soft, so he's on them in the half-light before they even know he's there.

"Well, look at this," Shane says. "I get it. 'We all dance around in a circle and suppose, but the secret sits in the middle and knows.' That's what's going on here, right, fellas?"

Shane stares at Beckley, expecting no answer. The reform school that regurgitated Beckley into the working world didn't have a curriculum that included Robert Frost's poetry.

"From what I heard of your conversation," Shane goes on, "none of you is exactly overburdened by curiosity as to how somebody's head ended up right here."

Beckley returns Shane's stare. "I'm surprised to see you, Kinnock. I didn't know songbirds came out this early in the Park." He looks over at O'Dell and Ackerman: "Except this songbird here seems to spend a lot of time singing to committees on Capitol Hill." He turns back to Shane. "My wife saw you on TV and said you look just like Tyrone Power. Or maybe some other homo actor. That's what she said."

Shane feels his right fist clench and spasm but keeps his voice level. "Beckley, it's good to see you're still managing to keep up with the news, in between banging fat barmaids and taking skim from every hood on your beat."

Beckley glances again at O'Dell and Ackerman. "You know, Kinnock, when the lieutenant said he'd call for a detective to meet us down here I thought we'd get ourselves a real one, not this reject from the homicide squad. You know, a *re-ject.*" O'Dell and Ackerman look back and forth between Beckley and Shane like puppies deciding which big dog they should follow.

Beckley: "Sorry to have to take you away from natural death duty, Kinnock. Heard on the radio over here that an old lady over in Petworth seized up this morning dragging her kitty cat out of the garden – you better hustle on over there, right? Get on *over* there." He guffaws, and the others, now confident in picking a winner, laugh too.

Shane moves to Beckley and jabs a finger into his chest: "You – " He stops. A few seconds go by. "O'Dell, Ackerman." He keeps his eyes on Beckley. "One of you needs to tell me what you know about this thing that brought us all here."

Ackerman, in shaky voice: "Our lieutenant got a call from Park Police that somebody found it. He told us to get right on it."

"Three of you."

"Yeah, three of us."

Shane can picture the scene: Beckley, O'Dell and Ackerman with an hour left on the overnight shift, hanging around the station trying to dodge any action on a Friday-night-into-Saturday-morning. A call comes in to a lieutenant, who sends them all out here just to get rid of them.

Ackerman, suddenly more assertive: "Why're we even here? Why isn't Park Police on this all by themselves? I mean, this is a park, and they supposedly got all the parks, right?"

"Maybe Park Police doesn't have a detective available so they asked us to help."

"No, maybe they know this is going nowhere. So they're trying to get us to tend to their shit."

Shane's reminded of the story that's made its rounds in the department, about how these three once dragged a dead body over the D.C. line into Maryland so some other cops would have to deal with it.

Ackerman squints at his watch. "Park Police at least says they've got a beat guy coming up here. Should be here soon, said he went to interview whoever it was that found this thing."

The skull rests on its jaw line on a small patch of gray-yellow grass that spring's touch hasn't brought back to life. As the others back away, Shane bends down over it and feels a chill. He's killed men before but quickly left the carnage behind, never seen bone stripped of flesh. He would've expected a bare skull to look like a fossil, but this one doesn't. Instead, it somehow looks both unknowing and omniscient, static and timeless.

The mouth is agape, as if frozen in terror.

He leans down to it. *What scared you so?*

Beckley, from behind him: "Looks like it's laughing at you, Kinnock."

Shane doesn't reply, just reaches to touch the skull, but then it seems to catch a slant of the morning light and glows golden for a moment. He jumps back.

Ackerman steps forward. "Shane, you think there's any need for us to stick around?"

Shane keeps staring at the incandescent skull.

"I said, is there any –"

"What? Oh, yeah. It depends. On whether this Park Police guy comes back."

Ackerman coughs. "No offense or nothing but you really think there's anything to this? We're standing under a bridge people throw themselves off of all the time. I ain't saying it's a good thing or a bad thing, it just ain't a crime when they do."

"If it's so clear that this one just went from up there to down here, then where's the rest of him?"

Shane can't keep his eyes off the skull.

"Look around you, Shane. There's all kinds of animals in them woods. The guy coulda bounced, no disrespect or nothing, into the bushes over there and then nobody saw him for months. And all these creatures get after him – geez."

"So you're all-fired certain this is a suicide. And all the murders that've happened here in the Park over the years, they don't make you at all suspicious?"

"It's not like – it's not – hey, here comes the Park Police guy." Ackerman's relief is palpable.

In the distance, a man on horseback rides slowly up the long path at creek side. He looks tall and rangy in the saddle and sports the wide-brimmed hat of the mounted policeman. His snap of the reins is sure handed, his shoulders roll easily.

Shane circles the skull and looks on the ground around it.

How'd you get here? If an animal dragged you here, where are the tracks?

He bends over it again, and the world falls away.

****

"Howdy!"

The horseman dismounts and lands with a thud. He's young, too young, with a belly that hangs over his belt and a wet hank of hair he wipes off his brow. Breathing hard, he walks up to Shane, says who he is – all Shane catches is something like "Shipley" – and sticks out his right hand: "Real nice to meet you, sir."

The horseman snorts, works something to the back of his throat, and spits behind him. "Sorry about that, sir. Better out than in, like they say."

Behind Shane, one of the cops starts laughing.

The horseman hitches up his pants but they fall right back where they were. "Sir," he says, "you want me to tell you how I got into all this?"

"In a minute. How long have you been with Park Police?"

"A year, sir. Actually, 13 months." He sniffs again.

"And what do they have you doing at the Park Police?"

"Well, sir, pretty much nothin', sir."

Beckley calls out. "Looks like you got yourself a sidekick, Kinnock."

Shane ignores him, again. "So Shipley, whoever it was that found this skull, you have them holed up somewhere?"

"It's Shiflett, sir, Bobby S-H-I-F-L-E-T-T. And yessir, they're at our Park Police office, around the bend there."

Shane pivots to Ackerman. "This thing needs to be guarded for a few minutes while I take a walk with Shiflett here to talk with this witness. Think you can handle that?"

Ackerman shrugs and looks over to the others.

"I get it," Shane says. "Okay, after that I'll call your lieutenant and tell him you're clear here and you can check off and go home." Ackerman nods vigorously, O'Dell nods, too. Beckley goes back toward the skull, slouching.

Not even fifteen minutes later, Shane is walking with Shiflett and his horse back up the path from the Park Police office. "So whaddya think of my witness there, Mr. Kinnock?"

Shane keeps walking.

"Mr. Kinnock, you're not thinkin' she might know more about how that skull got down there than she's lettin' on, now, do you?"

Shane stops and waits for Shiflett and the horse to catch up. "No, I don't. Surprisingly enough, I don't think a 65-year-old woman would know too much about the skull she happened to trip over while she was on her morning walk."

The sun has broken through spaces in the treeline and the ground mist is rising.

In Shane's mind he can see the white-gold orb in the yellow grass patch and he quickens his pace.

From around the bend he hears music, faintly at first, then louder. Soon, the piercing vocals of Rosemary Clooney are unmistakable.

Come onna my place, my place-a come on!
Come onna my place, my place-a come on!

Shiflett's horse grunts. "Mr. Kinnock," Shiflett says, "That sounds like it's coming from where your police friends are."

Shane says nothing for about five steps.

Then: "Shiflett, I don't know how long you plan to be in this line of work. But for as long as you are, don't ever get to be like those losers."

Rounding the corner, Shane can see O'Dell, Beckley and Ackerman up ahead. One of them has brought out a small radio and cranked it up. Beckley has put a stick through the eye hole of the skull and he's in a fencer's stance, waving it toward the others, and they're doubled over laughing.

The skull falls to the ground and rolls to a stop, upside-down.

Shane passes straight by the uniforms and goes to the skull, turns it over and holds it. He means to put it back down but keeps on holding it. He runs his fingers around the eye sockets, over the nose gap and across the teeth.

Suddenly his hands start to shake until he has to let go of it, and he feels his skin tingle from a thousand prick-points on his neck and back and across his body, and then comes a surge of life-juice, long dormant, that propels him from his haunches to his feet in a quick hop.

In a flash of clarity he steps up to Beckley. "What the fuck is this kick-the-can routine all about?" O'Dell and Ackerman take small steps away from him.

Beckley blinks once, then again, but doesn't move. "Fuck you, Kinnock," he says. "You know if you take this too far, I'll be in the Chief's office in an hour and he'll have your badge and gun five minutes after that."

"You want my gun? Okay, you can have it." Shane turns away.

Then he turns back and grabs Beckley's hand and twists it behind his back, grabs Beckley's throat and shoves him down. Beckley's head hits hard and he grunts and Shane bends over him. "You wanted my gun, right? Well, here it is." He puts his revolver to Beckley's temple and cocks it. "Now are you ever going to come on a crime scene of mine again and do something like this?"

Beckley says nothing.

"Are – you – ever…"

Beckley shakes his head.

"*What?*"

Beckley shakes his head again, twice.

Shane hears Shiflett's voice. "What are you even *thinkin'*, sir?" He feels a hand on his back.

Looking at Beckley, it's as if Shane never saw the man before. He moves the gun around Beckley's head, then draws it away. He plants his knee on Beckley's sternum and pushes off of it to get up, uncocking the gun and holstering it.

Ackerman and O'Dell-Gets-Fucked-Again look at him, then look down. "All three of you all, get the hell out of here," Shane says. "And take your shitty music with you."

Beckley rolls over, tries to rise, slumps.

"You might be well advised," Shane says to him, "not to talk to anybody about this. I heard what you said back there and I don't think you'd want the police brass to find out that you use your off-time guarding the door for a big-time numbers boss and a murderer. Now get out of my sight."

Beckley drags himself to his feet and walks back towards the cruiser that brought the three of them here. Ackerman calls back over his shoulder. "You're a crazy fucking bastard, Kinnock." He stops at a safe distance and nods his head toward the skull. "All this over *that*. And if anybody asked you, you wouldn't even be able to say for sure that it's human."

Shane picks up the fedora that he lost in the rush towards Beckley, pulls his tie all the way up to his neck, and brushes the grass and brambles off his suit.

An engine buzzes overhead. The sound builds to a roar, then subsides. No plane appears on the horizon. There've been three airline crashes on the east coast since January, two in a month just near Newark, jet planes dropping out of the skies on sunny days and wiping out whole neighborhoods.

As if people don't have enough to worry about, even a cloudless sky can still pose a threat.

Shiflett is standing still, dumbstruck. Shane offers his gun to him. "Take a look at it. Not a bad-looking piece for department issue. It's a .38."

Shiflett takes the gun, doesn't answer.

"You go through marksmanship training with the Park Police, Shiflett?"

"Naw, but I did a lot of shooting in the service, even though I never saw no action."

Shane nods towards the gun, which Shiflett is holding gingerly in his right hand. "Point it in the air and fire it, see how it feels."

"Don't wanna do that."

"I said, fire it. Fire it in the air. Pull the trigger and fire it."

"Sir, but –"

"*Fire it.*"

Shiflett fires, once, hands the gun back.

"Did you feel the trigger pull there, Shiflett? Pretty heavy, wasn't it?"

"Meanin'?"

"Meaning it wasn't going to go off by accident."

Shane leaves unaddressed the other possibility.

Deep in the woods a bullfrog groans once, twice. Geese fly overhead in V-formation, late arriving from the south. The creek has come back to splashing life, carrying last night's rainwater on a twisting journey towards the Potomac and beyond.

Shane hears a series of clicks coming from his car, followed by a muffled voice: his police radio, needy and nagging. He doesn't even have to hear the words to know what's coming next, and the tedium that'll come with it.

"Shiflett," he says, "I've got to go to a death scene. The Park Police gave you some training, right?"

"You mean like teachin' me something? Not nearly."

"What do they have you doing over there?"

"Right now, just ridin' around Rock Creek Park all day, supposebly watchin' out for trouble. But really, I spend a lot of my time just cleanin' stuff up." He pauses. "Truthfully, sir, I don't think they're takin' me all that seriously."

"So I'm to assume they never taught you the procedure for dealing with a dead body?"

"Uh-uh."

"Well, from what you've picked up here and there, what do you think we do next?"

Shiflett thinks for a second, then answers firmly. "We call the coronator."

"The what?"

"The coronator. You know, the doctor that says how dead people died."

It takes Shane a second to realize that for the first time this day – this week, this year – he's smiling. "No, he's called the *coroner*. Shiflett, where'd you grow up, anyway?"

"North Carolina, sir. Town called Roanoke Rapids."

"So when you were growing up down in Roanoke wherever, and somebody got killed, didn't you ever hear of a coroner taking care of the remains?"

"Nobody ever got killed where I grew up, sir."

"Well, I'll call the coroner and have him come down here, and you just sit on this until he gets here. And if anything else comes out of this down the line, maybe I'll get back to you."

Driving away, Shane catches a glimpse of himself in the rearview mirror.

He's just assaulted another cop, made him think he was going to kill him.

He should feel ashamed, but he doesn't.

In fact, he hasn't felt this good in a long time.

2

"Let's say this was a jumper and the head popped off on impact. Sorry, Shiflett, but it can happen. Some of the rest of the bones may've ended up being taken by animals but you'd think we'd find at least something in this grass on either side of the bridge."

"Unless the rest of him bounced into the creek, sir. And then it's long gone downstream."

"That would've been one hell of a bounce."

Two hours have passed and Shane is walking briskly towards the Calvert Street Bridge from the yellowed patch where the old lady found the skull.

To his right is Rock Creek, now running swiftly. To his left is a wide strip, lush with tall grass, wildflowers and weeds. Behind the strip is a steep hill that leads up to the bridge's eastern end.

And following devotedly behind him is the underused Shiflett, on foot with his horse stabled elsewhere, and an overanxious spaniel named Spike that Shiflett saw fit to bring to the Park, "just to help, sir."

Before coming back out here Shane called Shiflett, having no one else to call. He neglected to tell him not to drag any more animals along with him.

"Shiflett," he says, "Every other Southern boy I've ever met had a *big* dog. At least a big dog might do us some good out here."

"Used to have one in North Carolina, sir. But the landlady at my roomin' house don't allow pets, no way I could keep a big dog there. She don't even know I've got this one, on account of I trained him not to ever bark inside my room. Or ever, really."

The Shane Kinnock of just a few hours ago, a man without a mission and long lacking peace of mind, would've thought that training a dog not to bark anywhere, anytime was impossible. Right now, he sees the proposition as being just about as certain as the time-tick of the earth's course.

He counts the steps as he goes and stops when he's directly under the bridge. *Exactly 150 paces from the skull-point. A hundred yards, give or take.* He turns to Shiflett. "Let's just get started looking." On hands and knees they comb through the grassy strip while Spike the spaniel torments small frogs on the creek bank.

After an hour of coming up with nothing he tells Shiflett that they need to expand their search area. They start back up the dirt path, with the creek now on the left and the hill on the right, and scan both sides.

"How well do you know Rock Creek Park, Shiflett?"

"I'm out here pretty much all day, sir. Got to know pretty much all the trees, and there's pretty much every kind of animal in these woods that you can think of."

"Every kind of animal? You ever see any elephants out here, Shiflett? Some elephants, maybe a stray tiger or a lion?"

"You got me there, sir."

They come to a chain-link fence topped by barbed wire.

"Sir," Shiflett says, "that's where National Zoo's territory starts. For what it's worth, sir, that's where you'd find your elephants an' lions an' tigers. *Sir.*" He works his mouth around on something.

"The Park," Shiflett goes on, "it starts up again on the north side of the zoo and it goes on for miles. Alla way up to Maryland, and the parts up north are even wilder than down here."

"I've been in those parts."

"You know, sir, they got me out here ridin' during the day, of course. But I like it out here so much, lots of nights I come out here on my own time."

"Some strange stuff happens in the Park at night, Shiflett."

"I've heard some stories."

"It's not as if there's a killing here every week, but it's had more than its fair share, going back years."

Shiflett is peering at Shane with a newborn's gaze. Shane has no idea what he's thinking but at least he's listening.

"Some of the cases have never been solved," Shane goes on. "There was a girl named Meslin, stabbed in the chest, happened about five years ago. White dame, so naturally the papers went crazy on the story. And then there was the Walker boy, a Negro boy killed here in the Park a few years ago."

"Sir, how'd he die?"

"Somebody stabbed him 17 times, broke his skull. Then they did something else to him I can't even say."

Shiflett slows, looks down at the ground. "What happened to the case?"

"The Chief had Homicide put in about a week on it and then let it die. He has this creep of a deputy, his name is Calvin Rector, and Rector's got a thing for queers. He right away had us brace every one of them who ran around the Park. The Chief even came close to having us charge one of them but I convinced him not to do it."

"On account of --"

"On account of we had no evidence on him. Kind of a sticking point."

"They ever find out who did it?"

"No. It's pretty much been forgotten."

"Forgotten? Why?"

"Why do you think, Shiflett? You heard me say he was a Negro boy, right? I wouldn't think anybody who comes from down your part of the country would need much of an explanation about things like that."

Shiflett winces.

"Sir," he says, "how you know about all these cases in the Park? You work on any of the others?"

Shane slows down. "No, I just grew up in D.C. When I was a kid I used to come over here to the Park all the time with my family. My sister, really. There wasn't a weekend during summertime that we didn't find our way over here."

Shane comes to a halt.

"When it'd get real hot at night," he says, "lots of people would make their way down to the Park with sleeping bags, to get relief. Still do, for that matter, the Park might as well be a hotel when the weather's warm. But me and my sister, we were never allowed in the Park after sundown."

"Your sister younger or older?"

"Twins."

"So I figure you and she're close."

Shane picks up the pace. "Not anymore we're not. She died."

"Sir, I'm sorry. What did your father do?"

"He was a Congressman, still is. Jesus, you ask a lot of questions. Why don't you drag your dog off that dead squirrel he's showing so much of an interest in."

After another hour they've covered the whole strip for a half-mile in each direction and are coming up again to the yellow patch. Spike runs towards the patch and starts pawing at something in the undergrowth next to it.

"So what's next, sir?"

Shane lights a Camel, his first since early morning. "Probably nothing, if we don't find something else. All we'd have would be a nameless skull with no body attached to it."

Shiflett just nods. He takes out a tin of chew and shoves a wad in his cheek. "This little experience here today has been the most interesting thing I been in since I joined up with the police. I can't see myself stayin' in this job too long."

"Stick with me, Shiflett. I'm not giving up yet."

Shane is watching Spike burrow into the ground – at first just a couple of inches, then more, until after a time the dog has dug a hole so deep that only the tips of his ears can be seen.

Shiflett's dog is on to something.

Shane trots up to him, sees him trying to climb out of the hole he's made. The dog has something in his teeth, then loses his grip, falls back in the hole, starts all over again.

Shiflett runs over, grabs the dog, pries open his mouth and snatches a small, white object that Shane strains to see. "Could it be a bone fragment?"

Shiflett works viscous dog spit from it. "Naw," he says, "it's just paper. Ain't nothin'."

A part of a newspaper is poking from the bottom of the hole. "Not necessarily nothing," Shane says.

He works his fingers around the paper for several minutes until he can expose an edge he can hold onto without tearing it. Lifting it gently, he thinks it might flake away in his hands but it stays intact. It's a page full of ads from the Washington Post. He scrapes some caked dirt off the top right corner until the date shows **May 1, 1951.** "This is barely a year old," he says. "How'd it get buried so deep in the ground in so little time?"

Shiflett stares into space. Then he answers, as if the secret to the universe is evolving in front of him and he's trying to wrap his fleshy arms around it. "There was some big mud slides in the Park last year, not long after I started on the job. One of the biggest was right here, from on up the hill – happened the same night the river flooded real bad. You can even see from that long ridge from up there how the mud came down."

"Isn't there a walkway," Shane says, "that we can take to get up there?"

"Yessir, down that way."

Shane takes off in a trot, and Shiflett and the dog follow far behind.

At the top of the hill, at the end of a winding quarter–mile walkway, is a clearing where the woods end and the city street begins. The clearing opens up on a playground with teeter-totters and hanging tires and shiny swing-sets, and behind the playground are two baseball fields with bronzed infields, manicured turf and foul lines marked with a draftsman's precision.

A couple of minutes pass before Shiflett arrives, wheezing and carrying Spike, who's gone limp.

"Shiflett, you wouldn't have any idea when they dug out these fields, would you? They look new."

Shiflett hands the dog to Shane, bends over and puts his hands on his knees. Finally: "They was doing the excavations last year when all the heavy rains hit, and this is where they had a bunch of huge piles of sand and dirt. Some was what they dug out, some was the sand they brought in for the sandboxes, the piles was like 10 feet tall here. And they all washed down the hill."

A rolling stone. A rolling stone gathers – what. It gathers something, goddammit. Shane can't think of the rest of the phrase. But it doesn't matter. He's seeing it all happen.

"What if that's not all that washed down the hill, Shiflett?"

Baby stare from Shiflett, with no sign of any universal secret about to be solved.

"All this time we've been looking for the rest of the body down there by the bank. But what if it was never down there to begin with? What if it started out up here, it was at rest at the top of this hill, but then the skull came loose and rolled down there?"

"Somebody's skull just comin' loose like that?"

"Yeah, it could and it would, when the soft tissue that connected it to the body decomposed. You know, fell apart. Which means that the rest of the body could be up here somewhere, on a line with where the skull landed down there."

About 30 yards down the slope is a grove of bushes that guard a small cliff. In front of the grove is a mound of dirt that looks to be about four feet high and ten feet or so across. It stands out because it's lighter-colored than any of the soil around it.

"Tie the dog up," Shane says to Shiflett, and starts towards the mound.

The incline is steep and the turf still muddy from the rain, so Shane inches his way down slowly. He's a few feet from the mound when his left foot hits a root and he turns his ankle, then his feet give way and he feels himself falling and he braces himself against the mound with his right hand. The mound is soft and sandy and gives way and crumbles at the top, but he's still able to brace himself against it. "Goddamn it!' he says as he gets up and rubs his ankle and looks back at Shiflett, who's perched precariously on the hill a few feet behind him.

Shiflett is gazing past him. "God almighty. God almighty."

Shane looks down at the mound, which is still crumbling.

Four finger bones are sticking out of the top, pointed upwards.

The pile keeps settling, revealing a fifth bone, maybe a thumb.

Then one-by-one the bones all drop into the shifting sand like dying rose petals falling from a wilting stem.

Shane and Shiflett stand still. A minute passes, maybe more. Finally Shiflett speaks.

"So what's next now, sir?"

"Shane. And from now on, to me you're Bobby whether you like it or not."

"Yes, sir."

"So you want to know what we do now, Bobby?"

"What's that?"

"We call the coronator."

3

Just an hour after marching past that "Welcome to Washington" sign, Emily was in the vicinity of the U.S. Capitol building, scouting out places to live and work.

The living part came surprisingly easy. A family was moving out of a house just three blocks from the Capitol and another was moving in, and the new renters needed to sub-lease a basement room. It was a dreary place, and she had fellow tenants that crawled around on four legs and bounced wildly off of her walls. But she'd seen worse, and at least it was within her means.

Taking care of the working part took longer, but she was soon waiting tables at a small restaurant – more of a bar that occasionally served edible food. The Tune Inn had just opened, and two things about it drew her to it. It was close to home and management would give her a waitress uniform. If not for that, she'd have had no working clothes.

At the Tune, as its staunch patrons called it, Emily worked the late shift, which left her with most of the day to roam the city and take in everything that she could – museums, libraries, even college classes that she infiltrated, passing as a student. From the first classes she sat in on – about public speaking, writing short stories, the U.S. Civil War and how Negroes were treated after it – she was thrilled by the amount of information that was within her reach, if only she had the means to grasp it. On the side, she took a course in secretarial shorthand – a language all its own, made up of symbols that stood in for groups of letters, all to let a hand moving a pen match the speed of a mouth uttering words –just so she could better record everything she was learning, as she was learning it, and then look back on it later as she was learning more.

She kept to a frugal budget and in a few months she'd saved enough to buy something that served as a business dress. After another couple of months she had a second dress, and it was only then that she felt ready to look for a better job – with "better" for the moment being defined as any *place where she had a name other than "Toots," her behind was spared from constant squeezing, and she didn't have to nightly rebuff demands for favors in exchange for money.*

The place that she chose to look for "better" was the U.S. House of Representatives, and her hunt started on a summer day. She could've chosen the U.S. Senate but she'd never before walked on high heels, she was sweating though her dress, and the Senate side was a longer trek from where she lived – even forward-thinking people sometimes make a consequential decision based on what pains them at the moment. She went to a building, with no real direction – there didn't seem to be an application office and none of the guards were of any help in answering questions – and then to an elevator.

She pushed the "up" button, for no reason other than that it seemed to be a better choice than "down."

The doors opened, and in the elevator was an operator and another man who was tapping a toe and looking at his watch, as if the stop had interrupted some master plan.

The man looked at her and took her measure. She took his with a side glance.

The operator turned to her: "Going down, right, ma'am?"

"No, up. To the top floor." She didn't know what the top floor even was, and the operator rolled his eyes. "This elevator is going down."

Before she could say anything more she heard the man behind her. "Sir, I don't need to go down right now. Since the nice lady wants to go up, I'll go up with her."

In the time that it took for the elevator to travel to the top the man identified himself as a Congressman, determined that she was looking for work, and invited her to apply for a job in his office, saying something along the lines of, "We can use another pretty face around here."

And so she got the job.

On her first workday, she was put on a switchboard and tasked by the office manager, a woman named Claire, to say one sentence to every caller –

"*Congressman Joseph Barry's office, how can I help you?*" – and then direct the call to another staffer with a half-sentence: "*One moment please.*" After two weeks she wondered whether she'd ever do anything in Washington that was more vital than passing somebody else's voice to somebody else's ear. After three weeks, the cord on her telephone was beginning to look like a noose.

In week four, the same office manager gave her a promotion: answering letters and telegrams from the Congressman's constituents. She was elated, even though she was shunted off to a windowless room and given a typewriter with keys that stuck. This would give her a view of American democracy at its most basic and personal level. But she soon learned that any correspondence that had to do with actual constituent services – in other words, anything that could help someone, directly – had already been diverted away from her, as well as any letters that the Congressman might be moved by, or might want to include in a speech. On top of that, she was ordered to make up a separate file for correspondence from war veterans and told that they'd be answered exclusively by office manager Claire. So Emily was left, day-to-day, with a pile of communications that largely came from the forlorn, the dispossessed, or the crazed.

Even when she felt most thwarted, she never lost sight of where she was, and where she had been. Four months into it, her requests for more challenging work were being ignored, and she still hadn't even seen the Congressman whose cause she was supposedly serving.

That changed abruptly on an autumn Friday when she was called by Claire, who was in need. The Congressman was giving a major speech in a week on public housing for war veterans. His secretary had gone home sick. They needed someone to take dictation, and somehow no one else in the office knew shorthand.

Claire led the way to the Congressman's office, her yellow hair bouncing in perfect rhythm with the clackety-clack of her high heels on the hardwood floor. She moved with the aplomb and entitlement of someone who'd never lacked access to any place, anywhere.

Emily had figured that the place where a U.S. Congressman did his work would be expansive and grand. The office she entered was small and resembled what she thought a man's college dormitory room might look like: books and newspapers randomly strewn about, discarded clothes lumped in a pile in a corner, an inside-out umbrella sitting tilted on a rug, walls covered with sports pennants not artwork. One pennant was blue and white and bore the word "Yankees."

"DiMaggio!"

The Congressman was reclined on a couch. He was working the New York Times crossword puzzle and at the same time watching a television across the room.

"DiMaggio's up," he said. "Everybody pipe down."

Of course, *Emily thought.* Dodgers-Yankees, World Series, fourth game.

In Brooklyn her uncle had been an ardent Dodgers fan and in just a few months taught her the sport, to the point where she not only knew all the players and their numbers and positions, but also their averages and tendencies. Baseball offered to her what was best about religion – ritual, adherence to form, and, yes, passion – without all the rest of it. In Washington she'd continued to obsess over the Dodgers' progress game-by-game through daily checks of newspaper sports pages and frustratingly faint broadcasts on her bedside radio.

Claire moved closer to the screen. "Which one is DiMaggio?"

"You're not a window." Claire quickly moved out of the Congressman's sight line.

"And if anyone is looking for DiMaggio," he went on, "look for this."

He rose lithely from the couch, seized the inside-out umbrella, and wielded it like a baseball bat. "Look at his stance" he said, mimicking it. "How far apart his feet are. No other hitter stands like that, only DiMaggio has it all figured out. When he strides to hit the ball it's barely a step, and it keeps his head from bouncing. He always has his eye on the ball."

"Keeping his eye on the ball," Claire offered. "Just how you approach politics."

The Congressman didn't answer, he just kept watching the TV. "Look at that," he said, "how he got around on that fastball low and inside. And have you ever seen anyone run so gracefully?"

For the first time since Emily had met her, Claire seemed confused. "Sporting events on television, it's something new."

The Congressman let his umbrella-bat drop. "It isn't new at all. This is just the first time the World Series has ever been on television."

Emily was riveted. She was hoping that the camera would scan the field to second base and Robinson, the first Negro allowed in the sport. It didn't, but she was drawn to what she was seeing of DiMaggio, and to beauty encountered unexpectedly.

The Congressman settled back onto the couch. "Bevens has a no-hitter going."

Claire looked quizzical. Emily started to respond, but demurred.

"Bill Bevens," the Congressman went on, "is a pitcher for the Yankees, he hasn't let any of the Dodgers get a base hit, and no pitcher has ever been able to do that in a World Series game. And just by the way, I wish I didn't always have to explain everything to everybody."

He went back to the Times crossword puzzle. "Okay, here's one – nine down, 'Extinct species, prehistoric.' I'm thinking the right answer is…"

Claire started to laugh. "We all know it's --"

"RAYMOND KINNOCK! But that doesn't fit, goddammit."

Claire nudged Emily and whispered: "It's a running joke. Every time he does a crossword he finds a clue that could apply to Kinnock and he yells out a fake answer. So funny."

"It's actually a dinosaur species," the Congressman said, "in the lizard family. So, I wasn't far off." He scribbled on the newspaper page, chuckling. Emily made a mental note to find out more about Raymond Kinnock.

Another man, an aide to the Congressman, walked in tentatively with a stack of papers. Emily had crossed paths with the aide, and he'd never looked her way.

"Applicants for summer jobs, sir." The aide dropped the stack on a table next to the couch. "I assume you'll need a few days to go through them."

The Congressman grabbed the stack and flipped through it briskly. "No. No. No. Yes. No. No. Maybe. No. No." He turned back to the TV. "Now can anyone tell me what's going on in the game? Sorry, rhetorical question there."

Emily didn't hear him, she was watching the television, still transfixed. "Just need to get a couple of runners on," she muttered.

The Congressman stopped flipping through pages. "What?"

Emily was jarred back into the room. "I'm sorry, sir. I'm actually something of a baseball fan. And I couldn't help watching the game for a moment." She tried to compose herself.

"I meant," he said, "what's happening?"

"Alright," she said, wanting to get it all straight before she spoke. "Bevens is still pitching, the Yankees are up 2 to 1. It's the bottom of the ninth. The Dodgers have the tying run on first – oh my goodness, there's a second out."

She moved closer to the Congressman's couch, to get a better view of the set.

"This one's finished," he said. "Yankees' ballgame."

"Not just yet," she answered, glancing back-and-forth between him and the TV. "Now the Dodgers have first and second. And a decent pinch-hitter coming up."

"Don't even try to tell me you know who he is," he said.

She did, his name was Cookie Lavagetto. But she stopped herself. "A player with an Italian name, I think. Or maybe somebody else."

He didn't move, just tossed a question over his shoulder. "So Dodger girl, how'd you get to be such a baseball fan?"

She tried to think of an answer that would get around having to talk about where she'd come from.

"Goddammit! Goddammit!"

The game was over, just that fast. Emily's player with the Italian name had doubled in two runs. Bill Bevens, so close to doing something that no one had ever done before, had been summarily dispatched to the ranks of people who do the same things everybody else does. And Emily's Dodgers had beaten the Congressman's Yankees. Inside her heart leaped, but she kept a poker face.

The Congressman stared at the screen, as if it were a board with election precinct results. When he spoke it was in the voice of someone whose rooting interest was, at least for the moment, on the side of the practical. "Bevens was in trouble, he had nothing left in the tank. But Harris didn't want to cost him his no-hitter and his place in history."

Claire had been mute for long minutes. She seized on an unspecific reference, a name like any other, to get back in the conversation. "Who's Harris?"

"Bucky Harris, the Yankees' manager. He's like you in this office. Or actually, like me. He should've taken Bevens out of the game for the good of the team. Too much loyalty to one player."

Claire shuffled papers in front of her. "A little entertainment is wonderful but don't we still have veterans' housing to think about?"

The Congressman stretched out his arm without looking at her. "Okay, lifeguard, I guess this means we've got to get out of the pool, right?"

Claire handed him a sheaf. "This is what I came up with," she said. "Add your own thoughts as you go through it, and Emily here can take it all down. I understand she's good at that."

He leafed through the pages and started reading out loud, and Emily dutifully recorded his words. The speech started with a reference to "the bill before the House," meandered through "guarantees for private investment" and "formulas for public contributions," ended with "on behalf of all veterans, thank you." It wasn't clear to Emily if he'd added any changes of his own.

"Just like every other speech I've given," he said absently, "and it's worked for me so far. As my friend at the Post would say, let's print it."

He started to hand the sheaf back to Claire, but stopped.

"Just out of curiosity, what do you think about this speech, Dodger girl?"

Emily raised her pen from her pad, didn't raise her eyes. "I don't think it's necessarily my place –"

"I agree," Claire said. "This speech has already been reviewed --"

"Reviewed," the Congressman said. "Which just means that you wrote a draft and proofread it."

"Of course, but you read it too."

"It can go through one more review. What do you have to say, Miss ..."

"Rose."

"Of course, Miss Rose."

Emily had waited for a question like this and in her head, a hundred or more times, she'd come up with answers that would show that hers was a voice that was worth being listened to – that's all she wanted. It was why she'd come to Washington, why she'd wanted a job in a place like this, why she'd spent hours sitting in classrooms where she didn't belong, furiously taking notes while others around her were nodding off.

But then and there, she seized up and couldn't find words.

"That's all right," Claire said to her. "We understand, you're being put on the spot here. Congressman, what we need to do next..."

"A person."

"What?"

"A person." Emily said. "You need to tell the story of a person."

"What are you possibly talking about?" The Congressman's tone was softer than his words. He swung around on the couch.

"What I mean is – and please, Claire, don't take offense, I'm just giving my opinion. It seems to me that a good speech should tell a story. And at the heart of every story is a person. You tell the story of one person, and people will see themselves in them. That's the way to reach people. That's the way to persuade people."

Claire shook her head. "And where do you propose that we find a person..."

"He gets hundreds of letters from people every day. I read the ones that are funneled to me, and I answer them. They tell their stories. Some are off on tangents, some are insane. But all of them matter."

"But this is a veterans' issue –"

"Claire, you know that I have to return all the vets' letters to you, I'm not allowed to answer any of them. But I have to imagine there's one that has a message that could make this speech more real."

Emily had seen so many letters, from so many people that she'd known she couldn't help. Then one came back to her.

"A letter came in last week," she said. "From a vet in Hempstead. He was wounded at the Battle of the Bulge, lost a leg, came back home. Now he's out on the street because he can't go anywhere else."

Claire looked at the Congressman and shrugged.

He was silent for a time. Then: "Miss Rose – what brought you to this office? How'd you come to work here?"

He'd either forgotten about his elevator encounter with Emily, or he was choosing for the moment not acknowledge it, for whatever reason. She chose to pass it off as well. "It was …"

She searched in her mind for the best phrase to use.

Good luck? Good fortune? Chance?

"It was … serendipity."

He looked at her squarely, and she felt for the first time the full force of his focus. "What a wonderful word. One of the most beautiful words in the English language. And so underused."

"Perhaps it's underused," Emily said, "because of the rarity of circumstances in which it actually applies." She clasped her hands on her lap, and at the same time crossed her legs, concerned that she'd taken liberties, and somehow at the same time hoping that she had.

The Congressman put his crossword puzzle to the side. "Well, your presence in this meeting of ours is both serendipitous and – felicitous." Did I use that the right way?" He smiled, and it was as if no one else were in the room.

"If you're saying that it was appropriate and even, shall we say, propitious, I'm very flattered." Emily glanced over at Claire, who was looking down. "But let's go on."

"Wait," he said, "this interests me. Words matter, don't they? How they sound, and how so often the sound matches the nature of the word."

"As in, mellifluous?"

I'll see you and raise you with euphonious."

Claire broke in: "Shall we get back to the speech?"

The Congressman's eyes met Emily's.

Depending on who's saying it, just one word can change the course of a battle in a war (advance! retreat!) or tip global markets (buy! sell!). Just one word has the power to save a life, or cause a life to be lost. For Emily Rose, just one word set in motion a chain of events that would ultimately end in her losing her life, and the irony is that the word was " serendipity."

"So Claire," he said, "why don't you go through the vets' letters that Emily here is talking about, and you can take the one that she's remembering and work it into the speech. And then--"

Emily interrupted. "There's one other thing I should say. The letter that I'm remembering, it was from a Negro *veteran. And what he wants is fair housing, along with everybody else he fought alongside. And for."*

The Congressman waited a bit before getting up.

"I have another idea," he finally said. "Claire, just get the letter to Miss Rose here and we can see what she can do with it. Taking a crack at speech writing will be good practice for her." To Emily: "Just nothing about the Negro issue. Not yet. There'll be a time."

Emily almost pressed the point but didn't. There *will* be a time.

Claire left the office and walked back down the hall, the click of her heels less assertive.

The Congressman hovered over Emily, put his left hand softly on her left shoulder. "I hope to be seeing more of you in this office – such as it is."

He breezed out. She exhaled.

****

4

THE WASHINGTON POST
Sunday, May 25, 1952

NO BONES ABOUT IT
By Bran Bentley, Staff Reporter

A 65-year-old widow made a grisly discovery during her morning walk yesterday in Rock Creek Park: a skull. Officers assigned to the Metropolitan Police Department and U.S. Park Police responded to the scene and claimed custody. But the police are downplaying the significance of the find. "Some people are getting all worked up about it," said veteran Metropolitan Officer Mark Ackerman, "but right now, we don't even know if it's human." The skull was transferred to the office of the District Coroner for analysis.

****

Shane's in the Park. He's holding a bone, buffing it with a rag. A box of bones sits next to him. Other bones are scattered around him.

He has to examine every one of them. He takes each in turn, buffs it, eyes it, buffs it again and runs his fingertips up and down its surface. Now and again he thinks he sees something but when he looks closer he sees it was nothing.

Don't think about the whole skeleton. Just think inch-by-inch.

He's vaguely aware of a voice. Bobby: "I said, you been here all night?"

"Yes."

"How come?"

Because after he sent Shiflett home yesterday he called for the coroner to come down and take the bones from the pile, and a crime scene officer to come down and take the clothes and any other evidence. Then a fresh murder took priority and nobody showed up. Meanwhile, somebody had to stay with what was left of whoever this once was.

"Why didn't you call me back down here so I could spell you? I done gave you my number." Bobby sounds wounded.

"Because it was my job."

My job, first and foremost.

It's been awhile since Shane heard himself say anything proprietary about something having to do with his work.

"So you went and got the box here…"

"And the rag, and this flashlight, and that thing over there." He gestures towards a tarpaulin that's covering the sand pile.

Bobby fingers the edge of the tarp. "Why'd you put this here?"

"It started to rain a while ago and – it just seemed like the right thing to do."

Shane slowly pulls the tarp off. A woman's jacket and blouse are sitting upright in the pile. They're filled out in the chest, where the rib cage was, but both sleeves of the jacket are empty. The jacket is a faded pink – maybe it was once bright red. The jacket and blouse are in tatters. The rest of the body, whatever is left of it, remains buried.

Bobby backs off.

"See what I spared you," Shane says. "You should be glad you weren't looking at this by flashlight in the dead of night."

Bobby lightly rattles the bone box with his foot. "So what're you lookin' for here?"

Shane rubs his eyes hard. In a night fog he fought sleep to a standstill but now it's gaining the upper hand. An hour ago he popped a couple of bennies and he's waiting for them to kick in.

"What I'm looking for," Shane says, "is something that shows she was killed. Maybe on whatever flesh that's left, some sign of a wound. The girl didn't just wander into the Park to find a place to curl up and die. This is a murder case, pure and simple."

"And why does it matter to you so much if it's a murder case?"

"Because if she's just another Jane-Doe-unexplained-death, nobody will care past tomorrow. But if she's a homicide victim in a homicide case then the case gets worked and we have a chance to get some answers."

"Bunch of people die in this town every day. Why does gettin' some answers on this one matter so much to you? "

Shane picks a chunk of sand from the pile and holds it at eye level. Little by little he releases the sand. He gazes at the grains as they tumble through the damp morning air.

"It just does."

In the middle of every night, wherever he is and whatever bed he's in, he jolts awake and claws at his blanket and sheets. He's digging through holes filled with the dead-eyed, looking for the one face that he knew since his earliest days – never finding her.

Bobby falls silent. "Don't this coronator – this coroner – he has to say first whether this was a homicide or not, right? He ever comin' back down here?"

"Oh, he finally came and went, and he made it pretty clear he's not going to be an easy mark on this. The Chief used his pull to get him his job and he repays the favor. So whenever the murders are up, like they are now, all of a sudden he starts calling all the close ones an accident or a natural or a quote-unquote no-call instead of a homicide. So the press stays off the Chief's ass."

"So you need to find –"

"If we don't find flesh on any of these bones, it's going to be a lot easier for the coroner to make a no-call."

"But you think you're gonna find any flesh? Look at what you got so far, just bones."

"Then I'm looking for something on a bone, a cut or a nick from a knife."

A strangling case that Shane worked a few years ago comes back to him. "I suppose we could also find a broken neck bone. That would do it."

In a flash he can see it all happening.

The neck, thin and brittle as a goblet's.

The hands, rough and dirty as a mechanic's.

The crack, the convulsion... another crack. A heave of breath.

"Aah, forget it," Shane says. "The neck bone, it's too small. Needle in a haystack."

"How about a blood stain off the clothes?"

"Long gone. All you need to know is, the coroner says we've got to find something in the pile here that he can hang his hat on. Or we need to ID her and come up with a witness, or a motive, or something. Or else he won't call it a homicide."

There's a long, low rumble in the distance. Thunder. Or maybe another misguided jet. Bobby doesn't seem to notice. "Howdya think she got under the pile?"

"Probably ended up dead here late one evening, and nobody saw her through the rest of the night. And then the rains came and the mudslides happened and she got buried."

Now from behind Shane comes a rustle, and a second voice, a familiar rasp.

"So Kinnock," the voice says, "it looks like I didn't get the whole story from Officer Ackerman, did I? He didn't even think there was a human being up here, let alone a decked-out broad."

Shane doesn't have to turn to confront the voice. "That story today in the Post, it's not the first one you got wrong and it won't be the last."

Branford Bentley dismisses this with the same wave that he uses to pass off everything in life that he hasn't quite yet figured out how to make his own.

He's been working the crime beat for the Washington Post for the last couple of years, chasing bylines with the mad zeal of a frontier bounty hunter. His ambition is vast and imperialistic – write for a newspaper, own a newspaper, own a newspaper chain, own the world – but he wears it as lightly as he does the flower that always garnishes his suit jacket lapel.

He tools around town in a Jaguar and has slicked-back black hair and a grin like Errol Flynn's. But no pretty-boy Hollywood actor ever had eyes like Bran Bentley's. Sad and cynical, haunted and hard.

"You know, Shane," he says, pushing past Bobby, "you should've been happy with my story today on this skull affair. At least I kept your name out of it."

"I wish you would've done me the same favor when you wrote up my hearing on the Hill last month."

"That was shit luck for you," Bran says absently, in the way of someone who thinks it's a man's business to avoid shit luck.

"How'd you find us here?"

"The same way you ended up here. I got a lead on where the skull was and then I worked my way up."

Shane fires up a Camel and promptly forgets he's still holding the lit match.

Bentley circles behind him, claps Bobby on his shoulder as if he's a long-lost frat brother – "How's things, my friend?" – and bends over the pile. He runs the back of his hand across the jacket. "Used to be a cocktail suit, " he says. "I recognize it. A saleslady at Garfinckel's told me this is made from something called Capri satin. There this'll run you as much as a couple hundred."

"Garfinckel's," Shane says. "I'm assuming you priced it out as a present for your wife?"

Bentley rolls his eyes. "Something like that, pal."

He steps back and takes in the flashlight, the tarp, the bone box. "It looks like you've invested some energy in this." He slides next to Shane and grasps his arm. "You know you've only got a few hours left on it, right?"

Shane's match is burning to the nub but he's not paying attention to it. "You don't see anybody getting in my way right now, do you?"

"That's only because Big Chief Charlie Moran doesn't know yet what he has on his hands. A well-dressed dame getting dumped dead in the wildest park in the city. Do you know how huge this could be?"

Bentley's on to something and Shane knows it. In the middle of a crime wave, with all the papers all over him, the Chief will do everything he can to avoid having to take this case on as a homicide that he'll probably never close.

The match flame catches Shane's fingers and he winces and throws it down. "You know if the Star or the Daily News have gotten wind of this?"

"Right now I'm alone on the story. But I won't be for long."

"So when do you have to go to Moran for comment?"

Bentley answers carefully. "Our first edition hits the streets at 2 a.m. Meaning my deadline is midnight."

Shane feels his chest tighten. "So that means I've got about 16 hours before Moran tries to take this in his own direction."

"Maybe less. Don't hold me to anything." Bentley pulls Shane close to him. "Listen, I've heard you've had a hard time on the job lately. I know you're dying on the vine, you want a comeback case. But something tells me this isn't the right one."

Shane breaks free. A plan born of desperation is coming to him. "I'll keep going over all these bones, something's got to be on one of them. Then I'll get my sergeant to push to get Glover from the crime scene squad down here, he's the best, and he'll get all the clothes over to the Homicide office, and the bones over to the coroner. And then we'll go to missing persons and get all their files on dames who disappeared last year and we'll see if we can find something there."

"Something. Something like fucking what?"

Shane doesn't answer. The only voice he hears now is the one in his head.

We'll see if the clothes match up with any of the descriptions in the missing persons reports. Maybe a red suit, if we're lucky.

And if we don't get a hit, we'll look to the descriptions of each missing girl and see if the clothes here would fit her.

Or if she'd ever be caught dead in them. Literally.

Bobby sits on his haunches by the pile. "Shouldn't we box up all the sand, too? I mean, there could be something, right?'

"No. That won't be necessary. We'll find something on the bigger bones."

"But –"

"No, that's what we'll do. And I swear to God that before midnight I'll figure out who this girl was, or at least what happened to her."

Shane walks up the hill towards the playground. It's raining now and he's getting drenched, but he doesn't care. At the top he takes off his hat and raises his face to the rain and he feels the water rolling down the nape of his neck. He makes his way back down the hill, passes Bobby and Bentley and looks down at the dirt pile, which is starting to melt under the drip-drip-drip from the trees overhead. He reaches down and picks up a sleeve on the jacket and rubs it gently between his fingers. Pieces of it flake off and settle into the moist ground.

He puts the sleeve back in its place. He feels himself banging the outside of his right thigh with his fist, softly at first and then harder, like a jockey taking the whip to his mount. "Let's get after it," he says. "We've got to fill up these clothes with a real live woman, don't we?"

5

A straw hat, gray, probably once black.

A broken chain with a locket that may have once held a photo.

A tattered suit jacket. A blouse and a skirt and a belt.

A bra and underwear, a girdle with garters. A slip and nylons.

Jewelry and a wristwatch, a shoe, just one.

Shane's taken all the clothing from the hill and put it on a table in the homicide squad room.

He rearranges it to mimic a life-form.

The only sound in the room comes from the radio in his sergeant's office. It's an opera singer, Mario Lanza, in full voice.

Bobby's next to him and next to Bobby is the sergeant, Nunzio Roncalli. Sarge is stolid and sober, grounded by family: an Italian earth-mother wife and five boys he's grooming for police work. He's so fervent in his faith that his men call him "The Nun" behind his back. He's a man of only one known extravagance, which is playing opera garishly on his office radio. He's everything that Shane isn't. Shane loves him anyway.

It's been two days since Shane slept, and his head is aching. He goes in his pocket for two more bennies.

He pulls Glover's evidence report and picks up the one shoe. "Report here says it's a high-heel, brand name Natural Poise, size 7. Which is, what, about a medium? Sarge?"

"Yeah, that's my wife's size. Which in her particular case means that her feet are the only thing on her that's still a medium."

Shane picks up the hat, which is topped by what look like brown stems. "Guess these used to be flowers. Name inside the hat says Breton, pretty fancy brand if I'm not mistaken."

"Was the hat in the pile?"

"No, it was under some leaves around 15 feet away."

Shane's running scenes through his head.

She's walking down Calvert Street, and some goon catches her by surprise and pushes her, and she catches a heel and falls backwards down the hill. She hits her head and her fresh-bought hat flies into the brush. She's his for the taking.

Shane reaches for the jewelry. "We've got a ring and earrings and a pin and they've all got blue rocks in them. They look like, I don't know, topaz."

The sergeant holds the earrings up to the light. "I think we can say for sure this wasn't a robbery."

"Not necessarily. There's no sign of a purse, and you'd think that'd still be there. We can't rule out anything."

Sarge: "What about her drawers? Anything notable?"

A garter belt, hose and underpants are fused together in a congealed ball. Gingerly, Shane separates the underpants. "Rough as sandpaper."

"Any signs of tearing?"

Shane pulls the ends apart and they crackle. "Not that I can see. We found them in the pile right near the pelvic bone, so it doesn't look like they were taken off her and then tossed away."

The goon starts to work the ring off her finger, but it sticks. He reaches under her skirt and works his way up. But then he hears a siren, and he runs into the woods.

Sarge: "What's the report say about the watch?"

"It's a Seth Thomas, so-called Sweetheart Brand. Looks like she was at least somebody's sweetheart."

Say she had a husband, and a lover on the side. And her husband trailed her to Calvert Street, and now he's lying in wait. He sees her leaving a bar and bum-rushes her, grabs the wrist that wears the Sweetheart watch. He says to her, How can you have the nerve to wear anything I gave you when you're out catting around like this? He twists her arm behind her back and forces her down face-first.

Bobby's holding the bra, eyes wide. "What's your report there say about this?"

"You've gotta love Glover. Report actually notes, 'D cup.'"

Shane lifts up the blouse and skirt, which are crumbling on the edges, and inspects the suit jacket. "Glover must've taken a magnifying glass to this. Says the collar was velvet, not that you can tell anymore."

And the fabric, as he now knows from Bentley, is Capri satin. Two words that Shane never heard put together, and from now on they'll always evoke something just beyond his reach.

The sergeant works his fingers around the jacket to where the label should be. "Do we know what size this stuff is?"

"Yeah, the report says medium. An average-sized girl."

Bobby's still eyeing the bra, fixated. "An average-sized girl, but geez. Them things shoulda been in the guidebooks, like tourist attractions."

The Sarge laughs. Shane doesn't.

She has a shape to her and she knows it. She gets off the streetcar at twilight and she sees a man in a nice wool suit. She turns just so, and she sees him eye her up and down. Later, backed against a lamppost with his tongue dancing around hers, she feels his hand against her breast and she thinks, this is going too fast. She moves his hand, he moves it back, and grabs harder. And he doesn't let go.

Shane throws the evidence report on the table. "There were two items in her pockets that the property clerk sent straight over to the fingerprint squad. He thinks maybe they can get something off them. One's a makeup case, the other's a receipt from a restaurant, dated May 1, '51. And no, there's no name on it."

"What restaurant?"

"The Calvert Café. It's about a hundred yards up from the pile where she was found. So we know where she was that night."

Bobby rises. "Let's run on over there and talk to the manager."

"We don't have a name of the girl, we don't have a picture. So what do we ask him? Sir, do you remember seeing a woman in red wandering through here on some vague night in the distant past?'"

On the radio in the Sarge's office Mario Lanza's opera tenor has given way to a Broadway voice, singing about an enchanted evening, seeing an unfamiliar woman across a crowded room, and somehow knowing he'll see her again and again.

Shane grabs the box of files that he got from missing persons and empties it on the table. The files obediently fan out in alphabetical order. "All the broads reported missing last May. Let's see if we can make any kind of a match with our clothing here."

Roncalli picks up the first file. "Ella Bertram, age 25, secretary with the Treasury Department. Last seen on April 28, 1951, getting into a cab after leaving Duke Zeibert's on L Street. That's not that far from the Calvert Street Bridge."

"Was she with anybody?"

"The report says she was known at the restaurant and a waitress there said she was with a serviceman, some oily guy the waitress had never seen before."

"Any clothing description?"

"Nothing specific. Waitress said it was cold in the restaurant that night, and Ella wore a heavy coat through the whole meal."

"Did they ever find the serviceman?"

The sergeant takes a scrap out of the file. "A note here says that they got a lead on him over at Fort Belvoir, but there's nothing here to say that anything came out of it."

Shane sits up. "Physical description on the girl?"

"Subject is described as five foot seven nine inches tall and weighing about 175 pounds."

Shane shakes his head. "She's not our girl. There's no way this one would've gotten into a size medium." He's drumming his fingers loudly on the table. "Next, Sarge."

"Lou Ann Campbell, age 22, student living at 724 8th Street, Northwest, reported missing on May 4, 1951. Report doesn't give any physicals and it doesn't say when she was last seen."

"Student, 22 years-old, meaning she's in college. Living over on 7th Street. Howard University, right?"

"You got it."

"She's not our girl. Next."

Bobby: "Why?"

"Because it's a Negro college. These are fancy white girl's clothes."

"But –"

"Bobby, that's just how it is. Move on, Sarge." Shane's fingertips are beating faster on the table, tap-tap-tap.

"Okay, next. One Maureen Collins."

"Maureen?"

"Yeah, Shane. Maureen.

Maureen.

Shane hasn't seen his wife in more than a year, in fact more than five, give or take. It was a separation that Shane both provoked, and didn't choose. At the end, he signed papers. Has she gotten remarried, changed her last name? He remembers going to the Park with her once when they were barely teenagers and finding his way with her into bushes off a path. What if some other frolic took her back there?

"What's the DOB on that Maureen girl," he says, flushed.

"Doesn't matter," Sarge says. "Maybe you didn't hear. It was a bad report. Collins girl never went missing."

Shane settles back.

It goes this way for more than an hour, from the A's through the J's, with the sergeant throwing out 20 names and Shane rejecting each in turn.

He can picture each of them. He sees her moment of panic, then her moment of clarity, as she watches her life-thread slip from its spool and fall gently into black.

Shane just can't put the dead girl's clothes on any one of them. And so for each one he says, "She's not our girl."

"Okay," the Sarge says, "here's another. Barbara Kaplan, age 25. Last seen on the evening of Tuesday, May 1, 1951, which would be the exact date we're looking for. Disappeared after leaving her house on 6th Street, to go over to her sister's in Blue Plains. Mother of six."

Bobby spits tobacco juice into an empty coffee cup. "Can I just ask something here. Just askin', right? Was this Kaplan girl workin' at the time?"

Shane's thinking, I don't need to hear from Shiflett unless cracking this case is somehow going to involve horses or farm animals. But Sarge answers. "It says here she was a housewife."

"What about her husband," Bobby says. "How'd he make a living?"

"He was a butcher."

"It ain't her, neither," Bobby responds. "Our girl was dressed up real nice. A butcher's wife with a houseful of kids ain't gettin' dressed up to go nowhere at night in the middle of the week, and especially not just to go see her sister."

Nobody says anything for a few seconds.

The sergeant nods and smiles. "I think you're right, Shiflett. How'd you come up with that?"

"Just watchin' Shane do this. The way he thinks, it brings a whole world to life."

But Shane isn't listening. From outside he's hearing a bell. It's coming from Sarge's dago church a few blocks away, and it's tolling six, seven, eight, nine.

We won't even be done with these files before 10. Bentley sees the Chief in just a few hours, and then the Chief will know all about this, and then everything will change and I'll never see this case again.

The Broadway voice fades into a station break.

Tap-tap-tap-tap-tap. "Come on, Sarge. We can crack this."

Shane has another vision, this one more lyrical.

A young woman is getting ready for something. Maybe it's a date, maybe it's a show, but whatever it is, it's something special. She goes to her closet, puts a blouse around her shoulders and feels its softness on her skin. She looks for a crimson jacket, doesn't see it at first – where's it hiding? – then finds it, plucks it off the hanger. She puts on the jacket and a matching skirt, cinches a belt around her waist, admires herself.

She goes to her mirror and dabs on makeup and lipstick. She leans in close and smacks her lips twice – just the act of doing it is a small pleasure. She looks one last time in the mirror and fusses with her bangs. She puts on a pair of patent leather high heels, then another and another before choosing the first, eyeing the line of her legs in the closet's full-length mirror. She swings a purse over her shoulder, tilts her head back and walks out her front door to take on the world.

Roncalli turns back and forth gently in his swivel chair, his half-circuits regular as a metronome's. His phone rings and he gets up to answer it.

Bobby spits again into his cup. "Ain't it amazin'," he says, "our girl's family wasn't down here the day after she went missin'? How can it be in America that a girl can just disappear into nothin' and nobody cares?"

Shane listens for the sergeant's voice from the other room, but the only sound he can hear is the death rattle of his own fingertips.

The sergeant comes back to the table. "That was Glover. When they scraped some dirt off of the makeup case they came up with a single letter monogram, the letter R. So we can just hone in on the Rs."

Shane flips through the pile of files. "There's still eight girls here with last name R. And then there's all the girls with first name R."

"Well, there's something else you should know. Glover found a groove on one of the bones. And from what he's seen in his other cases, he thinks it came from a knife. The coroner's examining it right now."

Shane leans back and closes his eyes. Bobby nudges him. "And this means..."

"It means," Shane says, awakening to a world of possibilities, "that I'll get my homicide classification from the coroner. It means the Chief won't kill this. It means I'll have a case to work. It means I'll get to find out who the hell she was."

★★★★★★★★★★

Day 1, foam at the mouth, pink in color, and flies appear.

Day 2, maggots at the nose and mouth, structural breakdown, eye orbits crumbling.

Day 3, darker maggots arrive.

Shane recognizes the words he's seeing in his head. At some point in his shifting past it was important for him to know what they meant.

Day 5, skull bone visible, hair loosening.

Day 6, second round of flies arrive.

Shane recognizes the words but he's never seen them look like this, rolling in front of his eyes as if they've been inscribed on a long, lighted ribbon.

Day 7, mold on nose.

Day 8, beetles arrive, skin erodes, mouth deteriorates.

A skull is floating in front of him at waist-level. For once, just once, he wants to be able to fight disintegration to a draw. So he grabs at the skull with both hands to hold it together but it starts to move in circles. He loses his grip.

****

The steering wheel is moving as if it's spinning on its own. Shane turns it hard-left, hits a curb and rocks to a stop.

He puts his head on the wheel. *Fuck, where have I been.* He feels pressure rising from his gut, opens his door, stumbles outside and lets everything out.

He sticks his rolled-up Post under his arm. There's a lamppost at curbside and he leans into it, fumbles a Beechnut into his mouth and tosses the wrapper. He coughs. *I've been coughing all goddam night.* He brings something up from the back of his throat and hocks it to the street. and it collects in a crack and works its way towards the wrapper slowly, slowly, like a raindrop sliding down a windowpane. All he can focus his wits on is the course of his spittle. A minute goes by, maybe five, maybe 20.

I'm here to see Chief Moran. He advances towards headquarters, placing one foot in front of the other with the care of a tightrope walker. *I'm here to see goddam Chief Moran.* The hallways are a maze. *I'm here to see –"*

"Shane, what the hell are you doing here?"

Shane hears Roncalli say, it's five o'clock in the morning. You're not due back in for at least a few more hours on account of the overtime you worked last night. And he hears him say, it looks like you slept in your suit, you miserable lush.

Roncalli says something else but the words are lost as soon as they hit the air.

"Pay attention, Shane." The sergeant grabs him by both shoulders and keeps his hands on him. "Okay, that's better. Come in here."

He guides Shane to an office and forces him into a chair. "I'll never be able to figure you out. Just what are you thinking?"

"I'm not giving up, goddammit. I'm here to see the Chief."

"Like hell you are. As if the Chief's even in the building, and a good thing for you, too. He'd have your behind in a second if he saw you like this, and he wouldn't give a crap who your old man is."

Roncalli runs his hand through his dark, wiry hair. "Mother of God, you were flying high just as few hours ago. How'd you even find anyplace open on a Sunday night?"

Shane trusts his sergeant, more than he trusts anyone anymore. Alone among the brass, the Nun has one distinction: Shane's never caught him in a lie. In his years on the force Shane has won his share of medals and certificates. He once saved them but now they're all gone, except for the pin the Nun ceremoniously fixed to his lapel when he closed his first murder case: the sergeant's own 20-year service pin.

Yes, he trusts his sergeant. Which doesn't mean that at this particular moment it should go both ways.

Shane takes off his hat and carefully balances it on one knee. "I just went to Tony's for a couple of quick ones, Sarge. But I've been under the weather lately." Here, the cough comes in handy.

Left out of the story is that after the two quick ones he downed five more, then closed down Tony's, then closed down the after-hours joint on Fourteenth Street.

Also left out of the story are the downers he dropped when he left work.

"Jesus, Shane," the Sarge offers. "Jesus." The way Sarge says the name, you're convinced he knows the man personally. "When you were on your game, you were the best detective on the whole force. Look at the Uline case. And you're going to say you don't remember it, like you always do."

Shane doesn't, really, just the basics. A white guy killed a Negro girl not far from Uline Arena after the circus let out one night. The only witness was a white hooker in the neighborhood. Somebody on Shane's squad had to break her, and it wasn't exactly what you'd call easy, but he ended up bringing her around.

As for the rest of the story – how he found out her whole history so he knew how to get to her, how patiently he worked her, when his voice rose and dropped, how he played on what little was left of her best instincts – it's all lost to Shane, except in the occasional retelling of the sergeant, who somehow maintains a memory of all the interrogations he ever saw or did. To Shane, they're just like the trials he once handled as a lawyer, in another life.

At the time, here and now. Forever after, there and then.

The Sarge is still talking. "You saw things no other detective could see."

Shane thinks back on a Christmas Eve night spent in a holding cell at D.C. Jail, getting a confession from a rapist over a shared tin of corned beef hash, when every other cop on the squad was home trimming trees and doing God knows what else. "Bullshit," he answers. "I just worked harder than everybody else."

And if he could find a way to the words, he'd say this: I'm a lawyer, and if it wasn't for the fucking war that's what I'd still be. Best detective – I wanted more than that. I'll never do this job as well as I could be doing that one. I might as well be playacting.

The Sarge goes on. "You went downhill on me there for a while. But then the last couple of days, I thought you were back to your old self. Now I see this."

"It's not as if me going out last night made any difference."

"But you know what might make a difference? I've never come out in so many words and told you to try to find God. What have I said?"

"I know. I should let God find me. I got it."

Shane's knee jerks and his barely balanced hat starts to fall but he snags it. "If God's really looking he knows where to find me every night. I can't wait to see him. The water into wine thing will come in handy."

Everything's starting to come into focus for him. "Look, Sarge," he says, "I came down here to see the Chief. If I can't see him, I need to see Rector."

"This is about that girl in the Park, isn't it?"

"Yeah. Yeah, it is." Shane shoves the newspaper across the desk. "First edition. Came out just after 2 a.m. Read the back page."

THE WASHINGTON POST
Monday, May 26, 1952

POLICE ABANDON PARK BODY CASE
AS PROMISING CLUE PROVES WORTHLESS
By Bran Bentley, Staff Reporter

No further police action will be taken regarding the skeletonized remains found in a dirt pile in Rock Creek Park this weekend. "The bones were closely inspected by the coroner and experienced Metropolitan officers," MPD Chief Charles Moran told this reporter by telephone. "An officer thought at first that he saw a knife wound on one of the bones. But as it turned out it was just a defect and had nothing to do with whatever happened here."

The Chief went on to say that since there were no other signs of foul play, and the coroner's office has specifically refused to classify the case as a homicide, "I've told my men to close it out and move on to more pressing matters."

"Jesus Christ, Sarge, how much do you have to read to know what it says?"

"Pipe down."

While police recovered almost all of the skeleton, still missing are the bones of the victim's right ring finger. They will likely remain lost in the forest. A high-ranking police official observed, "We'll probably never know what happened to the girl. Sometimes strange things just happen in Rock Creek Park and there's no rhyme or reason to them."

The sergeant grimaces. "It would've been nice if somebody had told me they're closing this out," he says bitterly. "Just a few hours ago I went around and around with the Chief on this. I thought I'd bought us some time."

"What the fuck happened?"

"I guess I shouldn't be surprised."

The Sarge rubs his face. No matter what he's saying, it always comes out in the tone of a man wearily rubbing his face.

"What it comes down to is, nobody around here wants to deal right now with all the flack a murder in the Park brings. The press is already in a fever about the hearings on the Hill, and the crime rate's just gone up again. And then on top of all that, there's what happened earlier this morning."

Just past midnight, U.S. Marshals were dispatched to a bungalow in Northeast and a rowhouse in Northwest, rousting two veteran MPD vice officers on graft charges.

"Faye behind this?"

"Yeah," the Sarge answers. "Who else?"

Jeremiah Norris Faye is the city's top federal prosecutor, on the job for just under a year. He does his work with the grand jury in secret, silent as Coolidge and reclusive as a Trappist, while all the other DAs before him just bent over and said "take me" to anybody with a press pass. Quietly he's working his police corruption cases up through the ranks of MPD. Rumor has it that he has his sights set on none other than Jake Kaufman, friend of compromised cops throughout the city and most likely their real boss as well.

"So what you're telling me," Shane says, "is that with everything that's going on, Moran won't stick his neck out on this."

"Shane, just accept it."

"So who're the vice guys who are getting indicted?"

"You know them. Stan Carper and Jimmy Taylor."

Shane thinks back, the haze is lifting. Carper and Taylor. He met them both right after he came out of training – rode around with them once, saw them drag an old Negro drunk into an alley and force his face into a sewer grate until he told them where some drifter witness was hanging out.

Shane pretty much avoided Carper and Taylor after that.

The sergeant circles behind him, closes the door and pulls a chair next to him. "Shane, I know you got a raw deal on that lagoon case. I want to help you. But my hands are tied on this thing."

"Your hands are tied on pretty much everything."

"Especially this. As far as the Chief is concerned, all this Park case will do is whip everybody into a frenzy and then they'll start pointing fingers at him. The girl's been up there in the Park dead for a year. Even if it's a murder, you think anybody's ever going to get to the bottom of it?"

"Not if nobody tries, they won't. It just isn't right to play politics with this girl. Shit, if we stop now, we won't even know who to give the bones to. Just get me a week and I'll have something."

"I took my best shot, Shane. I don't think anybody could reach the Chief on this."

"Sarge, I can be that guy again. The guy that broke that hooker witness, and a lot more than that. I can do anything I want, I just feel it."

The sergeant clasps his hands behind his head and stares at the ceiling.

"I take that back," Roncalli says. "There's one man who can reach the Chief. Your father. You of all people don't have to be reminded of all the things he can get done in this town."

"I'm not doing it, Sarge. I wouldn't go up there and see him even if I was stone cold sober." Shane rises too quickly, sways, falls back in the chair.

"You might have to sack out awhile before you go to his office. But from everything you've told me about your father, he's a pot of black coffee and a long cold shower rolled into one."

"No."

"Listen to me. I can't figure out why this one case matters so much to you, Shane, you haven't told me. But whatever it is, let this sink into your saturated brain. If it means so much, you'll have to do everything it takes."

"You're not telling me anything I don't know."

The sergeant gets out of his chair and stands next to Shane. "I know you're prideful, son. But you know what the Church says about pride."

Shane doesn't want to wait around to hear what the Church says about anything.

6

In an office not far from where Shane and the Sarge are talking, a man is hovering over a typewriter.

The man is someone Shane's never met, though like most informed people in America he's heard of him, and the two actually have friends in common.

The typewriter is an Underwood, vintage 1920's, with a raised carriage and polished silver keys: a church organ in miniature. The room's walls are adorned with precise oil paintings of birds of all types, from the common sparrow and thrush to the exotic umbrella cockatoo and ruby macaw, even the obscure Nazca boobie.

Thanks to television, Haynes Nickens's face and name are known to millions. They have some idea about the hours he devotes to whatever task is given him, always for the greatest good – often 40 or 50 or 60 sleepless in a stretch, and one time a full 72, not that he was counting – and his reputation for righteous discipline is legendary, even feared.

Now, he's going back through what he's just typed, making sure, as he always has, that what he writes will exceed the bounds of his assignment and stand the scrutiny of time.

And if somehow there's some puny imperfection in this report that he should've long since finished but never got to before, given the press of all his business, who'll ever notice?

His fingers hang like claws over the keyboard.

MEMORANDUM

DATE: April 1, 1951

TO: Chairman
    Committee on Un-American Activities
    United States House of Representatives

FROM: Haynes Nickens
      Investigator

RE: Surveillance of Target No. 1

On this date, the reporting investigator has completed his surveillance of Target No. 1 and the female subject who was made a part of this investigation due to her association with Target No. 1. The following is a complete memorialization of the information that the reporting investigator has developed on the female subject.

She was born Emma Hadassah Rosenblum in Bonn, Germany on December 3, 1927 and raised there until age 10. Her father, Siegfried, was a merchant and a leader in his community.

In October 1938, the female subject, her mother Hanna, her paternal grandmother Hilde, and three-year-old sister Leah escaped from Bonn to avoid Nazi persecution. Her father stayed behind, planning to rejoin his family after assuring escape for other Jews in his neighborhood, particularly his employees. He was subsequently terminated.

The female subject and her surviving family members eventually ended up in Shanghai, China, along with thousands of other Jewish refugees, believing it would be a safe haven. Shanghai was an "open city" before the war and did not have restrictions on immigration. Certain Chinese officials sympathetic to the Jews issued mass "protective passports" to them; by 1941, nearly 20,000 European Jews had found shelter there. The female subject attended the Jewish Youth Association School in Shanghai. Already fluent in German and Hebrew, she learned English quickly and acquired an American accent from U.S. teachers at the school.

Unbeknownst to the female subject and her family, shortly after their arrival in Shanghai a plan was devised to exterminate Shanghai's Jewish population. Ultimately they were crowded by the thousands into a small area where raw sewage and rats ran uncontrolled, and they were treated like animals by their military overseers.

Evidently, in the words of the idiom, the female subject had fled from the frying pan into the fire.

7

Shane's in his father's office. Ten minutes ago he was in the backseat of his car, sleeping off his bender. Still, he's here, and the old man is keeping him waiting, as always. In the meantime he has to listen to Louis Carlsberg rail about what a "this goddam dilettante," one Joe Barry.

"If Joe so much as comes close to setting one foot in the U.S. Senate, Shane, I swear to you I'll shoot him first."

Washington is a town full of hatreds and none is more fevered than Raymond Kinnock's, held vicariously by Louis Carslberg, for Matthew Barry and his son Joseph.

Louis was Raymond's first hire for his Washington office more than thirty years ago, an energetic and servile 17-year-old. Raymond promptly tapped into him and began the long, slow process of bleeding him dry. Now Louis sounds like Raymond, dresses like Raymond, and every night drifts off to sleep comforted by thoughts of Raymond.

Shane tries to make his point quickly. "I'm just up here about a case I'm working and I need to get back on the job soon." But Louis is having none of it. "Do you really think, me boyo, you can come up here and move things along like you might a vagrant on Ninth Street? You're up here now, don't you know, where everything moves at its own pace."

They go to an anteroom behind an unmarked door. It has no windows and just three pieces of furniture – two chairs with no armrests and a squat telephone table – but on its walls are photographs of Raymond Kinnock on just about every square inch, with everyone who's mattered in the American half–century, Babe Ruth and Lillian Hellman, Albert Einstein and Arturo Toscanini, every President since Wilson, and on and on.

There are at least a hundred pictures mounted, going back through Raymond's entire career, and he appears to be about the same age in all of them. In his 30's, prematurely gray, he's wise and inscrutable, in his 60's, ruddy and barrel-chested, he's vital and potent. He dominates every photograph no matter who happens to share space with him. Even his teeth intimidate across the years: garish white, showing just a hint of the incisors, the smile of the beguiling predator.

The photographs send a message to anyone who's ushered into this room by Raymond or Louis. This is a man who's known everyone worth knowing in America, and what's good for him is good for America, so what's good for him has to be good for you too.

"So how's the old man's campaign going?" Shane takes the lead, putting off for now the moment when the talk turns to him, and what happened to him at the Senate crime hearing a month ago. He'll need to have a completely clear head then, and that's still a distant goal.

"Aye," Louis says, blessing himself, "I think your Pop's in for a rough one."

"You say that every two years."

"But he's actually got a Republican opponent this year, and the boy's got a lot of money in the coffers. Word is, that bastard is putting a big chunk of his millions behind him."

"Jesus, Louis. You've heard all the rumors. That bastard's gone crazy as a loon. It's been one long, slow breakdown for him since the accident. Have some mercy."

"I don't have it in my heart and neither does your father. There's no keeping that bastard down."

That bastard. Matthew Barry, blood enemy of Raymond Kinnock and another 60–some- year-old Irish Catholic who's used to getting his way. Matt is second-generation Irish, the sole heir to millions that the Barry family earned in shipbuilding while the Kinnocks were still pushing mule carts around in the old country. He runs the Barry family empire from an estate that occupies prime beachfront in upper-crust Southampton, Long Island. He hasn't been seen in public since his youngest son died in a car wreck.

Raymond Kinnock and Matt Barry locked horns 30 years ago and began a feud that's partly political, partly personal, and entirely tied up in stubborn, petty grudges. Suffice it to say that it started when one or the other made an offhand remark at the raucous wake of a friend in common, and the remark got back to the other one, and the question of which one sprang from lower-rung "shanty Irish" forebears was permanently put in play – that's all it took. Now Matt controls a newspaper, the New York Herald Sun, and he deploys it to attack Raymond at will. Raymond, House Majority Leader, controls every Congressional committee that can hound Barry and his monopolies.

And neither one will be satisfied until he annihilates the other.

Shane shakes his head. "There's no way the old man loses this one. There's practically no one in his district who doesn't owe him, he's made sure of that."

"I'm just saying, me boyo, he's got a fight on his hands and I don't even know if he realizes it. He spends less time on his own race than he does trying to figure out how to keep that bastard's boy out of the Senate."

That bastard's boy. Joe Barry is Matt's 35-year-old son and his last great hope. Joe's running for a Senate seat in New York, Raymond's state, circling the territory and pissing all over it to mark it for his father and his family. Raymond's trained himself to hate the son as much as the father, if that's possible.

"I keep telling your Da," Louis says, "just let Matt put his boy in there, it doesn't matter as much to you as to does to him. But your Da keeps fighting, and so that bastard keeps fighting back against him in his newspapers, running all these stories, putting him in the worst light. And if somehow that bastard caught hold of some monstrous lie and ran with it, God knows what could happen to the bill."

The bill, of course, the bill: Raymond's new life mission. Shane's as distanced from his father's work as he is from the man himself so he only knows that it has to do with civil rights, and Raymond says it'll change America forever. Since it's an election year, the bill has to pass before all the wavering Congressmen go back to their home districts at the end of summer and hear their constituents tell them, We've already done enough for the nigras, and where'd you get it in your head to think we sent you up there to go off on your own on some high-minded whim?

Which means, to hear Raymond's followers tell it, he's the only man to get the bill through, and any public challenge to him between now and August should be taken as nothing less than an attack on Negroes everywhere. Mind you, no one can quite figure out what's made him so gung-ho about Negroes all of a sudden – up until recently he hasn't exactly been Frederick Douglass on race issues. So why now?

He's an aging man with much power but no promotion in sight. He's next in line to be Speaker of the House, but the Speaker is wily Sam

Rayburn, with a death grip on the job. He's moved by a vision of himself in the oval office down Pennsylvania Avenue. And the only way to get there is to seize someone else's dream to stake claim to his own.

Unless Raymond's actually sincere about what he says he wants to do.

"And you know, Shane, the bill is all your Da lives for now."

Shane doesn't give an answer right away. Then: "I'd listen to what you're saying about this bill if I didn't already know exactly why my father's usual grubby maneuverings are being devoted to something noble."

Louis hasn't heard a word. "All I know," he says, "is that it's not going to be any easier for your father if his only son keeps finding his way into the news for the wrong reasons."

Shane knows what Louis is about to say, just as any other son of a famous man would. *Everything you do reflects back on him.*

He tries to head it off. "It's not as if I wrote a letter to Senator Kuykendall saying, 'As long as you're holding your hearings on crime and corruption in D.C., let me have the honor of giving humiliating public testimony about the dishonest sons of bitches I work for, and how they fucked up a murder case and then lied about it. And while you're at it, Senator, can you please set it up so I can end up being the fall guy for the whole goddam thing."

"Don't swear."

"Somebody on Kuykendall's staff found me, I'm sure it wasn't hard. All I know is, I didn't want this."

"You should've just come to us. I know your father and Harlan Kuykendall have had their disagreements, but these things can always be worked out. It's just lucky for all of us that your father has his District committee on this side, and he could talk to people and try to make it right for you."

Shane steps towards Louis. It's all he can do to keep from wringing the man's neck. "You forget I've actually practiced a little law, and I know enough to know what it means when you get a subpoena. I couldn't just come to you, I had to come to the committee. Christ, Louis, I didn't come here to get into all this."

Where the hell is the old man?

"Look, me boyo, no need for this to get unpleasant." Louis reaches out and squeezes Shane's arm. "I just want what's best for you. Can you at least tell me –"

"– that I'm not planning to spill my guts in public again and ruin what's left of my police career? Yeah, Louis, I can say that."

"That's my good man." Louis smiles for the first time. "So what brings you here? You're looking marvelous, by the way."

"Just some police business, like I said. We found a skull in Rock Creek Park yesterday."

"Aye, and I'm sure your Pop will love to see you." Louis glances at his watch. "Come, take a seat in his main office. There's something in there you might like to take a look at."

Shane can find the main office just by following the stale cigar smell. It looks pretty much the same as it did years ago, just a few knickknacks have been added here and there, and some photos that have spilled over from the anteroom (Mae West, Douglas Mac Arthur, Ernest Hemingway).

Louis points proudly at a television in a wooden console. "Isn't it a beauty?" He touches the top lightly. "Top of the line. I just got it for your father a couple of months ago at Dalmo's, not even three hundred. You know how he is, needs to know everything all the time." Louis beams like a father who's just bought his boy a new bike.

Louis isn't worth even a tenth of what Raymond is, but he bought his boss this high-priced television, and Raymond took it.

"Anyway," Louis says, still glowing, "make yourself at home, feel free to watch it. The Senate crime hearings are on again this morning. Your Chief is up right now."

Louis leaves and Shane settles into his father's leather chair and turns on the set.

A small white dot appears in the center of the dark screen and stays there, flickering slightly, for five or ten seconds before flaring into a close-up of the beefy face of Charles Patrick Moran, Chief of the Metropolitan

Police Department. The subject is gamblers, and whether they might have anything to do with the city's rising crime.

"You've asked me about this Jake Kaufman fellow," Moran says. "From everything I know, he's a legitimate businessman."

"And not just that," the Chief says, "he's the American Dream in human form. Born to poor immigrants, he taught himself the barrel trade, built himself a business, and earned himself a fortune that he now gives back to his hometown by way of donations announced every year with a press conference in front of police headquarters."

"From the barrel business," the Chief concludes, "Jake Kaufman moved into the entertainment business and is now a highly influential *impresario*." Moran's eyebrows arch as he says the word as if to say, look here, this old flatfoot knows his way around the language.

"But Chief Moran, one question has to be asked."

From off-camera comes the sound of papers being shuffled.

"What about this Washington Post article from March of this year? It says that, quote, Mr. Kaufman's numbers business here got so vast that last year it attracted the attention of a Philadelphia gangster family, the Rick – the Rick –"

The microphones pick up whispering back and forth.

"– I'm saying, the Riccobene family, that's R-I-C-C-O-B-E-N-E family. And that the Kaufman organization retaliated so violently that the Riccobenes from Philadelphia had to turn tail and run. What do you have to say about that?"

Moran takes off his eyeglasses – which Shane knows he doesn't need to see, he just wears them when he thinks the occasion calls for him to look more serious – and examines them intently. Finally: "I just thought that was our revenge for their Eagles beating our Redskins nine out of the last ten times."

The questioner doesn't bother to follow up. Moran delivers a haymaker. "Senator, if you end up being lucky enough to spend as many years in this town as I have, you'll learn that you can't believe everything you read."

The camera pulls back, revealing that Chief Charles Moran is at the long witness table by himself, the man in charge with no entourage needed. He's the second-best actor in town, eclipsed only by Raymond Kinnock, the man from whom he learned the craft.

The Chief and Raymond Kinnock are friends, of a sort. When they're together in public the Chief will call Raymond his very best friend, and Raymond will graciously nod and return the favor. In truth, the friendship is a marriage of mutual necessity. Raymond runs the House committee on city affairs and gives Charlie Moran everything he says he needs to run the police department and keep his command. In return, Charlie deploys his department's infantry of street snitches to dig up dirt for Raymond: this Congressman seen coming out of a bottle club with a stripper, that Senator spotted in a homo joint, a cabinet official hanging around with egghead friends who might be tied up with Commie front groups.

Thanks mainly to Charlie Moran, Raymond Kinnock knows more about everyone in official Washington than anyone else knows, including J. Edgar Hoover – someone else that Raymond knows a lot about.

"Chief Moran, sir," says a voice in a Southern drawl, "if there's no threat from organized crime in the city, why is the murder rate going up?"

The Chief is ready. "Senator, twenty percent of our violent crimes occur in just one of our thirteen precincts, the Second. That area is exactly one-point-two square miles, and exactly fifty thousand, eight hundred eighty-seven people live there."

"And what," the voice interjects, "makes the Second Precinct so bad?"

"The main reason is the heavy proportion of colored people there. I'm sure there are many upstanding citizens among them. But the better elements are moving out and the worse elements are moving in."

Blame the Negroes, Charlie, nobody does it better than you do. Throw in some condescending bullshit to cover yourself.

The camera jerks to bring one of the senators into the frame: Harlan Kuykendall, committee chairman, Raymond's counterpart on the other side of Capitol Hill. A few months ago, as these hearings caught on with the public, the press started dubbing him the city's top crimebuster, and Kuykendall wasted no time in launching a campaign for the White House.

Naturally, Raymond Kinnock despises Harlan Kuykendall.

"Chief Moran," Kuykendall begins, in a twang that sounds as if it's been plucked from an Ozark banjo. "You must know that in a hearing before this committee just last month, one of your detectives made some very serious allegations against your department."

Shane puts his hand over his eyes. *Christ, why do I have to go through all this again?*

"According to this detective," Kuykendall goes on, "a very well-publicized murder case, the so-called lagoon murder, was handled in a dishonest and corrupt fashion by members of your staff."

"I am familiar with those allegations." The Chief lowers his voice to show concern. "We're all imperfect men. If mistakes were made you can rest assured we'll get to the bottom of them and we'll deal with them. And just so you know, the very detective who's making these accusations hasn't been cleared of anything."

The image of Louis Carlsberg's florid face floats before Shane.

Isn't this television set a beauty, Louis said to him. *I got it for your father a couple of months ago.*

Which means that just a month ago his father was likely watching this television, from this same chair, when Shane was in Charlie Moran's position, getting grilled in live broadcast by this same Senate crime committee. And not handling matters nearly as deftly.

Detective Kinnock, you're telling us that other members of the police department, including a senior detective, forced you to charge a colored man with what's come to be known as the lagoon murder, correct? Even though they had no real evidence he did it?"

"It actually went higher than that, sir. I –"

"This was the same colored man who reported finding the victim's body in the lagoon near the Jefferson Memorial, correct?"

"But in the course –"

"Detective, isn't it true that at the time that this was allegedly going on, you never made any public statement about the matter and you just let what you now say was an injustice perpetuate itself for months, while the man that you now claim to be so concerned about sat rotting in jail?"

"I tried –"

"Answer the question, detective."

"Sir, I –"

"Answer the question."

Shane can picture how his father must've looked here in this room, on this plush leather throne of judgment. He can see him turn to Louis, can see him shake his head disdainfully.

"Detective, are you willing to answer questions today about your own past? Specifically, are you willing to answer questions about your war record and the circumstances of your discharge?"

"Senator, I must respectfully state that as to such questions, I refuse to answer on the grounds that I may incriminate myself."

Shane hears loud voices coming from outside.

Raymond Kinnock bursts in, ruddy-faced and swivel-shouldered, wearing a seersucker suit with a baby blue pocket square and white spats.

He's followed by Louis, a man who's in the habit of trailing a respectful two steps behind everything in life.

"Well, look who's here," Raymond purrs. "So Shane, me boyo, you're trying my chair out for size, are you now?"

Shane rises, smooths out his trousers and comes around the desk. Raymond's already on the other side of the office, hanging his suit jacket on a coat rack and then thumbing through a sheaf of papers that he plucked from his in-box. "So, Louis," Raymond says, "I assume you called our friend Drew Pearson today?"

"I did." Louis smirks.

"And so I'm assured," Raymond presses on, "that our friend Mister Barry will have a surprise in store for him when he opens up his newspaper in a couple of days?"

"He surely will."

"Wonderful, just wonderful."

Raymond turns to Shane. "Son, I know how little interest you have in anything I do, but Drew Pearson – "

"I know who Drew Pearson is, he's in every paper in the country. And I know how to read."

Raymond commandeers his leather chair, takes a box out of the drawer, draws out a long, fat cigar and passes it back and forth over a lit match. "Sublime," he says to himself. "Batista's favorite."

He goes back to his mail and Shane paces to the oak cabinet. "Should I just help myself to a Bailey's?"

"Son," Raymond says, "I've been inexcusably inhospitable. Louis, run and get Shane a small coffee. As I recall, you like it with sugar and – "

"Black."

"-- a dash of cream --"

"No. Black. Black. Just like always."

"Black, then."

In less than a minute Louis fetches coffee in a cup that looks dainty enough to be part of a little girl's tea party set. It's fine china and it has writing on the side, the bold signature of Raymond Kinnock, fashioned in gold inlay as if it were John Hancock's.

Louis stands by while Raymond indulges himself on Battista's favorite cigar. Neither speaks.

Louis finally leaves, shoulders sagging.

Shane lights up a Camel and starts right in. "I know you're busy and I'm busy, too. I just might need for you to help me out with the Chief on a case I want to stay on. There was a skull found in Rock Creek Park the other day, and – what are you doing?"

Raymond's put down his cigar, propped up one foot on his desk and removed his spats, shoe and sock. "Look at my big toe there, the monstrous corn I have. Lanced it the other day, all kinds of pus and sap and whatever else flowed out of it, I thought for a second I was a maple tree in Vermont.

For a day or so the toe was as smooth as a debutante's behind but then the corn came back fierce."

Shane starts to frame a response, but Raymond holds up his hand. "Listen closely," he says. "A living creature approaches, demanding nothing from me. Come here, Rover!"

A sleek white cat with a shimmering coat sidles up to Shane's leg. He leans down but the cat slinks away, emerald eyes glowering. It glides towards Raymond, who chuckles: "Rover, is that any way to treat a guest?" Raymond reaches to take a small ball from the bottom drawer of his desk and proffers it to Rover the cat, who's suddenly animated. "Fetch, Rover!" Raymond tosses the ball across the room four or five times and each time Rover dutifully retrieves it.

Raymond admonishes, "Now sit down." Rover stares at him. Raymond says, "If you want to eat this week, sit *down*." Rover submits meekly. Raymond goes into the drawer and produces a bowl of dry cat food.

Rover raises his head. Raymond glares at him and hides the food.

"So, Shane," he says, "before you get into your grievance tell me how you're doing generally. Chief Moran's treating you well, I'm sure."

Shane looks down at Rover, who seems to be stealing glances at Raymond and quivering. "It depends on what you mean by being treated well. If you mean, am I getting any good work, the answer's no, not at all."

Raymond takes a letter opener from his desk drawer and starts to pick at his big toe. "They say this can cause an infection, but I don't believe it for a minute. I know an instrument like this may not be the cleanest, but it's not as if I've dragged it through a horse flop."

"God almighty, you're not even listening. I'm on ice. And I just want to be back in the mix again."

Raymond picks up an envelope from his desk, surgically divides it crosswise with the letter opener, holds one half to the light. "You couldn't possibly think that you could come up here to that hearing last month, say the things you said about the people you work with, and then expect those same people to welcome you back with open arms. You still have a job, don't you? Just bide your time, wait for the dust to settle, and everything will turn out fine."

Raymond slowly puts his sock and shoe back on, goes behind his desk, takes out the cat food bowl and holds it over Rover, who stands up on his hind legs. "Higher, Rover." The cat extends himself on his paws like a ballet dancer. "Alright," Raymond says, and settles the bowl onto the rug. Rover eats ravenously.

Shane downs the coffee and flicks his cigarette into the cup. "And what happens when everybody's forgotten about the hearings, and nobody's looking at the department anymore, and I'm left to Charlie Moran's mercies?"

Raymond stands up. "Everyone I see, all day long," he said, "they want something from me. Are you no better than them? If you don't mind me saying, things would be a whole lot better for you if you were still married."

"You – you." Shane starts to stammer, stops and starts over. "You didn't even come to our wedding, for God's sake."

"Your mother was ill."

"She was bedridden for just about all the time I knew her, if I can even say I ever did. Her being ill was always your excuse for not doing something you didn't want to do anyway. And half the time you weren't even with Mom, you were up in your district."

"All I'm saying is, maybe if your personal life was more stable, you wouldn't get yourself in scrapes like this." Raymond bends down and plucks Rover's ball from the cat's clutch. "Besides, you and me, we have a history, don't you know. It's not as if I haven't gotten you out of trouble before."

"Do you think I wanted –"

"No, Shane, do you think I wanted. To have my son to be branded a possible war criminal. To have to bow and scrape to a cabinet secretary just to get my son a dishonorable discharge and not something worse. To have to go to the Chief – "

"*Don't say it.*"

"– just to get you a job after you lost your law license?"

Shane wants to throw the tea party cup against the wall and shatter the Raymond Kinnock name. But he doesn't.

He goes to the door to leave.

He doesn't leave.

Raymond breaks the silence. "So, what is it you came here for? I take it there's something you wanted to talk to me about."

There's only one man who can reach the Chief on this, Shane. Your father. Your father.

"There was a skull in the Park yesterday. I got sent down there because they didn't think anything would come of it. Maybe it was some hobo who drifted into the Park and died of exposure, or even some animal. Who knew, you know? Christ, this is pointless."

"So?"

"So, we traced the skull to a pile and then when we dug into it we found bones inside women's clothes. And common sense says that the girl was killed. But the department wants to drop the case --"

"I saw the Post this morning."

"-- because they don't think there's any evidence --"

"I saw the Post."

"I just need a week – get me a week and I can solve this. At least I can prove it's a murder and needs to be investigated. At the very least I can find out who she was, you know?"

Shane's voice hasn't wavered. In the moment when a beaten man's future hangs in the balance he's never thinking, here's my future hanging in the balance. At that moment he's no more aware or conscious or anxious than he's been at any other dire point in his recent past. This is only because he's already become so used to the feel of desperation sweat and endured so many failures that he doesn't sense the coming of the setback that could set him back forever.

Rover's finished lapping up the food. "You know, Shane," says Raymond, "it's been years since you called me father. Or Dad, or Pop, or

Da. Why is that?" He pushes Rover away with his foot. "Ah, it doesn't really matter. Jesus, Shane, whatever you want from me, I can't give it to you."

One beat. Two beats. "I just want to follow this through," Shane says. "I don't want to be pulled off this case, I can't explain why. I put my goddam hands on the girl's skull --"

"Don't use profanity around me."

"I put my *goddam* hands on her skull. Look, it just means a lot to me. I just want the Chief to let me work this even if it's a real homicide, not some heart attack or suicide."

Raymond has sat down and closed his eyes. "What kind of police department would Charlie Moran be running if any old Tom, Dick or Harry could get him on the phone and tell him how he should handle each of his thousands of cases?"

Shane palms the dainty delicate coffee cup and grinds it down onto Raymond's desk and feels the small eggshell bottom crumble. "That was somebody's daughter down there in the Park. Dammit, have you forgotten what it's like to have a girl buried in a bunch of rubble and have nobody care – "

"I don't want to hear this."

" – nobody care what her name was or what kind of burial she gets, or whether she even gets a burial? Goddammit, have you forgotten what we went through?"

Raymond's put a hand over his eyes.

Thirteen years ago, Shane's sister Erin joined the Red Cross as a nurse and went to England.

Twelve years ago, the Nazis bombed the building where she was living in London. Thirty-five of her neighbors were killed, but she survived. She ended up, along with hundreds of others, in a trench that was excavated to serve as a public shelter in a London park named Kennington. There in the park, she went on tending to the sick.

Eleven years ago – actually, 11 years, seven months and six days ago – the Nazis bombed the public shelter. Fifty dead bodies were dug out the first day, but so too were a few survivors. Then heavy rains came, and the walls of the trench started crumbling, and somebody in charge decided it was too dangerous for the recovery workers to continue digging. So, they covered up the smoldering hole, covered up everybody who was still left in the shelter from before the bombs hit. And maybe a few of them, maybe more, might still have been alive.

Somebody made a calculation for the greater good. And the greater good didn't give a shit whether Shane ever saw his twin sister again. The Brit government never even put an exact number on all the dead. Bad for public morale, you know.

This is the way things can go in war, in life, whether you're in a park in London or a hill on Guadalcanal, or anywhere else, really. No one person matters all that much, and some people end up mattering not at all.

"I never told you this," Shane says to his father, "but I flew over there a week afterwards to get answers. And the authorities wouldn't let me anywhere near the park."

I should've pushed them, made them let me go there. I never should've taken no for an answer.

"Shane," Raymond says, "I won't hear this."

"They kept me about a half mile away, but I could see smoke still rising off the pile. Maybe it was from the bomb, maybe it was mist. Hell, all it does over there is rain."

Why the fuck didn't I push them to let me get closer, at least to see?

Raymond has pivoted his chair the other way.

"Whatever it was, I couldn't help thinking about what might be in all that smoke." Shane's throat narrows and his eyes fill up and for the first time in his life he's glad that his father has turned his back to him.

"Do what you have to do," Raymond murmurs.

"What?"

"I said, do what you have to do. And I'll do what I have to do."

"Call the Chief?"

"Yes, yes. I'll call Charlie. Right now." Raymond leaves.

Why doesn't he just make the call in front of me?

Raymond comes back not five minutes later, a different man. He takes Shane in a full two-armed hug. "Great news, me boyo."

Shane knows by now to brace for the worst.

"The Chief is going to give you until midnight tonight to get what you want. If you can prove it's a murder by then, he'll let you stay on it. It's barely past dawn right now, so that's almost a whole day. And he did it just as a favor to me."

Shane watches Raymond bounce over to Rover, who's chewing on something he pulled from under the rug, and he thinks: There's no worse feeling than getting down on your knees and then rising to the knowledge that you have next to nothing to show for it.

A minute later, he's standing in the hallway outside his father's office. Louis is squeezing his arm – "Come back soon, me boyo" – and then vanishes.

On the weighty walnut door to his father's office is a gold plate that bears the number "161" and Raymond's name. It has a loose edge. Shane puts a fingernail under it and works it, works it, until he's able to take it and rip it off and as it clatters to the marble floor he says, "Fuck." Again: "Fuck, fuck, fuck!" He bangs his head against the door once, likes the clean feel of it, does it again, harder. He strides out the door.

Only later, looking in his car's rearview mirror, does he see the blood trailing down past both sides of his nose.

8

"Number one and number two were suicides," Shane says.

It's Monday evening and Shane and the Sarge have been working the missing persons files all day.

"They weren't missing," Shane says. "Never missing. They were somewhere. Maybe with a hole in their head, but somewhere."

Shane gropes for the sergeant's files. "Number three went home to Cleveland to die from tuberculosis. Number four ran off with a guy from the Navy Yard. Number five, it turns out, is being hidden by the prosecutor's office, she's a witness in the police payoff case."

This afternoon they got down to ten women who fit their first requirements, such as they are – date reported missing, clothing size, all that – and carry a first or last name starting with R. They split them up and did their legwork and now they're back in the Sarge's office, winnowing down the list. With the clock ticking.

If we don't make this girl by midnight ...

"So number six is Kim Roberts – "

"And I went over to the address we have for the guy who reported her missing. Turns out she was a broad that the guy got to know last year, and one night they shacked up and she rolled him. He didn't want to have it go to court, he just wanted to find her, so he just filed her as missing."

"Any chance this guy actually offed her and this is just his cover story?"

"Nah. Kim's very much alive and well, dancing in Baltimore under the name Georgia Belle. Got it straight from her mother who lives over in Brookland."

This is the essence of a good cop's job. Put aside the smart uniform with its creases as sharp as if they were hard-carved from slate. The badge that serves as a ticket to anywhere in the city. The crazy chases and the flashing lights, all the heroics and all the Sherlock Holmes bullshit about gut feeling and deductive reasoning. The job comes down to this: A good cop knocks on doors.

"Alright," Shane says, "so here's numbers seven, eight and nine. Helen Richardson, Roberta Wilkins and – Martha Reynolds."

"The first two are in the sanitarium, and the third I'm almost positive is dead. I've got Shiflett over at public records getting a death certificate on her just to make sure."

"So we're down to one, an Emily Rose."

Shane opens the last remaining folder.

"Missing persons report filed by one Claire Montgomery on May 28, 1951. That's a little late for us. But the physical could match up – height between 5-foot-4 and 5-foot-6, weight around 120. Dark hair, dark eyes. No residence address listed. Employment address just listed as 'U.S. House of Representatives.' This Claire Montgomery gives her own residence as 2131 O Street."

Shane looks up from the folder. "So did you go over there?"

"No," Sarge says, "I flew over a carrier pigeon to drop off a note for her. Of course I went over there. Woman who runs the place says Claire's never there, she works around the clock for a Congressman."

"Which one?"

"Some young guy. Jim Barry. Guy from New York."

Shane chuckles. "It's Joe. Joe Barry."

"You know this guy?"

The sergeant doesn't own a television and he skips through everything in the newspaper to get to the crime stories. He knows who the President is and maybe the Vice President, but the names of any of the backbenchers are lost on him. Unless one happens to end up killed, or too close to somebody who ends up killed.

"I don't know Joe Barry," Shane says, "but my father does. And I sure do know of him."

"Well, apparently all the broads in town know of him too. This landlady could barely keep her britches on when she was talking about seeing him on the television."

"So will we be able to talk to this Claire dame?"

"I called for her a few times at Barry's office," Sarge answers. "Got the feeling she was ducking me."

Shane leans back. "I'll take this one, Sarge."

"She probably doesn't want to be interviewed in Barry's office, and there isn't enough time to bring her back to headquarters."

Shane knows where he'll take her.

"When Shiflett comes back," he says, "tell him to come on over to room 161 in the old House building. That's where I'll have her."

In the Washington, D.C. of 1952, all roads lead to Raymond Kinnock's office, one way or another.

****

Shane's eyes are closed. He's in his father's photo room, tilted back in a folding chair. Below him is a drink, one-hundred proof Old Forrester straight up, and his feet are propped up on another folding chair. Grasped, just barely, between his right thumb and forefinger, is a Cuban cigar.

He takes a quick inventory. The drink is from his father's liquor cabinet. The cigar is from his father's humidor. He owes his job to his father. Which means he owes his father what he's earning, and everything he's wearing except for the maroon socks that are from a bagful that he managed to buy for himself at Woodies' before going off to college an eon ago.

Shane Kinnock, 34 years old. Made in America by... Raymond Kinnock.

"Detective! Sir!"

It's Bobby Shiflett, closing in on the photo room. He's looking for Shane, who doesn't answer.

"Detective Kinnock?"

Bobby comes in. "Your sergeant said I should come over to your father's office."

"There's nothing for you to do here." Shane takes a long drag on the Cuban.

"Where's everybody at?"

"Gone for the day. After a long day. What time is it?"

"It's about 10:30. I woulda come over sooner but there was a report of a shootin' and everybody got called in. Not that there was much for me to do there. I was about as useful as tits on a truck."

"It wouldn't have made a difference if you'd been with me. I've been tracking this girl Claire all evening, back and forth between her office and her rooming house. Finally got hold of her by phone from here, and she told me she had no idea what I was talking about."

"Maybe she was lyin'."

"Maybe. Probably. But it's too late for me to get behind it."

Shane picks up the glass and stares into it. Whether it's Old Forrester or Fleischman's or West Virginia grain, it all tastes the same in the end.

"No, Bobby, you and I have just been like Punch and Judy on this one." Shane struggles up from the chair. "You ever hear of them, little puppets dancing around in a box in a sidewalk show? Except we've got the likes of Charlie Moran holding our strings, and he's going to shut down this little puppet-show-in-a-box tomorrow morning."

Shane goes to Raymond's inner office for a refill and comes back to the folding chair. He's decided he'll quit police work for good tomorrow, when he really won't have anything to devote the best of himself to, such as his best still is. Or maybe the day after, just to ease into whatever's coming next.

He thinks, this is probably the last time I'll ever see Shiflett. If Shane were a different man, he'd at least be able to tell Shiflett that he has an honest quality in him that Shane hasn't seen in anybody for – oh, a long time. But Shane isn't that man, not now, and he doesn't tell him. He goes to the simplest thing he can talk to him about: his dog.

Bobby looks away. "Don't have Spike no more."

"You don't have him?"

"Naw. Since Saturday morning I've been workin' double time, what with helpin' you out on this case and all. He made some noise, and the landlady told me I had to get rid of him."

"So what'd you do?"

"Let him run. She told me to."

Shane says, "God *damn* it" and he means God damn everything, and most of all God damn the circumstance where a good old country boy loses his dog on account of him helping Shane out with all his shit.

He goes over to Raymond's photo wall. A minute passes.

Bobby says, "You know, Detective, we coulda found out what happened to that girl, if only we'd had more time."

If only we'd had more time. *If only I had more time.*

"That's what everybody's last thought is, isn't it, Bobby? As if it comes as a big surprise, right? There's never enough time for guys like us to do anything, really, because it's not our clock. It's somebody else's clock."

"Like, you mean it's God's clock."

Shane laughs and shakes his head. "God's the last guy that has anything to do with it. It's whoever else is all the way at the top, they set the clock and if you're not up there with them, you might as well not even wear a wristwatch."

"I don't like thinkin' like this," Bobby says.

"Sometimes what's on top is simple fate, or just pure fucking luck, right? But it's never guys like you and me that's on top. And it sure as hell isn't God. Come over here a second."

Shane points to a gilt-framed photo in the center of the wall.

"The gray-haired guy is my father. Handsome son of a bitch, right? Now, you know who the other guy is?"

"That's –"

"That's the Pope, Bobby. Pius the Twelfth. The Holy Father, the Supreme Pontiff, Jesus Christ on earth. Well, when the Nazis were slaughtering all those Jews during the war, you know what he had to say about it? Nothing at all."

Shane flicks a long cigar ash on the carpet. "Was the Pope a bad guy in all that? Sure he was. But he also knew he wasn't really all the way at the top. The guy with the little mustache and the stiff-arm salute was all the way at the top and that was that."

Shane reclines against the wall, settling into surrender.

His eyes stray to a photo on the bottom row, smaller than the rest.

It's the only photo in the room that doesn't feature Raymond. A boy and a girl are in the picture. Shane and Erin at age nine, him in shorts with dirty knees, Erin in pigtails and droopy socks. They're outside Griffith

Stadium, home of their beloved Nats, and bending over them is Walter Johnson, the legendary Nats pitcher, his uniform shirt with the formal team name "Senators" scrunched up against the top of Shane's head. The picture was taken 25 years ago.

In that quarter-century, Shane went to Yale and then breezed through Yale law school, passed the bar and tried a lot of cases in a little time. Got married. Went to war, killed people and saw them get killed. Came home, met his son, watched his wife and son leave him, lost his law job. Got a police job, put some killers in jail, almost lost his police job, and now is about to leave his job altogether for God-knows-what. Not exactly an uneventful life.

Even given all that, the image that lingers in his head as much as any other is of the great Walter Johnson ambling from the ballpark after a game, wading into a cluster of coarse, sweaty fans yelling out demands, then suddenly brightening on seeing him and Erin standing to the side with their cameras and seeking them out – seeking *them* out – to have his picture taken with them.

Just behind Shane in the photo is the bicycle that he rode to the game that day, a bright red Rollfast 20-incher.

And Shane remembers, oh, he remembers, how he struggled to learn how to ride that bike just a few months before.

Wobbling down the street and coming to a stall and teetering. Flinching, falling. Re-mounting. Teetering, falling again. Pain.

The bike – the enemy – lying complacently on its side. Then, the long car ride home. His father's stinging rebuke from the driver's seat.

Sitting in the back, young and solitary. His hairless legs fused to a hot car seat, his shoulders heaving.

Then, the feel of a hand on his back. His seatmate, reaching out. His twin, whispering. "It's really just you and me. It always has been. Always will be. Never forget that. You'll ride it next time. Just don't give up."

Shane finds the framed picture of Raymond and the Pope, lifts it from the wall, holds it in both hands.

In one motion he raises it over his head and slams the picture over his left knee, breaking the glass and splintering the wood, takes each side of the frame and breaks it in two, stomps and grinds the glass into the hardwood floor until much of it is powder, then picks up the picture and rips it into glossy confetti.

Bobby bends down over the mess, but Shane takes him by the arm and lifts him up. "We still have time before 12," Shane says. "We're going back out to the Park. This girl was strangled, and that neck bone is out there, broken in two, and we're going to take a shot at it. I don't give a shit if it's too goddam dark to find it, or if the rain might've washed the whole goddam pile away. We're gonna try."

Ninety minutes to find a bone in the night. Such is the reckless surge of hope that near-hopelessness can breed.

Bobby bends over again, then starts to sway back and forth.

"Jesus, Bobby. Are you okay?"

Bobby looks up. His face is a Halloween mask, white and fretful. "You don't know, do you? Ain't nobody never even looked at it, right?"

"Looked at what?"

"I messed up. You mean Officer Glover never told you? Somebody was supposed to tell you to get somebody to look through it."

"Look through *what?*"

"The pile, the whole pile of sand and dirt from the Park. I saved it that first day, in a buncha boxes. Even though you told me that it didn't matter."

"I told you the pile didn't matter?"

"Yeah, when y'all was goin' through the girl's clothes, I came in and you shushed me. I just thought it might be useful."

"Jesus Christ. Where is it *now?*"

"It's prolly in storage at our office in Rock Creek Park. It's in three big boxes. Somebody was supposed to pick them up but I bet they never did. You must want to kill me."

"*Kill* you? I should kiss you. We can go through it all in good light, inside."

Shane bolts from the chair. He has no time to muse about the secrets that can slip right through your fingers, or the second chances that life sometimes affords you to find them.

"Bobby," he says, "we're back to where we started. In the Park, digging in dirt."

9

THE WASHINGTON POST
Tuesday, May 27, 1952

BROKEN NECK BONE PROVES HOMICIDE IN PARK CASE
Miracle Find Puts Pressure On Chief to Re-Open Case
Identity of Murdered "Mystery Girl" Still Being Sought
By Bran Bentley, Staff Reporter
BULLETIN

Investigators have determined that the skeletonized remains found in Rock Creek Park on Thursday morning were those of a young Caucasian woman who was strangled before being dumped there last year. Definitive evidence that the girl's death was in fact a homicide was developed early this morning when a neck bone, broken in two pieces, was found in dirt that police had preserved from the area where the body was found.

The victim – known now throughout the city as "the mystery girl" – remains unidentified.

Sources close to Sen. Harlan Kuykendall, Chairman of the Senate District Committee, said that he will take steps to "zero out" the police department's budget if the Park case isn't re-opened.

Metropolitan Police Chief Charlie Moran is expected to address the matter later today when he appears before Rep. Raymond Kinnock's House District Committee.

****

Television cameras that look to be as big as PT boats are circling into place around the committee hearing room. Glaring klieg lights have been set up overhead.

If it's any less than 90° in the room, it's not by much.

Even from where Shane is sitting with Bobby, thirty or so feet behind the witness table, he can see that the back of Charlie Moran's round head is wet with sweat.

A group of secretaries is clustered at the end of the front row just a few feet from an empty place on the panel marked by the nameplate "Joseph F. Barry." They keep glancing at the door and nattering among themselves. One of them is a bit on the plump side but pretty enough. Bobby nudges Shane. "Look it the one on the end."

"Don't even think about it," Shane says. "She's not here for you."

The members are entering in twos and threes. A Capitol security guard closes the heavy doors and they settle together with a groan.

Bobby whispers, "Your Chief wanted to walk away from the Park case and now it looks like he was wrong. How bad is he gonna get roughed up here?"

Shane doesn't answer. He knows where all the allegiances lie. House versus Senate. Raymond versus Kuykendall. Raymond and Charlie Moran versus the rest of the world. And he knows Raymond has it in his power to look after his boy Moran and turn the hearing into a lovefest for him. A lingering flicker of faith in his father hopes for something more.

Raymond is approaching the presiding chair. On the wall behind the chair hangs an immense painting of the man himself, sitting in the very same chair. On the wall as it's captured in the painting, there's a smaller version of the painting itself, and in that smaller painting a still smaller painting, and so on and so on. An absurd infinite progression of Raymond Kinnocks, forever in power.

The chairman is now seated and raises his gavel and the room falls silent. "Chief Moran," Raymond says, "I understand you have a prepared statement to read before we ask questions?"

"I do, Congressman."

"Then why don't you –"

The heavy doors open again and Joe Barry enters as if propelled by a rush of air. He's tall and lithe and he's wearing a light gray suit and a rust-colored tie that play off his suntan. As he walks to his seat the girls in the front row smooth out their dresses and cross and uncross their legs.

Raymond follows Barry's progress across the room. "I see," he says, "that we've now been joined by the next Senator from the great state of New York. Excuse me, I guess we're all getting ahead of ourselves. So tell me, Joe, are we just back from an early summer foray to the beach?"

The crowd laughs briefly, then falls quiet. *What's Joe going to say?*

The sweet answer is, nothing.

Joe Barry moves easily to his chair. He runs a hand through his hair, looks over at Raymond, and gives him a toothy smile. Then he flicks an imaginary speck from his lapel.

A roomful of people surely miss the gesture. Raymond, who never misses anything, surely sees it, and sees it as the public fuck-you that it was meant to be.

When it comes down to Raymond versus Joe, Shane's supposed to have a clannish rooting interest for the Kinnock side. But at this moment he's finding it hard to see why.

Charlie Moran clears his throat. "Members of the committee." He perches his eyeglasses on the end of his nose and reads from a rumpled piece of paper.

"As you all know," he begins, "I directed last week that a full investigation be mounted into the case of a body that was found in Rock

Creek Park, and under my command it's been learned that the body was that of a Caucasian female and that she was murdered."

He pours himself a glass of water from the pitcher in front of him.

"This is a very grave matter. Our girls have to be able to know that they can walk around in our public parks without getting jumped by some thug."

Moran takes a long drink from the glass then settles it easily onto the table. "I consider this matter so grave, in fact, that from this point forward I'm taking personal charge of this investigation on a minute-by-minute basis. If anyone asks you, who's the lead detective on the Rock Creek Park case, you can say proudly, 'My Chief of Police is.'"

Everyone on the panel is now smiling – except Raymond Kinnock, still seething over Joe Barry's slight. Barry's distracted by the girls.

The Chief drains his water glass. "I swear to you, gentlemen, I'm not going to be satisfied until we get the degenerate bum who did this off the street" – here he inclines forward – "and sitting and sizzling in old Sparky."

A couple of the Congressmen start to clap but the Chief holds up his hand: "Not to say I can do all of this myself, because I can't. I'm going to need the help of the public."

And then he disgorges pretty much everything that's been turned up so far. That the girl was wearing a red cocktail suit and a flowered hat when she was snatched up. That the body was buried in a mudslide on the second of May last year. That she was probably killed and dumped on the night of the first.

"So," he concludes with voice soaring, "if anyone in this city saw anything suspicious that night, they should get on the phone to us as fast as they can."

Shane gets up, climbs over Bobby and hits the big doors hard. He's still pacing in the hallway when the doors open and the Chief sweeps by, with Bobby not far behind him. "Hey, Chief," Shane yells out, as Bobby tries to pull him back. "What was that all about?"

Moran turns. "I called your father this morning and told him you'll still have a role to play in this case. I just haven't figured out yet what it's going to be." He draws close, his tone is kindly, the soft touch of his hand on Shane's arm is benevolent. People may be watching, of course.

"I don't give a shit about who does what," Shane says. "I just care that it gets done right."

The gallery has emptied from the hearing room and a woman in a loud polka-dot dress wielding a camera is coming near. The Chief guides Shane around a corner. "Let's talk this through. It'll work out fine."

Then, once they're by themselves: "So what's your fucking problem, Kinnock?" They're nose-to-nose.

"Why the fuck are you putting out all that information? The whole investigation is out there."

"It's called good police work, Kinnock. Something they wouldn't have taught you in your fairy law school. What the fuck else would you do?"

"Maybe try to do a little more legwork. Before we just up and tell everybody everything we've found out and invite all the crazies out there to offer up some bullshit that'll take weeks to sort through."

The Chief waves his hand. "I don't need a lecture from you on how to run a dragnet. I told your father you'll still be working on this so you're going to have to be. But I don't like it, and if you buck me you'll be out on your ass on an insubordination rap."

Shane goes to the men's room and nods to the Negro attendant. His name is Rodney and he's been stationed here since Shane was first old enough to use a toilet.

He hears Bobby come in: "I'm thinkin' your talk with the Chief didn't go too well."

"Just the usual horseshit.." Shane steps to a urinal and unzips. He feels strangely buoyant. "Main thing is, I'm still on this."

"So what happens to me?"

"What do you mean, what happens to you? As long as you're willing to keep on doing this in your free time, you're on it."

"Won't your Chief mind?"

Shane finishes, goes to the sink and turns on the water. "Not if we use you the right way. Shit, Moran could probably look right at you and not even notice that you're not with MPD."

"He was a detective back in the day."

"And one time he had a case where he put the suspect in a lineup with five fillers. And the victim picked one of the fillers. Didn't bother Charlie, he went out and locked up the filler. Said he had a positive ID. Tells you something."

"So how'd he get to be Chief?"

"He has a gift. There's a small point in the back of his throat that acts as a suction. And it somehow manages to always activate itself when he's on his knees in front of a Congressman."

Shane flicks water off his hands and Rodney glides next to him with a towel, then turns to the side when Shane goes in his pocket for a buck to palm to him, then glides back to his chair around the corner. A series of movements executed wordlessly, the choreography of the constantly repeated routine.

Shane looks in the mirror and passes a wet comb through his hair – still no gray. *At least I have that on the old man.*

"So, what do you see yourself doing on this, sir?"

"Staying close enough to the Chief to keep him honest."

"And me?"

"Staying close enough to me to keep me honest." Shane pockets his comb and touches Bobby's arm. "I found out the hard way in the war. You can never be too sure about the guy next to you."

"Why do you want me for this?"

Shane starts to voice his first thought. *Who the hell else do I have?*

Instead: "Because you're a hell of a lot smarter than anybody's ever thought you were, including yourself. Now just go home and get some sleep. Because if I know my Chief he's going to use this thing as an excuse to run in every vagrant Negro in town."

If Bobby Shiflett from Bumfuck, North Carolina thinks our park is wild, just wait till he's on the front lines on our streets.

10

THE NEW YORK HERALD SUN
Tuesday, May 27, 1952

RAYMOND KINNOCK IN KICKBACK SCHEME;
FUNDS USED TO TARGET POLITICAL RIVAL
By Staff Reporter

The Herald Sun has learned after a six-month investigation that Rep. Raymond Kinnock (D-N.Y.) has been secretly getting illegal kickbacks from workers at his D.C. and New York offices and steering the money to Rafael Bellino, opponent of Rep. Joseph F. Barry (R-N.Y.) in the November Senate election.

Informed sources say that a number of Kinnock's employees have been told over the last year that they had to make regular "patriotic contributions" to the fund, or else find new jobs.

Shane creases his newspaper and flattens it on the counter. It joins his cigarettes, his coffee and his plate half-filled with sausages, cheese grits and collard greens. He reads on.

The Herald Sun has further learned that the matter has been referred to the prosecutor's office to determine whether criminal charges should be brought against Kinnock.

Shane hears a squeak and feels jostling next to him. Bran Bentley, settling onto a stool. "Nice story," Bentley says. "Front page, above the fold, nothing better than that."

"Is that all you came to ride me about, Bentley?"

"Hey, don't knock it. A lot of fuzz would kill to have their mugs on the front page."

Shane looks back at the Herald Sun. "The piece is all about my father, and it was all but written by Matt Barry. I'm not even mentioned in there."

"I'm not talking about that out-of-town rag. This." Bentley takes the morning Post from under his arm and lays it on top of Shane's paper.

"Check out the photo, we got you walking into headquarters last night with the news about that bone. I wrote the sub-head myself, about the quote-unquote mystery girl. It's a phrase that'll stick, at least until your people find out who the hell she was."

"And I'm thinking you're hoping we don't find out for a while. Goose the suspense. Heighten the fear. Sell more papers."

"You misread me, Kinnock." Bentley shakes his head ruefully. "I'm just like everybody who's ever lived, from the cavemen around the fire all the way down. I have a hard-on for a great story."

Shane scrapes at his greens. "How'd you find me down here?"

"I called your headquarters, told them I was working the skull story for the Post, and I talked to one of your officials, Rector. He said you might be down at one of the coon clubs you like to hang around in."

"Coon clubs?"

"His words, not mine. So I just walked around U Street until I found a place that's serving late breakfast. Mind if I stay?"

"I was just about to leave."

"Stay. Maybe I can make it worth your while."

The counterman comes up. "Whaddya have, sir?"

Bentley eyes Shane's plate. "Suddenly, not much of an appetite. Do you serve tea?"

The counterman looks at Shane, then back at Bentley. "Coffee, sir. We like to say to fellas like you, we only serve two kinds here. Black and high yellow."

Bentley laughs uneasily. The counterman doesn't smile. "I guess," Bran says, "that means the high yellow is for me."

The counterman goes to the burner. Next to it is a radio, playing low. He turns up the volume and a blues guitar riff swells and a voice rises as if from middle earth: *Got them highway blues, been down this road too long ...* Bentley perks up. "Who the hell is that?"

"His name's Chester Burnett, but he goes by Howlin' Wolf. He was here last night with his band."

"Never heard of him."

"There's a different kind of music out there and it's coming to us from right around the corner. If you ever got out of those chi-chi Georgetown salons, you might've heard about it."

The counterman slides a cup to Bran and slips away. "No, I haven't heard shit about whatever music you're talking about," Bran says. "But I *have* heard how you managed to hold onto the Park case by your fingernails. And frankly I wouldn't think the Chief would be letting you anywhere near anything that mattered to him."

"I'm going to stay on it. Bet on it."

"I'd bet, only if you'd lay me a week. Because after that you're off it."

Bran languidly stirs his coffee. "You know, when you were being grilled at the hearing about that lagoon case, it sounded as if you had more to say but you got cut off."

Bentley's gone to some trouble to find me. He wants something from me. Maybe he has something to trade. And, he's on my turf.

"Go ahead and ask your questions," Shane says. "Off the record."

"Just give me the whole story like you couldn't tell it before."

Shane explains it all, in a pinched monotone.

How a 42-year-old white woman was dumped naked in the lagoon across from the Jefferson Memorial, and the body was found by an old, drunken peg-legged Negro named Johnny Toland who lived on a houseboat nearby and called the police as soon as the dame bobbed to the surface.

How the press hawked the case hysterically, for all the same reasons that they're now going to hawk the Park case hysterically.

How his partner, Preston Rowe, the Chief's favorite, was put on the case and promptly turned his sights on Toland himself, on the flimsiest of hunches: The police had found stains on the boat that couldn't be proven to be blood, but then again they might've been, and when they braced Toland, a man who was in the habit of spending all his days floating on rocky waters and in a haze, he couldn't alibi for every minute of the week before.

How Rowe locked Toland up and sweated him, and how Toland finally gave himself up, with a story that didn't square with any of the evidence, but Rowe ran with it anyway.

How Rowe brought Shane into the case to do the paperwork on Toland's arrest, since Rowe couldn't spell his last name if you didn't spot him the first three letters, and how that was the first time Shane knew what had been done to Toland.

"Rowe thought I was just like him, Bran. That I wouldn't blink an eye."

"What happened next."

"I went to Rector, who did nothing, then to the Chief, who did less. Actually worse than less. He told me if anybody asked about any of this I should keep my fucking mouth shut or he'd have my badge."

Shane goes through the rest of the story, seeing Bentley's interest mount.

How Toland stayed in jail for months while Rowe, Rector and the Chief tried to concoct proof against him.

How even after the trial judge got the D.A. to drop the case to save everybody from embarrassment, and Toland hobbled out of jail a vanquished man, the Chief still ordered the Harbor Patrol to raid the man's houseboat weekly for the next six months.

How in 25-some raids, only one consequential piece of evidence was ever turned up. It was a long strand of rope, found in the last raid. One end was tied to the houseboat, the other to an anchor embedded in the river floor, with a loop wrapped hard around the neck of the submerged Johnny Toland.

Shane explains it all to Bentley, how he tried to stop it all from happening, but there was only so much he could do. And the more he says, the more he sounds to himself like a suspect.

Cops don't explain anything to anybody.

But Bentley is still taking it all in. "So how is it you got called before the Senate committee?"

It's the part of the story Shane doesn't want to talk about, but has to. He needs what he thinks Bentley has.

KEVIN FLYNN   93

"Kuykendall," Shane says, "is after the Chief."

"Everybody in town knows that."

"So somebody close to Kuykendall must've gotten wind that something rotten happened behind the scenes, so they dragged me up there. Then once I was there, they treated me like I was some sort of Commie, pressing me to name names. Which I had to do."

"I'm supposing some people don't see it that way."

"Just everybody I work with. Let's just say I'm not the most popular guy on the force right now."

"So, you gave up your partner, Rowe. But not Rector. And not the Chief."

"The questioning went in another direction. Almost as if somebody up there deliberately ran the train off the rails just to save the Chief's ass."

Bentley looks warily at his coffee, which he's yet to try. "And then, from what I hear, Moran went back-channel to the committee with the story that you were in on the lagoon case every step of the way, that you even took the lead in charging Toland."

"And that's how he got himself enough leeway to bust me down to natural deaths and push my ass off to the side."

"So, you got fucked," Bentley goes on. "But how could the Chief pull that off? You're Raymond Kinnock's son."

"He knew how to do it so my father wouldn't say much. You know, give me a horseshit job but keep me on the department."

"And nothing ever happened to Rowe."

Shane snorts. "No. Took the Fifth and walked away scot-free. Back on the job."

Bentley raises the cup to his lips, winces, puts it down. "So, if you didn't take the Fifth in the lagoon case, why'd you take it when they started asking about your war record?"

"Ah, Bran." Shane shakes his head. 'If you want to go off on a tangent, we won't have much more to talk about."

Bentley lightly runs his fingers over his lapel flower, first the petals and then a small thorn, and stares at the table. It's as if he has two visions of his future. In one he's tuxedoed at the gala Pulitzer Prize awards ceremony, mounting a stage, speech in hand. In the other he's in the dock in a libel trial, caught in Charlie Moran's crosshairs.

He finally speaks, his rasp now more of a wheeze. "If all this is true," he says, "it's dynamite. The Chief of Police obstructing justice like a common hood. But how can I trust it?"

Behind Bentley, Shane sees the club's front door swing open and three Negro boys burst through, broad-chested and boisterous. Bentley glances their way, a couple of times.

Shane puts both hands up. "You can't trust it just like that," he says, as if in surrender. "Nobody was around when the Chief said anything to me. It's my word against his."

"You have anything else on him? *Anything*?"

"Nothing else I can give you. Look, I'm sorry we even had this talk." Shane shifts, as if he's about to get up.

"I've got something," Bentley finally says. "It has to do with the Park killing. But I can't give it to you, because you're never really going to be on the inside in the case."

Now Shane does get up. "You offend me, Bran, when you underestimate me."

He pauses, one two… three.

"Jesus, Bran, there's been a plan in place to deal with this."

Actually, there's no plan in place. At least not until right now.

"The plan," Shane says, "is that anything I do on the case, we'll make it seem as if the Sarge did it and not me. What the Chief won't know won't hurt him. I'll stay in, I'll get what I want, everybody else'll get the glory. And we'll all go home happy. But as far as you and I are concerned – "

Bentley takes Shane by the belt and tries to move him back to his stool. Shane pushes his hand away. "I really have to be going."

"Wait." Bentley reaches for a smoke and fumbles for a lighter. "I need your word. You give the obstruction of justice story to me before anybody else gets it. Or else you get nothing from me now."

Shane feigns hesitation, as if he has a choice. "You'll get it before any other press guys get it, absolutely."

"Alright." Bentley looks around again, distracted by the Negro boys. "I'm hearing you're down to your last lead on who your mystery girl might be. Claire Montgomery. She's nervous, Shane. Classic good-girl, never had cops banging on her door."

Claire Montgomery. How does Bentley get this stuff?

Bentley goes on. "Not that she necessarily even knew the dead girl, she probably didn't. But I can at least hook you up with her, so you can cross her off your list one way or another."

All that run-around with Bentley, just for this. A possible lead to a possible lead. But if it's all he has I'll take it.

"I'm assuming you know her."

"I found out about her, Shane. Let's just leave it at that."

"And how'd you manage to find out about her? Only a few of us on the case even know about her."

"You guys kill me, pal. You think you can move around town in your MPD Plymouths, flashing badges and dropping business cards, and nobody pays attention."

Bentley gets up, goes to the phone booth outside, comes back maybe a minute later. "She'll see you, but not at home and not at work. She can be up at the Rib Room at the Mayflower Hotel at 3. Too late for lunch and too early for dinner, no one else there except for maybe a few stray tourists."

Shane waves to the counterman for the check. "So what do you have on the guy she works for. Joe Barry."

Bentley's tone changes, he's not used to having the tables turned. "She helps run his office, I think. That's all I know."

"I didn't ask about her, I asked about him. I just thought, you and he have been around town a few years. He's got a nice place in Georgetown, near yours."

"How do you know about my place?"

"Guys like you kill me," Shane says. "You think you can move around town in your fancy sports cars, dropping business cards, and nobody knows who you are."

"Do I know Barry? Yeah, we've crossed paths."

Bentley starts to go in his pants pocket, presumably to pay for his coffee, but his hand comes out empty. "Look," he says, "are you going to meet this broad at the Mayflower or not?"

"How will I make her?"

"Oh, believe me, pal, she'll stand out. I love my brunette wife. But there's something about an icy blond princess that makes the blood boil."

11

MEMORANDUM

Page 2 of 4

DATE: April 1, 1951

TO: Chairman
        Committee on Un-American Activities
        United States House of Representatives

FROM: Haynes Nickens
        Investigator

RE: Surveillance of Target No. 1

Not long after the forced relocation of the female subject Emma Rosenblum to a Jewish-only area in Shanghai, the Nazi government in Germany pressured the Japanese government in China to exterminate all 20,000 Jewish refugees living there. The Japanese delayed acting on the plan and the Jews were spared. Nonetheless, living conditions in the Jewish-only restricted area remained miserable.

The female subject's mother died in Shanghai in late August 1945, leaving the female subject and her sister Leah in the care of their grandmother Hilde. The war had ended but the Shanghai Jewish area was not immediately liberated. It wasn't until January 1946 that the female subject and her sister Leah were transported by ship to San Francisco and then by cross-country train to New York. By this time their last lineal relative, their grandmother Hilde, had died.

In New York, the girls were met by Mr. and Mrs. Jakob Siegel, their distant aunt and uncle, whom the female subject's family had known in Bonn before the war. The female subject took up residence with the Siegels in Brooklyn. Shortly thereafter she underwent treatment for melancholia and was considered a suicide risk.

In January 1947, the female subject left the Siegels and her sister Leah and moved to Washington, D.C., hoping to embark on a new life by herself, with no attachments to her troubled past.

****

Shane pivots into the Rib Room at the Mayflower. Sitting in the back is a woman swathed in yellow.

A piano melody drifts in from the lobby, playing an old tune he just heard recently, and now it's settled in his head.

He circles around the place and approaches the woman from the side. She's wearing a canary-colored cardigan and a cream-colored blouse, sipping on a drink and eyeing a menu. Blonde as advertised, with a pert nose and lips that look as if they were fashioned by God just to say the word no.

"For the life of me," Shane says, "I can't remember the name of this song."

She looks up, startled. "Detective."

"Kinnock. And you're Claire Montgomery."

He settles into the chair across from her. She holds out a hand and he takes it in his right and pats it with his left. "I know no one likes to meet up with a cop, no matter what the circumstances."

"I need to get back to work soon and I don't even think I can help you. Except I can tell you one thing that I'd think you'd already know. That song is 'No Other Love' and it was a hit for Jo Stafford a couple of years ago."

"Haunting."

She smiles, either vacantly or mysteriously. Shane inclines towards mysteriously. He's prone to giving a beautiful woman more credit than she deserves.

A waitress brings menus. Claire clears her throat. "I think the chances that I'll have anything useful for you are very small."

"But I take it you know more than you let on to me the other night."

"To the extent I know about this at all, it's only that I filed a missing persons report last year on one of my co-workers, an Emily Rose. I told you about that when you called."

She never said a word about a missing persons report when Shane called her.

He doesn't even think to ask her why she didn't come clean before. Fish swim, birds fly, people lie to the police.

"You have to at least know that a woman's body was found in the Park."

"It's been in the papers but the police haven't said much more than that."

Shane shoves his menu to the side. "Your friend probably isn't the girl we found in the Park. People move in and out and around this city every day and pretty much all of them manage to stay out of harm's way. But you filed that report on your friend for a reason."

"She was hardly a friend," Claire says. "More like a close acquaintance who just left town. If anything happened to her, I'm very sorry" – she looks to the side – "Nothing for me, thanks, I ate at my desk earlier."

The waitress has reappeared. She's pushing 50 and has a chipped front tooth. Shane points to Claire. "I'll just have what she's having, but make mine a double."

The waitress looks at Shane and puts her hand on his arm. "You got it. Ginger ale in an extra-large glass."

"I didn't think they even made drinks anymore without liquor in them. But what the hell, I'll be adventurous."

"Go ahead, Detective," Claire says. "I know you want a real drink. Don't let me stop you."

He shakes his head and the waitress leaves. "What else can you tell about me?"

"It's far too early for me to say." Her eyes are shining like polished turquoise.

He hears the first, halting notes of a song he recalls once liking -- "Fascination," he thinks -- but then the lobby pianist botches a couple of notes and the effect is lost.

He asks how she first met this Emily Rose. And she goes on in the dialect of the Capitol Hill staffer whose whole life is confined within one square mile of the famous marble buildings.

How she'd been working for "the Congressman" – not "Joe" or even "Mr. Barry" – for about a year when Emily came in.

How she became the Congressman's "AA" – administrative assistant, meaning office manager – and so she had the power to "engage or dismiss staff."

How she asked Emily to put together "an SF-171" – job application – and then eventually decided to "engage" her over the objection of the Congressman's "LA" – legislative assistant – because she felt that Emily would be "devoted to my Congressman's mission."

The first rule of a man on the prowl in D.C., whichever way he votes, should be to avoid any woman who can find it in herself to say the words, "my Congressman's mission."

The waitress returns and sets Shane's ginger ale in front of him. She puts her hand on his shoulder. "Hon, if there's anything else you want, just wave." She keeps her hand on him for a beat too long, then fusses over the table before leaving.

"So, Detective," Claire says, "do you always have such a devastating effect on service workers?"

"Waitresses, chambermaids, gas station attendants. They never let up on me." Shane already misses the warm languor he's afforded by a stiff drink in a dim place. "So how long did this Emily Rose work there?"

"All the way up until she didn't show up anymore." Claire crosses her arms around herself.

"And when was that exactly?"

"I filed my report with the police in late May last year, and some weeks had passed. I'd say it was around the first of May that she stopped showing up."

The first of May last year.

"Emily was an everyday employee and the last time you saw her was around May 1 last year. And it took you almost a month to file a missing persons report."

Claire takes off her cardigan and shifts in her seat, her blouse straining against her figure.

Finally: "When she didn't show up for work, at first I let it go. Then more time passed and I got angry because she was leaving the Congressman in the lurch. But that's just the way she was."

"Meaning."

"She could be unreliable. And the way she came to us, it was as if she just appeared out of smoke. She was very friendly and she had a smart sense of humor. But she never went out with us after work, and she avoided all questions about herself."

"So, why'd you finally file a report?"

"Something about the way she left just nagged at me. She never said goodbye, never called or wrote. I thought if there was anything fishy about it, somebody should look into it."

"And nobody in your office filed their own report?"

"I knew her the best. Everyone knew I'd filed it."

Shane reaches into his suit jacket pocket. "I need to show you something," he says. He pulls out a small paper bag wrapped in tape, peels back the tape and opens the bag. Inside is the makeup case that was found on the hill in the Park. He sets it down on the table. "Have you ever seen this before?"

Claire's eyes widen. "I gave her this," she said. She picks up the case and stares at the letter R. "One Christmas everyone on the staff exchanged presents. I took it down to a jewelry store to have them monogram it."

She slumps and her eyes water.

Shane looks at the case. There's a film of dust on the shiny gold surface but he can still catch a glint of his reflection in it.

The neck bone told me how she was killed. And now I know who she was.

"Do you mind," Claire says abruptly, "if I clean it up some?"

"Sure. It's already been dusted for prints."

She takes her napkin, dips it in her glass, and works the surface of the case until it gleams like new. "She was so young."

Shane gently takes the case back from her and puts it in the bag. "We found it in a pocket of her suit and we haven't found her purse. She kept the case separate for some reason. Maybe you made it special for her."

"She probably was in too big a hurry to put it back in her purse the last time she used it. She was always running, always moving." Her voice trails off.

"Honey. You and I now, we're going to work together, to try to find out who wanted to do something terrible to her."

Shane lowers his voice to a murmur.

"I know this is hard, so let's start with something simple. If somebody pressed you on how well you knew her what would you say?"

Claire takes her glass, starts to raise it, puts it down. Shane senses a tremor in her hands. "About as well as she wanted anyone to, maybe even less. She never talked about where she came from or where she lived or who her friends were outside the office or even if she had any friends outside the office. When I went over her 171 –"

"Her job application. Do us both a favor and try not to talk to me like you're a Soviet party functionary." Shane locks eyes with her and smiles, to take the edge off the words.

"Yes, her application. It had no references, no background information, it was as if she'd dropped down on us from another planet. All it said was she was taking night classes at a local college. Nothing even about what college."

"Any home address?"

"Yes, I believe. But then she moved and we tried to get more from her but never did."

She's holding her glass in both hands, hard enough to break it. "I'm sure you've already looked into all of this, haven't you?"

Shane ignores the question. His first rule in an interview: Get, don't give.

"With all the gaps in her past," he says, "why'd you hire her?"

"I didn't right away. I put her on the phones for a couple of days and I told her she'd be working for nothing until I made my mind up. Before I knew it, she was handling the phones by herself and not long after that it was pretty clear she was –"

"A star?"

"A potential contributor to the Congressman's efforts."

"And a potential rival to other staffers."

"Which I could understand. In just a few months she went from the phones to helping him write speeches and draft bills, for gosh sakes."

"So, the Congressman let this girl who wasn't even a college grad help him draft legislation."

"She was pretty good at it. Alright, I'd say very good." It's an admission that comes grudgingly. "Smart in her own way. Picked up on things quickly enough. Asked a million questions about politics. She wanted everything we could offer."

Shane tips back the last of his glass and by habit starts to look for the waitress, but then he stops himself. No reason to rush for another ginger ale. "You said earlier she was unreliable."

"Just after she'd been with us for a while. Say something had to get done on a weekend, forget about trying to get her in. It was as if she ceased to exist after Friday at 5, poof, she was gone. She seemed to have bigger things going on someplace else."

"Did she ever talk about what she did when she was away from work?"

"I remember her saying she loved doing outdoor things. But she never elaborated."

Claire squeezes her glass again.

"She could swear like a sailor. And her clothes. She wore pants to the office sometimes, because she said they were more comfortable. She would talk to anyone, I think she was on first-name basis with all the elevator operators. It was like she didn't observe any of the traditional –"

"Boundaries."

"Yes, boundaries."

"You're painting a picture of someone who was very unusual and very ambitious."

"I think she had her eye on every job in our office from the time she got there."

"Including yours."

Claire sets her jaw. "She wasn't going to get that one anytime soon."

She puts one hand over her mouth. "That sounded harsh. I did very much like her, all things considered. And she had the most wonderful laugh. The way a laugh is described in books but you never really hear one like it. Lilting, I guess that's the word."

An image is expanding before Shane, as if from the flaring beam on a television screen: the skull in the Park, ossified as a dinosaur bone, locked in a strangled scream. And sitting across from him is someone who knew the skull when it had a face affixed to it. A face that seems to have known every emotion but fear.

"So what did she look like?"

Claire takes a small sip of soda and pats her mouth with her napkin. "I suppose she was a perfectly nice-looking girl."

"And what did the Congressman think of her?"

Claire folds her napkin, aligning the corners with military precision. "He thought well of her." She looks past him. "Listen to this piano player, he keeps hitting the wrong notes. What's wrong with him?"

Shane doesn't turn around. The bars and clubs where he spends most of his nights don't have a tinkling grand piano, and every time he hears one he feels as if he's in Satan's waiting room.

"Did she have any romantic relationships?"

"I think all the men in the building wanted to be with her. But I don't think any of them ever got anywhere."

"Sounds as if she may have been a little more than just perfectly nice-looking."

"I'm not a very good judge of the appearance of other women."

"So she had no boyfriend that you know of?"

"No, not that I – no."

"You hesitated."

"Who ever knows about those things, Detective? It's not like I ever followed her around on dates."

"It was a simple question and you answered it. So did she owe anybody money?"

"Not me, and no one I knew about."

"How did she present herself in the office?"

"Perfectly presentably."

"More presentably earlier or later? Were things getting better or worse for her?"

Claire draws down the last of her ginger ale and puts on her cardigan. "To the extent it might matter," she says, "she was kind of dowdy at first. Over time she wore more and more expensive clothes to work. I knew what we were paying her and I finally asked her how she managed to be so finely turned out on her salary."

"And."

"She just said she was very frugal and spent her money wisely."

Claire slides from the booth and reaches for her purse. "I really have to be getting back. Congress is still in session and I'm needed. You know where you can find me if you have any more questions."

Shane takes her arm and holds it. "I just have one or two more." She tenses. "Did you ever see any indication that she ever had any sort of relationship with the Congressman?"

She pulls away. "No. And if there had been, do you really think I'd say anything about it to a Kinnock?"

"I see you've done your homework about who my father is."

"Part of the job of a political staffer is doing good advance work."

Shane settles back in the booth. "When all this gets out, it's not exactly going to help your boss's Senate campaign, is it? At the very least it's a distraction."

Her neck tightens. She takes her meticulously folded napkin and pushes it into her empty glass. "Just a while ago you brought me up short for sounding like a government functionary. Now you're the one who's sounding as if you think politics is everything, even when there's a dead girl in the picture. Maybe you and your family have been in this town too long."

"That may or may not be true. But I'm not running around doing my family's business. And no, I don't think politics is everything."

He doesn't add the obvious, that everything eventually comes around to politics.

Claire stands stock-still.

"I can give you a ride back."

"I'll take a cab," she says, holding her purse tight against her chest.

"I almost forgot," he says. "You don't happen to know where I might be able to get a photograph of her, do you?"

"No. Actually, I take that back." Claire opens her purse and muddles through a wallet. "You might not think it's a very good one but it gives you a sense of her. It's a group shot."

"What was the occasion?"

"It was a lunch we had early last year for a secretary who was leaving. Somebody had one of those new instant cameras and after we took the shot we all sat around in a circle and watched it come to life." She hands the picture to Shane. "Emily's in the center."

Five people in the picture are sitting at a semi-circular table. Four of them are talking, laughing, eating, smoking. Two of them are already fading to gray. Only one from among the group is looking right at the camera, smiling slyly, immutably. Shane stares at her hair. Coiffed, black, lustrous.

Just a couple of days ago, he held this head in his hand.

In the picture she has her left elbow propped on the armrest of her chair and her right arm is poised on the table in front of her. Everything about her features is excessive. The dark eyes too wide-set, the regal nose too long, the full mouth too wide. Yet somehow it all comes together.

"You can keep that if you need to, Detective."

Shane starts to put the picture away, but keeps it out.

He never met her.

Now he can't believe she's dead.

12

Emily had a corner booth all to herself.

There was only one other diner in the place, a solemn- looking man who was paying no attention to her, preoccupied with some sort of book that he was scribbling in. For at least a bit, maybe, she could feel safe being alone.

About four hours before, the Congressman had called her on the line that connected his office to her workroom and whispered that they should meet at this place at 9. It's on 16th Street, he said, right near the park. She said, there are lots of parks in the city. And he said, there's only one that matters and that's Rock Creek, just bring good hiking shoes, I'll have a surprise for you.

She owned four pairs of shoes: the high heels that she wore to work every day, two pairs of light flats that she'd worn as a waitress and still wore when she was padding about the city, and the rubber-soled winter boots that she'd worn on her night journey to Washington and hadn't worn since. The boots would have to do, even in the heat.

It was now past 9:30, the Congressman hadn't shown up, and the boots stayed stashed in her bag. She waved to a waiter, and just like that she ordered herself a Cosmopolitan. She'd never had an alcoholic drink in her life, but she'd heard of this one and the name carried an air of sophistication – in this setting, it appealed to her sense of irony. The drink went down as smoothly as the name suggested it would.

A clock outside chimed ten. The staff was upending chairs on top of tables, closing time was nearing, so she ordered and downed a second, then a third.

The room around her was getting hazy, but she found clarity in the small acts of paying her tab and setting her escape route: The 16th Street bus was still running, and she could take a transfer to get back home.

She walked out of the place and into a summer night cauldron. She took a deep breath and fanned herself, cursed having to carry a bag with useless heavy boots all the way to a bus stop, and cursed the Congressman for good measure.

"I said we'd be going hiking. I didn't say anything about skiing."

Emily swung around and his face was in front of her. The Congressman had his hand in her bag and was lifting one of her winter boots out of it. "At least nobody can say that these aren't stylish."

She didn't know whether to slap him or kiss him. She kissed him. "Joe Barry, you're incorrigible."

"So don't incorrige me."

"Funny. That's not even a word and you know it. Try to find that in one of your crossword puzzles."

She pushed at him and laughed, and just that quickly the last woebegone hour was forgotten, without any accounting.

Joe took the bag off of her shoulder with one hand and brought the other from behind his back. "I got you these, for what it's worth." He held out a group of violets. "I went by the Park on my way up here and they were growing by the entrance. But it took me awhile to find ones that were in full bloom."

She joined hands with his around the flowers. "So, you're saying this is why you're just getting here now?" She didn't even try to suppress a smile. "It took you an hour to pick these?"

He plucked out one flower, put it into her hair, and propped up the others against the base of a streetlight. "They'll make somebody walking by here tomorrow happy. And you and I will find more just like them in the Park tonight."

"Come on," he said, pulling her behind him.

She started to teeter – from her three sophisticated drinks, and the high wire of her high heels that, to the end of her days, she would never be able to master – and he halted. "I can help."

Sitting next to her on the sidewalk he knelt down and took off each unsteady shoe. He started to talk about work – maybe to come clean on why he was late – going on about this or that bill, and what he was doing to try to reach across the aisle and get it passed, and so on.

She cut him off: "Tonight we're not solving the country's problems. No big stories. It's just you and me, alright?"

He didn't say anything, just rubbed her feet for a minute or so before putting her winter boots on. Then he rose from his knees and grasped her shoulders. "Alright then, let's get going." He looked down at her legs. "At least those hideous boots aren't knee-length."

He took her hand and led her so deep into woods that she could barely see him ahead of her.

"Don't people in Washington sleep in parks on hot nights like this?"

"They do," he said. "Just not where we're going in this one."

She still had on the beige dress that she'd worn to work. She now regretted it as she brushed across branches still wet and grimy from an afternoon rain. Regret quickly passed into resignation, and then relief – an unfamiliar sense of letting go. Why care about anything like that now? With Joe's guidance she navigated across gullies and gnarled roots, but she didn't miss a step. The boots were ungainly, but functional. The sound of cricket-chirp filled the air, and small creatures leaped gracefully back and forth across the path as they walked deeper into the Park.

They came to a place where twisted tree branches formed a canopy that was high enough to crawl under. "We're not far from a lovely spot," Joe said.

Had she been a naturalist, her head occupied by science and not romance, she would've caught the scent of the next seasons in the air: seeds from trees and flowers beginning to spread, preparing for autumn and winter, even though summer had barely started. But all she could think about was that not long before, she was on a city street, and now she was enveloped in this state of nature, and rapture.

All of a sudden she could see a gleam – from a full moon, still half-shrouded by foliage – and she could hear gurgling, accompanied by birdsong.

With a few more steps she was in a place the likes of which she'd never seen before. The moon cast a light so bright that it rivaled the sun's, and it seemed to catch every glistening ripple of the water that rushed in front of her and every stone that it ran across.

"I thought Rock Creek was just a creek," she said.

"It's much more than that," Joe answered. "Let's just call it a river here."

He edged close to the water. "A little bit of history for you. President Roosevelt came up here all the time, knew every trail. And this is the exact spot where he used to skinny-dip."

"He'd do what?"

"Swim. Naked. The best way."

"FDR would do that?"

Joe chuckled. "That would've been a sight. No, Teddy."

He cast aside his suit jacket, removed shoe and sock from one foot and then the other, unfastened his pants and unbuttoned his shirt, dropped everything to the ground. He stood before her, unclothed and unabashed.

"I'm going in," he said. "Come in with me."

"I can't."

As soon as she said those two contemptible words she wanted to take them back. She reclined on the ground and looked up at the sky, watched a cloud pass across the moon and then retreat, listened to the water surging.

She rose up on her elbows: "Can I go halfway?"

"Halfway in," Joe asked, "or halfway off? Either way, the answer's no."

"Are you sure no one's around?"

"I'm a U.S. Congressman and I'm naked as a jaybird. Do you think I'd be doing this if anybody was around?"

She said to herself a Hebrew phrase that roughly translated as,"Why not?"

Joe turned away from her, towards the water. Emily disrobed, at first awkwardly, then boldly. In as much time as it took for a second cloud to challenge the moon and then take a pass, she'd become as committed to this as she'd been to her winter walk across the Williamsburg Bridge. Her only hesitation showed when her left hand glanced across her right forearm. What if he sees my Shanghai number? *There was no reason to stop now – if he saw it, she'd find a way to explain.*

When she was finished, all she was wearing was Joe's violet in her hair. She waded into the river, which was less bracing than she'd feared. She let it run across her shoulders, dipped her head into it. In a moment she was one with it.

He swam to her side but she paddled away from him, to a place where the water was calm. "Not yet," she said.

She lay back, and she closed her eyes, and she just let herself drift, maybe for the first time in her life.

She still held onto enough about religion to know about baptism, and the absolving power of being immersed. But she didn't think about her own sins, just those that had been committed against her. She felt them washing downstream and out of her life.

Her hair fanned out on top of the water. Too late she remembered Joe's violet, and when she reached for it, it had already joined the downstream flow. She felt herself getting pulled by the current, righted herself and fought against it, started to flail. Then she felt one of Joe's arm around her waist. "I've got you," he said. With his other arm he drew them back upstream, to the place where they'd left their clothes.

He took her hand and led her around rocks on the shore. In the June night heat, the chill on her body faded quickly, then became an exhilarating tingle. He continued to hold her by the hand. "There's a flat patch over here with soft sand."

"Wait," she said. "Can I just go back and get my boots?" She giggled and broke free from his grasp. On the sandy patch she fell, prone, and Joe moved over her.

In the middle of their lovemaking she felt alive to everything, not just the man who was atop and inside her, undulating gently, but everything beneath her, around her and above her. Something grazed across her arms – which were over her head – she imagined it was a breeze-tossed butterfly and she saw herself in the butterfly's body, being blissfully carried to unknown places.

Afterwards they lay side-by-side and she came as close to saying the words "I love you" as she ever had, or ever would. She rolled over towards him. He was snoring lightly, spent.

She rose quietly, retrieved her clothes and slowly dressed. She let a minute or two go by and then nudged him in the side. "Joe honey," she said, "wake up. Show me more of this enchanted place."

He opened his eyes, rubbed them, reached up and touched her face. "What time is it?"

She held up her watch to the moonlight. "Just past 12."

"Oh my God," he said. "Jesus Christ. We've got to haul it on out of here." He trotted over to his clothes. "I told my wife I'd be home by midnight."

While he dressed, Emily walked to a tree and leaned against it. Someone in the distant past had carved into the bark two sets of initials inside a heart. More recently someone had painstakingly carved an obscenity next to the heart. Emily idly mused on whether the carvings had been done by the same person.

The walk out of the Park was labored, and she found herself losing ground to Joe. They were taking the same path from the river that they'd taken to it, but now its course was uphill, and her ponderous boots were a hindrance. She reached a point where she had to catch her breath. She propped her hand against a wooden post and felt something slither beneath it – a water snake that jumped as she did, then vanished into the darkness. She cried out but her voice rang hollow.

She continued trudging uphill. She heard a rustling of leaves ahead and then to the side of her, and someone jumped from the brush and grabbed her.

"Scared you, didn't I?" Joe tried to hold her but she broke away from him. "I wasn't going to leave you behind," he said. "I told you before that I have you." They went on with their walk, separated by a few feet.

On many nights to come, she would return to the Park with the Congressman, and she would find in this ritual much more delight than disenchantment. But for the rest of the time that was allotted to her, it was the night of the full moon that she would most cherish among all of her memories, and most of all what it felt like to be bare and innocent in the embrace of welcoming waters.

13

Shane's settled in his place, a Florida Avenue rooming house. He's lying back on what passes for a bed, a fold-out hassock with rusty wheels. His ember Camel ash is hanging uneasily as he's drifting off.

He's always looked at sleep as his enemy, death's warm-up act. Lately it's been returning his disdain, visiting unpredictably. So, he's doubled up on the barbs. They're starting to kick in.

The drugs come courtesy of one Dr. Kales, who beat a back alley abortion charge a few years ago. It was Shane's case and Kales now serves as Shane's cut-rate pharmacist. The irony is that Doc has no idea that Shane pressed the D.A. over and over again to nail the quack bastard on the abortion rap, but he wouldn't do it. Maybe the D.A. needed his own barbs.

Shane raises himself up and snuffs out his cigarette in an empty tuna fish can. Something is making him fight the pills. He throws off his rough military-issue blanket, navigates his way around all the books stacked next to the hassock, then around the room's functional furniture – fold-up chairs and metal card tables, everything collapsible, easily moved and easily abandoned – before he finally arrives at the window.

On warm nights, a young Negro in the building next door sits out on his fire escape and plays the sax. Tonight's program starts with "Misty" and segues into "I'll Be Seeing You."

Shane goes to his wallet and takes out Emily's picture. When day breaks he'll put it in play for the case, starting by taking it to the Calvert Café to see if anyone there recognizes her. Maybe they'll remember something strange about the last time they saw her there.

For the moment, he just looks at it. He puts it in his pocket, takes it out, looks at it again. He hasn't been able to stop himself from looking at it.

He hears the phone ring down the hall. It's the only one in the house and it sits on a wooden table outside the room of his landlady, Almeta.

Shane's known her for most of his life, beginning when he and Erin would pass her house on their walks to Nats and Redskins games at Griffith Stadium and she'd invite them in for lemonade. After Shane split up with his wife Almeta took him in.

He's the only white person in the place and he pays his rent by way of on-site protection and peacekeeping, which means every so often having to draw his gun to break up a knife fight or separate husband from wife, boyfriend from girlfriend, husband from wife's boyfriend.

Almeta's hard of hearing and has a bad hip so it always takes her awhile to get to the phone. Fortunately, no one in the place seems to get many calls.

"Mr. Shane, it's for you!"

It's been months since he last heard those words. Nobody on MPD except the sergeant knows where he lives, and nobody else in his life has a clue – the stray barmaid or dancer doesn't get the number – so it's either the sergeant calling, or it's trouble.

It turns out to be both. "You might want to get down here," Sarge says. "Seems the Chief's got himself a witness in the Park case and we've got a lead."

"What kind of a witness?"

"I haven't talked with him, but I'm told some guy came forward with information and the Chief's running with it."

"You mean, some fucking nut came forward to send us all off on a wild goose chase and it all goes back to the Chief running his mouth on the Hill this morning."

"Son, I didn't have to call you. You're on your own time and the Chief didn't say anything about bringing you back down. I just thought you should know."

At headquarters, Shane trots straight to the Homicide squad room. The Sarge is reliably in position, poring over paperwork. Shane puts his fists down hard on the desk. "So, what the hell did this witness say?"

Roncalli takes his time putting down his papers. "*Did* he say? I'd watch my past tense if I was you. The fella's still here." He waves towards an interrogation room with a closed door. "The Chief told Rector to pull photographs of possible suspects to show him, and Rector's off looking for them."

"Have you talked with him yet?"

"Nobody has outside of the Chief and Rector. All I know is, he says he saw somebody who matches up with our girl around the first day of May or so last year, and she was right near the Calvert Street Bridge with a guy who looked like he might be up to no good."

"And he's saying this guy was colored, right?"

"Yeah, Shane, colored. In case you haven't noticed, they're just as capable of doing bad things as white folks."

"And the only people who've talked to him are Moran and Rector. That's a couple of first-rate sleuths we're putting all our money on. Somebody needs to flush out this guy's bullshit."

Shane starts to pace back and forth until the Sarge loses patience: "You walk like that in front of me, I feel like I'm in a shooting gallery with an air rifle in my hands."

"Nobody knows the facts here like I do. Let me just have some time with him."

"The Chief looked at this fella and thought to himself, he can close this Park case for me and ice my job for years. So, trust me, the Chief doesn't want you going anywhere *near* this guy."

"Where's Moran now?"

"All I know is, he wants to give something to the newspapers tonight. He said he's coming back here by 11 and that's just ten minutes from now."

Shane goes into one side of his suit jacket, then the other. *Where is it? Where'd I put it?* He pats his front pants pocket and finds it: "I've got a photo of the dead girl. I know who she is now. Somebody needs to show the photo to this guy and I'm the only one that has it."

"Give it to me."

Shane thinks back to the plan he concocted on the fly for Bentley at the U Street club. "Let's do it like this," he says. "Whatever I get from the guy, if he ID's the girl or whatever else, you can just say you got it out of him. Don't say a word about me to the Chief."

"No."

"Better yet, Sarge, say you had to cuff the guy around first. The Chief'll like that even more."

"No, I said. I can't rush it. Plus the Chief is looking to have the guy with him when he meets the press."

"Are you fucking kidding me? This case is already about on its last breath. Put this guy in front of the press before he's been fully braced, you might as well rip out all the tubes."

The sergeant glares at Shane for a long second. "Alright," he finally says. "But be out of there in five minutes or I'm coming in for you. If the Chief catches you in there, you're through. And I won't be far behind you when your behind gets kicked out the door."

* * * * * * * * * *

Shane walks into the room without knocking. The man's back is to him. He's holding a folding chair, moving the back of it like an iron over a blazer that he's stretched out on the desktop. He's humming to himself.

Shane clears his throat. The man turns. "Wrinkles," is all he says.

He puts down the chair, meticulously drapes the blazer over its back, and sticks out his hand: "Quentin Dalton." His grip is soft and moist.

Dalton sits down, gingerly settling against his blazer. Shane takes the other chair. Dalton crosses his legs at the knees and puts both hands on his lap. He's wearing a gabardine sports shirt, chinos and penny loafers. He has clear eyes, a long, straight nose, and auburn hair that laps over his collar in the back.

Shane recalls a phrase he once heard: "The man walks into a room looking like he smells something."

Shane takes off his hat, puts it on the desk and pulls out his Camels. "Want one?"

"Sure." Shane lights up, tosses the pack and a matchbook to the man and watches him light up. His hands are steady.

Shane has just five minutes here, but he can't size up the man's story until he first finds out something about him.

Thirty-three years old and divorced, "her choice not mine." Has two girls but doesn't see them much, they stay with their mother. Works for D.C. government as a housing inspector.

Shane tallies the balance sheet on the Chief's star witness. Loser in love. Indifferent father. Sucks on the public tit working a soft job.

"You grew up somewhere in the Midwest. Am I right, Mr. Dalton?"

Dalton tweaks at his nose, once, twice. "What are you, a boardwalk fortune teller?'

"It's how you talk. Not Chicago, but not too far from there. Someplace to the east."

"Evansville, Indiana. You're good, detective, I have to say."

"I've just met a lot of people from a lot of places."

Shane asks where he lives and he says on Blagden Terrace, off Colorado Avenue, near the new amphitheater. Shane knows that's just a few paces from Rock Creek Park.

"You live by yourself I assume?"

"Yes. As if that's important." Dalton tweaks at his nose again.

Shane glances at the clock on the wall behind Dalton. One minute gone by, four left. "Mr. Dalton, I know you've gone through this before, but not with me."

"Of course." Dalton looks for an ash tray. Shane opens a desk drawer, seizes a stained coffee cup, knocks his own ash into it and passes it to the center of the desktop. "I saw the article in the Star this evening, about the police chief's testimony on the Hill, and it brought to mind something I saw last year."

"Which was?"

"The Chief mentioned May first. That night I was down on Connecticut Avenue, near the bridge on Calvert Street. It was close to midnight and I'd gone down to get a bite to eat."

"Dinner. At midnight."

"I needed to get out of the house. I'd parked at the corner of Calvert and Connecticut and as I was going to my car, I saw this gal standing near the end of the bridge. She was dressed to the nines and she was talking with this man."

"Could you see his face?"

"Not at that point."

"His back was to you?"

"Yes, and she was facing me, and the streetlight was on her. And there was something about the way they were talking that didn't seem right."

"So you did what."

"I walked by them and went down the bridge a bit, even though my car was back the other way, and then I crossed over to the other side so I could keep an eye on things."

"When you turned back around and looked over at them, had anything changed between them?"

"Not really, they were still just talking. Then as I was coming up on them I saw him reach out and touch her shoulder a couple of times and she seemed to pull away from him. They were going back and forth like that."

Shane glances again at the clock. "Was anybody else around?"

"Nobody on foot but there was a lot of car traffic on the bridge. And if you're going to ask if the two of them saw me, I don't think they did. Neither one of them ever looked at me, anyway."

"How was the gal dressed?"

Dalton flicks his ash and pauses. "Just the way the Chief described on TV, at the hearing. Red outfit, flowered hat."

"Did you get a good look at the man?"

"It was almost funny how it all worked out."

With his spare hand, Dalton fusses over some lint on his lapel.

"Just as I got to the point when I was closest to the two of them, there was no traffic on the bridge. And for the first time I could see him clearly, and he looked like a guy I'd seen before."

"From?"

"My job. Up until the last year or so I did a lot of inspection work in the shanties over there in Northwest. Freedmen's Court, Glick's Court, Logan Court."

Alright, maybe he's not sucking on the public tit after all. Spends his time going in and out of the shanties, for as little scratch as the city pays, not an easy paycheck.

From outside, down the hall, Shane hears a rumbling voice.

Is Moran coming back early?

"Describe this guy for me," Shane says to Dalton.

He smooths down an eyebrow with a little finger. "Like I told your Chief earlier, he was in his early 20s or so. Colored man."

"Dark? Brown? High yellow?"

"Dark. Close-cut hair."

"Mustache, beard?"

"Not that I could see."

"Build?"

"I could see he was a strapping man. With a good build. Not that I was really paying much attention to that."

"What was he wearing?"

"Khaki pants and a sports shirt, but don't ask me about color. Nighttime, it all melds together."

"What'd you do next?"

"I went to my car. I looked back over my shoulder and they were going back over the other side of the street."

"Crossing the Calvert Street bridge?"

"No, staying on the same side over there, just crossing the street."

"There's a restaurant there, the Calvert Street Café. You familiar with it?"

The place that gave her the receipt that was found in her pocket.

"Yes, I believe that restaurant is right there."

Shane presses him. "Where that new school playground is?"

And the big sand mounds that washed down the hill the next day.

"Yes," Dalton says, "I believe so. I'm all over the city every day, but I'd say yes."

The rumbling voice outside our room is getting louder. Shane hears the voice say something but all he can make out are two words: "*Post reporter.*" Then: "I'll deal with the guy from the Evening Star at midnight. And by then I'll have kept all those ink-stained bastards happy."

It's the Chief and he's not far away.

Shane puts his weight against the door and rests his hand on the knob. "Where'd you go then?"

"I was going to just go home but the whole thing still nagged at me."

"So?"

"So I made a U-turn. I drove around some, but I couldn't find them."

From outside the room, silence.

What's Moran doing? Where's the Sarge?

Shane trains his attention on Dalton. "You have a pretty detailed memory of what happened that night."

"It stuck with me. It's not every day you even see a pretty white gal and a colored anywhere near each other, let alone talking like that."

Shane lets a moment pass. "That was over a year ago, right?"

"It was."

"And a lot of days have gone by since then, right?"

"You could say that."

"So you can't really say for sure that what you saw was on May first, as opposed to May second, as opposed to April 30th."

Dalton looks Shane in the eye and doesn't blink. "No. I know it was May first, for two reasons. That's my mother's birthday. I'm sure that would stick out in your mind."

Would it? I'm the last one who'd know how to answer that.

"And what else," Shane asks.

"And I filed a police report the next day. And that'll tell you it was May first." He turns his head to blow out smoke. "You can look it up if you want to, Detective."

"Did you tell anybody else tonight about this report you say you filed?"

"I'd forgotten about it, to be honest with you. And your Chief and his assistant there, they never asked."

Shane feels a bump on the other side of the door and hears Moran's booming voice, aimed at no one in particular. "I'm going to get my witness here over to meet the press and then we're all going out to hit the streets." Shane clamps his hand hard on the knob. He feels it move and struggles to hold on. "Goddammit," the Chief says, "Who locked this goddam door?"

Shane strains to hold onto the knob. His hand is wet, he's losing his grip. He plants a foot against the desk and pushes off from it.

He can see a sliver of light in the crack in the frame. It's getting wider. Slowly, slowly, the knob starts to turn and the door starts to budge.

He hears a crack.

Then, Sergeant Roncalli's voice. "Wait, Chief. I let Dalton take a smoke break. I thought you wouldn't need him right away."

"Jesus Christ," Moran says, "I didn't tell you to do that at all. Goddammit, you dumb guinea, can't you even follow an order?"

The door eases back into place. Shane hears the clump-clump of rubber heels on a dull floor until finally the sound fades to nothing.

He turns back to Dalton. "So you actually filed a police report. On what?"

Dalton is staring at Shane. "What exactly was that all about? I hate people when they're not polite."

"I'm asking the questions here," Shane answers, for lack of anything better to say. "So what did you report to the police?"

Dalton tamps out his cigarette in the cup. "I knew I hadn't seen the fellow do anything illegal, but I wanted to get something on the record. Just in case what I saw ended up going bad, you know? So I remembered hearing that the police have this unofficial policy."

"Which is."

"That coloreds aren't supposed to be allowed to stray west of 9th Street, where more of the rest of us live. And the cops keep records, and the third time they catch a particular colored west of 9th, they find something to lock him up for."

"And so you called in this colored guy for being too far west."

"Yes."

"You know, Mr. Dalton, if you're a colored and you're in the jail for even a day you might not come out the same. No wonder they all end up pretty much staying within their borders."

Dalton purses his lips. "Look, Detective," he finally says, "I don't hang around with any coloreds, and if it turns out that this one had something to do with this gal getting killed, then hang him from the nearest tree, right? But if all you end up getting him on is this west of 9th Street thing, just let that one go, alright?"

"Deal."

"Even if he is a colored."

"I said, deal. Leave it at that."

It's almost 11 o'clock. Shane takes the photograph out of his pocket and hands it to the man. "You recognize anyone in this group of people?"

Dalton holds it tight in both hands. "That's her," he says. "The woman in the center there is who I saw that night."

Shane reclaims the photo. Dalton sits back in his chair and shakes his head. "It never had to happen, did it? I hate to say it but it's her own fault in a way."

In one motion Dalton sweeps some stray ashes off the table and into his palm of his right hand and deposits them in the wastebasket.

"Looking like she did," Dalton goes on, "and standing in front of the wrong kind of man, something was bound to go wrong."

Shane picks up his hat and tells the man to sit tight.

The sergeant is in his office, with his opera. Shane asks him if the coast is clear.

"Yeah, it is." Sarge puts his head in his hands. At least he's smiling, a little.

Shane takes out his notebook and scribbles on a page, rips it out and hands it to the sergeant. "Put this in your file. Dalton ID'd our girl."

"But what did you think of him?"

"He ID'd our girl. Nothing else I say matters. This is the Chief's lead and we all just have to ride it home."

"Jesus, Shane, can't you answer a question?"

"Okay, he has a great memory, nailed the ID, and right after he saw what he saw he did everything he could to alert the police to it."

The sergeant stays fixed in place. "There's always a *but* with you. What's the *but*?"

"*But*, he has a strange take on our girl. Says she might not have been all that innocent, that whatever it was that happened she might have had it coming to her. He's good. He might just be too good to be true."

Shane pats his back pocket, and the photo that he knows it holds. "So what's next?"

What's next is that Sarge is sending him home – "Get some sleep, you look like hell" – while the Chief leads 50-odd squad cars on an all-night raid on the alleys in the Second Precinct, all the places where housing inspector Dalton could've seen the suspect before.

"Fifty cars," Shane says. "A hundred cops."

"Yeah. Moran had me pass out mugshots of a bunch of known hoods that generally match the description that Dalton gave. I'm staying back here showing duplicate mugshots to Dalton himself. If I get a hit, I'll call out there and we'll try to make a collar."

"And if you don't get a hit, the Chief'll still have a hundred cops running around the Second, turning the place over and breaking heads and showing who's boss. I get it."

"Jesus, Shane. I tried to get you involved. And I saved your behind back there."

"Yours, too."

Shane puts his hand on the sergeant's shoulder. "Give me a couple of mugshots so I'll have something to do out there. I want to be part of this."

The sergeant reclines in his swivel chair and closes his eyes. Then, without comment, he hands over a mugshot, a young, dark-skinned Negro, in full face and profile. "Identifiers are on the back," he says wearily. "Glick's Court. You know it. Have fun."

Shane takes the Negro's picture and holds it close. He notes the eyes, which are luminous.

He takes Emily's picture. He holds it up next to the Negro's mugshot. The Sarge is talking. Shane isn't hearing him.

14

MEMORANDUM

Page 3 of 4

DATE: April 1, 1951

TO: Chairman
        Committee on Un-American Activities
        United States House of Representatives

FROM: Haynes Nickens
          Investigator

RE: Surveillance of Target No. 1

After staying with the Siegels of Brooklyn, N.Y. for a year, the female subject left for Washington, D.C.,

where she took up residence in 1947. She changed her
name from "Emma Rosenblum" to "Emily Rose," dropping her
middle name "Hadassah" and hiding her Jewish origins.

In June 1947, she began working in a clerical capacity
under Target No. 1, U.S. Representative Joseph Barry.
In the course of surveilling the target the reporting
investigator developed information as to the personality
and habits of the female subject, including the following:

1) Unlike the target Barry, whose father's company
is now known to have had business ties with Communist
governments in the 1930's and beyond, the female subject
seems to have had no associations with Communists or
other political subversives; and

2) The female subject maintained an ongoing intimate
relationship with the target Barry.

****

It's past 2 a.m. and Shane's driving with Bobby up to Glick's
Court. In front of them, then next to them and soon far behind them, is
the incandescent Capitol. It commands the skyline with its shimmering
permanence, and tonight it looks as if it's captured the whole radiant moon
in the windowed space beneath its dome. A lone flag at its base snaps to
attention with each rush of wind.

And Shane feels about as noble and patriotic as he would if he were
cruising down a dirt road in Dixie with a bunch of cracker cops, on what
they'd call a coon hunt.

He winds his way over towards Glick's, then to an alley. It's lit by two
long strands of bare bulbs hung on rusty poles planted in uneven rows: a
block within a block, two columns of 40 or more broken-down, two-story
wooden shacks facing each other along a strip that makes up the middle third
of the court, with tall chain-link fences separating the strip from the better
housing on the outside. Each shack holds five, six, ten people, all Negroes

naturally, where electricity is an occasional visitor and indoor plumbing just a hoped-for stranger.

In this alley more corn liquor is downed, more dope is shot, more tricks are turned and more people are killed than in any other strip of its kind in the city. The only competition comes from the next alley over, or the next one, or the next.

A small, smiling Negro boy meanders around the shacks, unattended. His belly pokes from under a threadbare shirt that his nose is running all over. The only reason he's smiling is that nobody's had the heart to tell him what life has in store for him.

The Capitol's white shining light doesn't reach this part of town.

Shane pulls into a spot where he can see down the alley and still stay mostly hidden behind low-hanging trees. He turns off the engine and the lights. Shrill sirens are sounding relentlessly all around. Charlie Moran's invading army is fanning out through enemy territory.

Bobby looks down the alley. He blows on hot coffee he's brought in a mug from home. "What's gonna come outta all this tonight?"

Shane doesn't answer at first. He seizes Bobby's mug, takes a sip from it and hands it back. "MPD will run in as many Negroes as the paddy wagons can handle. One-fifty, maybe even more."

"Run 'em in over what?"

"Open arrest warrants, some of them. Others, whatever they're doing when one of our goons jumps out on them – a dope deal, pissing up against the outside of a building, whatever." Not to mention, he thinks, the ones who'll end up getting hauled in for just doing whatever a man will do to try to defend himself when he's getting knocked around by a cop over nothing.

"But what about Emily's case?"

"I almost forgot. Just maybe at the end of all this we'll have enough real evidence to charge one of them with the killing."

"And if we don't?"

"We'll charge one of 'em anyway. No, not really. I guess not really."

Shane coughs. A warm, wet day has become a cool, wet night.

"The Chief's already come up with a fancy name for all this," he says. "'The Sweep in the Second,' something like that. Tomorrow he'll say the whole thing was a smashing success and we've got the criminal element on the run. Then he'll sit back and see what happens next on the Park case and if he has enough of an excuse he'll send everybody out here again."

Bobby rests his mug on the dashboard and runs his hand around his waist. He's feeling for his gun, for about the fourth time. "So," he asks, "Who're we over here to catch?"

Shane fishes in his shirt pocket for the mugshot Roncalli gave him. "All you need to know is, this boy was what was left over after the Sarge assigned out 50 other hoods in this area. So that says there was probably nothing about him that jumped out at anybody." He turns on the overhead light. "His name is William Washington Robinson, he goes by Willie, and he's 23."

"That's funny. My best friend when I was growin' up was named Willie Robinson. He'd be a little older 'n 23 now, though."

Shane glances over. "Not too many white kids running around with the name Willie Robinson."

"He wasn't a white kid."

This boy's full of surprises.

"Anyway, he's six-one and 190. One arrest, shoplifting, December 23, 1951. Looks like he jumped bail so he's got a warrant on him now. That's a mistake he's going to be sorry for."

"So how're we gonna handle this here?"

"We've already got him on the bail jumping but that's picayune, we want more." Shane turns off the light, lowers his voice and looks squarely at Bobby. "Over there to the right there's a gap between the two shacks. It's a big dope area and there's always used needles lying around."

Bobby cranes his neck to see.

"You go down there and pocket one of them. Watch your finger, don't get stuck. Then we'll go collar Robinson's black ass and shake him down. If he's clean we'll put the needle on him and take him off on a dope charge, and if he's carrying something we'll lock him up for that and toss our needle. Either way we win."

Bobby looks down. He turns toward the window.

"So now the cat's got your tongue," Shane says. "Grow the fuck up, Shiflett. It's a rough world out here. It's our job to clean up this hellhole and we're not going to be able to do it by playing nice."

Bobby shifts around and puts his hand on the door handle. "I didn't think," he says – "I didn't –"

Shane takes a long drink from Bobby's mug and smiles. "Jesus Christ, Bobby, I'm kidding about all that. You should know me well enough – well, hell, maybe you don't yet."

Bobby looks dumbstruck.

"We're going to go up there," Shane continues. "We'll knock on the door, we'll say who we are and we'll see if he's there. If he is, we'll take him off for questioning as quietly as possible, and hopefully we won't even have to unholster our guns."

"And if he ain't there?"

"Then we'll apologize for coming around so late, and if we think he's in the area we'll ask if we can stay until he comes back there."

"And if they say no?"

Shane puts Willie Robinson's photo away. "If you play it right they never say no."

Bobby starts to stammer. "Look, Detective Kinnock, I'm sorry, sir."

"Don't worry about it. This isn't your regular line of work."

Shane hears a siren coming closer and a cruiser races by with cherry light blazing. He gets a glimpse of the cruiser's backseat area through the rear window and sees the downstroke of a nightstick. He knows the cruiser by its number, knows the cop who's driving it. "You're just lucky, Bobby," he says quietly, "you're in my car here and not the one that just passed."

Outside Shane's car, hell is being visited upon hell. Inside the car, it's peaceful.

There's a loud bump against the car. Bobby starts and Shane reaches for his gun.

Shane eases back. Somebody's walking along the side, holding on for support. From inside the car he can't tell if it's a man or a woman. He just knows it's either a wino or a hophead and they're too out of it to realize that their crutch is a cop car.

"Let him get out of here before we get out to go down the alley," Shane says.

Bobby gets a tin of tobacco from his jacket.

"So, tell me," Shane says, "how is it that a Southern white boy ended up with a Negro friend? I thought that's not supposed to happen down there."

Bobby shoves a pinch into his cheek. "It may not be the way it's supposed to happen, but it's the way it goes when you put dirt-poor crackers and dirt-poor colored folks not far from each other in the same fields, and you tell 'em all to work the land for close to nothin'."

Shane lights up a smoke. "You ever been to a jazz club?"

"Naw, ain't never."

"I ought to take you down to the Negro clubs sometime, down around U Street. Some of those boys can really play."

Bobby weighs Shane's offer. "Don't you stick out in them places?"

"I stay in the shadows. And the boys in the band are all used to seeing me there."

The boys in the band. A few words that can describe any rag-ass group of players anywhere, all the way down to the sadsacks who play weddings in American Legion halls where they double as clean-up staff when the nuptials are done. But to Shane the words conjure up so much more.

When he was no more than ten years old, his father started taking him up to Manhattan and handing him off to a man that Shane only knew as Uncle O. The man ran a hot club in Harlem and he'd take Shane there to see all these colored folks playing in bands.

A few years went by and Shane came to learn that Uncle O was a murderous Irish gangster named Owney Madden who ruled Hell's Kitchen, and Raymond Kinnock stayed in office by keeping Uncle O happy.

Balanced against all that was this. The place that Uncle O ran uptown in Harlem was the legendary Cotton Club and among those colored folks who played there were Duke Ellington, Louie Armstrong, Billie Holiday and Coleman Hawkins. So everything else Shane came to know about Uncle O was like background static on the radio.

"So," Bobby says, "them fellas that play in the clubs you go to. You get to be friends with any of them?"

"Friends? No. Maybe a little."

Truth is that Shane can't say he's ever spent more than a passing few seconds with any of the players he's watched except one, and that's Chet Freeman, trumpet player for Coleman Hawkins and native of Glick's Court. Shane locked Chet up on a dope charge in '46 and cut him slack, partly because he needed a snitch in the Court but mostly because he loved the man's sound.

Chet spends most of his time now touring with Hawkins, but word on the street is that any weekend he's in town he still comes down to the Glick's alley, out of hometown loyalty. But also, for sure, to help him feed whatever it takes for a man to grip hold of a mournful thought and make it into a joyful noise.

"You know," Shane says, "there's more Negroes crammed together down here than anywhere else in the city. They're poor and they got no education and nowhere to go. This is all they'll ever know."

Bobby cranks up his window and drains his mug. "Sure," he says. "But there's more'n just them shacks down here. Like there's a church across the street over there and at the end of the block down yonder there's a school."

Shane hasn't heard. He takes a flashlight from the backseat and turns it on and off to make sure it works. The drunk has fallen off to the side of the alley, harmless. "We need to be making our way down the alley."

Loud voices and singing are coming from the first shack on the left end. A man staggers out, sees Shane and Bobby walking by, pivots and goes back inside. "That's where the gin joint must be tonight," Shane says. "It floats up and down the alley. A big mason jar of corn whiskey just costs a quarter. But if you're there for most of the day it adds up."

"How we know where we're lookin' for this Robinson?"

"It says on the back of the photo here, the boy's at 16 Glick's." Shane shines his light on the front of the shacks, one-by-one, sees no house numbers. Finally, a big "11" painted in black on a rotting front door that's mostly off its hinges. "If there's any pattern here we're not far." An old woman in a housecoat stands next to the door of 11, staring at them as they pass before retreating into the dark.

In the distance, a single siren trails off wanly.

A loud crash sounds behind them – a stray dog tipping over a garbage can, pouncing on the spillage.

They come to what has to be number 16 and Shane tries the knob. It's locked but the jam is corroding. A hard shove will open it.

Instead Shane knocks. "Open up, it's the police."

A light, probably from a kerosene lamp, flickers under the crack and he knows somebody's in there. He moves the flashlight to his left hand, draws his gun and nods to Bobby to do the same.

"I said, open up. Police, goddammit."

Footsteps come fast towards the door and Shane plunges against it. He hits a body hard and they both sprawl on the dirt floor and the flashlight flies out of his hand. He knows Bobby is behind him somewhere, but he can't see him in the dark and he can't hear him over the shrieking and crying. He feels around the struggling body he's on top of and he puts his gun next to where the head is. "Don't shoot me," says a high voice, "I ain't done nothing. Please don't hurt my babies."

Shane's eyes adjust to the dark space, and he room comes into focus. Bobby draws next to him with the flashlight. The body under Shane is a woman, she could be any age. He puts his free hand on the dirt and gingerly pushes away from her and rises. "Just take care of those kids," he says. She hustles over to the hysteria in the corner of the room.

Bobby shines his flashlight along the bottom of the walls, where empty Coke bottles have been shoved into gaping spaces. "Rat holes," Shane says, getting his bearings, brushing himself off.

The woman walks back to them with a toddler slung over her shoulder, catching her breath. "Cat used to get most of them rats," she says. "Cat was all over them creatures. Then he up and went."

Shane holsters his gun and shows his badge. "Sorry for the ruckus, ma'am. Just down here looking for a Willie Robinson. You know him?"

She pats the child on the back. "Yes – no. I mean, I know him but I ain't been seein' him. He's my son. Hush *up*, Luther." Another child has started whimpering.

"First, he don't live here, and second, he won't be comin' around here no time soon. Went down the country yesterday, won't be back for the rest of the summer. What you want him for?"

"We need to talk with him is all. He may be in some trouble and we can help him."

"Help him?" She moves her child to her other shoulder. "Ain't never seen no police come around here to help nobody."

"I'm not just any kind of police, ma'am." Shane takes off his hat and holds it to his chest. "Tell me, what part of the country are you talking about?" He puts his hand on his hip and his jacket draws back just enough to show his holster.

"North Carolina," she says after a second or two. "Tarboro. Where I grew up, where he was born, where our peoples're from." She pushes her hair back. She's wearing a sleeveless smock and Shane can see she has old lady arms, skin hanging off the bottoms like turkey necks.

"You have a number for him down there?"

"He goes down there, he's his own man. I can't be expectin' to have him sit hisself down for long in one place."

"You expect to be hearing from him?"

"Maybe, maybe not. Ain't like I don't have my hands full without him."

There's another bang outside and she looks quickly over Shane's shoulder.

"It's nothing, ma'am," he says. "Dog out there running wild."

"Good," she says, as if to herself. "I mean," she goes on, "why don't nobody tie up them mongrels?"

Shane eases towards the door. Bobby bumps against him once, then again. Shane ignores him. "What do you mean by summer, ma'am? He be back by September?"

A third child joins the howling cacophony, then a fourth. "Most likely he'll be back," she says. "Then again, he finds steady work down there, who knows?"

"Ma'am, I understand." Two dead roaches lie on a folding table. Shane places his card squarely between them. "My number's on there. You hear from your son, you call me." He steps around a child wrapped in burlap on the floor and leaves.

Back in the car, Bobby says, "She's lyin'."

Shane just stares out the window down the alley.

"The boy may not live with her," Bobby goes on, "but he ain't far away. You see how she looked when she heard that noise outside? She thought that was him comin'. And that thing about him takin' the train to Tarboro yesterday – I been on that train, it don't run but once a week, on Saturdays."

"I figured all that." Shane doesn't look over.

"Well if you figured, why didn't we stay?"

"Did you want to have to put up with all that yelping? It wasn't going to get any better."

"So, what do we do now?"

"Sit here and watch. I agree the boy's close by, maybe out somewhere stealing for the rest of them. And who can blame him for that."

The police radio cackles with gibberish.

Bobby slumps in his seat. "We gonna take shifts?"

"I'll watch first. I'm not tired."

Again, the radio cackles.

Bobby rests his hand on his waist. "I ain't tired neither and if I was, I couldn't sleep right now anyways."

"One-sixteen, Kinnock, answer up!"

Roncalli is on the radio.

"Jesus, Kinnock. Advise as to status of Robinson."

"Responded to his home but he wasn't there. Believe he's still in the area. Currently sitting on his house."

"Be advised that witness Quentin Dalton made a positive ID of your man Willie Robinson from a duplicate photo he was shown. List Robinson as now officially wanted for the Rose murder."

So this is the guy.

If that mother thinks her life is hard now, wait until she sees how it gets when her boy gets locked up for killing a white girl who had friends in high places.

Roncalli again: "By order of the Chief, do not, repeat, do not proceed further until multiple backup units are on scene there. Do you copy one-sixteen?"

Shane lets a couple of seconds pass. "Yeah, I copy."

A wind gust rolls a bundle of chicken wire across the street in front of the car. The stray dog bays like a coyote. Close by, sirens are reclaiming the night. The blue cyclone is re-gathering strength.

Shane reaches under the car seat and pulls out a pair of binoculars. "We're lucky there's nothing to block our view down there," Shane says. "Most nights everybody's out on their front until all hours. The rain must've driven them all in."

"Here comes somebody," Bobby says. A figure, walking from the end of the alley. "Where'd he come from? I thought it was a dead end down there."

"It's easy to get into the alley."

Shane doesn't finish the thought. *As easy as it may be to get into the alley, it's the toughest thing in the world to get out of it.*

Through the binoculars he can make out the figure. "Negro male. Right size, maybe the right age. I can't see his face until he comes under a light." The man's walking slowly and looking around furtively. "There you go," Shane mutters. "You're dark enough but I can't tell for sure." He trains Bobby's flashlight on the photo, then looks back through the binoculars. The man stops at number 16 and has his hand on the door.

Shane hears a familiar voice outside the car. "There he is! Get his black ass!" Two uniforms run by the car and race into the alley.

"Goddammit," Shane says. "It's Moran and Rector."

Bobby bolts forward. "You mean..."

"They're coming in to get the collar all by themselves. Guess the Chief doesn't think he needs much backup." Shane takes out his gun. "He's going to get his fat ass killed if somebody doesn't help." He runs from the car, with Bobby right behind.

Up ahead, Calvin Rector trips on a tree root and sprawls on the ground, sliding face first through the mud. Shane vaults over him and lands in a puddle, keeps his feet. He sees Moran's pink round head bouncing along in front of him, the treasured "Chief" hat already lost in the chase. A small, wailing boy runs naked from number 16 and Shane tries to dodge him but can't. He knocks the boy down, and the boy's head hits the ground. He hears the mother yell at him, "You motherfuckin' monster!"

Moran is at the end of the alley, trying to crawl through a gap in the fence, his big behind barely squeezing its way to freedom. Shane feels something grab him and looks down to see the mother's old arms wrapping themselves around his ankles. He falls, gets up and kicks her away. "You motherfuckin' monster!" she yells again.

He emerges on the other side of the fence, side-steps a chamber pot and runs around an outhouse. In front of him is a row of ramshackle brick rowhouses, poor but not alley-poor. On the other side of the rowhouses is another alley full of shanties. He doesn't see Moran or the Negro who ran away.

All of a sudden it's quiet. There's a gap between rowhouses and he runs towards it.

He hears gunshots – one, two – maybe three and four, maybe echoes.

The gap leads to a dead end but there's another gap further down the court, and that one leads to a small clearing.

The Chief's on his back on the ground and the Negro's standing over him with gun in hand. The Chief's slobbering on himself and his hands are clasped together. The Negro's holding the gun loose by his side. "Please don't kill me, son," Moran's saying. "I'm a god-fearing man."

Shane aims his weapon at the Negro. "Drop the gun."

He's not going to shoot me, look at his face, he's scared.

"Drop it now."

If he flinches, go for center mass and drop him. Shoot to kill and nothing less.

They stare at each other for a long second and then the Negro's gun hand flinches.

Shane lowers his weapon and fires and the man drops. "My leg," he yells, "my leg," and he collapses, dropping the gun. Shane goes over and kicks the gun to the Chief, who's now sitting up.

Jesus Christ, he could bleed out right here. I haven't fired a gun at anybody since Guadalcanal. You'd think I'd have learned.

Moran shakes his head and shudders. "You saved my life, Kinnock." He rises to his haunches, puts his head down and shakes it again.

The Negro man's bleeding on the asphalt and squirming in pain but Shane doesn't have a radio on him so he has to hope the squad cars in the area heard the shots and are on their way.

Calvin Rector runs up, breathing hard. "Everything okay, Chief?"

Moran stands straight up and eyes him. "You didn't see what happened, Rector?"

"Naw, Chief. I heard the shots but I was on the other side of the fence. What'd he do to you?" Rector walks to the man on the ground and kicks him in the head, falls over backwards and rights himself. "That's just what this nigger deserved."

Moran paces around the Negro, who's breathing but unconscious. He puts his right hand in his back pocket and jingles his change. "You know, Calvin, I had the nigger cornered. I was right up on him, and he gave the whole thing up to me about killing the girl in the Park."

He walks closer to the man, turns back.

"Then he started to break on me and Kinnock here ran up and grabbed him and his gun went off. Next thing I knew the nigger had Kinnock's gun and was standing over him about to shoot him. Thank God I was able to take the nigger down."

Moran turns to Shane and winks. "We make quite a team, don't we, Kinnock?"

Shane takes off his jacket and tie, tosses them to the ground, then takes off his dress shirt. He walks over to the man, wraps the shirt around his leg and knots it to stop the bleeding. One of the man's arms is splayed awkwardly under him and he straightens it out.

He walks back towards the courtyard. He hears Moran call out to him. "You got nothing to be ashamed of, son. You did everything you could possibly do." He hears Moran say to Rector, "I guess Kinnock's a little embarrassed. Nigger got the better of him."

Shane sees the first of many squad cars roll into the block and stands in front of it: "Kinnock, Homicide. Get on the air as fast as you can and get an ambulance down here. The nigger's leg is hurt bad and he's probably also got a bad concussion. Then we're gonna lock the nigger's ass up."

He learned on the job long ago that to make some people do what you want them to do, sometimes you've got to be willing to speak their language even if the words taste foul on your lips.

A Negro girl runs up to him, pigtails flying. She spins him around and pounds on his chest with her fists. Shane takes hold of her hands. She cries, "I seen it all. Fat white policeman shot at the boy trying to hit him in the back, then he tripped and dropped his gun and the boy just picked it up. Boy didn't shoot at nobody." She tries to get another breath but can't.

Shane walks her into the shadows so nobody can see he's stroking her head. He whispers to her. "Please be quiet, honey, please. Please, if you know what's good for you, please."

The courtyard's filling up with cops. A couple of press hounds sprint past, fresh from monitoring the police band and hearing about the big chase.

Shane keeps walking away from everybody. He stops and looks back. Moran's standing over the Negro and he's lit up by the flashbulbs popping poosh! poosh! poosh! in the night air.

Right now old Charlie's acting like he's Rocky Marciano, heavyweight champ. Only the Rock never needed anybody else to jump in the ring to help him.

Even from his distance he can hear the Chief say, "Boys, this thing was *over* before it even started."

An ambulance appears. Shane waves it down and flashes his badge. "There's a nigger up there laying in the street." He grips the car's window frame. "We think he killed a white girl. Ride up in there fast, we need to keep him alive in case he starts to talk."

The driver looks skeptical.

"You know," Shane goes on, "so's he can give it all up and then we can fry him good."

"Okay, boss," the driver calls out and pulls off.

Shane watches the driver get out a litter and load the man on it, roughly. When the ambulance comes back up, Shane stops it, gets in the back and squeezes next to the litter.

He cradles the man's head and rests it on his lap.

The drive to Gallinger Hospital is bumpy and slow. He rubs the man's hand the whole way.

And in stray moments he's thinking.

You can play the hero right now, Charlie. But I know what really happened.

I'm not sneaking around anymore on this case.

Don't fuck around with me now, Charlie Moran. And don't think anything is over.

15

THE WASHINGTON POST
Wednesday, May 28, 1952

GIRL KILLER TO FACE
MURDER GRAND JURY,
MAYBE THE CHAIR
By Bran Bentley, Staff Reporter

After giving the matter just a few seconds of thought, a D.C. judge decided to send off Willie Robinson – now identified as the confessed killer of Capitol Hill secretary Emily Rose – to a grand jury. It's Robinson's first step to his date with the electric chair.

Only one witness testified against Robinson, but it was a big one. Charlie Moran, MPD Chief, detailed all the evidence against Robinson, including the boy's own confession, and added something unexpected. Since the boy's arrest he's steadfastly refused to say anything in his own defense. "If somebody leveled these charges at you and they weren't true," the Chief said to the judge, "don't you think you'd deny them?"

Asked during the hearing if he wished to testify and fight his charges, the Negro youth just made an inaudible comment and smiled. His appointed lawyer, Paulie Donovan, stepped in to say that he'll be talking with the D.A.

about setting up a quick plea bargain to spare the boy's life, but he knows nobody's promising him anything.

Prosecutors are said to have developed additional connections between Robinson and Miss Rose but didn't divulge details.

As if things weren't already bad enough for Robinson, Chief Moran has announced that he'll be investigated for possible involvement in the 1946 killing of white female Janet Meslin in Rock Creek Park. Reports at the time stated that Miss Meslin may've been seen in the company of a Negro youth shortly before her death.

****

"It all starts with working like a motherfucker to be the best that's ever been.

"Thing is, you end up on the same stage with a dude like Charlie Parker. You on, hotter than a motherfucker, and then Bird stands up and it's like God himself reached down and touched his horn.

"Since you was nine or something, you been feeling the music all up in your bones and shit. You wake up in the morning, it's the first thing you think about, and you reach right past your old lady to grab at your horn, same thing at night. You work your *ass* off, right? Still. You always been straight and shit, basically.

"But Bird, he does smack like it's morning cornflakes and he just plain hears shit you don't, and he plays the shit he hears like no one else.

"And so you try it. And you do the shit again, and then again, and each time it feels better than the time before, until Bird's pretty much the *last* thing on your mind. And by that time, well, it's like they say in a war. You don't hear the shot that kills you."

This is how a heroin addiction starts, at least according to jazz trumpeter Chet Freeman, son of Glick's Court, in confidences he shared with Shane one night. Back when he was still in the mood to talk to Shane, which he might never be again.

Shane's sitting at his main club, the place where pretty much everybody who knows him knows they can find him, most every night when he's not working. The Coleman Hawkins Band is in rare form but he's just watching Chet, and it's one of those nights when Chet's finding a way to make his demons pay service to his talent as opposed to the other way around.

A waitress is flitting about just off the stage. She's slight and pretty, with knowing brown eyes and hair that falls to her shoulders just so. Chet would say she's fine, but too yellow for him. To Shane, she's just fine.

She's clearing off one of her tables. Some kids from Howard U. rolled in earlier and left a mess behind. She can't keep from stealing glances at the clarinet player undulating on the stage. He has coffee skin, pressed hair and a Billy Eckstein mustache. He's winking at her, moving his piece below his waistband. He's missing most of his cues.

The band winds down in a move to the break.

Shane walks over to the side of the stage, just outside the spotlight. Chet's working a cloth around one side of his trumpet. Shane tries to catch his eye but he's not looking up. "Chet," he whispers.

Chet raises his head, then goes back to his horn.

"Chet, over here."

He turns slowly. "Don't be comin' 'round here to see me."

"We need to talk."

"Got nothin' to say to you." Chet snaps the cloth and starts working the other side of the horn.

He's high, not to say that this is a reason to call a news wire. "If I take you in the back and shake you down, Chet, you and me both know that I gotta run you in. You want me to do that?"

Chet just shakes his head. He sets his trumpet down in its case and walks behind a big, black curtain.

Backstage, Shane scans the area for eavesdroppers. Everybody's gone outside for the break, it's too hot to stay in. Nobody's around but the pretty waitress and the clarinet player, in the shadows by the back door, maybe twenty feet away. They're up on each other and he's running his tongue along her neck and she's unbuckling his pants. They're reliably preoccupied.

Chet's leaning against the side wall, doped up but angry. "I heard about you lockin' up Cat Eyes from the Court."

"Cat Eyes? You mean Robinson?"

"You shoot a boy down, and then you work him over in his hospital bed, and you don't even know the boy's nickname. Shit."

"The Chief shot that boy," Shane says. "Everybody knows that, right? It was in the papers."

"I know just what happened over there. Knew it all by fuckin' sunrise."

Shane's just about the only cop that Chet could say "fuck" to without getting beaten down, and Chet knows it.

Shane lowers his voice. "Well, maybe you didn't hear that your boy Cat Eyes got off lucky. If a colored boy's standing across from just about any other cop on this force but me and his trigger finger starts to look itchy, he ain't living long enough to even get sent to the hospital."

"Maybe you wanted him dead, but you just a bad shot."

"You know, there's a fair number of Jap motherfuckers who might say otherwise, if they still could."

Anytime Shane talks to Chet, the word "motherfucker" starts sailing past his lips like "and" and "the."

Chet wipes his mouth with the back of his arm. "So, if you know everything already, what the fuck you need from me?"

"Talk to me," Shane says, "about Robinson. Willie. You know, Cat Eyes."

"What's he sayin' for himself?"

"That's a problem. That's a motherfucking problem."

Behind Chet, the waitress has pulled the clarinet player's pants around his ankles and dropped to her knees. Shane comes around to Chet's side and leans into him so he won't be distracted.

"He's not saying a word and he's got a lot he needs to talk about. Chief Moran of the Metropolitan Motherfucking Police Department is in court today saying the boy confessed to him right there on the street."

"And did Cat Eyes even have a chance to talk after that?"

"He sure did. He got knocked out when all that shit was going on – "

"So I heard."

"-- but he came to just before he got to the hospital. The doctors finished up with his leg and he was awake and in a room an hour later. We spent all day taking turns to try to get something more out of him."

" Takin' turns, hah. That's a motherfucking joke. More like y'all were takin' shots at him, I'm bettin'."

Shane feels flush. "Fuck you, Chet. You've been down that road with me and you know I treated you right. And I made sure everybody down there treated this boy right. Shit, Moran knows not to cross me for right now."

Chet starts to turn towards the lip-smacking and the soft moaning behind him. Shane puts his index finger to his forehead. "Right here, Chet. Willie, Chet. Tell me about him. Because I gotta tell you, there's more to the case against him than what's come out from the Chief so far."

"Newspapers don't say that."

"Newspapers don't know everything. We found out Willie could've crossed paths with the dead girl. He's been doing one of his two jobs up there up in the lowest level of the Capitol building. In a place called the folding room. It's a factory like something out of a hundred years ago, and it cranks out thousands of letters that the Congressmen up there send out to the voters."

"Don't mean Willie and the girl ever saw each other, ever."

"He's up there every day, and you know for sure if he ever did have any dealings with her we'll find out. But there's even more to it. Come to find out your man Willie had his second job as a dishwasher at a place uptown called the Calvert Café, where the dead girl ate her last meal. And it's just a stone's throw from where her body was dumped."

Chet bends down. Puts both hands on his knees. Straightens up. "Okay, I'll talk to you. But same deal as always. I don't tell nothin' –"

"-- that's gonna get nobody locked up for nothing. Right."

"So, what the fuck can I tell you? He's a good boy, cares most of all in life about his family – will do anything in the world for 'em. Works them two jobs, brings shit over to 'em whenever he can. Whatever it takes to put food in their bellies, he'll do, you get me, on account of that's all he cares about."

He stops. Footsteps sound on the stage side of the curtain.

The steps move away. "Not gonna say he coulda never done somethin' like this. Suppose you don't really know about anybody. But I'm damn sure not gonna say he coulda. You mean to tell me he's not saying nothin' about his case at all?"

Shane shakes his head. "I tried to talk to him first, then Moran, then my sergeant, then I went in there again. None of us got shit out of him. He said the most to me."

"And you got that by sayin' what?"

"I went in his room and told him I was sorry I had to do what I had to do. I told him I wanted to get his side of the story. And he just mumbled something about a hymn."

"Him who?"

"No, a hymn, h-y-m-n. Like a church song."

Chet smiles for the first time, as if he's hearing something meant only for himself. "I know the word, you don't have to go spellin' it for me. Now what exactly did the boy mumble about that?"

"Just that thing about a hymn or something. Made me think that maybe I was supposed to go to church and open up the book and listen for some song. And then he closed his eyes and from then on he wouldn't say anything, just kept his eyes closed."

Chet presses both hands to his brow. He can't seem to stop smiling.

"All I can say to you," he says, "is you a man, and a man's got to figure some shit out for himself, and I can't help your ass out with everything. But I'll tell you this, about whatever Cat Eyes said about what you call that hymn word. That's Reverend Williamson talkin'. Shit, I didn't even know Cat Eyes was seeing the Rev over there."

Shane pictures the church that Bobby talked about last night, across the street from Glick's Court. It's just big enough to fit fifty on the high end and it has a sign out front that dominates the building that it's meant to honor: **Bible Way Congregation, Reverend Fulwood Williamson, Pastor.**

"So, what does the Reverend have to do with Willie not talking?"

"Seriously, for somebody who hangs around our places as much as you do, you don't know shit about us. Like about the Reverend being into all this silent protest and shit."

"It hasn't made the Post," Shane says drily.

"But it's sure as shit made the Afro-American," Chet shoots back. "Look, all you need to hear is a story."

Chet takes a long breath. It's becoming clear to him that Shane's not taking him off to a cell tonight.

"Last year the Rev called to the private school closest by his house and pressed them about lettin' his boy in even though he knew they wouldn't, of course. So the Rev just marched his boy into the school on a Monday, walked him right down to the first-grade classroom, told him to sit his ass on the floor, and then sat his own ass down next to him."

Chet tells how the Reverend let everybody at the school know he was a preacher and talked about all the important white folks that he knew all over the city – even President Truman, though the Rev might've stretched the truth on that one a bit – then just sat by his boy, didn't say another word that day. Somehow the Reverend got himself and his boy back into the school Tuesday, then again Wednesday, and sat silently with him in the classroom.

"Thursday," Chet says, beaming, "the crackers who run the school had a meetin'. Friday, the boy was in the classroom, right up front, yellin' out his A-B-C's and kickin' everybody's *ass*, and the Rev was back home with a big-ass grin on his face. Ain't that some shit?"

"It's some shit, all right. I just don't know if what you call silent protest works so well if you're not six years old, and you're not in school but you're in jail for murder, and your daddy's nowhere around to help you out."

Chet makes a face and slouches against the wall. "Cat Eyes knows his daddy'll come around for him when the time's right."

"How long have you known Cat Eyes?"

"His whole life, just about. His mama and me grew up next to each other. I know her real well."

"*Real* well?"

"Well enough."

From behind them Shane can hear the sound of a pulling zipper, and a few seconds later the pretty waitress bustles by, head down, on the way back out to the restaurant side.

"Boy had a bit of a mean streak as a young'un," Chet goes on, "but that's not exactly unusual for anybody who had to grow up fast in the alleys."

"I take it he ran around with some lowlifes?"

"No. I mean, now, the boy – no."

Shane grabs Chet by the shoulder blades and squares him around. "Don't hold back now. The boy's in about as much trouble as a boy can be in, so nothing you say can make it worse."

"Naw, I'm not –"

"What's in your pockets, Chet? Want me to look?"

The rest of the band can be heard tuning up on stage. "You know, the boy just…"

Chet stops as the clarinet player moves out of the shadows and passes by them.

"The boy just runs numbers sometimes for Sweet Pea, that's all. To get himself a little money on the side. Nothin' to do with any of this."

Sweet Pea. Right.

Jimmy "Sweet Pea" Johnson commands the numbers racket in the Second Precinct and works for Charlie "Three Finger" Brown, who commands everything between the Second and the Eighth. Three Finger works for Tyrone "Big Ticket" Blackwell, who commands most of Northwest and Northeast. And Big Ticket works for Jake Kaufman.

So, Willie Robinson basically runs numbers for the city's biggest gangster.

Maybe it has nothing to do with any of this, and maybe it does.

Shane circles behind Chet, says "They're going to be missing you out there," and starts to shove him lightly towards the stage.

Chet wheels around. "Y'all ain't got shit on that boy."

"That's just not true, Chet. We got what the Chief will say he confessed to him."

"You really believe that shit?"

"Whether I believe it or not doesn't matter, Willie's still gotta face it. Plus we got a witness who says he saw him with the dead girl the night she went missing, right near where she ended up."

Shane doesn't even mention that he's heard from the Sarge that a second witness came up to headquarters just a while ago to say that he saw the girl in the restaurant where Willie worked, and then saw Willie leave right after the girl left.

"And on top of all that," Shane says, "your boy isn't saying a word to defend himself."

"He got himself a lawyer, right?"

"If you can call him that. Paulie Donovan. Down at the courthouse, free lawyers get given out off a wheel, like it's the lottery. And your boy Willie got fucked with a bad number."

Chet trains his bloodshot eyes on Shane. "You really think he killed that girl?"

"Yeah, I do," Shane says, with more conviction than he really feels. "One of the men who saw them together, I talked to him, looked him straight in the eye. And besides that, if your boy had nothing to hide, why the fuck wouldn't he say something?"

Just don't ask me why *he would've killed her. Because I don't know that at all.*

"What you got on the boy, it wouldn't be nearly good enough to take down a white man, would it?"

"That's not really important right now."

A shout comes from the stage. "Chet, get back out here!"

Chet waves a hand and keeps looking at Shane. "You and me, we go back. If you was all that sure that Willie's done this, you wouldn't be down here. I can tell you're lookin' for somethin' *good* about the boy, not somethin' bad. And if a white cop is lookin' for somethin' good about a poor colored boy who's up on a murder charge – well, shit."

Shane doesn't give an answer because he doesn't have one.

"If you got any heart in you," Chet goes on, "can't you try to keep him out of the chair, at least? Like, he's a young fella, right? Okay, I'm not sayin' he did this shit, 'cause I don't think he did, but *if* he did, what if he was just doin' it for somebody else? What if some powerful-ass person wanted this shit to happen and played on him, slipped him some money for his family or some shit like that?"

"It's the D.A.'s case now, Chet. I can't go off on my own."

From stage-side: "FREEMAN!"

Chet grabs Shane by the shoulders, just as Shane grabbed him a few minutes ago. "You an' me both know," Chet says, "that you work for some corrupt-ass motherfuckers. If you got any doubts about this charge y'all put on Cat Eyes, you gonna have to find a way to follow up on this shit on your own. You as much as said that the boy's got himself a sorry-ass lawyer who won't lift a motherfuckin' finger for him."

Chet clamps down harder on Shane's shoulders.

"You say you all about justice an' shit," he presses on. "Well, justice says somebody's gotta make sure this boy don't get railroaded. Shit, you're smart enough, you even told me when you first locked me up, you remember, we were talkin' about what kind of deal I could get for myself an' you said – "

"Yeah, that I knew more law – "

"Than the motherfuckin' D.A., right. Well, I know you got the *brains* to make sure the right thing happens here." Chet eases his grip. "But do you got the *balls* to do that, mister?"

Shane meets Chet's stare, reaches down and pats around one of Chet's pants pockets, feels the sharp point of a needle through the cloth. He takes Chet's hands off of him, one by one, and touches Chet on the arm. "Have a good set," he says.

Chet starts back towards the stage, then turns. "You know, if you really be all about justice and shit, then right now you gotta almost *be* his motherfuckin' lawyer."

He walks off into the unsparing stage light.

16

THE WASHINGTON POST
Thursday, May 29, 1952

MOUNTING SCANDALS COULD DOOM JOE BARRY'S NEW YORK SENATE BID
By Drew Pearson

The New York Senate campaign of Rep. Joseph Barry (R-N.Y), cruising into the late rounds of the fight virtually untouched, is about to be dealt two powerful body blows.

Sources say Rep. Barry's father, industrialist S. Matthew Barry, will soon face tough questioning from a Congressional committee about his companies' transactions with Communist governments. A high-ranking government official says that the hearing will produce a bombshell that could even result in criminal charges being brought against him.

On top of that, there are growing indications that Joe Barry himself had a too-close friendship with Emily Rose, the Capitol Hill staffer found dead last week in the city's Rock Creek Park. A high-ranking government official who's viewed documentary evidence of the relationship says it's "potentially devastating" to the married Barry.

****

"It's been a great week for you, hasn't it? First there's the Time magazine cover story we haven't even talked about. Then this column you fed to Drew Pearson, tucking it to Barry. Very clever."

"So how *are* you, Shane, me boyo."

It's 7 a.m. and Shane's at his desk with the Post on his lap, opened to Pearson. Raymond's at home and for a change he's answering his own phone.

Shane usually has to contend with his father's latest transient girlfriend when he calls, or a Negro housemaid. Raymond has said publicly that it was the maid's stories of her struggles in the South that awakened him to the civil rights cause. As far as Shane can tell, her main role in Raymond's life is to make sure Shane's calls never get through to him.

Raymond goes on. "That was quite a piece that Time ran on me, I must say. Made even this ruddy Irishman redder than a virgin on her wedding night."

Shane's read the story. It was titled, "The Negro's Man of the Hour." He stayed with it almost to the end, when he came to this:

Safe and secure in his office retreat on a warm night in the capital city, Rep. Kinnock blithely dismisses the possibility that his progressive dream will derailed by his own budding scandal or by allegations of criminal misconduct by his son, Shane, in a D.C. homicide case. "There's a saying that the sins of the father are visited on the son. I've never known it to go the other way, and it won't now."

"I called about the Pearson column."

"I'm still stuck on what exactly you mean, son, when you say I'm so clever.

"He ran the item about Matt Barry that you had Louis leak to him. And on top of it all, he even threw in a mention about Joe and the dead girl in the Park. Nice."

"I have no earthly idea what you're talking about."

"I was in your office the other day. I heard it all."

"An enterprising journalist followed up on a lead and found there was something to it."

"Isn't it kind of unusual for somebody as big as Drew Pearson to run an item like this? Guys on the Hill are screwing around every day and all the reporters in town look the other way."

"Well, it's not every day that one of the girls that's getting screwed, to use your phrase, ends up dead in a public park."

"Pearson says there's documentary evidence on Barry and the girl. Have any idea what that is?"

"Why are you asking me, of all people? Son, I have a breakfast meeting with the Speaker at eight and then an early lunch with the President. I have a job to do."

"You're not the only one. Somebody supposedly has documentary evidence that a married Congressman was screwing the dead victim in a case I'm on. That's relevant information to my investigation."

"Your investigation." Raymond chuckles. "That part's over, isn't it? You have your man, that Negro boy you all locked up. Now it's been referred over to the U.S. Attorney for grand jury, so it's the prosecutor's case now, right?"

"Not exactly," Shane answers. "Yesterday the Chief was perfectly happy to call this a closed police case and give it up to the D.A., but then your Pearson story about Joe hit the streets. And the amazing thing is, when I got into my office this morning the Chief himself was already waiting for me."

"And to what end?"

"To the end of telling me that maybe the colored boy didn't just act on his own wild impulses. To the end of telling me we need to do some more investigation on our end and not just leave it all to the D.A. To the end of saying the real key to the case just might be the Joe Barry angle and I should go at it hard. You know," Shane goes on, "if I didn't know better I'd think somebody put an idea in Charlie's head to change his mind and try to bring Barry into this."

"Son," Raymond says, "the police chief can read a newspaper just as well as anyone else. He sees a reference to his case and he sees a name and he runs with it. For the life of me I can't see how any of this has to do with me."

He's still feigning ignorance. The typical politician tries to survive by making people believe he knows more than he really does. Raymond Kinnock, in no way typical, learned a long time ago that the secret to survival lies in making people believe he knows much less.

Shane measures his words. "I just had a few thoughts, maybe a hunch or two is all. Keeping in mind that if I go wrong on this, I wouldn't want any of my sins to be visited upon you."

Raymond doesn't rise to the bait, not that Shane was really expecting him to. Your ordinary father, caught in the extraordinary circumstance where he's quoted in a national magazine distancing himself from his own son, might think to say he's sorry or at the very least explain. But most fathers aren't politicians, and most of those who are still have some capacity for feeling guilt. Raymond Kinnock doesn't.

Shane moves on. "I was just saying, Drew Pearson may be a muckraker but he's no fool. He's not going to run with something like this on a Barry unless he knows for certain that there's something to this evidence."

"Of course, of course."

"And the only way that there's something to this is if it's official. Reports by some undercover officer in a real law enforcement agency. Somebody who's followed Joe Barry around and really gotten the goods on him, not just some scribblings by a private dick or anybody like that. So, I just thought, with you being close to Hoover –"

"*Hoover,*" Raymond says sharply. "Why *Hoover*?" Just that quickly, he pulls back. "It just goes to reason that if reports like what you're talking about exist, pretty much anybody could generate them, right? Even your MPD force."

"Not MPD. There are exactly two people in my department who know the Hill well enough to run an operation on a Congressman. One's the Chief, and he's too public to get away with it. And the other one's me and nobody asked me. No, this is FBI, all the way."

Raymond forces a laugh. "So you want me to get J. Edgar Hoover on the line, just like that, and ask him to tell me about some reports that you don't even know for sure exist?"

Shane wants to say, How long are we going to play this game? You know I've figured out you had Hoover get one of his boys to follow Joe Barry around, you've been seeing all the reports, and then once this girl turned up dead you leaked the story to Pearson.

Instead he keeps talking in circles, as he usually does with his father, because there's never been a straight line in their relationship, ever.

"So tell me," Raymond says, "if I had all the information you think I have, why wouldn't I long ago have just trotted it over to your Chief?"

"Because when this gets played you want it to be played right. And you know Charlie Moran's limitations."

Finally, Shane's had enough. "You're going to bleed all these reports that you have on Joe into the press, aren't you? Kill his career little by little, death by a thousand paper cuts. But just think about how much more you could get out of your junior G-man exercise if everything that comes out of it could find its way into a murder investigation, with a motivated detective following up on every detail."

He feels a rush of shame. All his life he's tried to steer clear of his father's business. Now he's offering to help him take down a Barry.

Then he thinks of Emily, and the promise he made to Chet about Willie, and the feeling passes.

"You're probably asking yourself," Shane says, "why you should share it with me. And the answer is, because I'm a Kinnock. Which means I'm smart and I'll work it. Hell, you should've shared it with me before but that's another story."

The line seems to go dead. Shane taps on top of the receiver, once, twice. Then he hears his father's voice, more muted now. "Good God, just listen to yourself, nattering on about Joe Barry." Raymond leaves the phone, claiming that his ride to the office is outside his front door. Maybe it even is.

He comes back strong, inquiring about Emily, what a special a girl she must've been, and what a horrible death she suffered, and does she have family around to see she gets a good burial and all.

Then: "With all this time gone by, there's only so much that can be done to get to the bottom of this. But if there's anything any of us could do to help, they'd be remiss if they didn't do it."

And then: "Anything I might do, of course, could be looked at as meaning that I actually know something about any of this foolishness. People following each other around, all of that. So I'll just have to think about it."

From long observation of his father, Shane knows that a no from him actually means probably no but possibly yes, if circumstances change. Yes is never yes beyond a few hours or so. Which leaves "I'll just have to think about it" as the answer closest to yes.

Raymond will get the reports to Shane. Maybe not directly, but circuitously. Or maybe not at all.

"Sure, just call me," Shane says. And he's left to wonder, not for the first time, what it might be like to be a son who can have a conversation with his father that doesn't end up sounding like an exchange between wartime envoys.

Shane waits a moment before going on.

"By the way," he says, "your man Joe Barry is going to be up at National Cathedral this afternoon, speaking at St. Alban's graduation. A mick speaking at an Episcopal church. Something of an honor, isn't it?"

"Oh sure, it is. Next thing you know, a Barry will be standing up running his mouth at a pagan sacrificial rite." Raymond grunts. "You know, the Protestants wouldn't give the boy the time of day if his father hadn't given thousands to their building fund for that monstrosity. God, what the old man won't do to try to kick dirt over his roots."

"I just thought you might like to go up there with me. So you could see what the opposition is up to." Having to squirm through a Joe Barry speech to a bunch of snot-nosed high school prep boys in a Protestant church – to Raymond Kinnock that would be a journey into the innermost ring of hell. Shane settles back and waits for the inevitable rebuke.

But his father just grunts again. "I know you've got things to be getting off to, me boyo, so don't let me be keeping you."

To Raymond Kinnock, the present is long past. He's already leaning into the future, moving his chair next to it, grasping its pliable right hand in both of his, looking soulfully into its eyes and plotting its submission to his will.

The phone that Shane is holding to his ear might as well be a seashell.

If I bring Joe Barry's head to you on a platter, Shane thinks, *then maybe then you'll want to talk to me, you old bastard.*

17

When Shane was a schoolboy and under the sway of the nuns who taught him, he had a running nightmare about being kidnapped by Protestants and trapped in one of their churches.

Now he's inside one for the first time, a cathedral still under construction after 50 years, soaring over the hill it commands, and Rock Creek Park, nearby.

He takes it all in. Mosaics and tapestries and alcoved wooden saints. Stone sculptures perched in canopied niches. Jesus and his apostles and everyone else who ever knew him, stretched to the ceiling in jewel-colored stained glass. All in all, it's remarkably similar to what he saw in all the bygone Sundays of his childhood.

Shane gives this National Cathedral his blessing and decides he could stay away from it every day of the year just as easily as he stays away from one of his own.

The graduation is underway. At the pulpit is a droning cleric with a purple sash draped over sloping shoulders. The first ten rows of pews are filled with the graduates. They're chattering to each other, waving around their caps and programs sending up a sound like moths beating against a porch screen. In the pews behind them are their parents, less appealing, if it's possible, than what they spawned. The city's rich and distracted, fidgeting restlessly on hard oak benches, wanting nothing more than to be anywhere else.

Shane feels a moment of sympathy for Joe Barry, the next speaker up. The graduates won't give a shit about him, their parents will see him as a mick intruder, and on top of it all he'll be in a room that's way too big for him.

Shane soft-steps down the aisle. Halfway down on the right side a seat is empty. Shane glides to it.

"Is this place taken, miss?" he says.

Claire Montgomery looks up with a start. "It is, by one of Mr. Barry's assistants."

"I'm sure he won't mind." Shane takes his place and glances to his right just long enough to see a smile pass quickly on Claire's lips. With another stolen look he sees her in full: black tweed suit, dotted gloves and black sling-heel pumps, veiled hat sitting proudly on her golden head.

He feels a sharp jab in his left shoulder blade. "Out of my seat, buddy."

"Keep your goddam hands to yourself."

Shane's never seen the man standing over him, but he still knows him: the bulldog Congressional aide who wields his boss's power as if it's his own. Shane glares at the man, who's holding his ground. Claire raises a hand in the charged space between them. "Please, Billy, don't make a scene. The gentleman here didn't know and I should've said something."

The man scowls at Claire. "I'll deal with you later." He looks back at Shane. "Don't ever do this to me again," he says, just to save face, and pivots crisply.

Shane leans over to Claire. "Who the hell was that?"

"Billy Steele. Goes everywhere with the Congressman. Would run through fire for him."

"Seems to have a problem with his temper."

"Sometimes a little aggression is a good quality in a man if he has to get things done for his boss."

Shane starts to answer but then hears the words, "Joseph Barry," from the front of the cathedral. The Congressman is stepping slowly from the side of the stone altar steps. He's in a solemn navy suit and drab necktie. His beach tan has faded.

The moth-flapping from the front rows continues. A paper airplane arcs across the center aisle and sparks a small ruckus.

Shane plucks an overworked leather prayer book from the holder and starts to thumb through it, because that's what you're supposed to do in church when you're waiting for something to happen that never does.

Barry assumes the pulpit, looks all around the church, smiles – and launches into the oldest Irish joke ever told. It's a Pat-and-Mike yarn about two church-painters and their drunken, stumbling climb to the top of a scaffold inside a Dublin cathedral.

Seems that Pat bet Mike a pint of Guinness that he could carry Mike on his back all the way to the top of the scaffold's summit. Halfway up, hundreds of feet from the bottom, Pat slipped and it looked for sure like they were both going to plummet to the church floor. Miraculously, Pat was able to grab hold at the last minute and climb to the pinnacle, where he claimed the money for his pint. But Mike had the last word. "Sure, you won your beer, but I do have to say that about halfway up I had a moment of high hope."

Joe, Shane thinks, your kind of Irish have been here a hundred years, when the rest of us were still over there suffering. Why play this farce, and to these people?

Then a loud snort sounds from the front rows, followed by unexpected laughter. Barry brushes his forelock aside and looks down. The moth-flapping starts to fade.

"That story is meant to be whimsical," he goes on. "But underneath the humor is an acknowledgment of man's eternal desire to bear great burdens and climb great heights to achieve his goals. This glorious cathedral will be the product of many people's labors over many years and there'll be slips along the way. But human beings have an endless capacity to create, and then to cherish the things we've created."

He pauses and looks down again.

"And we've also always known, ever since Cain killed Abel, that we have an endless capacity to destroy the things we should love the most."

Shane puts down the prayer book and leans forward.

"Twelve years ago," he continues, "at the beginning of the war, there stood in a place called Coventry, England, a church called St. Michael's."

He tells the church's story. How it was built over the course of 25 years in the early 15th century, how it stood as a cherished landmark for over 500 years until in a matter of minutes it was reduced to rubble by Nazi bombs.

"St. Michael's was but one of thousands of structures demolished in England during those terrible days. But far more important than any of those buildings, or the expanse of the dreams of the people who first imagined them, were the living and breathing human beings who failed to find safety within their walls when it mattered most. Hundreds of them, thousands, buried under those buildings."

Barry scans his audience. "Who can say what greatness the world lost to that siege. Another Da Vinci? Another Mozart, a Madame Curie?"

He stops for a moment and his gaze lands on Shane and lingers. "Or maybe someone like Clara Barton, a nurse moved by grace, to tend tirelessly to a country's wounded warriors. Who can say?"

Shane's eyes are burning.

What would Raymond say if he knew Joe Barry just invoked the memory of his dead daughter Erin? And what, for God's sake, would Matt Barry say?

A bird is flitting from perch to perch on a beam in the church's upper reaches. The rustle of his wings is the only sound in the place.

Joseph Barry lowers his voice. "We've always known of the violence that lurks in the shadows of the human soul. But to those of you who aspire to political leadership I say, remember that there are other ways people can destroy each other. Not violently, but even more insidiously than the masters of war could ever contemplate."

The bird swoops from his beam perch to an alcove above and behind Barry, who glances over his shoulder and nods.

"They do this," Barry says even more quietly, "by taking people's freedoms away from them, little by little. By using patriotism as a bludgeon to attack their political enemies. By doing what one of my colleagues is doing, day after day after day. It has to stop."

For two years Joe McCarthy from Wisconsin has been on his anti-Commie crusade that's swept up blameless people in its wake, but he's gathered too much power for anyone inside or outside the Capitol to take him on. Until now. In this unlikely setting.

The moths are quiet, oblivious. But surely the parents caught the reference and Shane waits for their boos and catcalls. Instead, silence. Maybe they're less angered by what Joe Barry just said than stunned that he said it at all.

Barry nods gently, the corners of his mouth turned up just ever-so-slightly.

Claire nudges Shane hard and whispers. "Just tell me he isn't good."

Shane nods. "But why is he saying this? It could kill him in his campaign."

She reaches her left arm around Shane's shoulder and pulls him close. "Maybe because he knows he's going to win anyway. And just maybe because it's the right thing to say."

" – *but because of the people who sit and let it happen*."

Shane thinks these last words from Barry may've been part of a quote from Einstein, but he's not sure, and he's actually sorry not to have heard all of it.

"In the end," Barry says, voice rising, "it all comes down to something that was said most clearly by a theologian and scientist named Teilhard de Chardin. He was a man of God but also a man of the earth, and in a moment of wondrous inspiration he captured his life philosophy in two sentences: 'Someday after mastering the winds and the waves and the tides and gravity, man will harness for God the energies of love. And then, for the second time in the history of the world, he will have discovered fire.'

"I thank you for the privilege."

The audience – the moths, their parents, the tedious cleric, everyone – start to rise and cheer. Shane pats Claire on the arm and bolts out of the pew, wanting to make sure Barry doesn't get away from him. Walking up the center aisle he leaves the chaos behind him.

Shane looks over his shoulder. Barry's engulfed in a cluster of black gowns. "Thank you, thank you very much, thank you," he's saying, in the broad-A, Park Avenue accent that Shane was brought up to think smacked of privilege and pampering, but right now, at least, seems to resonate of something exalted. He steps off to the side and leans lightly against a statue of Moses, brushing a stray leaf from one of the stone tablets of judgment.

Just like that, Joe Barry's in front of Shane and the crowd drops away.

"You're Shane Kinnock," Barry says, and he grins and shakes Shane's hand and grips his shoulder. "I've been hearing about you for years."

Barry holds onto Shane's hand. It's as if they're alone on an island. "You know," Barry goes on, "if my old man could've gotten away with kidnaping you at Yale and adopting you as his own, he would've. There was something in what he heard about you that made him think you would've been a worthy successor to him."

Joe Barry's smile fades into an expression more rueful and he leaves unsaid the obvious next thought which is: We all have our fathers to deal with, don't we.

Hangers-on in the crowd are regrouping for another advance. Shane has just a few seconds to make his pitch but reaches for the words. "Congressman, look." He sees the approaching throng and goes on. If you've kept up with me through the years you know what I do now. And I'm guessing you know what case I'm working on. We need to talk, you and me."

Shane leans in. "You know there's trouble for you in Drew Pearson's column today."

Out of the corner of his eye he glimpses Billy Steele. "You again!" Steele bellows. "Get away from the Congressman!"

Shane plants his right foot – *I'll drop him if I have to, even here* – but Steele manages to grab hold of Barry and whisk him away in one motion. Barry looks back, the smile in place. "You should talk first to the girl who runs my office," he says, and he's gone.

A middle-aged woman, left breathless in the wake, turns to Shane. "If you're looking for an autographed picture they're great at getting one to you right there in the office."

Claire appears. "Did you get a chance to speak with him?"

"He wants me to talk to the girl who runs his office."

They walk outside and see a black Lincoln trailing exhaust fumes onto Wisconsin Avenue: Joe Barry leaving in a puff of smoke.

"I'm taking this to mean," Shane says, "that you're going to have to stand in for him for now."

If Claire's troubled by the prospect she isn't showing it. "I suppose, if it's still necessary."

"Yeah, it is, honey. Now more than ever."

18

Her ceremonial black suit is gone. Now she's decked out in ivory, her right hand bears a small emerald, and the ring complements her earrings and the pendant that graces her long neck.

She's with Shane in a booth in a dark, smoky joint called The Neptune Room, three blocks from the White House. It's only a floor below street level but it might as well be lower than a coal mine. Today it's filled with late lunchers, early drinkers, and anyone in the area who's left work early but isn't looking to head home soon.

It could be any month of the year, any day of the week, any hour of the day.

A sign on the wall outside the place bears a portrait of Neptune himself, the Roman god of the sea. He's sporting a full red beard and wielding a bronze trident that points to an inscription: *Here lie the secrets of the deep.*

Shane's in the best suit he owns and it's not much, a light gray glen plaid he bought on sale at Hecht's. Claire's outmatched him, but all he's thinking about is, who the hell gave her all her rocks?

A lime wedge straddles the edge of her glass. He leans over: "Something stronger than ginger ale this time?"

"Still ginger ale." she says. "I think they just put the lime there so I wouldn't ruin the image of the place." She has immaculate diction and her sentences flow as smoothly as fountain water over stone pebbles. "So, what kept you overtime? Damsel in distress? Killer on a rampage?"

"I got off at three and I had a few warm-ups at a place close by." Something about her has him straying too close to uncomfortable truths.

"You have to watch yourself, don't you, Detective?"

For a moment her concern seems real, and for a moment he's moved.

A waitress comes to the table. Shane orders a Fleischman's straight up. He may've been moved, but not to abstinence. "No point in hiding anything anymore, right?"

"If that's going to be the theme of the evening, Detective, then tell the truth. Weren't you at least a little impressed today?"

"I assume you had a hand in writing his speech for him."

Claire shakes her head. "Not a word," she says. "If you haven't already realized it, he's brilliant."

"If he was all that brilliant, I wouldn't have to be sitting here talking to you. I assume you saw Drew Pearson's column in today's paper."

"I said the Congressman is brilliant, I didn't say he's perfect." She reaches across the table, picks up Shane's glass and rattles it gently. "We all have our vices, don't we? I should think you'd relate to him. Another handsome, imperfect man."

Shane takes in her fragrance: floral, maybe lilac. He takes out a Camel pack, draws two out and proffers one to her. "Sure," she says, after a measured pause. He extends his lighter. "Careful, don't get too close."

"I'm not planning to."

She takes a long drag on the Camel and settles it into a ceramic ashtray that bears another image of Neptune. "I'll be back," she says suddenly. "When the girl comes back around, order me something I'd like."

She returns to find a double martini in place in front of her. Her cigarette is half-spent. She eyes it, starts in on it again and takes a sip of her drink, wincing faintly before taking another.

She came in with the scent of flowers, she'll leave with the smell of tobacco and liquor.

Shane starts in. "Were you surprised by what you read in Pearson's column?"

"Only that a big-time reporter like him would sink to running an item that you'd expect to see in some tabloid rag. And I have no idea why it's of any interest to you. You already have your man in your murder case."

"We have one man, sure. One."

If she caught the implication, she's not letting on. "It's such a shame," she says. "That Willie fellow would come around picking up boxes of newsletters all the time. He was so quiet, he seemed like the kind who'd never get out of line."

"So, people in your office knew Willie Robinson."

It won't be long before Bran Bentley and the other reporters get onto this.

"Don't say people. I had contact with him. I ran the office and I had contact with everybody."

"Did Emily?"

"I can't speak for her. And if you're about to ask if the Congressman knew him, you know as well as anyone. Congressmen and delivery boys don't mingle."

Through all of her answers, her eyes never leave Shane's.

There's a new theory in policing. It says that liars in the act of lying can't stop themselves from looking to the right because they're reaching out to the left side of their brain, the one that's better at concocting a story. If you buy into the theory, then Claire's vouched for by the flat, impassive gaze she offers to Shane.

He thinks the theory is bullshit. Better to watch her for other signs: a faltering pause, a moistened lip, a quick draw of breath, observed north of her sternum and south of her emerald pendant.

"You've convinced me," he says, "that your boss never met my suspect. Are you as convincing at denying the Pearson story?"

"Who's to say what the truth is about that sort of thing? Like I said before –"

"You weren't in anyone's bedroom, how were you to know." Shane pulls the ashtray to his side of the table and raps his Camel on it three times and an orange ember jumps to his pants leg. He brushes at it quickly, but it's already left a hole. So much for the glen plaid from Hecht's. "I should tell you that I've spoken to people in your office."

"I don't see how my name could've come up."

"None of them say much. But they do say you knew the Congressman and the girl better than anybody else in the office."

"Not anywhere near enough to know it all." She's trying to control her voice, almost getting there, not quite. "Besides, he was an adult, she was an adult."

Claire reaches over towards Shane's cigarette pack, but he heads her off, grasping one of her hands and then the other. "Sure, she was an adult and she made her choices like we all do. And her choices somehow led her to getting dumped on a hill like she was nothing, I guess by this Negro. But the problem is that he doesn't seem to have had any reason to kill her."

"Which means he didn't?"

"Maybe he didn't do it on his own."

Claire tries to pull her hands away but Shane holds on to them.

"And while I don't know much about her," he says, "I do know that just last year she may've had something going on with a very ambitious and very married Congressman whose career could've been killed if anything about this girl came out. And the one person who knows the most about all of that is trying as hard as she can to hold out on me."

He turns Claire's hands over, palms up. "Look at your pores. See how open they are."

If they are, the light's too low for anyone to see them. She looks at her hands anyway.

"That's the first sign of deception, Claire. You're a decent girl and you don't want to live your life in the shadows."

He lets go of her hands and she claims one of his cigarettes.

A band is on the bill tonight – "The Bill Thompson Quintet, Featuring Fabulous Fern Mathewson" – and they're coming back from a break. A plump girl that Shane pegs as Fabulous Fern is striding to the stage and he braces for the worst, a strident set of show tunes that'll drown out everything he's trying to build with Claire.

Fabulous Fern takes a long breath and settles in close to the mike.
You took the best that I ever had
Sunday through Saturday, you treated me bad
So tell me, oh why am I here?

Fern turns out to have a voice like Billie Holiday's, redolent of old grudges and recent passions.

The waitress is at the table. Claire downs her drink and orders another. "I can't say it any than better this," Shane says quietly. "Stop fucking around with me."

A lonely, crystal tear runs down Claire's cheek. "I don't think anyone's ever said anything like that to me before."

Her hands are clasped together on the table. Shane pats them, then takes hold of them, more gently than before.

"I'm sorry," she goes on. "I haven't meant to mislead you."

"None of this is easy," Shane says. "Cleaning up after a murder never is." The waitress returns with Claire's drink and retreats. Shane presses forward and Claire draws away.

If she comes around, he thinks, it'll only be on her own terms.

He changes direction. "Just help me out here. This thing has me turned upside down. I'm not sleeping, I'm not eating."

"And you're drinking like there's no tomorrow."

"Which there isn't, on what I'm working on." He drains his glass and looks for the waitress. "So how is it I can't even find out where she lived or where she was from, or any fucking thing that went into her being what she ended up being. Excuse the language."

"Maybe she never wanted to be figured out. And maybe she wouldn't want to be figured out now either, at least not like you want to."

"Did she ever say what she did during the war?"

"Along with a thousand other things," she says drily, "it never came up in our conversations."

Can't stand not having you, can't stand having you near
Can't make myself say the three words you wanna hear

They both pretend to listen to the music and a ponderous silence drops between them.

"Let's start over again," Shane finally says. "You're from up north. Philadelphia, I'd say."

"And how did you figure that out?"

"Detectives detect things. Here I have an advantage – all through my childhood I was terrorized by nuns from an order in Philly so I know the accent. As for you: Main Line, I'm guessing?"

"If it matters to you, feel free to go off and do more detecting."

She starts to say something more, then stops. She reaches out for his arm, then takes her hand back slowly.

Shane looks at the retreating left hand. "I don't see a ring on your finger."

"No."

"Boyfriend?"

"Yes. No. Nothing so committed as that." She picks up her Camel, and the long ash disintegrates in the tray.

He feels his seat shake. A beefy young guy has settled hard into the booth next to them. Football player type, big enough even to be a pro. Hatless, maybe because he wants to show off his wavy, thick blond hair.

The beefy guy turns to take a long look at Claire. She pats her mouth with her napkin and lightly runs a finger along the neckline of her blouse.

A couple sitting two booths over get up to dance and Shane can tell they haven't been together before. The man tries to touch the woman's shoulder but misses, then she lurches into him and he pulls her out of a fall.

The waitress brings back their drinks, and an unexpected bonus round.

"Here I've been going on and on all this time," Claire says, "and you're not saying anything about your story." She moves to rest her elbow on the edge of the table, but it slips, and she has to prop it back up.

She's trying to turn the conversation back to Shane. He'll go along for a bit, feigning an air of shared confidences. "My story? Same as millions of others, nothing special. Unlucky enough to have to go to war, lucky enough to come back from it. With a lot of stuff in between."

"It's been seven years."

"It wouldn't matter if it'd been seventy."

"So, what did you do before that?"

"I was a lawyer, if you can believe it. Then some events occurred – my sister died – and, I ended up enlisting."

"So why didn't you take the law back up again when you came home? Not that there's anything to be ashamed about in being a cop."

She bumps the heel of her hand on the table. "Don't even answer that. I'm sorry to be getting so personal."

She peers over at the dance floor. "Those two are really making a mess of things out there."

Shane feels flush. "Let's just say I didn't have quite the charmed existence during the war that your boss did – induction, flight school, a few months of missions, shot down, welcomed back home a hero, best-selling book."

The war's like an attack dog that's never put away securely, it always finds a way to break free through the fence and rush him. Now it's leaping towards him again with eyeteeth bared.

"At the end, something happened when I was in the Pacific. A killing. Somebody could say that it could've all been avoided."

It could've all been avoided. What a refuge the passive voice provides. It sounds like something one of the Nazis would've said at Nuremberg.

Shane feels his throat constrict. He can't go on, he wants to go on. "I took all the blame. Everything fell apart when I came home. She – left."

"Who left? You were married?"

"Yes. We're not together anymore. And I have, we had, a son, he was born just before I shipped out. He'd be, what, eleven now." He rubs his eyes again. *God, I sound like a broad.*

"It's alright, Detective –"

"Shane, please."

"It's alright, Shane. We all have things in our lives we're sorry about, things we wish had come out differently. The end of the war gave everybody a chance to start over. We all thought everything was going to be better than it was before."

Claire stares blankly at her glass. "Then we ended up just getting swept along by the same things as before and we lost sight of everything that matters. And we're all just looking back and regretting things we've done, same as ever."

Her diction is suddenly less than immaculate. "I'm making no sense now, am I? It's Emily. I should've stopped her."

"So, you knew she was with Joe."

"Yes. I did. She'd come talk to me. She loved him, but –"

"He didn't love her."

"No, he very well may have. The problem was his wife, Sheila. And I knew Joe would never leave her."

"Because it would kill his career."

"Which would kill his father. And also, because Joe really cares about Sheila. Or should I say, he feels badly for her."

She describes Joe's marriage and then something that the Barrys have managed to keep under wraps. Sheila's sick with some degenerative disease, maybe lupus, and stays in New York for much of the year because she doesn't like to travel and she wants to stay close to her doctors.

"That's the way to put it," Claire says. "Joe feels badly for her. It's not the same as love, but sometimes it can tie you down even more than love does."

Joe Barry's had it rougher on the home front than Shane had thought.

On the other hand: a lot of nights with an empty bed to fill.

A look crosses Claire's face. Shane sees it and pounces. "You're thinking that Emily could've gotten killed over the problems she caused. For Joe, for his career, for his wife, for his father."

Claire's having none of it. "Heavens no. Joe Barry has his faults but he'd never do something like that."

She downs the last of her drink. "No, I was just then thinking that maybe if I took more time with her she might not have ended up so – disappointed." She shifts, about to get up.

"By what, Claire? You've come this far. Jesus, I can draw the rest of the picture myself if I have to."

"By Joe. God. I think it probably became pretty clear to her towards the end that there wasn't a future with him. She didn't say so in so many words, but I think that's one reason why she was talking about leaving town."

And then she changed her mind at the last minute, and she decided to stand her ground and fight for what she wanted. And then she had to be gotten rid of.

He starts to ask a question but she's looking past him at the bandstand, and he loses the thought.

"Listen to this," she says. "It's 'Blue Tango.' You probably know it. But just listen to it closely."

A guitarist is now fronting the band. A swarthy, smirking Latin with long fingers that glide up and down his axe like a cat tiptoeing across a tiled floor.

Claire's staring at him. Shane says, "It pains me to say it. He looks like a gigolo. But I have to say he's good."

She waves him off. "No," she says. "It's not him. Listen to the other instruments."

He's heard this tango before, everyone has, but now for the first time he's aware of the interjections of an ominous horn part, propelled by an insistent rhythm that grows more intense as the song gathers strength.

Claire works her way around the booth to him.

"I hear this," she says, "and it's like what we're all going through right now. On the surface everything is fine and pretty, but underneath everything's about to break apart and it feels as if something terrible's about to happen."

"It's a tango, for Christ's sake, don't read too much into it. Listen, do you want to dance?"

Right away, Shane's sorry he asked. Even in the best situation he's not especially nimble, and this isn't the best situation.

"Let's wait," she says, "for something more conventional."

She tips back her glass, forgetting she's already finished her drink. From under the table Shane hears her shoe fall to the floor, then feels her foot rest on his left and stay there.

They both happen to turn their heads and exhale smoke at the same time. Shane watches two gray, wispy ribbons lazily intertwining above the booth before rising into the dark void above.

The Latin beat fades into silence and a few people clap.

The beefy blond guy in the booth next to them is straining to look over at Claire. He has a dimpled chin and piercing eyes. Claire swirls the stirrer around in her glass.

A single piano begins playing slowly and Fabulous Fern starts in.

"Detective Shane," Claire says, "I think I'll take you up on your offer now." She bumps lightly into him, moves him into the aisle, takes him by the hand and guides him onto the dance floor. Four separate movements combined into one. And somehow she gets her shoe back on.

All the other couples drift from the floor and take their places just off the parkay as if they're obeying the commands of a hidden choreographer.

The beefy blond guy moves to a seat just outside the spotlight.

Shane finds himself relishing the long-lost feeling of being the man that other men envy because of the girl he has on his arm.

No other love can warm my heart
Now that I've known the comfort of your arms – no other love

"Do you remember this?"

"I do," Shane says. "It's what they were playing at the Mayflower when I came in to meet you."

He draws her closer, they start to sway. He feels himself start to swell and pushes her away slightly, she pulls him closer. He hears her murmur. "You've probably never really listened to this, have you? Just pay attention to the words, they're beautiful."

She puts her head on his chest.

I was blessed with love to love you
Till the stars burn out above you,
Till the moon is but a silver shell

Shane runs his right hand along her bare left arm and his left hand along the down at the nape of her neck and she moves her left hip close to him. He spins her to the right and the room seems to take a turn in the other direction.

How many times did Emily dance like this with Joe? How many nights did they spend like this?

The spotlight starts to pulsate.

"What was her favorite song?" Shane asks.

"What? What did you say?" She sounds like someone who's just been awakened by a shrill alarm clock.

"I was just wondering. Never mind." The crowd ringing the dance floor seems to advance and retreat in waves.

Claire pushes back to look squarely at him. "You asked what her favorite song was, right? You're talking about Emily. My Lord, don't you ever give up?"

"Look, I'm sorry."

She digs her left fist into the small of his back. "You can't keep trying to chase down the past. Eventually you have to deal with what's in front of you."

Shane starts to feel sick. He mumbles that he's sorry, pulls away from her and heads for the men's room. He hits the door and steadies himself against the cigarette machine. His hand pushes against the Camel button by accident and the machine spits out a free pack, good luck being parceled out to him tonight in small portions only.

The door opens again and closes behind him.

At the urinal he stares at the old English script on the top edge -- "Hendrickson Co., Piscataway, NJ" -- and he wonders what sort of family gets themselves into manufacturing pissers for a living.

He feels a hand grab hard at the back of his neck and an arm grab hard around his throat. He hears the crack his forehead makes when it hits the word "Hendrickson" just an instant before he feels the pain, which is fierce. He blacks out, until he feels himself being dragged and he hears a stall door slam and then he feels cold water running up his nose, and he can't breathe, he's gasping for air. He feels the hand clutch his neck harder and then he feels the cold water again and hears a gurgling sound, the sound a man that makes when he's giving up. He takes a big heaving breath and settles his face against something white and shiny. He hears a door slam behind him. He hears a man say something but it takes some time – a minute, an hour, somewhere in between – for him to put it together, and when he does he just keeps thinking.

Jake Kaufman says back off.

Jake Kaufman says back off.

That's what the man said.

He gathers the strength to push himself to his knees and stand up. He hears a voice in the distance – *Emily?* – calling to him but he doesn't answer. He stumbles to the mirror and takes a cloth towel to his hair, which is wet and tangled, and he probes the bulging, bloated welt on his forehead.

Outside the men's room he sees Claire. She puts both hands on his chest. "Are you all right? I've been calling for you. I couldn't find anyone who'd go check on you. I was worried sick."

He feels himself getting reoriented. "You shouldn't have been," he says. "You know what everybody says when somebody spends too much time in the bathroom, right? 'Hey, did you fall in?' Well, I actually did."

"Was pushed in, more like it," Claire says. "A couple of men said they heard a ruckus. I couldn't get them to tell me anything more. Was that big blond-haired man in there, the one from the booth next to us?"

"I don't know." Shane runs his hand along the seam of his left pants leg, which has been split wide open. "Why?"

"Because I saw that man get up when you got up and he headed where you were heading. Now he's not here anymore. He'd been giving me the creeps before that, to be honest with you." She reaches out and gently touches his welt. "Let's get you some ice to put on that."

He pushes her hand away. "I've been through worse." *How could I let that happen to me?* He curses himself for being complacent. For being careless. For being.

"Please, let's –"

"No."

"I just want to help –"

"I understand that."

"Do you have any idea why someone would – "

"No."

"I get it. You'll handle it all yourself, right?"

"Something like that."

They stand in silence outside the men's room for a minute or so. "Look," Shane finally says, "let's go back in the lounge and start over. I'll buy you another drink."

"Another drink isn't what either of us need. Be a dear and hold this." She hands him her purse and takes her suit jacket off the crook of her arm and puts it on. She takes back her purse and counts out change for the streetcar. He knows there's no point in even offering her a ride.

She abruptly snaps the purse clasp. "I'm going to do everything I can to keep my boss away from you. You're a zealot and you're obsessed. Go solve your case some other way. You just want his head because you're a Kinnock and he's a Barry." She puts on her hat as if it were the crown of the Queen of England. "You really don't have anything on him anyway. So good luck with all this, Detective."

It's a speech that calls for a response but in truth he's not really listening, because nothing she's said has anything to do with the question that at that moment is rattling around in his whiskey-saturated brain.

What the fuck does Jake Kaufman have to do with me?

19

Once the vision of a defiled boy planted ass-high in a trash can has taken hold of your thoughts, it's hard to rid yourself of it.

"Maybe it's just me, Sarge," Shane says. "I've had my two eyes set on either side of my face for a long time and I'd rather not find myself in a situation where somebody decides they'd look better in my mouth."

Roncalli barely looks up from his morning Post. "You didn't even get a glance at the face of guy that did this to you. You know how many two-bit hoods want their marks to think they've got Jake Kaufman behind them?"

Shane and Sarge and Bobby are in the waiting room at D.C. Jail. Shane's hard wooden bench is giving him no comfort.

He eyes the headline on Sarge's Post.

MATT BARRY, JAKE KAUFMAN GO ON HILL, BOTH TAKE FIFTH

Raymond's stooge House committee is going after Barry, and the Senate crime committee is going after Kaufman.

As if any of it matters. As if Barry and Kaufman and everybody close to them won't still be standing when it's all been sorted out.

Another side of town, another world.

Sarge tosses his paper on the bench next to him. "You still haven't told me why you think Kaufman would all of a sudden take an interest in you."

"How about this case, for starters."

"You're so wrapped up in this thing, you think everything comes back to it. So this boy Willie Robinson runs numbers for somebody, who works for somebody, who works for somebody else, who works for Kaufman. A bit of a stretch, I'd say."

"If you have any other ideas, I'm all ears."

The sergeant settles back in his seat. "Occupational hazard. Probably some thug you locked up years ago and now he's out. Or a jealous husband, there's probably at least a couple who'd love to dunk you in the crapper."

"Jesus Christ, Sarge, all I want to do is get Kaufman's measure. If he has his goons on me I want to know why, and if he doesn't he can say so and I'll take his word. I know where he lives, he's got a whole floor up at the Shoreham Hotel. How hard can it be to get to him?"

"Jake Kaufman eats guys like us for breakfast. Jesus, think about the Riccobenes. They tried to muscle in on him and Kaufman hit 'em so hard last spring, really savage stuff, that even they're scared to death of him."

"Some guinea gangsters from Philly, they're not the police. And I am. We shouldn't be scared of anybody."

"Then listen to this," the sergeant says slowly. "In this town Jake Kaufman is king and if you take a shot at the king you'd better hit him. This isn't a good shot for you."

Sarge goes back to his morning Post. "In the meantime," he says, "you need to know something. The boys at the lab were able to lift a fingerprint off that receipt we talked about, from the Calvert Café."

"So fucking what. It's probably just hers."

The warden comes around the corner. Shane and Sarge have known him for years and have used him enough for favors that they've gone to great lengths to treat him as their equal in law enforcement ranks. Which they don't see him as at all, of course.

"I shouldn't be doing this," the warden starts out, just as they knew he would. "Your Chief told me he don't want no one talking to that boy except him."

The sergeant grips the warden on his shoulder and slides a bill into his shirt pocket.

The warden knows the drill, doesn't even look down at the pocket. He points to Bobby. "You a first timer here?"

"Yeah, "Bobby says. "Does it always smell like this in here?"

"Just years of piss and shit and puke and blood that's seeped into the floors and the walls." The warden sounds proud.

They all walk down a narrow, unlit corridor before arriving at a point where the walls more or less come together. "He's in a holding cell here. The boy got mouthy with the guards on the way up from the block so they had to set him back in line, know what I mean? That's why he's late."

Shane shakes his head. *Quiet as a monk up till now, then all of a sudden Robinson gets mouthy with some flunky guards? What a load of shit.*

Just inside the cell is a folding chair, and a man who's chosen not to sit in it. Robinson is cross-legged on the floor with eyes closed and cuffed hands set placidly on his lap. A shaft of light from the mid-day sun beams down on him through a small hole that's been gouged into the wall.

Shane doesn't know any more about him than he did 36 hours ago. Robinson's mother wouldn't give Shane the time of day, and the most he could get out of anybody at the boy's jobs was that they don't find out anything more about the help than they need to.

So everything Shane knows about Willie Robinson comes down to what he took off the police blotter, read in the paper, or wheedled out of smack addict between sets in a bebop joint.

The warden advances on Robinson. "Boy! Look up here."

Robinson doesn't move. He has a lump on his forehead that's growing to the point of bursting. Shane touches the lump on his own head.

The warden spits on the floor where the bars meet the concrete. "He had that thing on his noggin when we brought him up yesterday."

"Yesterday," Shane says. "Who saw him yesterday?"

"Some reporter. Anyway, the boy's all yours, come get me when you're done." He walks away whistling.

Bentley, Shane thinks. *That son of a bitch is everywhere. How much of the Post's money did he throw at the warden to get the chance to spend time with this kid?*

Shane presses up against the bars. "Willie, we're back because you need to talk to us about some things."

No response. Shane looks down at Robinson's hands. The fingernails are long, smooth and shiny. The boy hasn't been picking at them or biting them. Either he has a clear conscience, or he's resigned to his fate.

"Not to tell you how to run your life or anything but you'd better talk to us as long as we're here. One of these days the Chief himself will be back over here and he can make it real rough on you."

No response.

"Willie, I saw Chet the other night. I've known him for years."

Robinson keeps his eyes closed. A scream comes from outside, where the courtyard is, then a moan and another scream and a long, baleful silence.

"I started seeing Chet," Shane goes on, "back when I was a kid, in Harlem, that's right. I saw him in all the Negro clubs up there, then in all the Negro clubs down here, too."

Shane talks about Coleman Hawkins and his band, about Louis Armstrong and Lester Young, about how pretty Billie Holiday was up close, about seeing all the great tappers when they came through the Cotton Club.

"Willie, I've been to your people's places. I'm not just another cracker cop. You can trust me."

Robinson shakes his head and lowers his chin to his chest.

Shane asks him about his work on Capitol Hill. He tries to show him a picture of Emily, but the boy won't even open his eyes to look at it.

Shane asks him about running numbers for Sweet Pea Johnson, and whether he's ever heard the name Big Ticket Blackwell or even Jake Kaufman. Shane tells him, "I've talked to your ma, and the people you work with, and none of them's come up with anything for you. Give me something to help you out, will you?"

Shane asks him about the Calvert Café, asks him whether he knew where he was on May first a year ago, presses him on whether he really could've said what the Chief said he said on the night that he got shot.

All these questions, and nothing's coming back.

Shane tells Robinson about the fingerprint on Emily's restaurant receipt. "If we're going to find out it's yours, tell us now and hope you can get some credit from the judge for at least being honest. Because if we have to go to the trouble of finding that out on our own, you're as good as fried."

No response.

As a last resort, Shane uses Raymond. Tells Willie about how his father is a friend to Willie's people. Talks about his father's bill, gets busy in the details. Makes Raymond out to be Abraham Lincoln with an Irish brogue.

Robinson's silence now seems contemptuous.

Shane runs his fingers around his shirt collar and pats his brow with his suitcoat sleeve while Robinson sits coolly below him. A foot behind

Shane is a wall, a foot to his left another, a foot in front, iron bars. *Who's confining who here? Who's shackling whose hands?*

Finally, Shane asks the most obvious question of all. "Why the fuck won't you talk, son?"

No response.

"I know you have it in you. You said something to me that first night, in the hospital, something about a church hymn. Ever since, I haven't been able to goddam figure out what you said. But I know you have it in you to talk."

Bobby steps up. "Maybe it was – ah, never mind. Just go on, Shane."

"Maybe it was what?"

"Maybe it was…" And he says a word Shane's never heard before.

"*What*? Spell it for me."

"I'm sayin', Shane, maybe it was A-H-I-M-S-A."

Shane tries to put the letters together in his brain.

Bobby digs into his back pocket and pulls out a folded-up piece of paper. "It's ahimsa, right, Willie?'

Robinson tilts his head back, looks at the ceiling and smiles. "Oh, Lawdy."

Shane glances at the sergeant, who's staring at Robinson. "And how the heck," Roncalli says, "did you know that?"

"Last night I went down to Willie's church. Saw his preacher talk all about it, name of Reverend Williamson."

Bobby crouches down so he's on Robinson's level.

"He was talkin', Willie, about this Indian word that means not bein' violent. Turnin' the other cheek, like Jesus said. Your preacher said it's what your people have had to do over a bunch of years. Fight back but quiet-like."

Robinson leans forward, peers at Bobby and nods. For the first time Shane can see Willie's eyes, and how he got his nickname. Even under long, shrouding lashes his eyes gleam light green, almost yellow, a one-in-a-million genetic mismatch with his mahogany skin.

"So, I'm guessin'," Bobby says, "that's why you ain't saying nothin'. You ain't gonna be no part of this."

Robinson stops and squints to the side, as if he wants to get this just right. "Darkness," he says, then stops. "Darkness," he begins again. "It can't drive out darkness, only light can. And hate can't drive out hate, only love can." His voice is feathery. "What's your name?"

"Shiflett. Bobby Shiflett."

"Why'd you go to my church?"

"I been goin' to church since I couldn't even walk. Sometime or another, I been to pretty much every Baptist Church 'thin 50 miles of Rocky Mount."

"Rocky Mount, huh." Robinson takes it in. "You ain't never been to a church like mine though, right?"

"Naw, and last night I did kinda sit way in the back and make myself as small as I could."

Robinson throws his head back and laughs.

"But listen," Bobby goes on, "Your Thursday night service is wilder'n anything I ever seen before."

"Who they have singin' the other night?" Robinson raises himself to his haunches and starts rocking back and forth.

"He was great, a young boy from out of town, him and his group. Boy named Sam, didn't catch his last name, singin' with a group that called themselves the Soul-somethin'. This Sam, he could sing 'em all like I never heard 'em sung. 'Jesus Gave Me Water,' 'It Won't Be Very Long,' 'I Couldn't Hear Nobody Pray.'"

Robinson's expression changes. "Did he sing, 'Were You There When They Crucified My Lord?'"

Bobby looks at the floor. "Yeah, he did. He did."

Robinson tilts towards the bars just so. Bobby reaches through though the bars and touches Robinson's arm.

"Yeah, Willie," he says, "he sang that one too. You know, they prayed for you down there, an' the Reverend told everybody to bring you some books, on account of you likin' to read an' all."

"Nobody'll come. And if they do, I'll never see no books, the warden'll see to that. Listen, did the Reverend ever say anything like, he's sure I didn't do this?"

Bobby looks to Shane, then back to Robinson. "Naw, he didn't really say nothin' like that. Listen, you wanna tell us --"

"No."

"Lemme finish, you wanna answer some of them questions that the detective over here –"

Robinson rocks back on his behind, re-crosses his legs and closes his eyes. He murmurs something.

Bobby asks, "What was that?"

Robinson gathers himself and speaks clearly. "Mark, chapter 4, verse 21. That's all."

Shane goes down the hall to shout out for the warden, who comes down the hall whistling the same tune as before. He unlocks the cell door and grabs Robinson by the arm. "Get up, boy."

Robinson stands up in stages, the warden still holding onto him. Then, just that fast, he shakes the warden's hand free, steps to him, butts him with his chest and glares at him with those eyes.

The warden stares at him impassively.

Down the hall is the guard who'll take Robinson back to his own cell. Robinson walks towards him with the hint of a swagger. The warden follows a few steps behind, content to seem uninvolved as long as he's being watched.

Back in the waiting room, Bobby turns to Shane and the Sarge. "He bucked on the warden and he shouldn't have. But it may not mean nothin', and we don't know what to make of it."

"I don't know," the sergeant says, "what to make of anything that happened in there, son. But I do know one thing. One man here found a way to get into this boy's life and into his head. And one didn't."

Sarge turns to Shane. "You spend all that time at the Negroes' clubs. Maybe you should've thought to drop by one of their churches."

Shane has no comeback. "Bobby," he says, "I also know a thing or two. One is, I've still got a lot to learn. And another is this."

He takes the pin off the lapel of his suit jacket and puts it on Bobby's uniform.

"Sarge over there gave this to me a long time ago. It was his and now it's yours, you've earned it."

He walks a few feet then pivots. "That quote from the book of Mark. I assume you know what it says, Bobby?"

"Yeah. It goes, 'Everythin' now hidden will one day be revealed.'"

"I thought it'd be something like that."

Shane walks out of the jail.

On the sidewalk, just outside, stands a young woman. Her clothes are too dark and heavy for a hot day: a long-sleeved blouse, a skirt that touches the tops of her shoes, a scarf tied tightly around her head. She looks like the orthodox Jews Shane saw years ago, when he was walking around New York with his father.

Shane wonders what she's doing over in this neighborhood, dressed like that. The Jews in town are clustered in a three-block area, miles away.

Maybe she's visiting somebody at the jail – a husband, maybe a brother or a friend – and she's steeling herself before she goes in.

As he passes her, he tips his hat to her. She says nothing, just follows his progress with her eyes and when he looks back, she's still watching him. He speeds up, then breaks into a trot.

****

Two blocks over and one down, he stops at a gate topped by a wrought-iron sign: CONGRESSIONAL CEMETERY.

He unlatches the gate, quietly closes it behind him and follows a zigzag path. The grounds are adorned by splotches of red, Memorial Day poppies left on soldiers' graves. He finds the row of dogwoods that he always uses as a landmark. At the end of the tree row is a large headstone that bears the name **KINNOCK** in six-inch letters, with three smaller inscriptions beneath.

MARY FRANCES CLANCY KINNOCK
January 9,1894 – January 7, 1929

ERIN SHEILA KINNOCK
November 16, 1917 – October 15, 1940

SHANE FRANCIS KINNOCK
November 16, 1917 –

Raymond bought the plot a month after coming to Congress more than 30 years ago. Even then, he was sure he'd be staying in town for a long time. Not ten years later he installed his wife as the first resident. A year or so after the Kennington Park bombing he had Erin's name inscribed on the stone, as if to will at least her spirit into the ground below. He left a sizeable gap under Erin's name for a tribute that he could never put into words for engraving.

Right below Erin's name on the headstone, Raymond added Shane's.

There's another blank space on the stone, next to the name of Shane's mother. Raymond hasn't gotten around to putting his own name there.

Shane hears the drone of a lawnmower in the distance. He's alone in the cemetery with the landscaper, a fellow caretaker of the past.

He stares at the words **SHANE KINNOCK** for a long minute.

All in all, he thinks, this isn't a bad place for a man to be when he's come to a point in his life where he's seeing all his options are dwindling.

A ceramic vase is set in the ground at the foot of the headstone. Inside is a bird's nest, maybe under construction, maybe long abandoned. Shane plucks a piece of straw from the lip of the vase and tosses it into the breeze.

I tried to get at the truth. The girl, she's always going to be beyond me. And the boy that supposedly killed her, it's as if he's a conscientious objector. A C.O. from his own murder case.

He's talking to his sister, same as always.

He pauses. Then, over and over: *I tried. I tried. I tried.*

He looks down at his mother's name, a life reduced to a few chisel strokes.

At that moment he can't bring to mind any special life lesson he ever gleaned from her, just a cloudy image of ailing benevolence.

Then a memory jolts him. A mud-skied October day, walking home from school. He was in Sister Rosamund's class – so, it would've been second grade. Making his way into towards his mother's bedroom and hearing one of his aunts – an alcoholic spinster who occasionally served as an erratic babysitter for him – start talking about some trouble he got into that day.

Her, saying how the nun said there was no point even trying anymore with him.

Shane, thinking he'd hear his mom join in and say something about how they'd have to send him off to one of those homes that his aunts were always talking about.

But all he heard his mom say was this. "My Shanie's just like a rubber ball. He always bounces back."

That's it. The whole memory.

But here's the thing. If you're stuck in the position of having one phrase in your mother's voice to call back at a rough time in your life, that's about as good as it gets.

Next to the headstone, half-buried in an anthill, is a rock the size of a fist. Shane picks it up and eyes it for a long minute as the wind surges and the lawnmower din swells and termites make a sound, shrill as a power drill, as they bore through the ground towards his mother's wooden box.

My Shanie's like a rubber ball, he always bounces back.

Shane puts the rock back in its place as his head quiets down and walks back to the cemetery's front gate.

He takes a streetcar to Dr. Kales's office on Washington Circle to get some demerol and some dromoran, more painkillers he's heard a lot about. He figures he'll be needing them over the next few days on the job.

The doctor calls out to him as he leaves with the pill bottles. "Take one every four hours."

Shane holds back the urge to answer: *You goddam quack, if I was going to take one every four hours, I wouldn't be coming to see you.*

20

As he enters the Homicide squad room one of the girls who answers the phones runs up to him, flustered. "A gentleman was waiting here for you. He finally had to go, but he left this package."

It's a plain manila envelope with five words marked in the top left corner. United States House of Representatives.

A package from Raymond. He sent me something after all.

Shane opens it and pulls out a sheaf of papers fastened with a metal clip. He ruffles through them quickly and words flash before him. Investigator. Committee. Un-American Activities.

These aren't FBI reports. Hoover wasn't in on the Joe Barry caper after all.

It makes sense. Of course Raymond would use a Congressional gumshoe to spy on Barry. Why waste a favor with the Bureau if he didn't have to, especially when he has legions of eager birddogs ready to do whatever he asks?

What's in here, might keep me in the game for a little while longer.

Maybe my father trusts me a little bit, after all.

For as long as a man lives, something like this matters. Even after his father is long gone.

He exhales and has the sudden sensation that he's been holding his breath for weeks.

The girl is still standing there. "That, and you have a phone call." The girl giggles. "It's Congressman Joe Barry. He's on hold. Do you *know* him?"

Shane goes to his desk and looks at the blinking yellow light on the phone, lets some time go by before lifting the receiver and pushing the button.

Barry starts: "You know, there's absolutely no reason for me to talk to you."

"If I was in your position I probably wouldn't."

"I've gotten the whole rundown from our friend Miss Montgomery. You made quite an impression on her."

"So, I'm a zealot, right?"

"Lost all perspective, just doing your father's bidding, trying to make it seem as if I actually might have had something to do with this murder case of yours. A zealot, and obsessed."

There's silence on the line.

Then: "Be at my house in Georgetown at six this evening." Barry chuckles. "I love a good challenge."

Shane cradles the phone. He pulls papers from the manila envelope, and he reads.

Page one, page two, page three.

Page 4, the last page.

MEMORANDUM

Page 4 of 4

DATE: April 1, 1951

TO: Chairman
        Committee on Un-American Activities
        United States House of Representatives

FROM: Haynes Nickens
        Investigator

RE: Surveillance of Target No. 1

Regarding evidence of an ongoing, intimate, and extramarital relationship between target Joseph F. Barry and the female subject Emily Rose, the former Emma Rosenblum: The reporting investigator has developed the following, which he is hereby making known to this Committee on Un-American Activities of the House of Representatives.

1) On Sunday, May 29, 1949, the reporting investigator surveilled target Barry's residence at 1400 34th Street, NW (Georgetown). At 2218 hours, target Barry and the female subject Rose, wearing a mink wrap and a salmon dress with low neckline, arrived at the front of the premises in separate taxis. Target Barry and the female subject Rose embraced in front of the premises and went inside, and at 0715 hours, some nine hours later, the female subject Rose emerged alone from the premises.

THIS WAS THE FIRST OBSERVED INDOOR DALLIANCE BETWEEN TARGET AND THE FEMALE SUBJECT.

2) On Thursday, June 9, 1949, the reporting investigator surveilled target Barry to an outdoor location, Rock Creek Park. There he observed target Barry meeting the female subject Rose, at which time the two embraced and proceeded together into nearby woods. The reporting investigator advanced in discrete pursuit as target and subject walked for approximately 15 minutes to a secluded location in the Park. The reporting investigator then observed behavior consistent with a physical romantic relationship between target Barry and the female subject Rose.

THIS WAS THE FIRST OBSERVED OUTDOOR DALLIANCE
BETWEEN TARGET AND THE FEMALE SUBJECT.

3) From Thursday, June 9, 1949 up to the date of
this memorandum, the reporting investigator continued
to conduct regular surveillance of target Barry, per
instructions issued within my chain of command.

On multiple separate occasions during this time
frame, as memorialized in logs, target Barry and the
female subject Rose met in various venues in Rock
Creek Park, presumably choosing those places because
of the privacy that their remote and secluded locations
afforded them for their clandestine activities.

The investigator routinely observed target Barry
and the female subject Rose engaging in physical and
romantic behavior similar to that described in paragraph
2) above.

4) On multiple other occasions, with dates
memorialized in the logs, target Barry and the female
subject Rose would end up together at a hotel in the
city, most notably the Wardman Park Hotel, located just
off the western edge of Rock Creek Park.

Shane takes it all in, every page.

Emily's years in Germany. Kristallnacht.

The flight to China, the Shanghai years, the boat trip to America.

The move to Washington and the name change, night school and
the Hill job.

And, in the end, Joe Barry.

The Sarge has come into the room. Shane hands him the report as
he reads it, page-by-page.

Shane goes to the last entry for April 1.

Per the reporting investigator's previous request, the date of this memorandum will be the last date on which he will be conducting surveillance on the target and secondarily, the female subject.

Surveillance on the date of this memorandum, to wit April 1, 1951, was uneventful. In the early afternoon target Barry was surveilled to a Washington Senators baseball game at Griffith Stadium, which he attended through its duration. Later in the evening, the female subject was surveilled to a restaurant off of Rock Creek Park. Target and subject were not observed to meet or interact in any way.

Having detailed all of the above, the reporting investigator respectfully requests that the HUAC formally relieve him of this assignment as of this date.

Sarge flips back to the top page of the report.

Shane leans back in his chair. He hears a low drone in the room, like he heard in the cemetery, a weevil-boring towards a wooden crate.

Sarge speaks over it.

"You mean *Haynes Nickens* was put on this? Somebody really wants to take Barry down bad."

Haynes Nickens is chief counsel and investigator for the House Committee on Un-American Activities. For more than two years he's been tracking down Commies, and families and friends of Commies, and anybody who might know a Commie, or might know what it means to be a Commie.

Thanks to him, one Alger Hiss was exposed as a spy, nailed for perjury, and ridden out of one of the top jobs in the State Department. Just one of many.

You might not be able to fully staff up the Soviet Central Committee with all the Reds Nickens has taken down, but you could probably get a quorum.

On the side, almost as a hobby, he's managed to chase down gangsters of every stripe across the country. Before working on the Hill he was an FBI agent for five years, Hoover's prize pet, a man of legendary energy and endurance.

All that, and nobody seems to know anything more about him than what he wants known. That he's a simple man with scant needs, That he's beholden to no one, belongs to no party, never even votes. And that he's driven by only one belief: that there are boundaries in life and people should stay within them, and if they don't they should be punished harshly.

The sergeant tosses the report back on the desk and the pages scatter.

"Amazing, isn't it, Sarge?"

"Yeah. Nickens has Barry dead to rights. All the meetings and all the whatnot, with everything papered. And one of the places where he has Barry meeting her is the same place where she ended up dead."

Shane gathers the scattered pages. "It's not what Nickens did that's so amazing. The girl faced down totalitarians in two places on opposite sides of the earth. Then she got out of China and came halfway around the world just to get here, the freest country anywhere, and this was where it all ended."

Sarge doesn't get it, he's already walking away. "Just remember, no wild goose chases. The Chief just wants you looking at Barry, nothing else. *Stay focused.*"

He calls back over his shoulder. "Maybe I should see if Nickens has some free time. I could use a man like that on this."

Shane just closes his eyes and calls to mind what Claire said.

The war gave everybody a chance to start over.

Isn't that the truth.

When it ended, a lot of people wanted to cling to what they'd had before. But millions of others tried to break with the past. They'd seen something or done something that they wanted to leave behind. Or, they'd been a part of something grand that made their past lives seem puny.

Guys who'd never even driven a car had all of a sudden found themselves running around Europe, gunning down huns. The girls who'd stayed behind did what they had to do with the guys who'd been left behind, and did work they never thought possible. A lot of people had ended up with something inside them that they didn't want to talk about. And at the same time they'd seen the gleam of a brighter future.

So the first chance they had, after all the madness was over, they picked up stakes and moved. Or they shaved a few years off their age, maybe even changed their names. They broke free of old constraints.

This girl tried harder than anybody. In 1946 she left what remained of her family, then went about changing her name and doing everything she could to transform herself into a different person, free of her sorrowful past. She was just getting started. Yet all of her insanely optimistic efforts came to nothing.

If identities had obituaries, hers would have a headline. *Emily Rose, Dead at Age 5.*

"So, Kinnock, this is how you go about a murder investigation? Sleeping on the job?"

Haynes Nickens is standing over Shane.

Shane's heard people say that he and Nickens could pass for brothers but he's never seen the man in person. He takes in the blue-black hair, sleek as sealskin, the eyes like hot asphalt and the Dick Tracy jawline, all in the same mix with the trademark three-piece suit, bow tie and pocket watch. He has the feeling that he's seeing a version of himself who's stepped out of, say, 1935.

Shane sticks out his hand but Nickens has already turned away. Some girls are tittering in the other room. Televised hearings have made Nickens a celebrity, to the point where he now has to do all his stakeouts and surveillances in disguise. Millions of daytime TV viewers know him as the grave young man who sits behind the main table and sometimes, not often enough, takes the microphone to grill a witness with more panache than any of the Congressmen can muster.

Nickens circles around Shane's desk, eyeing the clutter. There are only a few personal touches in Shane's work area. A baseball autographed by Walter Johnson, a wooden egg from a long-ago White House Easter Egg Roll, a postcard showing the Jefferson Memorial and Tidal Basin at cherry blossom time.

The postcard -- with "How's my little Bruiser?" scrawled on the back -- is under the glass on the desk, preserved like a butterfly. Raymond sent it to Shane more than 30 years ago, when he was in Washington after his first election, scouting housing for his family.

Nickens reaches under the desktop glass and plucks out the postcard. "Do you know the history?"

Of course Shane knows the history behind the Jefferson Memorial, and everything else in the city that's white and cold and backward-looking. He starts to answer but Nickens cuts him off. "The Japanese came first to the water with those trees, and their soft blossoms that flower and wither in just a few days, to show us the fragility of the present. Then came Jefferson in bronze, to remind us of our stalwart past." His accent is vaguely Southern. Shane now remembers: Richmond.

Nickens makes another circuit around Shane's desk, snapping the postcard. "You know, I was down there one day when the trees were at their peak and an early spring thunderstorm came upon us. And out of nowhere a bolt hit."

Nickens flicks the card against the side of his face. Shane starts to reach for it but holds off.

"I walked right to my car," Nickens goes on, "and got out a pad and paper and wrote something. *Nature lashes out. Brings a budding tree to earth. Leaves behind pink death.*"

Nickens snaps the card again. "Do you know it?"

"Know what?"

"Haiku. Japanese poetry. Three lines, five-seven-five syllables."

"I'm more of a Frost and Yeats man." Nickens crinkles his lip. "Now my question for you is, how do *you* know it?"

"I've been a lot of places."

Shane snatches the postcard back. "Evidently a lot of places where you can put your paws all over somebody else's stuff without getting your skull split."

"You can't blame a fellow for just wanting to get a sense for the man to whom he's giving his confidential work product."

"So I assume," Shane says, "you've checked me out."

"Naturally. You've left quite a paper trail behind you. Your war experiences made particularly interesting reading."

Shane stays on point. "Your report on Barry and the girl," he says, "is pretty damned detailed. Looks like this was a full-time job."

"Ach. This was like moonlighting, a hobby. There are a lot of hours in the day to get things done."

"So why give the report up to me? Why'd you come here?"

"I was told to. And speaking of the report." In one motion he plucks it from Shane's desk, folds it in two and puts it in his suit pocket. "I don't want it to get submerged in all this quicksand," he says, gesturing toward the stacks of paper. "You're a smart man, Kinnock, you'll remember what you need to."

"Detective."

Nickens brushes the shoulder of his suit. "Sure, if the title means that much to you. *Detective.*" He picks up the Walter Johnson ball, tosses it from hand to hand, flicks it like a top on Shane's desk, then brings the spin to a stop with a light finger touch. "The Big Train, they called him. Never anyone better."

"So you're a fan?"

"I used to be," Nickens says. "Lost interest about five years ago, or thereabouts."

"So who told you to see me?"

Nickens plucks the wooden Easter egg from Shane's desk. "My chain of command."

"And I'm assuming your chain of command ultimately includes my father."

Nickens shakes his head and smirks. Sits the egg on its narrow end. Watches it topple.

"So what is it that your committee could have on Joe Barry that would make you start tailing him?"

"Not much tailing," Nickens says, "mostly staking out. In my investigator role, I don't ask questions. In my lawyer role, I can say that the surveillance was deemed necessary because of the business dealings of Mr. Barry's father."

"So Matt Barry was the main target."

Nickens winks. "Let's just say you're an everyday commonplace citizen. You hear the richest man in America is selling ships to our most fearsome enemies, just so they can use them to take us over and kill thousands of our people. Wouldn't you want your government to pay a little attention to him?"

There's more to the issue than that, but Shane passes on arguing the niceties. "So where does the son come in?"

"Simple. We were looking at the father, and the son was taking money from the father, so of course he was tarred with the same brush. And if that wasn't enough, the son's views on other issues had the potential to compromise him."

"What other *issues*?"

"Start with civil rights. Mr. Barry took up with one side of the issue. There are fine people on that side, but as we both know there are also some undesirable elements."

"It sounds like somebody just wanted to trump up a subversion case on a rising star."

Nickens winks again. "My, my, a Kinnock leaping to the defense of a Barry."

Shane changes the subject. "So how many hours did you put in on this frolic?"

Nickens absently fingers his watch pocket. "I never count. Stakeouts are all the same to me. You stay in the same place, and the world is racing by, going in all directions, and you know eventually it'll slow down and get back in line. Or you make it so."

"I have no idea what that means."

Nickens just winks yet again, and Shane now realizes it isn't a wink but a tic. "This one," Nickens goes on, "was more enjoyable in some respects than others, since at least it put me into some city parks. It gave me the opportunity to observe an impressive array of bird life."

"So you're an ornithologist. Just like Alger Hiss was."

"Please. It was his only known virtue." Nickens takes from his jacket a silk pocket square, perfectly folded, and re-folds it. "Now as far as excitement is concerned, I can't say it ranked as high as, say, a Bureau black bag job. But the work had to be done."

He stuffs the silk square back in his jacket pocket and fusses over the points.

"So if it wasn't that bad a gig, why'd you ask to be taken off of it?"

"Other duties intruded. No, I'm not at liberty to tell you what they were." He takes out his pocket watch, looks at it, then dangles it idly by its gold chain. "I'm assuming that when you use this information you'll leave my name and the committee's name out of it?"

"Sure." Shane lights a Camel. Nickens says, "Must you?"

"And I'm assuming," Shane says, "that while we're working this angle, your side won't leak any more of it to the press."

"Leaking isn't how I operate. Anything I do, it's as if it's encased behind 200 cubic feet of concrete."

Over Nickens's shoulder, Shane sees that Sergeant Roncalli had moved close enough to listen in.

"I might actually be able," Nickens says, "to give you some help on the side. I know a lot about Joe Barry, and I saw quite a lot of your victim. If their relationship, if that's what you want to call it, becomes relevant to you, maybe I can help."

"Some people have said she was quite the beauty."

Nickens passes his hand across his face. "On the job, I'm like a gynecologist. I train myself not to even notice anything like that. In any event, I met your colleague, Shiflett, earlier. Just have him send me some of your reports and I'll see if there's anything that jumps out at me."

Shane starts to say thanks but no thanks, but the sergeant comes up. "Mr. Nickens, that's a wonderful thing for you to offer, just a wonderful thing." A bomb could go off at the desk next to him and the Sarge wouldn't notice.

Shane's seen it happen before, Roncalli's laconic reserve dropping for a celebrity. The two of them met Ted Williams at a police benefit dinner a few years ago and Shane thought the Sarge was going to fall to his knees and fellate Ted on the spot.

Now the Sarge fawns over Nickens for a couple of minutes while Shane cools his heels. "Shane," he finally says, "have Shiflett work with Mr. Nickens here. No harm in having another set of eyes on this, especially his."

Nickens moves towards the doorway, then stops. "By the way, Detective, you didn't ask me something I thought you would. I understand you've had a hard time finding the Rose girl's place. She had an apartment in Foggy Bottom, on Washington Circle, 2430 Penn Avenue to be exact. I tailed her there once from the Wardman Park Hotel to see where she went when she left Barry."

Nickens puts on his hat and delivers a parting shot. "Not that I would've expected it to occur to you just now to ask me."

And with that Haynes Nickens leaves the stage.

They stand by the desk, the sergeant and Shane, now alone together, not looking at each other. Finally the sergeant speaks. "Why couldn't you find that place? Jesus, Shane, you're slipping. And I don't know what to do about it."

Nickens re-enters for a curtain call. "There's one more thing you didn't ask me about, Detective. Maybe you'll remember to talk to Mr. Barry about it. I have photographs of him and the girl. Lots of them."

21

"You know that I know."

S. Matthew Barry has Shane's business card in his hands. He's taking it in his fingernails, which are really more like talons, folding it lengthwise with a knife edge.

"And," he says, "I know that you know I know."

He creases the card again and then again.

Shane answers. "Know that I know you know what?"

The card is now reed-thin and Matt Barry fixates on it as if it's a rare gem and he's a jeweler with a drill. All the while, he's talking in a near-whisper.

"I know this is all about your God-damned father. That's why you're here. And why you're going after my boy. You just have no idea what you're getting into."

Shane and Matt Barry are sitting in the front room of the Georgetown mansion where Joe Barry lives. It's a four-story brick Colonial that dominates a city block on 34th Street, with an expansive second-story patio above a three-car garage and an elaborate front entrance flanked by black torch-lanterns.

"It's you and your God-damned father's shanty-type that gave the entire Irish race a bad name, coming over here behind the rest of us with all your dirt and your drunkenness."

Matt twirls the card between thumb and forefinger. "And what a travesty it is that a man of my station had to be called before Congress to justify a few business deals, every one of them perfectly legal to anybody with more than mulch for brains."

And about those deals. "They were brilliant in their own way, anyone can see that, and your God-damned father wouldn't be able to understand them if you gave him a fresh Univac and a month of free time."

Shane says nothing.

Matt holds the folded business card in front of his face. He takes off his wire-framed glasses. For more than a year he's been secluded on his New York estate. He's in emotional descent. His lined face marks the tortured journey. But his eyes are as blue and fresh as aquarium water.

He goes on in a hushed rant. "Your God-damned father hates me because I wouldn't play his game in that Godforsaken city, and I moved out to Long Island and went over to the other party. And now I'm taking over everything out there, and I've got my boy set up to go places that Raymond Kinnock can't even dream about."

Matt is slowly taking Shane's folded card and putting it into his right ear. He inserts it tentatively at first, then more forcefully, working it around and around like a plumber with a snake. Then he takes it out, examines the debris on the end of it, and tosses it onto the glass coffee table between them so someone else can dispose of it, presumably Shane.

Their encounter began so pleasantly – Matt coming to the door and saying, I'm staying here while I'm in town, and Joe's wife Sheila's up in New York, and Joe's out playing tennis but he'll be back soon, and by the way can I get you coffee? – that Shane wondered whether the man recognized him.

The fact that Matt Barry knew very well who was standing across from him became clear when the conversation veered into the distant events that gave birth to the Matt Barry-Raymond Kinnock feud. Shane's heard it all from his father, many times over, and now he's had to sit through The Other Side of the Story. He could no more be bothered with the past particulars than when his father visited them on him. But he does know how much it's all come to matter, as the stakes have grown far beyond the trifling.

Matt Barry and Raymond Kinnock are two men with boundless guile, uncommon intellect and a shared homeland. They've been locked for over a quarter-century in a pitched battle that smells of the jungle – two lions, the first marking his turf and the second kicking dirt over the mark – and what they're now fighting over is the biggest state in the country, the country itself, and everything the country can yield.

The woman in black, from outside the jail – she's up on Shane now, jostling him.

Ask him, she's saying, where was he on the first of May last year? Listen to his hatred, the expanse of his ambition for his son. He can move all his companies and thousands of his people around like peas on his dinner plate. He could've snapped his fingers and made this happen.

A hornet has strayed into the Barry airspace – "That God-damned butler must have left a window open" – and lands on the coffee table, buzzing about annoyingly. Matt keeps talking but is obviously distracted.

Shane sees the legs tense. He waits for the man to pounce on the hornet and in his mind's eye he sees the table shattering on impact.

Matt reaches out slowly, his hand hovering over the table as gracefully as a hawk in flight.

He pins the hornet on the table with a talon. He gently scoops the bug up, walks him to the door and releases him back to nature.

Professional courtesy, Shane thinks.

And he never stopped talking the entire time.

Shane has two questions. One is just a matter of curiosity. *If the business deals were so innocent, why'd you take the Fifth before Congress?* But Shane knows the answer will basically be, I wasn't going to give your God-damned father anything he could shove up my ass. So, Shane goes to the second.

"You know I'm here about Joe's dead staffer, the girl. You wouldn't have had any conversation with him about all that, would you?"

Shane waits for an outburst.

Matt looks as if he had a bead on another errant hornet. His gaze sweeps the room until it lands on Shane.

A moment passes. Then Matt laughs.

He grips Shane's shoulder and uses it to help him rise to his feet. "Even your God-damned father wouldn't be so inartful as to go at it like that, oh no, not at all. Oh no, the Barrys have nothing to worry about from you, we surely don't."

He starts laughing again, and he doesn't stop until he's made his way down the hall toward the back of the house.

Outside, a car engine can be heard at the end of the block, coming closer. It's past 6:30. Shane goes to the front door, looks out the narrow window on the side, and sees a white Caddie idling at curbside. He can see the cloudy image of Joseph Barry on the front passenger side, can't see the driver. Voices are coming from the car. One sounds like a woman's.

After a long minute Barry opens the door and emerges in stages. First the distinctive head, then the shoulders with a sweater tied loosely below the collar of what looks to be a Lacoste shirt, and finally the lower half, in crisp ivory slacks and pristine canvas shoes.

Barry slams the door and walks towards the house and Shane backs into the foyer, but keeps watching. Barry throws his racket hard on the stone steps and it makes a tinny sound, like a splintered ballbat pounded on sandlot turf. He's scowling.

Scowling, that is, until he opens his door and sees Shane standing inside his house and a switch goes on and the dormant grin is ignited. "Sorry to keep you waiting," he says. "Game took longer than I thought."

Barry leads the way into the front room and flops onto an antique sofa. To sit across from him Shane has to squeeze himself onto a pink-upholstered, three-legged chair that barely accommodates him.

"I was just thinking," Shane says, trying to regain traction. "The press says you're this heroic aviator, broke your back bailing out of your flaming plane, still managed to drop all your bombs on Jap targets. Today you're gallivanting around the nets like a pro."

Barry doesn't answer, just stretches out, claiming space. He starts drumming the edge of the sofa with his fingers, and one foot is bouncing up and down. "You saw my father, I assume?"

"I did. How's his health?"

"Just keep those pharmaceuticals coming." Barry bolts suddenly from the sofa. "Which way did he go?"

"Down the hall back there."

There's an intercom on the wall, on the other side of the double fireplace. Barry goes straight to it, pushing buttons until a voice responds. "George," he says, "find my father and steer him back to the downstairs bedroom." He turns back to Shane. "No need to have the old man nosing around any more than he needs to."

"Who's George?"

"My valet," Barry says, as casually as anyone could ever say those two words.

He offers a brandy and Shane accepts. An older Negro in a white coat appears in barely a minute with two full brandy glasses and a Waterford crystal ashtray.

Shane thinks of Nickens: *I have photographs of Joe Barry and the girl, lots of them.* He wants to jump on it – would Joe here be so breezy if he knew what was out there on him? – but he holds back for the moment. "So, how's your Senate race going?"

"Right now it goes back to your old man. He managed to slow things down in the House this week just enough to keep me from getting up to New York to do the rounds. I've got a dinner to go to tonight and a vets' event all day tomorrow, so I won't even get up there 'til Sunday. Have to hand it to the prick."

Barry stretches again. He's said his piece with no resentment. In the long chess match of a campaign he knows this amounted to little more than the early loss of a pawn.

"So are you going to win?"

"Sure. I've already gotten rid of Ives." Irving Ives was the incumbent who's already dropped out of the race, scared off by the Barry millions being marshaled against him. "The guy who's left, whoever he is, will take the city, I'll take upstate and the middle, and it'll all come down to the suburbs on the Island. All those thousands of ex-GIs in their VA tract homes."

"Your neighbors."

"Isn't that something?"

Two years ago Joe Barry bought a house in the Long Island suburbs, planning for this race, staking his claim to be a man of the people. It's where his wife spends much of the year, in a white Rambler, between two white Ramblers, on a street full of white Ramblers.

"And why will they all go for you? Other than maybe you're helping a few of the guys in your block with their crabgrass."

"Because they don't care about political parties, they care about bread and butter. They want us to hold off the Reds, but they want us out of Korea because they see the war's going nowhere. When all's said and done, they'll want a guy who's seen combat, so they'll know he's got balls."

"Truman saw action in the Argonne Forest, and that's not doing him much good right now."

"I'm thinking more along the lines of Teddy."

He's gazing at his ceiling as if it's the baby-blue sky and everything beyond it. "They fought a war to save freedom, so they're going to want to keep feeling good about themselves, fighting for freedom here and all that. Which means that they'll go with a guy who's going to be good to the Negroes."

"And that's *you*? The man with the colored valet? You're going to be the knight in shining armor for the Negroes?"

"Hey pal, aside from showing up at their jazz clubs and letting them entertain you, you don't seem to have much to do with them, from what I hear. Except for locking them up." The grin appears again, at lower wattage. "Besides," he adds, "a lot of the old generals from the war still have their valets. I hear Eisenhower couldn't wipe his ass without his."

It's a colorful image but Shane doesn't respond. He's been jolted by Barry's jazz club reference. *Somebody's briefed him pretty well about me.*

"Face it, Shane, I'm on the right side of history." Barry swirls around the brandy in his glass. "There's going to be thousands of Levittowns sprouting up all over the country, and millions of guys in 'em will see the world like I see it. I'm a vet, I'm not bad-looking, I give a decent speech. And I can pull the two parties together. Shit, by the time I'm done there may not even be a need for parties."

Joe Barry looks like a boy on Christmas morning with all the shimmering packages laid out before him.

"What about the Catholic thing?"

"Somebody's got to be the first, it might as well be me. Once people get to know me, they'll see all that old stuff is just so much bullshit."

Joe Barry writes off years of religious bigotry as if it's as frivolous as gossip traded between two housewives under hair dryers at a beauty salon.

Maybe, Shane thinks, this is the confidence that a man has when he's seen just enough of war to imagine he's been fully tested by it, but not so much as to have it ruin him.

"So, Congressman, if you're so strong for civil rights, I take it you'll be voting for my father's bill if it gets to the floor."

"Not if he doesn't ask me. And he won't."

"Even if it comes down to a late-night stand-off, and one vote means the difference between putting a bill over the top or putting it off for years?"

Barry leans back. "When I'm in the Senate next session I can work with fellows on the other side and come up with a *better* bill."

"Sometimes in life you only have one chance. But hell, maybe you know better than me."

Shane lights a cigarette and proffers the pack to Barry, who makes a face.

"There's only one problem with all your career plans, Congressman."

"And that would be?"

"The little matter of the dead girl."

Barry settles back further on the sofa. He's almost prone, tapping his front teeth with a fingernail, staring upwards. Clouds have drifted into his baby-blue sky and he's measuring their threat.

"Drew Pearson will be all over that for a couple of weeks," he says in a steady monotone. "I'm sure your old man already has him primed. But a lot of papers won't even run his stuff, they'll be scared as shit that my old man will sue their asses. So it won't have legs and I'll weather it."

"So it's just a political issue for you."

Barry lifts himself up. "I thought we were talking politics. So, what else do you want to ask? And, come to think of it, how do I know everything I say about this isn't going to get right back to your father?"

"Because I'm telling you it won't. Aside from that, you have no assurances," Shane runs his finger around the Waterford ashtray on the table next to him. "But you knew that when you said you'd see me."

"You got it, pal. There's an old saying that goes, a clear conscience is a good pillow. And I'm sleeping very well these days."

"So, tell me about her."

"It was terrible what happened to her. She was such a beautiful girl, with such a spirit."

"Were you screwing her?"

"No."

Neither of them moves.

"O-kay," Barry finally says, chuckling. He claps his hands on his knees and rises. "I've got to get out of these clothes. That's it, right?"

"Not exactly."

"Damn. Alright, I didn't think so. So, follow me upstairs and we can talk." As he walks from the room, he's humming to himself.

He lopes down the marble-floored hallway and Shane follows behind. The walls are hung with original artwork, and further down to the right is a dining room with a table for twelve and a large gilt-edged mirror that could've come from Versailles.

Shane catches up to Joe at the dining room doorway. "You have a beautiful house."

"Someday," Barry says, "I'd like to own a place like this." He rubs his chin and looks around. "My father bought it from another Congressman. He didn't even tell me who."

"So did your wife put together all the furniture and the artwork?"

"No, my father had some French decorator take care of all of it. All I know is, there's a lot of Louies sitting around here. Louie Fifteens, Louie Sixteens, hell, probably even some Louie Armstrongs, for all I know."

Joe Barry grabs Shane's forearm: "Don't let on to my old man, but none of this means shit to me."

His cool detachment extends even to the house where he lives.

Joe quickly mounts a spiral staircase. Shane takes his time.

On the curving wall are Barry family photographs going back through the century. At the top of the landing is a massive portrait, elaborately oiled, framed and overlit, of Joe's younger brother James leaning jauntily against a 1949 Lincoln Continental. A considerably smaller, black-and-white version of the picture ran on the front page of the New York Times in 1950, the morning after James, dead drunk from a party, drove the car into the Peconic River on Long Island.

Joe passes the portrait without a glance.

Shane steadies himself against the banister, goes in his pocket and gets two more demerols to pop, his fifth and sixth of the day, at least. "Hey," he hears from down the hall, "you want to talk or not?"

A mahogany four-poster dominates the master bedroom. George the valet is sitting on a chair next to the bed, pushing studs through the buttonholes of a ruffled shirt. Joe Barry is standing in front of the dresser mirror.

"Every year," he says, "my father puts on a black-tie dinner at the Statler for my birthday and tonight's the night." He's holding up two tuxedos, one in each hand, jet black and charcoal. "I guess it would be something of a stretch to say that either one of these screams out that I have the workingman's interests at heart."

He waits for a moment and then explodes in a laugh. Shane joins in.

Shane doesn't want to go hard against him. He likes him and, more dangerously, wants to be liked by him. Joe Barry is handsomer, funnier and richer than all the others, with a grander ego and dreams to match. He moves about in a world a science fiction writer might imagine, where everything looms larger, speeds along faster and looks shinier.

Shane sees Barry standing in front of the mirror with his tuxedos and his wry smile, enjoying the moment's beauty and mocking himself for enjoying the moment's beauty, and he sees himself as he might've ended up if just one or two things in his life had gone differently.

Joe drops the black tux on the bed and holds the charcoal number against himself. His eyes don't leave the mirror.

"You know," he says, "I really don't know what the fuss is all about with this case, why people seem so interested in it. I'm sorry about what happened to Emily, sure, but to read the papers it was as if she was Betty Grable and Rita Hayworth all rolled into one."

Shane's still looking at the tux on the bed; black and beguiling.

At first, Joe's words don't register.

Then: "What?"

"It's not as if she was the only nice-looking piece of ass out there. Christ."

Shane closes his eyes and when he opens them the light in the room seems dimmer. "There's no getting around it, Congressman," he says evenly. "I've talked with enough people to know everything you were doing with her."

If Joe Barry senses that the mood has changed, he doesn't show it. "George, I'll wear this one," he says, handing over the black tux. He turns back to the mirror. "And Shane, unless one of your people was following me around like a pervert every night for months on end, they can't very well know what I do when I'm not doing my job. Not that there'd ever be anything all that interesting to know."

George comes over and starts to untie the sweater that still hangs loosely around Barry's neck.

"Let's go at it this way. Your wife, she's not here today, is she?"

"No, she's up in New York. As you already know."

"She's not here a lot, correct?"

"No, indeed."

George helps him pull his Lacoste shirt over his head. Barry's bare back is as muscled as a dock worker's.

"Would it surprise you to know that I'd be able to tell you the exact dates that your wife came and left your Georgetown house over the last two years?"

"You're bluffing, Kinnock, and we both know it. My wife and I are public figures, for Christ's sake. You could've gotten this from anywhere. And I still haven't heard anything you have on me with the girl."

George helps Barry out of his shoes, then his socks.

Shane's head is pounding. He's trying to picture Nickens's report, with all its crazy details about Barry's exertions, but all he can remember are random, odd words. "Female subject." "Nocturnal." "Dalliance." "Low neckline."

Suddenly, a date. May 29, 1949. *May 29, 1949.*

Shane moves up behind Barry, invading his mirror frame. "The dinner you're going to tonight. Your father has it for you every year, right?"

"Sure."

You had it in '47, right?"

"Yeah, I suppose."

Barry unbuckles his pants and steps out of them. He's down to his shorts. He puts a hand on one hip.

What's the key to a good cross-examination? Take your time, don't jump to the point too quickly, stretch it out. Keep the witness on a string.

"And in '48, '49, 50, and last year."

"I guess. So what?"

"Do you remember three years ago."

Barry doesn't answer. "George," he snaps, "Are you bringing those pants over or not?"

George has them on his lap and he's working a needle and thread over a pocket he's turned inside out. Barry has both hands on his hips now.

"I know a Congressman has a lot on his mind, so let me help you out. Your wife didn't go to that dinner, did she."

"No, I told you, she goes up to New York --"

"And so you went to the dinner by yourself in your tux, and when you came home somebody was waiting for you on the doorstep down there, weren't they? Somebody in a pink dress that went down to *there*, and everything she had was all out there for you, right, Congressman? And you took her inside, and she didn't come out until the next morning. Remember all that, *Congressman*?"

Barry blinks once, twice.

"Do you still think," Shane says, "that I don't have the goods on you?

Shane moves so close to Barry that his head is almost touching the man's left shoulder. He stares at him in the dresser mirror and murmurs. "I know about how the two of you would sneak around in parks and hotels, cavorting all over. Public parks, Congressman. Ring a bell?"

"George," Barry says quietly. "Get those pants over here."

George doesn't look up, just goes on fussing with the pocket.

"Close your eyes, Joe. Maybe you can even see her. Standing right there in front of you just like she looked on your doorstep that night. You can say something to her. What are you going to say to her?"

Barry looks blankly into the mirror, then back at Shane. He's a dead man. Staring him down, Shane feels as if he's boring through his eye sockets all the way through to the back of his cranium, an unimpeded shot.

"I said, don't you have something you want to tell her, Joe?"

Barry finally closes his eyes.

"What was that, Joe?"

Barry's lips move.

"What, Joe?"

"Why would I kill her?"

Barry turns and faces Shane squarely. "It makes no sense. Think about it, it really doesn't make any sense at all. Why would I kill her?"

"What –"

"No, let me finish." Barry jabs Shane's shoulder lightly to back him away. "Say a guy is seeing a girl on the side but he wants to break things off and she won't take the hint. There's other ways to get her out of his life without killing her, right?"

"Sure –"

"He could pay her off, for one thing. He could pay her a thousand – a hundred thousand, a million – to make herself scarce. How many girls could pass that up? And even if she just wouldn't get out of the way, even if she got pushed past a certain point, would he really kill her like this girl was killed?"

Barry jabs Shane again, harder.

"He wouldn't do it himself," he says. "Would he, Kinnock?" Another jab, then another. "George!"

The valet brings the pants over and Barry puts them on. "Just leave the rest of it on the floor here." George walks out with his head down.

Barry pushes Shane with both hands. "No, he wouldn't. He'd hire somebody to do it and they'd dump her a hundred miles away or throw her in the Potomac. They're not going to leave her in a public park and take a chance that some *mudslide* might cover her up, are they?"

Another push, harder.

"No, this was impulsive, spontaneous. Somebody lashed out and killed her without thinking and threw her down like a rag doll. Maybe they weren't even in their right mind."

Barry stops abruptly, then presses on. "Why are you even here? You've already got a man locked up for this. I'm hearing you took another pass at him yesterday and he still won't say a word about it. Doesn't that tell you something? Why won't he talk?"

"Maybe the same reason you won't talk." Shane is scrambling now. "Maybe he's got something to hide and he's got his own reasons for not wanting to say what it is. And that doesn't mean he did it. He had no reason to, for one thing."

"And I did? Don't make me laugh."

Barry pulls on the ruffled shirt and buttons it. "Somebody put a tail on me. And if I had to guess I'd say your father had something to do with it. And you're trying to convince me that anything trustworthy is going to come out of that? What a fucking joke." He's gathering steam.

He wraps a satin cummerbund around his waist. "Your father lines up some hack gumshoe to follow me around, right? Is that guy going to go back to your old man and say, 'Nothing's turning up, he's clean as a whistle, goes home alone every night.' No. The guy knows what his marching orders are, and he'll twist the facts to match them."

He yanks the bow tie around his neck: the final piece. "So, you have this big pile of shit that somebody gave you and your old man and you expect me to add more shit to it? No way, pal."

Shane's seen a lot of prizefights over the years, but never one better than Rocky Graziano against Tony Zale at Yankee Stadium a few years ago. In the fifth round Graziano was just a punch away from taking Zale out but Zale went into a clinch, lasted out the round – drawing on resources from who knows where – and won the fight in the next round.

Say what you will about Joe Barry preening in his hand-me-down Georgetown mansion. This night, with Shane, he's Tony Zale.

"Look," Shane says, "if you're holding anything back --"

"I'm not." Barry pulls the bowtie back and forth, up and down. Perfect. "You've seen me," he says. "I've got nothing to hide."

I've got nothing to hide: The politician's art always comes down to that one sentence, and the best in the business can make you actually believe it.

Shane goes for the last word. "If you're holding anything back, you're going to have to talk eventually. Faye's going to put a grand jury subpoena on anybody who might know anything about this. You wouldn't lie to a grand jury, would you?"

Barry pats him on the shoulder. "I don't know if I have much to worry about from 'Four-F-Faye.' From what I hear about him, he was back home stateside pushing paper around while I was dodging flak in the Pacific. But if I have to talk to him I will. At least he's not a Kinnock."

Shane ignores the jibe. "So, all she was to you was a girl who worked in your office?"

"Exactly."

"You never saw her outside work, never even met up with her one-on-one outside the office?"

"No."

"Never had dinner with her?"

Barry snaps his cufflinks into place and puts on the tux jacket. "I hate to cut this off, but my cab will be here shortly, and I have a phone call to make before I go. And for the record, the answer's no."

Shane plods downstairs and lingers in the foyer before leaving.

The sound of footfall came from the steps. *Is it George?*

No, Barry.

Shane flattens himself against a wall. Barry goes straight to the kitchen and doesn't see him. It would be right and proper for Shane to leave, but he doesn't. He stays in the foyer, turning off the inside light.

A phone is being dialed. Silence. Then, Joe Barry's voice. "No, the wife's not here. Not here, babe, won't be here."

A few seconds pass. Barry's voice goes low and gravelly and Shane can't make out the words. Barry chuckles: "Do you want to miss all of that?"

Shane can hear fireflies careening against the outside of the front window.

Barry, louder. "Have it your fucking way, then." A crash.

Wham! Wham! Wham! Wham! Wham!

The phone is being broken, something glass follows.

Shane watches as Barry walks quickly out of the kitchen. There's an umbrella stand in the corner of the darkened foyer, next to the front door, maybe four feet high.

He tries to crouch behind it.

Barry doesn't come all the way down the hall but veers into the front room and goes straight to the intercom. "George," he says, still breathing heavily, "before you go to bed tonight, I need you to clean up in the kitchen. The phone's broken, I think my father had a problem with it. And he dropped a plate."

Shane watches Barry stomp down the hall towards the staircase.

Good detective work comes down to seeing enough of life to know how certain events repeat themselves in order as predictably as moon cycles and tide movements.

Man wants woman to do something. Woman refuses. Man lashes out violently. Man lies about what he did.

Shane looks in the front room. Two empty brandy glasses are on the end table, unattended. He walks briskly into the room, takes a handkerchief, seizes the glass Barry used earlier and pockets it.

At his car, he looks back at the Barry house. The black lanterns have flamed to life. Joe Barry appears at his front door just as a taxi rounds the corner to deliver him to the adulation that he's come to expect as his due.

Shane has just two things to do tomorrow.

Visit the apartment on Washington Circle where Nickens says he tracked Emily, to see if he can get any other leads.

Take the brandy glass and have Joe Barry's prints checked against the print on Emily's receipt from the Calvert Café.

And as far as Shane knows, Joe Barry has just one thing to do tomorrow, an all-day vets' function.

Which means that tomorrow night Joe Barry will likely be right here at his house, if Shane has to come back with handcuffs.

22

THE WASHINGTON POST
Saturday, May 31, 1952

"WORDLESS WILLIE" SPARKS A SIT-DOWN, HUNDREDS ARRESTED

By Bran Bentley, Staff Reporter

Accused murderer Willie Robinson, facing the electric chair on the charge of killing Capitol Hill beauty Emily Rose, continues to decline to put up a defense on his behalf. He now has at least one thing going for him. The 23-year-old Negro has a lot of friends he didn't have before.

A group of approximately a thousand Negroes convened outside D.C. Jail last night to protest the treatment of Robinson, whose street nickname was "Cat Eyes" but who's becoming known as "Wordless Willie." A prominent city religious leader, Rev. Fulwood Williamson, addressed the group by megaphone and lauded Robinson for refusing to participate in what Williamson termed "a corrupt, racist criminal justice system."

Rev. Williamson went on to call for Negroes "in this city and across the country" to engage in something he called "passive resistance" to challenge the government's prosecution of Robinson "on flimsy, trumped up evidence." The coming days will help determine if these displays spread further and whether law enforcement will be able to contain the lawlessness that may follow.

****

"I saw her again today."

"Who?"

"I've told you about her. The same one."

"Shane, I don't know what you're talking about. Honest."

"Damn it, Bobby, don't you go and make me doubt myself, too. The woman in black. The one that just stares at me."

"The one you saw before?"

"Exactly, the one I saw outside the jail the other day. The one who looks like she came straight from a synagogue. This morning, she was sitting on the stoop across from my place when I came out. I started to go over to her, but she turned and walked away fast."

"Was she wearing – "

"Yeah. Hot days like these and she's always pretty much all covered up."

Bobby sits with his hands on his lap. "You sure you're alright? Your Sarge says you're taking too many of them pain pills."

"So they're making me see things? Christ almighty, this woman was right there, she's been following me around. I don't know what she wants from me."

"I'm just sayin' that maybe you're hittin' them things too hard. I was callin' over your place this mornin' for two hours and couldn't get you up, and now there's this. Your Sarge says one of them things you take, they give to *horses*."

They're sitting in the rental office at 2430 Penn, the place that Nickens put them on to, waiting for the landlady to come back with Emily's lease. It's an apartment house that has all the charm of a reformatory: bricks and limestone and drywall and pipes and wires thrown together to handle the postwar glut of government workers, mostly single girls in low-paying jobs, a way station for dreams put on hold.

What's taking so goddam long?

It's past noon, the fingerprint office shuts down at three, and it's going to take awhile for the boys over there to make the comparisons.

How hard can it be for this woman to track down a goddam lease?

The landlady reappears with a file box in her hand, breathing hard. "No Emily Roses in here," she says.

Shane confirms that she looked back through all the records of last April's residents, some 250 or so, then asks if she minds if he checks for himself. "Suit yourself, mister."

The file in the front of the box is titled ZIEGLER, followed by CASTLE, then PORTER and FLEGLER. "Some alphabetical system you've got here," Shane says. The landlady shrugs as if to say, It works for me.

Shane goes through JEMISON and BENNETT and McCORMICK and KOCH, all the way to the last file, marked TALLEY.

But no ROSE.

But who the hell knows if this is everything this landlady's got?

"Let's try something else. Do you ever have a tenant just go missing on you?"

"Sure, it happens. You know the way it is in this town, folks comin' and goin'. Somebody ups and leaves in the middle of the night, usually around the end of the month with the rent past due."

"Do you remember it happening last year?"

"Coupla of times. Paperwork on 'em would be in another box down the hall. My 'Absconded Without Paying' box." She turns to lumber away.

Shane doesn't want to wait. "Don't leave. I take it if somebody just disappeared and left all their stuff behind, that'd be pretty unusual, right?"

"Leavin' some of their stuff, that happens more than you'd think. Maybe somebody's on the run, leaves in a hurry, can't pack it all up. But somebody leavin' *all* their stuff, now that's unusual. Fact, it's only happened once that I know of. Girl lived in number 201. Come to think of it, it was around – "

"Spring of last year?"

"Yeah. *Yeah.*"

"Sounds like it could've been the girl we're here about."

The woman draws back and starts nodding. "Sure, it was last spring."

"What happened to her?"

Girl just seemed to vanish. Not sure the name was Emily or nothin' like that. Pretty girl, real friendly, though I didn't see her much. With so many of 'em here, I don't see 'em anywhere near every day."

Shane blots his brow with his shirt sleeve. "You ever see her in her apartment with anyone, ever see her keep company with anyone?"

"No."

"Ever take any calls for her?"

"Didn't even know she was gone for about two weeks, when her mail had stacked up. Went in the place and everything was still right there, like she was just down the hall or somethin'. Left it all behind her."

"What did you do with her stuff?"

"Put it in all in our crawl space downstairs."

The three descend a tight spiral staircase to a lower floor. Behind a swinging door on a creaking hinge is a room about 20 feet across with a four-foot high ceiling.

The landlady hands Shane a flashlight. "You can go in there. My knees ain't feelin' so hot today."

He hits the floor and works his way towards the back of the room, which is at least 50 feet deep. He hears her call out. "It's the couple of boxes all the way in the back on the left, with her number on 'em." He creeps through a cobweb, past a dead mouse that he nearly presses his hand on.

It's hot and the air is dank. Shane feels as he's sweated right through his suit. He passes what's been left back from the lives that've gone through this building.

A child's bicycle with two flat tires, a broken-down crib. A rusting box spring, a pile of wooden planks. A cedar chest with a film of dust.

Two mildewed boxes marked "201."

Here sits everything about a girl's life that's still collected in one place, all encased in a couple of rotting cardboard crates that could easily fit into a standard-depth cemetery plot, with room left over for a couple of coffins.

This can't be all of it. But maybe it is.

No matter what you do with your life, in the end everything about it, once it's all been picked over and parceled out and sorted through, can be dumped into a small hole.

Shane gets on the other side of the boxes and uses one to push the other out, inch by inch, towards the rectangle of light that's the only sign that life exists beyond this graveyard of artifacts.

Outside the room, he takes a few deep breaths and then bends over the boxes. Bobby comes up on him. "Whaddya hope to find here?"

Something. Anything.

Bobby takes items out of the first box and Shane notebooks them. Some sweaters and slacks, a pair of pedal pushers, three bandannas and five hats, a wool topcoat. A tangled mess of nylons, two bottles of cough syrup, toothpaste, band-aids.

Why am I bothering?

Then, the second box: filled to the top with hardbacked books, volumes of American and European history, classic fiction and philosophy – everything you'd expect to see if you'd come to know anything about Emily's voraciousness.

Shane flips through a few of the books. The bindings of some are broken from overuse and margin notes appear on most of the pages.

Shane tosses through what's left. "Where's the rest of it?"

"I threw out some food," the landlady says, "and some intimate-type things."

"Where are the dresses?"

She peers into the boxes. "What?"

"I said, where are the fucking dresses?"

"Easy, Shane," Bobby says.

"I know about this woman," Shane says, staring at the landlady, "and she had expensive things. I know for a fact she even had a mink wrap. Where the fuck is the pricey stuff?"

"I don't like your tone, mister. I boxed up what was in there."

"You boxed it alright. It's just that some of the boxes made their way to your room upstairs, and some went to the pawnshop for some easy cash."

"I don't even know for sure that you are who you say you are, mister, so back off. Anybody can get hold of a badge these days. Why should I answer questions like this?"

Shane doesn't press the point. He's losing the capacity to feel outrage. In a world filled with fraud, this is small change.

Bobby steps in. "Let's get out of here, Shane. We'll take all this and go back to the office."

Shane starts to refill the boxes but sees a manila envelope wedged against the side and opens it up.

Inside is a rubber-banded package. The document on top is headed "Rental Application" and next to it is a small, leather-bound book titled "Day-by-Day 1950 - 1951."

On the first inside page of the book, the name "Barbara Earnshaw" appears five times, as if the writer was trying out a new pen. They're the last decipherable entries in the book. The rest are in secretarial shorthand.

Shane looks at the squiggles, loops and dashes, all the graphic pirouettes, and he wants to know everything they signify.

The landlady is combing through one of the boxes, as if pretending to look for the missing dresses. "This book has the name Barbara Earnshaw inside," Shane says. How'd some other girl's things get in this box here?"

"Whaddya mean?"

"This diary here. It belonged to somebody named Barbara Earnshaw."

"Yeah, so? That's who you're over here about, right? That's who all this stuff belongs to. I forgot her name until we came down here and started going through it."

"No," he says, trying to restrain himself. "We're over here about an Emily Rose."

"Look, mister, you're actin' like I'm dumb or somethin'. I'm smart. I used to work in a war agency. Told you upstairs, no Emily Rose ever lived here."

She takes the diary and thumbs through it. "That's shorthand, in case you didn't already know."

"I knew. So, Barbara Earnshaw..."

"Is the girl who up and disappeared last year." She snatches the stack of documents, pulls out the rental application and points to the first page. "I, Barbara Earnshaw, do hereby attest..."

Shane takes the stack back from the landlady and furiously thumbs through them: two unopened letters from a New York post office box, three power bills, a postcard from an "Irene" from Mexico, a bill from a dentist.

All addressed to Barbara Earnshaw. No mention of Emily Rose.

And, in the back of the stack, a subpoena.

You, Barbara Earnshaw, are hereby commanded to appear before a grand jury convened by the Municipal Court of the District of Columbia upon the twentieth day of April, nineteen-hundred and fifty-one, the year of our Lord, in reference to the matter of, In Re Violation of Anti-Racketeering Provisions, United States Code.

Shane pitches the documents into the box and goes into his pocket for Emily's photo. "You've probably never seen this girl before, have you?"

The landlady doesn't need to take a long look. "That's her, that's the Earnshaw girl. But she's got her hair cut short and dyed black in this picture here. Why would she have gone and done that? She had such pretty long blond hair."

No wonder I couldn't find this place. She rented it under an alias, and in disguise. But why?

"So," Shane says to the landlady, "this girl vanished just like that, abandoned all of her stuff. and you didn't even think to call the police, did you."

"I thought of it, but I didn't. Maybe I shoulda. I just figured, with her disappearing like that, it probably had something to do with who her man was. And I was scared, tell you the truth."

"Who her man was?"

"Yeah, you know. That's really why you're here, right? Her man, her boyfriend, whatever. You know, the one that's on the lease with her."

"You're not helping me. Her man that's on the lease? Who the hell are you talking about?"

"Oh, no, I'm not sayin' his name, no sir, no sir. Don't use no tricks on me. The name's right in the papers there, you don't need to have me sayin' his name."

She takes the lease application out of the box and hands it back to Shane. "There. Look at page 2. But you just remember, I didn't say nothin'." She crosses herself.

The application is dated June 1, 1947.

At the bottom of page 1: a reference, somebody named Phyllis Everton, work address 513 9th Street, Northwest.

At the bottom of page 2: two signature lines, with names and designations beneath.

"Applicant": Barbara Earnshaw.

"Co-applicant": Jacob S. Kaufman.

There's a foot stool next to the crawl space door and Shane sinks to sit down on it, letting the application papers drop to the floor.

Jake Kaufman set her up in this place. Jake fucking Kaufman.

He feels a welling in his gut, a void stomach seeking to disgorge. Bobby picks up the papers, looks at them and turns away.

It was better when the girl was just a skeleton wrapped in red and that was all Shane knew about her. Now he knows too much, and he kicks himself for ever having cared.

He's never met Jake Kaufman. But he's met the type and in his mind's eye he sees the man breathing his rank gangster breath on his girl's earlobes, moving his gnarly gangster fingers up and down her flesh.

"Look," the landlady says, "I'll take a chance that you're the police, like you say you are. The rest of her stuff, all the expensive stuff, is holed up in another storage room I got upstairs, okay? I shoulda said that to you, but you can never be too sure who you're dealin' with when it comes to – you know."

She fans herself with her hand.

"In case he comes back around," she says, "it's all still there. You think I'm gonna steal from *him*? Forget it."

The landlady starts kneading the cloth belt on her housecoat in both hands. "You're not gonna tell him you got any of this from me, are you?"

"The secret's safe with us." Shane gets up to leave.

Then he remembers Joe Barry.

What the hell, the world is coming apart, I might as well try to nail something else down.

"I won't say a word to Kaufman," Shane says, "but you've got to do something for me. You worked in a war agency, right?"

She nods.

"Secretary?"

She nods again.

"Then do me a favor and translate some of this diary."

She takes it and starts paging through it. He asks if she sees Joe Barry's name anywhere, and he can tell from the look on her face and the roll of her eyes that she knows who he is. She pages through the book some more. "Here, right here. And it keeps on going. There's lotsa mentions of him."

He points to a random page. "What does this say about him?" She reads it and blushes. "I'd rather not say it, if you don't mind."

"Then what's the last entry dated, and what's the meat of it?"

She goes to the back of the book, says, "April 29, 1951," and scans a few lines. "The meat of it basically is Barry wants her to get lost and she doesn't wanna get lost."

Nickens had it right. There it is, in the girl's own hand. So much for him just being a hack gumshoe.

Shane tips his hat and tells the woman to keep her mouth shut about the diary. She says something to him but he can barely make out what it is, it sounds like her voice is coming from another place. He hears her say, so is this Earnshaw girl dead or what, and he hears himself say, read the papers and figure out this fucking mystery out for yourself, and he hears Bobby say, don't take this out on her. He leaves with Bobby and the documents and the diary, and he tells the landlady, somebody will come around later for the rest of the stuff.

And now the rest of Shane's life will proceed to disintegrate, bit by bit. If he still had his command of metaphor he'd be reminded, watching it all happen, of the skeletal hand that he once came upon in a park, and how it all fell apart before his eyes, bone by bone.

23

He goes with Bobby to find Phyllis Everton, the reference on the rental application. They pull up slowly to 513 9th Street.

It's the goddam Gayety Theater. Why would Emily know anybody down here?

The Gayety is a strip joint in one of the city's seediest blocks. Its facade is dominated by a poster reading "Girls, Girls, Girls, Best in Town," with life-sized photos that sadly belie the claim. About a year ago a drifter was shanked here by a roving thug, just 15, making front-page news. Even the young ones know that if you're out to shake down a drunk with some money in his pocket who's looking to get something from a floozy, this is where you want to be.

A guard sits in front of black curtains. Shane flashes his badge and says, Does a Phyllis Everton work here, and the guard hustles to the back. Shane parts the curtains and steps into a dark room filled with smoke, trombones, catcalls and the steamy stench of a curbside sausage cart.

The place is packed.

He hears Bobby say to him, Don't these people work durin' the day, but he stays quiet. A minute later a broad-shouldered woman in pants comes up and sticks out a wet, beefy hand. Bobby shakes it, Shane doesn't.

Phyllis Everton, nice to meetcha, I help run the place.

Shane brings out the Emily photo. He says, We have some questions about this girl, you know her?

Phyllis takes off her glasses, missing an arm piece, and pushes them down her nose. Sure do, she says after a second. The Earnshaw girl, except last time I saw her she was a blonde. Been about three years, but can't forget her, heh, heh, heh.

How's that?

Well, look at her there, Phyllis says, and then look at *them*, and she motions over her shoulder towards the stage, where a couple of plump girls in pasties are doing a fan dance.

She says, The manager here is all about business, and he was always trying to get the Earnshaw girl to dance up there, but I don't know if she ever did. Quite a looker, that one.

So, what'd she do for you here?

Waited tables, worked the register. Then she did hostess stuff. When she first came here, it seemed like she needed the money.

Why do you think she ended up here?

Don't know. We don't exactly ask for much in the way of references. As for why in a dancing place, she seemed to think it was a backdoor into show business or something. Wanted to meet people who could help her out, and damned if she didn't do just that.

How so?

Phyllis looks around, just as the landlady back at the Penn building did. She says, Don't bullshit a bullshitter, alright? You know who you're really down here about.

Shane says, I don't have time for this shit, and goes to leave. But Bobby says, Alright, this fella you're talkin' about, you don't have to name him. But I take it he met Emily down here?

Phyllis looks around again, then pulls Bobby close, and Shane still ends up hearing everything they're saying even though he doesn't really want to.

All about how this man came in one night and saw the Earnshaw girl in her tight little hostess outfit that fit her ass just so. How the man came in every night after that for two weeks until finally she sat with him. How even then she seemed scared of him, shied away across the table. Then some time went by, and the man kept coming in, and all of a sudden she started sitting right up on him. Started telling people in the club about all the promises the man was making to her. All about how he was going to take her to wonderful places and put her name in lights. And the next thing was, she was gone, and she never came back.

Shane listens. And here's all he takes from what he hears.

Emma Rosenblum, the kind of girl they make movies about, spends her youth being chased around the world by totalitarian monsters.

Emily Rose, goes to Washington, sets her mind on improving herself, on changing whatever world was left.

Barbara Earnshaw, glorified barmaid in a blond wig, gets herself holed up in a nest fronted by a mobster and lives out a second life. No, make that a third.

Towards the end of the story Phyllis starts slipping and using Kaufman's name. It actually seems to give her a small thrill.

Bobby asks Phyllis, Did you ever see the two of them argue, ever hear about them fightin' with each other, did the girl ever come to work with a black eye or anything like that, and Phyllis says, No, no, no.

Shane says, Phyllis, I've just got one more question to ask you, you don't have to answer it if you don't know. Are you sure she never got up there on stage and danced?

Phyllis says, It's funny that'd be the only question you have left to ask me. But no, I can't be so sure she didn't. Maybe she just might've gotten up there. Lots of girls, you know, they just can't say no.

Shane tries to make a fist with his left hand but his fingers won't clench together.

He walks with Bobby out to the light. Bobby says, Ya know, we got that dentist bill, we can go to the dentist's office and get this Barbara's records and check 'em against the teeth in the skull that the coroner's got stored away, an' then we can take that lease paper and check the handwriting, right, against that paper she signed when she got her Capitol Hill job?

Shane just keeps walking.

It's not as if we don't already know that these two girls were just one girl. One girl, two different people, two different men. One girl, and a lot of lies.

Back in the car, he weaves through mid-day traffic to get from 9th Street to Indiana Avenue. He crosses yellow lines to give the slip to a red Pontiac that's suddenly following him, not that Bobby's even seeing it.

Shane drops Bobby off at headquarters. He tells him where he can find Joe Barry's brandy glass and who he should take it to at fingerprints to make sure the work gets done right.

Shane guns the Plymouth's engine.

So who killed her?

She had a grand jury subpoena in her belongings. Did Kaufman kill her because she was about to go downtown and rat him out?

Willie Robinson, low-level numbers runner for the big-shot numbers mover – maybe a hired hit man?

Somebody else in her life the police don't even know about?

All of a sudden, Joe Barry doesn't look so sinister, compared to the alternatives.

Shane's just this close to making a clean getaway from headquarters when he sees the sergeant flagging him down.

The Sarge is saying Shane's off the case, for good this time. He's saying, Here you were told you were staying on this thing just to look at Joe Barry, then you went off and started chasing down these other leads, like you're going after Kaufman or something, and the Chief and Rector got wind of it.

Shane wonders how word got back to headquarters. *Maybe that landlady called to complain about me.*

The Sarge is saying, It's the Chief's case after all and he's had it with you, Chief says you're off of it and he's going after your badge.

Listen, the Sarge is saying, I could go to the mat for you on this one but it's not worth it. If you want me to try to keep you on this I will, I don't care, but it won't do any good.

Faces and names, theories, possibilities and eventualities are still speeding through Shane's brain, which hasn't quite caught onto the fact that none of it matters anymore.

The Sarge is still talking. Maybe it's a good thing if you take a step back, Sarge is saying. I can save your badge with the Chief and negotiate this down to a two-week suspension. Take it and run with it is what I'd do, and besides, you need the rest, you hear what I'm saying?

All Shane says back to the Sarge is, Tell Four-F Faye that we found Kaufman's girlfriend that he subpoenaed last year, she's rattling around in a box over at the morgue waiting for somebody to claim her, he can put that in his goddam grand jury.

****

Shane drives into Georgetown. On the way he has to dodge the red Pontiac again and he's thinking, where's Shiflett right now, he acts like I'm crazy, he'd see that Pontiac now for sure. Shane goes to Martin's on Wisconsin. It's just down the street from Joe Barry's place but he's not thinking about that.

He's remembering a winter night when his high school friends dragged him down to Martin's and he got drunk for the first time and ended up wandering out of the place and passing out in a snowdrift. His friends formed a besotted search party and saw his brown Oxfords poking out of the white mound. In another hour he would've died of exposure.

And saved everybody a lot of trouble later.

He gets a table around the corner from the bar, off the beaten path. A hunchbacked bus boy tries to make conversation, but Shane gives him a look and he takes off. He orders two martinis and sets one up across from himself. It stays untouched for the next six hours while on Shane's side of the table he drinks lunch and dinner. The place is pretty empty, since it's a holiday weekend, and all through the afternoon only a few people pass by him.

Anyone noticing him would think that they're seeing a guy waiting for his girl to come back. In a way, they'd be right.

He gets up four times. Twice to hit the head, once to get a third pack of Camels after running through two others, and once to ditch two empty pill bottles he doesn't want to have out on his table. No one talks to him. He talks to no one.

So, what do you think of before you let go?

He saw an article in Life magazine a month ago.

A photographer got to a bridge just as a jumper jumped. Got so close that the camera's flash must've seemed to the man to be some sort of celestial welcome. It was the damnedest thing. The man had pushed off and he was starting into free fall and he looked calm, unconcerned. He looked like a man who was doing nothing more consequential than stepping across a gap to board a train.

After sundown Shane goes to his car and heads up to the Shoreham Hotel. He knows Jake Kaufman has a suite there, maybe a whole floor, and he has an idea of what the man looks like, from an old mug shot that the Post published sometime back. He parks off to one side of the circular driveway at the lobby entrance and waits, fixing the mug shot in his mind and adding some years to the image. For reassurance he rubs the butt of his gun, holstered for now.

An hour passes, then most of another. There's a lot of traffic in and out of the hotel. Conventioneers with fold-up luggage, tourists with boxy cameras. But no racketeers with pinky rings.

This is a fool's errand. I'm staking out a guy and I don't even know if he's in town. I should just go back to the bar.

He swigs from a flask he has in the car. He reaches out for the radio dial but his hand lands on the Plymouth logo on the lighted dash. The word Plymouth appears against a big red circle *and any goddam ignoramus can see it looks like a rising sun and who the hell wants to ride around in a car and look down and see a goddam Japanese flag?*

Then a man appears by the bell captain's stand outside the hotel entrance. Illuminated by a spotlight over the driveway, he's the mug shot come to life, but grayer, a bit thicker, expensively suited. Shane jumps from his car and advances. He hears the bell captain say to the man, Can I get you a car, Mr. -- a car horn obliterates the name. No, thank you, the man says, in a voice of surprising gentleness. I have people right here.

Shane steps up the pace. He sees a small group coalesce around the man and thinks he hears someone say the word Jake, and the man pivots. Shane calls out, Mr. Kaufman! but a tour bus engine drowns out his voice. He moves to claim a position in the circle but the bus drives in front of him and stops, blocking his path, so Shane starts to go around the rear of it but it backs up.

By the time the bus gets out of his way, the man has gotten into a midnight blue Buick that's heading up Calvert Street towards the bridge.

Shane races back to his car and takes up the chase. He sees the Buick take a right to get down to Potomac Parkway. It's a treacherous, unlit road that follows the course of Rock Creek. In seconds he's going south on the parkway and sees his target's red taillights about a quarter-mile ahead. Over his shoulder he thinks he sees the red Pontiac again and he floors the gas pedal and takes his Plymouth up to 80.

The parkway has more curves than a European road course. Shane isn't so much driving his car as aiming it, aiming to the right of the coiling yellow line, aiming towards the red lights speeding into the distance, aiming in the direction of something he couldn't really describe if you asked him to.

The red Pontiac moves in on him from the right and he swerves left, then oncoming headlights send him into a half-spin back to the right and he screeches off the parkway and then goes into a full spin. His car turns wildly before it careens down a long slope.

His Plymouth tumbles downhill and his head hits the steering wheel, then the side window, then the ceiling and the side window again. Something metal hits his cheek and the taste of blood wells up in his mouth. He feels the car skidding and then it hits something, and he hears a crack!

and then the sound of heavy limbs banging on the car's undercarriage. His face is squeezed against the dome light, his head is throbbing, his ribs are aching.

And he's thinking, Maybe it's best if it all ends right now.

He fades in and out. He sees himself engulfed in orange. "Bless me father, for I have sinned," he says. He starts to feel searing heat all around him. He doesn't know if what he's experiencing are his last minutes in this life or his first in the next, he just knows to try to pray himself out of the worst of it. He says, "Oh my God, I am heartily sorry," over and over again, straining for the next line. As his legs start burning, he finally gets to, "for having offended thee, and I confess all my sins."

Then everything goes dark.

He never gets to the part about dreading the loss of heaven and the pain of hell.

June 1952

1

Shane Kinnock spends his first minutes of prolonged consciousness in three weeks transfixed by a calendar page on a pale green wall.

His face hurts. He touches his cheekbone and winces. His left arm is in a sling. An ID band has ridden up close to his right elbow.

The inside of his left wrist bears a stitched wound, a line as a straight as the left-right slash at the top of the J.

He hears a voice.

Right here, the voice is saying.

Look at me, Shane, goddammit. Look right here. Goddammit, stop staring off into space. You know I'm here, goddammit, you've known every goddam day I've been here.

Shane slowly turns his head. He thinks, it's the Sarge. But the Sarge never talks like that. He never takes the Lord's name in vain.

That's all he thinks.

Still. A couple of moments of clarity.

More follow. Sergeant Roncalli. *What are you doing here, Sarge?* Shane starts to say something to him, but holds off.

He sits up in bed, half-covered by a sheet.

He's wearing a sports shirt that he recognizes. He forces himself to remember why. He can see the shirt on the rack.

On the rack.

On the rack at.

On the rack at the Sears on Bladensburg Road.

He walked the shirt to the register and paid, what. Paid the four dollars to the clerk he always went to. Stanley, the clerk.

Under the bedsheet he sees white socks and chinos. He hears somebody say, We brought those over for you.

The Sarge is crouched next to the bed. Behind him is somebody else he knows.

Shiflett. It's Shiflett. He has a dog. Shiflett – Bobby. Bobby.

Shane says, So Bobby, why didn't you bring the dog with you? Then he remembers that something happened to the dog.

But Bobby's beaming and nodding his head. Maybe, he says, I shoulda brought Spike over here. Ya know, he just showed back up. Don't know how he ever found his way back home to me. And the landlady says she's gonna let me keep him.

Shane doesn't react. He's looking to the end of the bed for a clipboard. He wants to see his chart, but it isn't there. His mouth is dry and he feels weak but there's no intravenous stand in the room, no fluids. He strains to see if a nurse might be passing by the window of his room door, but chicken wire is embedded in the glass and he can't see much of anything.

He asks, What kind of a damn hospital is this?

The Sarge looks over at Bobby, then back to Shane. We've told you, Sarge says. We've told you before, you're at St. Eve's.

Shane starts to say, there's no St. Eve's Hospital in D.C. Tell me Gallinger Hospital, tell me Casualty, tell me Georgetown or G.W. But don't tell me St. Eve's, there's no St. Eve's Hospital.

Then it comes to him. He said St. E's.

St. Elizabeth's.

St. Elizabeth's Hospital for the Insane.

So, Shane asks, Why am I in St. Elizabeth's?

The Sarge backs away from the bed.

You try, the Sarge says to Bobby, who comes closer to the bed. Bobby says, Shane, you had a bad accident.

I remember, Shane says. Even though all of what he remembers of an accident could be fit into the time it takes for a blinding light to flash in a nightmare. So why, he asks, didn't they take me to a regular hospital?

They did, Bobby says, they took you to Georgetown. That's who stitched up your face and fixed your arm up.

Which took all of what, an hour?

Right. But then you started talkin'. And don't take this wrong and all, but you started talkin' crazy-like. Sayin' you heard voices, you were seein' things, talkin' about doin' yourself in.

Shane just remembers a crater with no top or bottom, no way out.

So how long, he asks, did that go on for?

The accident was, what, in the early mornin' of the first of the month. So, all that went on for about a week. Then Georgetown couldn't keep you no more. You kept gettin' hold of sharp stuff and so they sent you here.

Shane tries to orient himself.

I know my name and my age and I remember my rank and serial number. Truman's the President. It's – June 17th. Which means, July fourth isn't far off.

He's a 10-year-old all over again, bending over the Post, looking at the standings and trying to find where the Nats are sitting at the season's mid-point.

He remembers Erin. He remembers his mom. He remembers Raymond – yes, right, Raymond.

I see eyes staring at me from unplumbed caverns.

Emily. Emily. Bones in a pile.

Shane remembers Emily.

He's always remembered her.

He turns back to Bobby and the Sarge. So, he asks, what brought me around?

It happened just like *that*, Bobby says. You just, y'know, came back, it was – amazin'.

Shane knows there has to be more to it. He looks to the Sarge, and the Sarge lightly swats Bobby and tells him, Just say the words. Say the words, Shiflett, there's nothing wrong with them. Electroshock therapy, Shane. They gave you five rounds of it and the fifth was just two days ago.

Somebody strapped my ass on a table and shot electricity through plugs in my head like I was a Frankenstein monster. What the fuck. So who said they could do that to me?

Sarge says, your father did. Your father had to sign the paperwork.

He was real upset, Bobby says, seeing you the way you were, so he said they can do it to you. Didn't think he had no choice.

Shane's thinking he should feel angry, but he doesn't. He wonders why not. He doesn't really feel anything. He says, So my old man's been around here, huh?

Yeah, Bobby says. Your father's been here – a buncha times.

The old man's actually come around.

Shane presses his hands against his head and a memory emerges. Erin at age 10, sitting in a hospital with something bad, and one of Raymond's flunkies sitting by her bedside for three days while Raymond toured somewhere with a bunch of other Congressmen. From then on Erin's private nickname for Raymond was "fair-weather father."

Now, all of a sudden, Raymond is Florence Nightingale. How did that happen?

What's Raymond been saying to himself about me as he walked out of here?

My boy, I bet he says. My boy.

My boy, he says, my flesh and blood, and he's no better able to manage life than that madman Matt Barry.

Bobby puts his hand on Shane's arm and says, You should know, every time your pop's been here he's left cryin' over you bein' here, and he's been spendin' more time at the chapel here than the chaplain does.

Shane replies, You've already lied to me once, when you said I came around on my own, Sarge had to tell me they zapped me. Now you're laying it on too thick. You'll do anything to keep me from falling backwards again.

Then. Wait a second now, Shane says to Bobby. How would you even know how often my father's been here?

Bobby looks down at his feet: 'Cause I been here every day.

Every day?

Every day.

Shane manages to twist his features into something resembling a weak smile. So, he asks, who else has come around here?

The Sarge, here, of course. And your landlady, what's her name, Almeta. And that reporter fella, Bentley, he came around once or twice. He wrote up a nice article on you, put it on the front page of the Post, talked about the crash and all. Made you out to be a real hero.

That must've been a slow news day.

Shane wants to ask about somebody else, but holds back. Ah, fuck it, he says, just like that. What about --

"Oh, and that Claire girl you told me about. She came by at least once, sure she did."

At least once. Which means possibly more than once. Shane still has enough juice in him to care about how many times a beautiful woman bothered to come around for him.

Shane turns back to the Sarge. I'm assuming whatever they did, it jolted the crazy shit out of my brain. I'm also assuming there's a price I'm going to have to pay.

Just some memory loss, Shane. That's what I'm hearing, but supposedly it'll all come back. And from what I saw of you in the last few weeks, if it comes back anytime, it'll be too soon. And they say there's some risk you might go backwards. But hell, any of us in this job is always just a stone's throw from the crazy house, know what I mean?

Shane sits further on the bed and looks at his watch. Half-past four. On the outside, in his old life, he'd be one hour and two drinks into his own time. The thought passes quickly.

So Sarge, what'd they say went wrong with me?

We talked to your doctor here last week, and he said all this headshrinker mumbo-jumbo, about melancholy or something. Like as if you were a broad or something, all sad and not able to handle anything. Me personally, I think it had to do with all those pills you were taking. I don't want to say I told you so.

So don't.

Shane has an image of empty pill bottles on a barroom table.

So what else have I missed, he asks them. And right away he's sorry he did, because for the next half-hour they insist on telling him.

Willie Robinson's still in jail.

Joe Barry's riding so high, some people even think Eisenhower will pick him for the number two job if he gets the nomination next month.

The Chief is working in secret with Faye on the Park murder and nobody else knows what's going on with it.

Rumor has it that Faye has two grand juries working at the same time. One has the Rose murder, the other all his government and police corruption cases. And both have terms that end on July second, and indictments will come out the next day. And some heads will be rolling.

And Jake Kaufman was named "Humanitarian of the Year" by the D.C. Chamber of Commerce, on account of all the money he's given to all the boys' clubs in the city.

Shane's responses are a series of, okay, that's nice, that's interesting.

All this news has as much connection to his life as a Times dispatch on a coup in South America.

The Sarge talks about Nickens. About how he's gotten to know the man.

The man's just so *smart*, the Sarge is saying. Knows everything there is to know about birds, for instance. Just yesterday he was talking about how the birds that live the longest are the ones that don't stray outside their limits, and there's a bird in South America. This bird never flies outside this certain area and it turns out the area is in the exact boundary of this earth plate that's thousands of feet under the ocean, and the bird just knows instinctively that's where he should stay.

Shane knows he must be getting his mind back because he's been able to focus on all this nonsense and keep it in his head.

Sarge goes to his notebook. He actually wrote down the name of Nickens's fucking boundary-observing bird, like it's a street lead on a murder witness. Nazca boobie, Sarge says painstakingly and proudly. That Nickens is a smart man, the Sarge says again, you can take that to the bank.

Shane says Sarge, you're just making conversation now, you're rambling, and the Sarge says, No, I'm just saying he's a smart man and all.

It's as if the Sarge is trying to get a rise out of Shane, telling him how smart Nickens is, doing anything to bring Shane's spirit to the surface.

Shane doesn't go along with the plan. He just asks, Whatever happened to Joe Barry's brandy glass. And the Sarge tells him that Nickens is taking care of testing it, the man's his own crime lab and he can get results quicker than anybody.

From the way the Sarge is talking, Shane wouldn't be surprised to find out that Haynes Nickens has taken Shane's desk at work, moved into Shane's room at the boarding house, and is screwing Shane's ex-wife every night on Shane's fold-out hassock bed.

Not that any of that would really bother Shane right now.

Bobby chimes in. The Nats are playin' the Indians tonight and they're goin' up against Bob Feller. Maybe we can start bringin' you the Post every mornin' so you can follow the team.

Shane says, That's nice. And no.

Then Sarge takes a final shot. Senator Kuykendall's presidential campaign is lagging way behind. So, he put on some hearings on the Park murder case just to try to get his mug back on the TV. And he charged the department with dragging their feet on it, so the Chief went up there and blamed you, said you went off course too many times, but he said the case is under control now you're off it.

Shane picks at some lint on the frayed blanket that covers his lap. Good for the Chief, is all he says. He pulls on a thread and the satin edge starts to unravel.

I just have one question, he says. What have I been doing with my days here?

The Sarge says, They have you doing stuff during the day with the patients on the floor. There's a guy across the hall who thinks he's Jesus Christ, just stays in his room and yells out the beatitudes and the Lord's Prayer and all that all day. Another guy down the hall who has a thing for the King of England. Woman across the way, only words she says are alpha and omega. Then there's a lot that don't do much of anything, just sit and stare for hours. It's a fun crowd you're with here, Shane.

Bobby says, Come on, Shane, let's take you out for a drive, we can get the doctor on duty here to give us a day pass.

No, Shane says, I think I'll just stay here with my friends.

He walks to the door with Bobby and the Sarge. You know, Bobby says, we were hopin' that electric stuff would bring you all the way back around, maybe it still will.

I guess it gave me back my rationality, Shane answers. And the rational thing for me to do is to stay right here.

Spend enough time at sea, they say, and the land becomes an alien place.

The Sarge tells Bobby, Run up ahead for a second. Then Sarge turns to Shane: I want you to know, that boy saved your life. He tracked you down to the Shoreham that night and he saw you peel off after somebody, then he followed you down the Parkway and he saw you crash. He pulled you out of your car just before it blew up, Shane, and then he got you to the hospital. And on top of all that, he laid just enough of a story on the doctors that none of them ever thought to check to see if you were drunk.

Yes indeed, that boy saved your life.

Shane stares at Sarge. Considering my current frame of mind, Shane finally says, I don't know whether to thank Shiflett or kill him.

He pivots and goes back to bed.

2

Days pass.

He eats and drinks what the hospital gives him, in baby portions. When the time comes for him to push it all out of himself he usually manages to rise from his bed but sometimes he doesn't bother. One morning he rolls over and a stench wafts over him and for a moment he pulls the bedsheets around himself in shame.

Soon he revels in his newfound, ordered world of stink and slumber.

People – nurses, doctors, orderlies, others – come in and out of his room and he pays them no mind.

Every few days he trades in a Sears-bought shirt and a pair of Hecht's-bought pants for another Sears-bought shirt and pair of Hecht's-bought pants, and he never for a second stops to think about who's washing all his clothes and getting them all back over to him.

The only times in the day when he's not sleeping are when he's trying to sleep, and it's during those times that he's thinking about everything but sleep. Everything he's ever known, coming at him faster than anything ever has. In his wakefulness his hands work constantly, clenching and unclenching, clenching and unclenching, as if they decided on their own to clutch at something that the rest of him didn't even know existed.

His one constant companion is a light beam. Most of the time it's a pinpoint in the distance, but when it flares it's as if he's seeing a flashlight in a mineshaft. And he runs to it. A few words from a poem – Tennyson? – camp in his head: Not of the sunlight, not of the moonlight, not of the starlight. After it, follow it, follow the gleam.

Follow the gleam.

He follows the gleam. He has it in his hands. The gleam will take him to a place where he'll feel no pain.

He can't figure out why he always ends up slowing down, opening up his hands, retreating back to the darkness.

Night after night, way past midnight and well past the time when Jesus Christ across the hall has finally worn himself out from his all-day line readings of the Sermon on the Mount, Shane stares at the ceiling – his ceiling, now – and tries to think of his thoughts as if they were sheep. But in his illusion, they aren't leaping gaily over a meadow fence but racing madly in a pack in front of him and he's trying to catch them and wrestle them into high grass and tie them down and if he catches enough of them then maybe he'll be able to get himself some rest.

Out of thousands of these thoughts, finally only one submits to his will, straining against his bindings. The thought is this:

Everything I'm experiencing makes sense, I'm not seeing strange things like I was before, I'm not hearing strange things like I was before, and if I can just take the world as it is long enough, I can. I can. I can get out of this bed.

Then the thought gets away from him.

****

Shane hears something scrape across his floor. He tries to keep his eyes closed. He feels something rustle against his bed and he hears soft breathing. He rolls over and faces away from what he hears.

Outside its nighttime. The streetlight is shining through the window behind him and on the opposite wall, as it appears every night, is his shadow, an inert lump. Now it's been joined by another shadow, a moving, dark specter.

He stays still. He stares at the other shadow.

He opens his eyes, rolls over quickly and convulses.

Aggh! Why are you here!

The Jewish-looking woman in black is sitting next to him.

Get away from me! Get away!

Please, she says, be calm. I didn't mean to startle you. The people at the front desk let me come back. I've been wanting to see you.

Shane takes his hands out from under the covers and looks at them, then pulls down his blanket and looks at his arms, his shirt, his pants. He puts both hands on his head, his face, his chest, then wraps his right arm around himself. Trying to get a last grasp on reality, in case it's just about to leave him forever.

It's alright, the woman says. She starts to reach out to him but then pulls back.

The two sit in silence for a time.

He asks, Who are you?

She settles back into a folding chair that she's brought over to the bedside.

I'm Leah Rosenblum, she says.

Leah?

Leah. I'm Emma's sister – Emily's.

Shane rubs his eyes. Why are you here?

Why do you think I'm here?

I can see right through her, to the wall behind her, and all the walls behind that wall. What's wrong with me?

You were following me, he says. *When was that?*

I was. Please forgive me. I came down here a few weeks back, and I found out you were handling my sister's case. Someone in your office told me where I could find you. I kept trying to summon up the courage to talk to you but I just couldn't. And then, your accident.

My accident.

Yes. On the day that I finally set my mind on getting this over with, I found out what had happened to you. And then it took me some time to track you down here. As you can imagine, this isn't easy for me – I hope you don't mind.

No, I don't mind, Shane says. He slumps back on his pillow and breathes out.

He's remembering reading about her, Emily's kid sister on the refugee boat.

How old are you, he asks.

Seventeen.

Seventeen and she could pass for 30. She rests her lands on her lap. They're the hands of a dishwasher, lined and weathered. Shane looks around her chair. She's brought nothing with her, no purse, nothing.

He says, You're living in –

New York.

How did you know to come down to Washington?

Ever since Emma came down here, I would often go to my library to see the Washington papers and read stories about people she was meeting. One day I saw her on the front page and I thought, she must be involved in something very important. Then I saw the headline.

What did the picture look like?

She was sitting with some people in a restaurant. And she looked so radiant. Like she was on to the world and the world didn't know it. Have you seen the picture that I'm talking about?

Yes, Shane says. Oh yes, I've seen the picture.

He thinks, it's long gone now, lost somewhere.

He's focusing on something outside himself. He's listening to every word this girl is saying and how she's saying it. German accent, with a trace of British.

Some people, Shane thinks, they change their accent, if they want to get past who they were before. Some people – Emily. Some people like Emily do that – Emily did that.

This girl hasn't done that, she hasn't changed her accent.

Leah's hands remain in repose. Her right hand is cupped and it's holding her left hand, also cupped. She isn't stroking her chin, or worrying over the crease in her coarse skirt, or working away at beads.

He looks at his own hands and he's surprised to see they're at rest.

So, he says, why didn't you come down sooner? Your sister was missing for a year.

I saw an article in the Washington Post about you a couple of weeks ago, so I know you're a good detective. I'm figuring that you've already tracked down how my sister and I were raised. How we separated once we were here in the U.S.

I know the story.

Well, I loved my sister. But five years ago she came down here and I had to stay where I was. She made her choice at a time when I didn't have the luxury of making one. I was placed with strangers and Emma went on to a bigger life.

Did you ever hear from her?

She would write to me every couple of months or so, generally. But long silent stretches would sometimes go by.

Would you ever see her?

Once in a while. I know that for some years she'd come back to New York every weekend.

To do what?

To dance. She had ambitions in show business and she'd get herself chorus jobs on the weekends, through some connection she had.

Shane thinks, some connection. Jake – Jake Kaufman. He remembers Claire saying that Emily would disappear at the end of the work week, and she could never reach her on the weekends. Now this explains it.

So anyway, Leah goes on, maybe two or three times she called me when she was in town. I'd see her dance in Manhattan and after the shows we'd get together for dinner.

You and she. What about the family you lived with, the…

The Siegels. She never asked about them. It was just the two of us, she didn't want to see anyone else.

Did you ever wonder why that was?

Mr. Kinnock, I may be just 17 but I've seen a lot and I can figure things out. The Siegels and I represented something that she wanted to put very far behind her. I think the only reason she kept in touch with me at all was that she may have felt guilty about leaving me.

What did you think when you stopped hearing from her?

I figured she'd finally just decided to completely abandon everything about her past, once and for all. And I'm ashamed to say this but I just thought, good riddance. That's what I thought.

You're very direct for a young girl.

There's no reason not to be. And I'm not so young a girl.

So why are you here?

I'm here to see if I can help in some way. I'm here to find out more about her if there's more to know. Mainly, I'm here to make sure she's not forgotten.

She looks right at Shane and her eyes never wander.

I thought, Leah says, about her being left on that hill. As important as I believed that she was here, it seems that she meant very little to some people here.

Not to me, Shane says, and looks away.

Leah Rosenblum came to Washington for the truth and she's entitled to get it all. So he tells her everything he's learned about her sister and he holds nothing back.

He tells about going through her sister's bones, about first figuring out what her sister's name was, back when he thought she only had one name and not three. He tells her about how Willie Robinson got fingered for the killing. He tells her about her sister's double identity, and muses about the thousands of small deceits that maintaining it must have required. He tells her about Joe Barry and her sister's affair with him, and Jake Kaufman and whatever you'd call what her sister had with him.

Yes indeed, he makes sure to tell her all about Jake Kaufman.

He finishes, expecting some reaction from her, but her expression doesn't change.

I just have one question for you, she says. I've only been here a few weeks, but I can see that Washington is a very small town compared to New York. How do you think she was able to get away with this, moving around as two different people?

Washington, he says, isn't a small town. It's a bunch of small towns, and they don't overlap. Rich white folks, poor white trash. Capitol Hill. The Negroes in the slums, the Negroes in what we call the Gold Coast. West of Rock Creek Park, east of Rock Creek Park. The bureaucrats, the diplomats, east of the Anacostia – there's even more small towns than that here. If you're willing to make the effort, you can cross borders between the towns. But most people never even try.

He hears stirring from Jesus's room across the hall. To the limited extent that Shane's imagination has been operating in the recent past it's been fixated on this man, envisioning him as swaddled in hospital green, a bedpan for a crown of thorns.

He studies Leah's face. Finally he says, Is that all you're going to ask? I've given you all this about your sister. Don't you feel like you've been let down by her?

No, but I see you do.

She leans forward. Mr. Kinnock, you must remember that for eight years, in Germany and China, my sister had no life. Can you blame her for wanting to live as full a life as possible once she was given the chance? Even if that life had to spill over into another one?

What about her working at the strip club?

Leah shakes her head. Think, Mr. Kinnock, what else was going on in her life when she was doing that?

She was working.

And going to school in the evenings at a university. Remember, there was no law to help my sister get through college. She had no family to go to and the Siegels couldn't have helped her. And there was no one else, at least not when she first came here.

Before I just told you, how much did you know about all the things that were going on in her life?

I knew about the Congressman, yes. Maybe not all the details, but I knew she was involved with a man who was smart and funny and handsome and she thought he was going to be President someday.

Leah's face glows at the rare memory of her big sister sharing a romantic secret with her.

And, she continues, I knew about Mr. Kaufman. Again, not all the details, but I knew she had a friend who reminded her of our father.

Your father?

Yes, our father. A man who filled our house with strength. Until we lost him.

What else did she say about Kaufman?

That he was a successful businessman, that he gave a lot of money to poor people and synagogues. That he worshiped the ground she walked on, and that he took good care of her. When you put it all like that, her choices don't sound so reckless or decadent, do they?

But Kaufman is a killer and a gangster.

Sir, my sister saw too much for violence at too young an age to get close to someone that she knew to traffic in it.

How could she not have known?

Leah looks away, for the first time.

My sister, she finally says, had a capacity for self-delusion. We all had it, that's how we avoided insanity. You had to make yourself believe that you were going to go on living for years even though in one part of you, you knew you could get exterminated at any moment. You had to look at your captors and believe that at heart they were merciful people and would spare you even though in one part of you, you knew they were monsters and probably wouldn't. The only way we could go on living a meaningful life, day by day, was to struggle to see the good in people.

She turns back to Shane: That might be one reason why I am what I am now.

She fingers her rough, artless blouse.

You're Orthodox, he says.

Actually, Hasidic. And one of the tenets of our faith is that God is in everything. Literally everything.

Your sister abandoned all the things she knew. She changed her name, changed it again, lived out her years craving power and attention. You've taken your life the opposite way, made it more simple, more Jewish. Yet you two had the same experience.

I live my life in this way to honor my culture. What happened to my family and my people happened to us because we were Jewish, so I believe what I believe and I dress as I dress because that's who I am. But my sister made different choices for the very reason that her experience was *not* the same as mine.

How?

Sir, when we were interred in China I was only eight and she was 15. The Japanese soldiers did things to 15-year-old young women that they didn't do to eight-year-old girls. So, if my sister spent the rest of her life trying to outrun the person who she once was, it was because she was trying to outrun the pain that person suffered. I have to respect that. No, I have to cherish that.

Leah touches Shane's hand lightly: You do, too.

She wears no makeup, no nail polish, and her form is hidden beneath her shapeless garments. She has her sister's features but resembles her only in the way that a bird without plumage resembles another of the same species.

Jesus can be heard across the hall. Judge ye not that ye not be judged, he's saying in a bullfrog growl, over and over.

Shane starts to cry, for the first time, maybe, ever. How did I ever get here, he says. Why was I so weak?

Mr. Kinnock, Leah says, strength has nothing to do with it. I know all about you. About the losses in your past. About your time in the war. About the things you've seen as a police officer.

You know all that? *Jesus*, he thinks, *Bentley's Post article must've done a number on me.*

And I know the ways that men can find to push things like that behind them, the habits they can fall into, and the way that they can end up making things even worse. What's surprising isn't that this happened to you. What's surprising is that you staved it off for this long.

You sound like you know something about this.

I've gone through what you're going through. In the places I've been, you won't find anyone who thinks they're the Messiah. But you would be prone to finding old women walking naked up and down the halls reciting from the Talmud. And in every other way the atmosphere is the same.

So, how did you find your way back?

With all respect, sir, the question should be, how am I finding my way back? And the answer is that there's no answer. The malady that you and I have suffered from is as mysterious in its comings and goings as any force of nature. It's possible, just possible, that it began to leave me at about the time when I heard a story about a sermon that one of our Hasidic masters, a rabbi named Levi Yitzhak, is said to have given on the eve of Yom Kippur more than a hundred years ago.

Please, tell me.

Well, it's said that Rabbi Yitzhak stood next to the ark. And he raised his head to ask God's forgiveness for the sins that he and his congregation had committed, as is our custom. But he then said, God, in the past year we've caused no deaths, we've brought no plagues, no earthquakes, no floods upon the earth. *You've* done these things, God, not us. Perhaps you should ask for *our* forgiveness. And he paused for a moment to wipe a tear from his eyes. Then he continued: But given that you are God and we are mere mortals, we have no choice but to pray. And only then did the Rabbi begin the service.

I haven't been to church in years. What does that mean to me?

Everyone has to figure that out for themselves, she says abruptly. All I can say to you is that things happen. The mystery of existence is inexplicable. We're here, other people aren't. Do what you have to do with your life without blaming yourself for going on living. Without blaming God for what you think he did to you. Without blaming my sister, or anyone else, for not having been what you would have had them be. Without blaming the present for not living up to some starry-eyed view you might have of the past. My Hasidic faith teaches that past, present and future are all one. But one thing I know about the past that sets it apart is that it can never be any better or worse than what it was. Which to you means, make your peace with it.

He lies back and looks up at the ceiling. I once had a wife, he murmurs. She was named Maureen. We grew up together, we went to school together, she was everything I could've wanted. Then I went to college because my family could afford it, and she didn't because her family couldn't. And from the time I saw her again, all I wanted to do was change her. When she didn't need changing. Then I went into the war and when I came back it was too late. Nothing could've made me happy. I had a son, too. His name was – I called him Buddy. Because that's what he was to me.

The thought is stark and simple, stripped of complication, and it scares him.

The room is still. Shane wonders if Leah heard anything he just said. Then she speaks, softly: We have a saying, Mr. Kinnock. The saying is, When God gave us the Torah, he gave us not only the words, but the blanks in between the words. And God has left it up to us to make a worthwhile life out of those blanks.

A worthwhile life from the blanks between words in a holy book. He's never heard anything like this and he's trying, straining, to understand it and he can't. It's too abstract, he'd have to see it play out in real people.

The growling from Jesus's room across the hall has ceased. For a few moments, Shane experiences silence in a way he never has before, not as the absence of sound but the absence of everything.

Leah gets up. I came here to help, she says, and to make sure my sister would be remembered. I have faith in you, that you'll do what you need to do. I can leave content.

Where have you been staying?

With friends of friends. And I need to get back home. Back to what I'm used to.

Wait, Shane says. One more thing. We have your sister's remains, her body. Do you want to take custody of it?

She hesitates. Then: No, first find out who took the life out of it. It won't rest easily until then, anyway. Then, just make sure it's taken good care of.

He smiles wanly. I will, he says. The Irish, you might know, they spend their lives thinking about death and they plan years in advance for moments like this. In fact, there's an old joke that when an Irishman proposes marriage, the question he asks the girl isn't, will you marry me? It's, would you like to be buried with my people?

Leah laughs: Buried with your people, that's good. Remember that.
What?

I said, That's good, I'll remember that.

She comes closer. Godspeed, Mr. Kinnock. I know from your story that you've done many courageous things in your life. But your bravest day will be the one when you get up and walk out of here on your own.

Is there anything else?

He looks down at his sports shirt, which is wet and wrinkled and stained, and in that moment thinks of Adam in the garden, embarrassed by his nakedness.

He looks up to say something to Leah. She's gone.

****

He closes his eyes again. No sheep are racing about in the meadows of his mind.

He sleeps for an hour, maybe less. Careless, dreamless sleep. Something raises him from the bed. He stabs his bare left foot towards the cold floor and then makes contact. He struggles to swing his body around to the point where he's on the edge of the bed and both feet are joined. He eases down, takes a step, then another, then another. His breathing is labored but he keeps on, until he falls against the pale-green wall across from his bed and braces himself on his right shoulder. He takes off his sling and slowly rotates his left arm – no pain.

The calendar is right in front of him.

He reaches out, rips off the June 30 page, crumples it and throws it to the floor. Then he rips the whole calendar off the wall and throws it across the room. He leans his head against the wall and starts to laugh. He laughs and beats his hands gently against the wall, and then he starts to cry, and he keeps on laughing and crying until a nurse comes in the room and asks him if there's something wrong, and he thinks, no, there's nothing wrong, for the first time in a long time there's absolutely nothing wrong.

She tells him he'll have to go back to his bed.

And he tells her: "That's not my bed. *That's not my bed!*"

For a moment he can't say any more, because he's just heard his own voice calling to him from a place that he wants to get to as fast as he can.

"That's not my bed, and I'm never going back to it. I'll sleep on the floor here, if I even want to sleep."

He picks up the crumpled calendar pages and hands them to her. "If you're looking to make yourself useful," he says, "you might as well start drafting my discharge papers right now. Because a doctor's going to be on you for them tomorrow and you're not going to want to be holding things up."

3

Shane snaps open the morning Post and starts to go through it just as he did when he was a kid stretched out on his living room floor, learning to read by newsprint. Back to front, light to heavy. Easing himself into the world.

In his hands, crackling to his touch, it's the best bargain around. Everything that you'd want to know, reduced to 30-odd rectangles, all for just a nickel. Or in the case of this particular newspaper for nothing at all, since he just fished it out of a trash can in the St. E's waiting area.

First, he goes to the comics, then on to sports – the Nats are fading but at least they're above .500 – then skips past the ladies' section to the front page, and the story that he knew all along was there, but wanted to get to on his own terms.

Tuesday, July 1, 1952

GRAND JURY PROBES STRIKE FEAR INTO D.C., CAREERS AND LIVES ARE ON THE LINE
By Bran Bentley, Staff Reporter

All of Washington's institutions, everything from Congress to the local police, soon stand to be shaken up by grand juries led by one ambitious prosecutor, Jeremiah Norris Faye.

Mr. Faye has his sights trained on three targets: local police corruption, Congressional graft, and the gambling operations of local businessman Jake Kaufman. On top of that, MPD Chief Moran is saying that he expects a separate grand jury to charge one Willie Robinson with the murder of pretty Congressional staffer Emily Rose in Rock Creek Park.

Whatever decisions these two grand juries make, they'll need to reach them soon. Their terms end tomorrow, with indictments to be decided on Thursday.

In the meantime official Washington sits and waits nervously for what's being called "Indictment Day."

Shane scans the columns for a reference to his father's civil rights bill. He doesn't see one and figures, it's already stale news, the old man got it all the way through Congress and Shane wasn't even aware of it.

And he can't help but wonder if he'll be half a beat behind the world for as long as he lives.

The name "Kinnock" jumps from an article at the bottom of the page. It's a short item, bylined again to Bentley. But it isn't about Raymond or his bill.

HERO DETECTIVE TO RETURN HOME

Shane Kinnock, the Metropolitan homicide detective who nearly perished in a flaming car crash while pursuing a suspected criminal down Potomac Parkway, returns home today from an undisclosed facility where he's been undergoing treatment for an injury he suffered in the accident.

Some facility, Shane says to himself. Some hero.

"*Jesus*, pal, could you be a little less fucking obvious about reading all your press clippings?"

Nobody would ever keep records of these things, but it can't be very often that the St. E's waiting room has been visited by a Washington Post reporter wearing a Brooks Brothers suit and smoking a French cigarette from a holder.

Bran Bentley snatches up Shane's duffel bag and whisks him outside as if they're both about to be chased down by orderlies with nets.

"I still don't know," Shane says, "how it happened that you're my ride out of this hell hole."

"I called over here, pal, and the girl on the desk said you'd be getting out soon, so I told them to tell you to sit tight."

Gratuitous acts of charity aren't in Bran Bentley's daily playbook. Sure enough, as they walk through the parking lot, Bran casually mentions that his editor has said he's only one big scoop from being nominated for a Pulitzer. "By the way, that story you were going to give me, about the Chief and obstruction of justice in that lagoon murder. Isn't that pretty much set to run with?"

Shane stares silent, he knows Bentley won't press the point right now. It's his first and only windfall from his crack-up.

Bentley guns the engine of his Jaguar and peels out of the parking lot. "You know," he says, "I did a nice piece on you a few weeks ago. I saved you a copy if you want to read it."

"I already lived it. I don't need to read it. But back in the hospital a girl came to see me and she'd read it. She made it sound like you really dug into my past."

"Dug into your past? Not so sure about that one, pal. I thought it was pretty bare-bones." He swerves to avoid an ice cream truck sporting July Fourth bunting. "So," he says, "how're you feeling?"

"Like, how does the phrase go?" Shane remembers reading something from a writer about his own nervous breakdown – Fitzgerald, of course. "I feel," he says, "like a cracked plate that's been glued up but still has to be handled carefully. Sound familiar?"

"Can't say it does, pal."

A woman with a laundry basket on her shoulder is starting to cross the street but jumps back at the command of Bentley's horn. "So, where do you think you'll end up working?"

"Back at MPD," Shane says. "Where else?"

"I heard you had an insubordination suspension."

"I think it passed while I was, how do you put it, confined. And if I'm not mistaken, that's called a concurrent sentence." Shane smiles. Just yesterday, he couldn't have come up with a line like that.

"Listen, do you think it's a good idea to go back to a police job? What with your frame of mind and all?"

"I saw a doctor. Showed me the blotchy pictures, asked me all the usual questions, whether I'd ever wanted to screw my mother."

"Tough one."

"I got a pass there, said I never really got to know her."

"Nice save."

"As far as the doc's concerned I'm clean. I'm probably the only guy you know in this town who's certifiably sane."

Bentley says nothing, just keeps driving.

"Wait," Shane says. "Turn around, will you? Make a U-turn up here."

"Downtown is down this way."

"Please, just turn around. It'll be worth it."

Shane directs him back to St. E's to an overlook. "Let's get out," he says.

They walk to a bluff above the Anacostia River. Before them is the whole panorama of the city.

Shane's never stood here before but he's been hearing, for as long as he can remember, about the view from this vantage point close by St. E's, the place where nobody ends up unless they've horribly lost their bearings.

He gazes at the scene and reaches his hands out in front of him. The Capitol to the right, the Washington Monument just inches to the left, the Lincoln Memorial a few inches further over, all three sharing a small space near the crescent of two blue rivers. He couldn't be more transfixed if he'd just stumbled from a tour bus and was seeing it all for the first time.

"Is there a more beautiful city," he says, "anywhere in the world?"

Bentley puts his hands on his hips and sniffs. "Sure, probably" he says. "Paris definitely. Rome maybe. Hell, I don't know, I've heard the broads in Havana are amazing. Can we go now?"

"In a second."

"You sure you're all right?"

"Never better."

It's as if the distant, supernatural light beam that he was seeing before, the light he was drawn to and repelled by and finally fled from, has somehow dispersed itself and is now bestowing a glow on everything he sees.

Back in the car, they turn back and head downtown. They pass a cop in full uniform, right down to the white gloves, jumping off his traffic box to flag down a weaving car. A bunch of Negro women in maid outfits stand at a bus stop. One's holding out her hand to the others, showing off a ring. A swarthy man in overalls is pushing a vegetable cart towards Eastern Market, leaving a trail of bouncing tomatoes.

As they approach Capitol Hill from the south Shane says, "Take a left up here."

Bentley shakes his head but takes the turn.

Above the billowy elms that line the street Shane can see the white dome getting bigger through Bentley's windshield. The building is disgorging clusters of men in twos and threes. Congressmen fresh from a vote, Shane guesses.

He looks for a familiar face topped by a ski slope of hair but doesn't see him.

"You know," he says, "Washington's the only town we have that's based completely on an idea. That's the whole reason why this town got dug out of the swamp. Some of those guys there may believe in the idea, maybe it's the first thing they think about every morning. But they don't make this city run. It's the …it's…"

He's just this close to being able to get out what he's trying to say but he can't, not quite yet.

And this is all it is. That it's guys like he and Bentley that really run the city. The people on the streets they just saw. The counterman at Save-Mor Drug, Eddie something. The Jewish guy, Juley, who takes all the orders at Central Liquor. The guys who work in the folding room up there on the Hill alongside Willie Robinson. The tall, friendly guy with the moustache who runs the men's department at Hecht's and all the night watchmen who walk the floors in all the dreary office buildings.

"It's all of us," Shane says. "We run this place. And there's thousands of us nobody talks about."

Bentley puts his Jaguar into a spin to get it back on course. "I'd like to be part of your picture," he says, "but I don't have anything to do with running this town. I just sit back and if I see one of the guys who really run it do a good pratfall, then I get a laugh and I write up a story about it. And if I see enough pratfalls then I get a bureau chief job out of it, and maybe down the line I get to run a paper or a magazine somewhere. End of story, literally."

They pull up to a light. "So, if you're looking to make your bones on pratfalls," Shane says, "why aren't you covering Joe Barry's big one?"

"Because I didn't see it," Bentley says, as if that's all there is to it.

Traffic is heavy at mid-day. Bentley turns on the radio but all it yields is soap operas and westerns and he snaps it off.

"Tell me how this goes," Shane says to him. "You went through the war just like I did. Why didn't something happen to you like it happened to me?"

Bentley doesn't pause to reflect. "Some guys are just wired to take things hard. I'm not."

A black Nash comes up hard behind them and stays on their bumper. Shane turns around, but the Nash drops back a bit and he can't get a good look at the driver.

"Geez, Bran, there's a guy following us."

"Please, Christ's sake, don't start with that again. I heard before about you with the cars following you all around town."

Bentley pulls the car to a stop in front of the Florida Avenue boarding house and Shane gets out. Almeta is on the porch fanning herself. She rushes up and throws her arms around him. "Praise Jesus," she says, "just a month ago I thought I'd never see you again."

Almeta pulls back. In her right hand is a clipped newspaper article with Shane's picture. "Here's a pen, Mr. Shane, please sign it for me. Gotta say, I didn't have no idea I had a hee-ro living in my house."

Shane still can't remember much about what happened to him, but he knows it involved a lot of drinking and a half-cocked idea about rousting Jake Kaufman. He doesn't see anything hee-roic in any of that. Still, he signs the article in the margin.

A couple of Negro kids, a boy and a girl, come up to him with scraps of paper, parents hovering nearby. Shane turns around to Bentley. "I didn't know your rag had such a circulation." He signs the papers and runs his hand over the boy's head.

A young man in a dark suit appears from behind the Negro boy. Shane thinks he's the man he just saw getting out of a black Nash parked in the middle of the block, but he isn't sure. The man's shuffling, he appears to be crippled. He comes close. "I don't have the Post article on me, sir, but could you please sign this for me?" He holds out a folded piece of paper and points to the bottom of it. Shane thinks, how do I possibly deserve to have a grown man coming up to me like this, when all I did was nearly kill myself in a reckless joyride.

He signs his name painstakingly and hands the paper back to the man. "No, no," the man says, "you keep it."

"It's yours, sir. I signed it for you."

The man walks away smartly. He looks back over his shoulder and tips his hat. "Jeremiah Faye sends his regards, Mr. Kinnock."

Shane unfolds the paper. At the top is a title:

SUBPOENA.

You are hereby commanded to appear before a grand jury on the second day of July, nineteen-hundred and fifty-two. Please be aware that you are a TARGET of the grand jury's investigation. You will be asked questions as to which the truthful answers may cause you to incriminate yourself in criminal conduct. You are advised to seek legal counsel.

At the very bottom of the paper, in exactly the right place, is the signature: "Shane Kinnock."

It's Bentley, of course, who offers the closing commentary. "Christ almighty, Kinnock, you're a grand jury target. They want to charge you with something.

Jesus, you can't win for losing."

4

"How about a double vodka martini?"

"Sorry. I can't serve you."

"So, you don't have any vodka. How about gin? Anything to set up a Tom Collins?"

"I wish I could, but I can't."

"Whiskey sour?"

"No whiskey. How many ways can I say it? This bar is closed."

Shane shakes his head.

What's done is done.

Claire Montgomery puts a hand on her hip and settles into a well-practiced pout. "My, my," she says. "Shane Kinnock, you really have turned over a new leaf. I have to figure that you had yourself quite a well-stocked cabinet here. What happened to it?"

"It all got flushed down the commode down the hall," he says. "It's probably burning its way through the pipes even as we speak."

Earlier today, in a fit of temperance, he rid himself of all temptation.

"So, what can you give a girl who's thirsty?"

"I think I still have some RC Cola, vintage May 1952."

He pulls a couple of bottles out of his ice box. Claire comes up behind him and rests a hand on his shoulder. "I don't need a glass," she says. She takes a sip from the bottle and leaves a small crimson mark on the rim. She lets her hand drift lightly down his spine.

"Just last month," Shane says, "it seemed as if liquor had never passed across your lips. Now you sound like a walking bartender's guide."

She says nothing. Women who look like Claire Montgomery can always get away with saying nothing, no matter what the question is.

She called about an hour ago and asked him how he was doing. He started to just say he was fine and leave it at that, but then he let it slip about the subpoena. With that, she asked if she could come over and see him. He let a few seconds go by before saying yes.

Truth is, Claire's been a warm presence in his mind, ever since he reclaimed his mind as his own. Yesterday he worried over facing his grand jury for just about as long as it took him to walk into his dingy boarding room, empty his duffel bag, and toss his subpoena. From then on, through the night, he relived every moment he could remember from the evening he spent with her at the Neptune Room, and he cursed himself for letting any of it slip away from him.

She was that close. She was my future, my green light on the dock. And I let myself be borne backwards.

At daybreak he found himself bent over on the floor, bug-eyed and breathing hard, moved close to convulsions by a fear that he'd never see her again.

Now she's standing before him in a cream satin dress, delicately holding her crimson-ringed RC Cola bottle in a manicured hand, and he's trying hard to hide his rapture for fear that it isn't shared.

She eyes the makeshift clothes pole that holds all of his suits, the card table that holds his sport shirts, the foldaway-this, the combination-that.

"It's like you're still on a mission," she says. "Like you're living off the land, still plotting some subterfuge. So, what have you been planning to attack; traveling light, ready to get out at a moment's notice?"

He bends low to sit down on the hassock that folds out to serve as his bed. It rolls a few inches on its casters. "I was at war with everything and anything. Now you might say I'm trying to make a separate peace with life."

For a moment he wonders if she'll get the reference.

"I've always thought," she responds, "that Hemingway could've had quite a time with a character like you."

She doesn't disappoint. She's not Bentley.

She settles down next to him and the hassock barely moves. Her light landing would make a jet pilot jealous.

From outside he hears the fire escape trumpeter start to warm up with the first notes of "Glow Worm." God Almighty, he thinks, all I used to do was bitch about Washington's god-awful hot summers, but if they drive somebody outside to make music like this, how bad can they be.

Claire gets up abruptly, goes to the half-open window and leans on the sill. "I'm worried about you," she said.

"Why now all of a sudden?"

"It isn't all of a sudden. I went to see you at the hospital because I'd read the article in the Post about your crash, and I made some calls to find out where you were. Seeing you there in such torment – I'm sorry, I couldn't go back."

She stops, winces.

"And now you've rebounded, just to get hit with this subpoena. I'm worried about what they can do to you."

He walks over to her and drapes his arm over her shoulder. She pats his hand.

"It'll be okay," he says. "What's the worst they can do? I've already been wrapped up in a straitjacket and zapped like a lab hamster. Jail's a picnic compared to that. It wasn't long ago I was thinking, I've got no control over anything, somebody's pulling my strings all the time. Now somehow it's different."

"So who's your lawyer going to be?"

"You're looking at him."

She turns and stares at him. "You mean – "

"I didn't hire any lawyer, there's no reason to. I know as much about my witness rights as anybody I would've gone to. Besides, it's not as if I need anybody's advice on what I want to do."

"So you're taking the Fifth?"

"No."

Claire looks at him as if he just told her he's been diagnosed with curable cancer, but is declining all treatment. "Shane, that's foolish. You know the police chief hates you, and it looks like Faye may be out to get you too. Not to mention, a grand jury does whatever the D.A. wants it to."

She's more animated than he's ever seen her.

"You can put them off," she says. "The grand jury's term ends after tomorrow and maybe they don't have enough on you to charge you with anything. If you don't play along, then they won't get any more than what they already have. But if you give them the chance to grill you for hours, they'll pick through all your answers and if they want to find something to pin on you, they will."

She talks about seeing how Joe McCarthy and his cronies play the game, lulling people into thinking that if they just cooperate with the government, they'll make out just fine, then stabbing them in the back.

He turns a folding chair around and sits down, propping his chin on the seat back. "It's not that easy, Claire." He goes off on the Fifth Amendment, reaching back into law school lessons learned years ago. He only has a privilege if a truthful answer to a question would incriminate him in a crime. No matter what they ask him about, the Robinson lockup or the lagoon case or all the police corruption, he hasn't done anything wrong, so he can't incriminate himself, so he doesn't have a "Fifth" option.

Claire presses him. "You went to law school and I didn't," she says. "But I can see the jails filling up with people who went blindly before grand juries and Congressional committees saying to themselves, I can't get hurt because I'm clean."

"So, you think Shane the lawyer isn't doing right by Shane the client?"

Nothing she could say would make any difference. Shane the lawyer knows that there's only one answer that Shane the client will accept.

Downstairs somebody yells out once, twice. The sound is coming from the back side of the building, where a lot of trouble tends to start. Something bad is just about to happen and Shane considers moving for his sidearm, until it occurs to him that it's locked in a safe back at the station along with his badge, waiting to be reclaimed.

It gets quiet.

"Listen," he says to Claire, "It comes down to this. The grand jury just needs to hear the truth about all these things and I can give it to them."

"And it's your truth up against the so-called truth that they get from the Chief, and everybody else that the Chief puts up there to testify. And guess which truth the grand jury ends up believing, and who ends up getting screwed. Pardon my language."

He just shrugs.

"What about your father's case? The campaign fund investigation. Faye's also got that going."

"I'm so far away from my father's doings, if somebody tortured me to try to get me to tell them about Raymond, they'd end up having to kill me."

"At that hearing before Congress, you *did* end up taking the Fifth. When they started asking questions about something you did in the war."

She's still standing at the window. She fiddles with the latch, pretending it's broken, as if she'd know how to go about fixing it.

"I did take the Fifth then," he says. "What they were asking me about had nothing to do with what I was up there to testify about. That probably won't happen again."

"And what if it does? What if they try to rehash it?"

He walks over to her, wraps his arms around her waist, and she eases. He rests his head next to hers. "I'm not running from anything anymore, Claire."

She closes her eyes. The trumpeter is in the middle of "Blue Moon" but it fades out.

"Come over here," he says, and guides her to another folding chair and sits across from her. "It's like this."

He starts talking about an article he saw in Life Magazine a couple of months ago:

A man went to the beach one year with his wife and baby daughter, and he had the wife take a picture of him with his girl down by the water. And the next year they went back and the wife took another picture of him and the girl in the same spot. The three of them ended up going back every year from then on for many years, and each year they took that picture. In the first set of pictures the man looked strong and handsome, he was wearing one of those old-fashioned sleeveless swimming tops, and he was really built. And his daughter looked tiny and vulnerable.

Claire breaks in. "What does this have to do with anything?"

"Just hear me out."

So, time went on, and the man started looking smaller and older. His hair got grayer and sparser, and you could tell that every year he was wearing the same swimming top, but he wasn't filling it out like he used to and his skin was starting to hang. And the daughter got more and more robust. She grew into a beautiful woman, and he got hunched over and wizened and frail. But he kept on having those pictures taken. And then he died, and somebody in the family found the pictures and sent them off to the magazine.

"I saw that article," Shane says, "and it got to me. That fella having all those pictures taken. And maybe it's just now that I've come to the point of understanding what it was really all about, beyond the story of a father and his daughter."

"Which is?"

"That once you start down the road of telling the story of your life you have to be faithful to the truth. No matter how it makes you look."

She pulls her chair closer to him. "So, if the grand jury asks you about the war, what will you say?"

"I'll say, 'Mr. Foreman, I refuse to answer that question on the grounds that it may incriminate me.'"

He laughs, she doesn't. "Lighten up," he says. "If I can see the humor in this, you should."

"No, tell me, I need to know."

He wants to look away from her, get up and circle the room, walk out and hop in his car and go to Hy's at 5th and Florida and get his Camels and then go to Tony's for the rest of the night.

"I'll say that I did what I had to do."

"Which was what. I need to know." There's a tremor in Claire's voice. "From the beginning. Please."

He cups one hand in the other on his lap and meets her gaze.

"I'd just landed on Guadalcanal."

His mouth keeps moving and words are coming out, but he doesn't hear them. Once again he's back there, feeling like he's living inside an undulating balloon of foul wetness, a balloon filled with sweat and rain and piss. Hearing a voice and making out words, barely. Hearing the squish-squish-squish of rubber boots through jungle sludge. Hearing a voice again, a radio voice. A radio voice giving him orders, his mission, his reason to keep on grinding. Take the hill. Take the hill, the Jap defense depends on it. Take the hill and claim every living and dead thing it offers up to you.

He pauses. It hits him. *I'm talking about all of this.*

Claire looks so tense that Shane strokes the side of her face, but her expression doesn't change. "It's okay," he says, as much to himself as to her.

She asks, "So what happened next," and suddenly he's no longer right there, but hovering over his past self.

"So, we establish a hidden position, just off the hill. At nighttime we can't use any flashlights or smoke a cigarette. In daytime we can't even use binoculars because the sun might glint off the glass and give us up."

Outside, the fire escape trumpeter starts again into "Blue Moon," again it drifts into nothing.

"Once it looks like we're ready to move, I take ten of my men forward to feel out where the Japs are holed up. We come to this ridge and nobody's saying a word. And your mind isn't supposed to wander at a time like this. But I can't help thinking it's ... beautiful."

"Beautiful?"

"I don't know if it's lit by the moon or the stars or what, but it's like nothing I've ever seen before. Primitive, green and lush and peaceful. Right here, for centuries, time has been holding its breath."

Claire hasn't moved.

"Just then I hear a thud a, little ways away. It's a grenade, and it goes off. One of my men, his name was Cushing, he's from the Jersey shore… scared all the time, paranoid, gone in the head from the war."

"So, there was a grenade."

"Yes, and Cushing, paranoid Cushing, he's closest to it and he flies backwards. Gunfire starts coming down on us and one of our other guys is hit and he just drops dead."

Shane is keeping his voice even but when he looks down at his hands he can see they're trembling. Then it all comes out, the words scrambling over top of each other.

"There are some small trees about 50 yards away and we drag Cushing down to them, but they don't give us much cover. Cushing's leg is a mess and he's gushing blood. We're still getting fired on. We can't go forward and we can't stay where we are because we're fully exposed. The only way I can get my men to safety is to retreat and try to use the tree line for cover, and we have to do it *fast*, before the Japs can get down to us.

We're trying to stop Cushing's bleeding, but it isn't easy and we're getting heavy fire – there are bullets hitting all around us – the shots sound like they're coming closer and closer. Cushing can't walk, can't even crawl, and if we try to take him with us the Japs'll catch up to us."

"So, you have three options," Claire says slowly. "Stay with him and lose everybody. Take him with you and lose everybody. Or leave him behind, lose him, but maybe save all the others."

"I have a fourth option. Which is the one I take."

Claire shakes her head, but he goes on anyway.

"I take my .45 and I put it in his mouth and I fire it. And it blows most of his head off. And you'd think the bullet would carry all the nasty shit with it, but it doesn't. There's all this blowback on me. A blowback of Cushing, all his blood and brains, and fear and his fake bravado and his paranoia – everything. We leave there and the next time we get to water I try like a son-of-a-bitch to get Cushing's shit off me, but I can't. Hell, I'm sure I'm still wearing some of it."

He feels a spasm start at his shoulders and it works its way through his body. He waits before saying anything more because he thinks his words will be strangled in a stammer, but when he finally speaks he sounds steady.

"It was the only thing to do. We couldn't take him, and we couldn't leave him, the Japs were going to get to him and they'd torture him to get him to give up everything he knew about our operation, including where we'd probably gone to next. And after torturing him they'd have given him a brutal death anyway. You already as much as said it, it was the only way to save the most people."

"So, you played God."

"Yes, I played God. All of us over there played God at one point or another. And we weren't up to the task." He can't stop shaking.

Claire leans towards him. He shies away, then goes to the window. The shaking slows down. From behind him he hears her say, "Did you ever have any doubts about what you did?"

"An hour or so later. And then every hour or so, every day, through all the years since."

"And how did you end up getting into trouble with the military?"

"One of my men reported it up the line later. He'd been shell-shocked and I'd had to carry him around the island the whole time like a sack of meal, for what it's worth now. But word got back to Cushing's family, and they made a stink about it, and the Navy started a court martial."

"Didn't your commanding officers do anything for you?"

"They didn't lift a finger. Or to be accurate, they did. They wet a finger and held it up in the air and when they felt the wind, they kept their mouths shut. My father got involved and got me a dishonorable discharge. He told me that the Navy told him that if I ever talked about it publicly they could bring it all back up."

"So you're still going to go in the grand jury tomorrow, knowing you could be asked about it."

"It's the only thing to do." Shane says. "Look Claire, I almost lost my mind over all this. But I'd like to think I never stood in danger of losing my conscience."

A silence falls between them. Finally, Claire comes next to him and takes his hand from behind. Her hand is smooth and moist. "I see so much shameless ambition in this town," she says in a near-whisper. "But reckless nobility – that's very alluring."

The trumpeter is playing again, a slow number that wafts through the settling summer-night haze. He's skipping quickly through some notes, lingering over others, adding flourishes, making it all his own. Shane doesn't pick up on the melody.

Claire said, "You know this song, dear."

Shane strains to hear.

She starts to sing dreamily. "No other love, could warm my heart ..."

He turns and takes her in his arms. "Would you do a man the honor of dancing his last dance with him?"

They gently rock back and forth until the song ends. They keep holding each other for long minutes until Claire pushes away from him and walks away.

He stays at the window, clutching the sill.

He hears some rustling behind him.

He hears Claire say, "Come, dear."

She's sitting up on the hassock, which she folded out. Back against the wall, chest barely covered by one of his rough blankets, flaxen hair swaying over her shoulders.

He moves to her quickly and they make love frantically, until a rusted caster on the rocking hassock breaks off and they tumble to the floor laughing, then start in again.

Later, she rubs his neck while he stares at the wall. "I don't have any cigarettes," he says, "and I can't even offer you a nightcap."

Claire gets up. Shane hears the snap of the clasp of a purse, then the sound of a lighter. She says, "See what you started here with me?"

A few minutes pass, then she nestles back next to him. "What about your wife and son? You never talk about them."

The question is jarring, and he avoids it. "You never talk about this steady of yours, either. Is he still in the picture?"

"Less after tonight," she says quietly. "But yes."

"I'm sorry I asked," Shane says. "I don't have a claim on you." The feeling that rises up inside him is something he once knew as guilt.

She rolls over on her back. "Don't think that I didn't notice that you answered a question with a question. Your wife and son, do you think about them much?"

He's seeing Maureen again as he saw her the first time.

He's seeing himself, gangly and pimpled, walking up to her at the Waffle Shop down from St. Patrick's, and he's talking with her, and he's amazed all over again that words are even coming out of his mouth.

He's seeing Maureen walking towards him, jeweled and gowned, on the morning he married her. He's seeing her walking towards him, jeweled and naked, later that night.

He's hearing words said together, sentences finished, silences shared.

He's seeing Maureen walk away from him on the morning he found out his sister had been killed.

He's seeing himself lurching against Maureen's baby bump, straining to kiss her as the troop bus behind him revs its engines, and he's seeing her turn her cheek to him.

He's reading the letter that tells him he has a son. He's fingering the inside of the envelope for a photo of the boy, an image he can carry through battle, but it isn't there.

He's seeing himself back stateside, stuck in the house he didn't have anything to do with buying, nursing a pain he can't share with a woman he doesn't think he knows anymore. He's seeing himself climbing out the side window of the house so nobody in the front room knows he's going out.

He's seeing his boy Buddy on the day Maureen moved them both out, and he has a pinwheel in his hand. Maureen's dressed him in a blue jumpsuit with a matching hat. Buddy waves the pinwheel at him and then he runs away, a vision in diminishing turquoise.

Shane says, "Do I think about them? Not much."

"Do you know where they live?"

"They're probably in the area. Her family was from here."

"That's some unfinished business that you probably need to resolve, isn't it?"

"I guess we both have things we have to sort out."

She rubs his back.

He feels her fingers run lightly up and down his spine as he falls asleep, his last thoughts awash in the color blue.

5

Shane spent all day testifying before a grand jury.

There are few sentences that can so easily capture how a man's life can go haywire than that one.

At the end, he walked out on the balls of his feet, spent but still trying to be buoyant, if only for appearances. Then he heard someone yell to the old marshal who sat in on the session: "Hey blue coat, how'd it go for him?" The marshal didn't reply, just pointed at the cuffs on his belt and rattled them.

Maybe it didn't mean a thing, but Shane can't help but think: The grand jury's in the pocket of Jeremiah Faye, and maybe this marshal in the frayed blue uniform is right up next to old D.A. Faye, maybe he's even on the detail that escorts Faye home, and tucks him in bed at night.

Maybe this old marshal meant that Kinnock's good as gone, throw him in a cell and lock it behind him.

It's nighttime now, and Shane's on the other side of town from the courthouse, inside his childhood home.

This is the house where he grew up, where he watched his mother die, and he's here for the first time since he left for the war. Over the years he's driven by it, walked near it, parked for hours outside it, but never come inside it. Raymond still lives here, and Shane wouldn't be here now if he didn't know for certain that he'd have the place to himself. It's a weekday night and Congress is in session, so no Raymond anytime soon.

In dim light he navigates around dark corners to the kitchen, tries to find a wall switch but can't, then moves by memory to his father's library. The door's open.

The room is oak-paneled, loaded with artifacts from Raymond's travels, and dominated by a desk that, according to Raymond, was built from the timbers of an old warship. For years the room was off-limits to Shane and his sister. Now he sits at the desk and idly picks up the Time magazine with the cover portrait of his father: The Negroes' "Man of the Hour." Beneath the magazine is a stack of newspapers marked with the stamp of the Library of Congress.

The top paper is folded to an inside page with a headline circled in pencil. "Abuses Cited in Shock Therapy."

Shane flips through the stack and sees more of the same. "Psychiatrists Seek to Replace Electroshock." "Shock Therapy Abuses Alleged." "New Drug Eyed to Supplant Shock Treatment." The dates at the top of the pages swing back and forth on the timeline.

At the bottom of the stack is the New York Times from June 13, 1952. Front page, far right side: "Doubts Persist, But Hope Still Lives."

"The truly depressed," Shane reads, "feel separated by an invisible barrier from everyone they've ever loved, every joy and or appetite they've ever relished. Friend from friend, mother from daughter, son from father. Electroshock therapy carries risks but it can break down that barrier."

In the margin at the end of the paragraph is a pencil check and a small star.

Shane settles back in the chair.

Son from father. Son from father. Son from father.

A noise comes from somewhere.

Shane opens his eyes, stays still. Footsteps are coming down the hall and he jumps up and touches his gun and races for the door, which is opening, and runs hard into somebody he can barely see. The impact knocks him to the floor. He looks up at a man in his undershirt and boxers: Raymond, with his hand over his mouth.

Shane pushes himself to his feet, chagrined. "Did I get you in the chops?" he asks, hoping.

"Not at all, son," Raymond answers, but he keeps his hand where it was. He stares at Shane for a moment, his voice is soft. "I was just wondering why I'm being given the pleasure. Twice in just a month, finding you alone in an office of mine."

"Why are you here? Congress is in session and I know everything you've got going on up there."

"I was in my own bed. Sorry to spoil your plan by coming back to my own home early."

Raymond moves to his desk chair and eases himself into it. His legs look sturdy, his arms rock-hard.

Shane's been on the receiving end of his father's barbs often enough to know what's coming next. *You went downtown to the grand jury today, and you stared into the future, and you came back for one last look at the past. Am I right, son?*

But Raymond says nothing like that. "Take a seat, son." He leans over. "Are you okay for tomorrow? Did you get any sense of what Faye is going to do with you?"

"I should ask you the same question. You're just as much in Faye's crosshairs as I am."

Raymond opens his mouth, words don't come out. He looks as if he's about to cry.

And Shane sees he has just three teeth in the front.

"Good fucking God. What happened to your teeth?"

"Lost most of my grin years ago, son." Raymond closes his mouth, gathers himself. "At least I can say I've had the best dentures money can buy."

"Who else knows?"

"Your mother did, of course, and a very discrete dentist. I take pains not to be taken off guard like this."

Throughout his career Raymond's triumphant, rapacious smile defined his public image. And all that time, the smile slept at night in a water glass.

Raymond is quiet, his eyes shut. He still looks to be on the verge of bawling. "I know what your sister called me behind my back. 'Fair weather father.' I should've been there more when you both needed me."

He works his mouth again. "Your mother could only do so much for you," he says. "Then less and less as the years went by."

"She loved us unconditionally and we knew it," Shane says. "That was enough."

"I just felt as if I had other paternal obligations."

"You mean you had – "

"Other children, like another family? Lord, no. I just felt like I was the father to every poor mick who washed ashore and landed hard in Hell's Kitchen. I had to serve all their needs and be their example. Of how to make it in this country."

Shane gets up and pats his father's shoulder. "And you did, Pop."

Pop. The word finally comes out, after all this time.

Raymond pulls the neckline of his undershirt over his lower lip. "I've sinned terribly, son."

"Politicians do things to survive. You're not the first."

"Not just that. I – shit, son. I can't say anything more. Shit, shit, shit."

"Pop, look," Shane says, "no matter what else happens tomorrow, go back and think about all the laws you've gotten through and all the good they did. Now the biggest civil rights bill in history just passed and it wouldn't have happened without you."

"You don't know, do you, son?"

"Know what?"

"You really were out of it, weren't you? The bill is dead."

"*Dead*?"

"Dead as Kelsey's nuts, as my own father used to say. In the end I couldn't keep the votes together. Matt Barry ran a story in his paper, it quoted unnamed sources in the DA's office, said I was about to get indicted. For whatever it is that I'm supposed to have done."

Raymond brushes absently at his boxers for several seconds.

"It just gave everybody who was still on the fence a good excuse not to have to cast their lot with the coloreds."

"When did this happen?"

"While you were –away."

"God, I'm sorry, Pop." Shane squeezes his father's arm. "Maybe next year."

"No, son. This was the last best chance."

Shane glances down at the Time cover. If his father was ever really the man of the hour, the hour has now passed.

Politics in America. For years to come Negroes will be swinging from trees without the law to help them, all because two old men couldn't stop fighting over whose dick was bigger.

"So what about that indictment story about you," says Shane. "Do you think it's right? Are you worried?"

Raymond waits before answering. He looks vacantly towards the door, then starts to speak, languidly. "Son, I'll tell you a story. It's about a time when you and your sister were still both little and we were all up in New York."

It was around Christmas time and they'd all just seen Santa Claus at a midtown store. And as they were walking through the city's streets, Erin would hold tight to Raymond's hand but Shane kept running away. "Impossible to control, even then, don't you know, and driving me to distraction." So they got all the way to Broadway and 42nd, the busiest street corner in the world, "and you just took off and ran straight towards traffic. And I watched you and thought, just let it happen, just let the boy get hit. Lord, let him get hit."

Raymond runs his fingers softly across his lips.

"It tells you something that I would even think such a thing. From the time when you and your sister were very young, you were the one I worried about. Always tempting fate, putting yourself in harm's way. I loved Erin as much, but everything always fell into place for her. Which is rather ironic – "

He stops and takes a deep breath.

"What I'm saying is that I worried myself sick every night over you, couldn't sleep, literally throwing up, fretting over all the things I couldn't control, all the bogeymen out there, and I had no say in any of it. It's why I ended up not being around as much. I couldn't take the worry and still do what I needed to. It's why at that moment in Times Square, I thought, 'Let it happen, let's get it out of the way, I've lived it a million times before anyway. Put me out of my misery.'"

You could ask a thousand sons and only a handful would've ever heard their fathers empty their souls like this. And Shane's still in the great majority. Because he didn't take in a word his father said after, "Let the boy get hit, Lord, let him get hit."

Time will pass and one day what Shane says next will rise up and hit him between the eyes. But at this moment all he can do is back out of the room until he feels his shoulders brush up against the door jam.

"I can't say it any plainer," he says to Raymond. "I won't be happy until you're dead."

Raymond looks confused. "I don't understand. I'm just saying, I'm not worried about myself. I'm worried about you."

Shane leaves the room.

He goes to his old bedroom, lies down on his old bed and passes time staring at the walls and the moving light-shapes cast through the windows by cars passing outside.

Half an hour passes, maybe more. He hears feet padding towards the hallway bathroom, hears the bathroom door open and close. He rises, walks into the hallway, sees the yellow light shaft under the door and hears the sounds of a bedtime ritual. Water run, soap rubbed, water splashed.

Quiet.

He presses against the door. He starts to say, "Goodnight," but the water starts up again and he stops. The water slows down to a trickle. Again, Shane says "Goodnight", but he can't even hear the word himself because the water starts up again. He waits for quiet.

He says, "Goodnight --"

Toilet flush.

"-- Pop."

He walks away. He lurches back.

He walks away.

6

THE WASHINGTON POST
Thursday, July 3, 1952

TITANS FACING POSSIBLE CHARGES TODAY
By Bran Bentley, Staff Reporter

As all of Washington awaits today's corruption indictments, sources say that they could topple two giants on the national political scene.

Within the last two days, Rep. Raymond Kinnock (D-N.Y.) testified before a federal grand jury after being advised that he's a target of the government's investigation into illegal kickbacks. On the heels of Kinnock's appearance, S. Matthew Barry – billionaire industrialist and political powerbroker, accused of selling retired U.S. warships to Communist governments – was taking the Fifth and refusing to testify.

A source close to the investigation says that its crosshairs are trained squarely on Kinnock and Barry.

Meanwhile, a separate grand jury is reported to be returning an indictment in connection with the Emily Rose murder, as well as one against a law enforcement officer in connection with the 1950 murder of one Margaret Fitzwater in the so-called "lagoon" case.

All of this drama will converge in two different courtrooms at the same time today.

****

Jeremiah Faye is a small man with stiff, centered-parted hair and a reedy voice who still has a knack for commanding center stage.

"Are you finally ready," the judge says, "for us to call the Willie Robinson case?"

Faye preoccupies himself with papers on his desk. Shuffling them, straightening them, re-straightening them.

Seconds pass. Still no response from Faye.

Shane knows that this moment of insolent delay is all a part of what a good prosecutor does: establish that he's the moral authority in any room that he's in, that he defers to no one, that events move on his clock and no one else's.

He had a front row seat at Faye's show yesterday, sitting through six hours in a grand jury. The late arrival, the dramatic entrance. The predatory circling of the witness stand, the head raised to high heaven and the eye roll. The final dismissive wave-off.

All bluster. But Shane also saw something else. The mastery of the art of asking probing questions, one-by-one, unwaveringly. The lacerating intellect, the command of detail. The righteousness of judgment.

Now Shane's sitting in a courtroom on Jeremiah Faye's terms.

Just an hour ago, Sarge called Shane and said that the Chief wanted him in the courtroom at two-sharp, along with everybody else in the Willie Robinson case. When Shane asked why, since all they'd see in court was Robinson getting arraigned on the murder indictment, the Sarge didn't answer right away. So Shane said to him, is getting everybody down there just a ruse to have *me* there, so it'll be easier to get me arrested-on-perjury-indictment or some other thing, so the marshals won't actually have to earn their pay and get off their asses and hunt me down?

And the Sarge had the same sound in his voice that a doctor gets when you ask him how bad the cancer is. "I don't really know."

So when Shane first saw the Sarge in court, he moved up close to him and squeezed his arm and told him that he's been the best boss he ever had, and whatever happens today, it'll all work out all right in the end. And then he told him the story about his mom and her rubber ball comment, about how her Shanie would always bounce back. Just to reassure the Sarge.

Now Sarge is sitting on his right on a courtroom bench, Bobby on his left. Sarge's foot is tapping wildly. Shane's already asked him twice to stop it but he hasn't. On the other side of Sarge is Calvin Rector and then Chief Moran, sitting on the aisle where until just a few minutes ago he was greeting well-wishers and underlings.

Bran Bentley's been in and out. Shane sees him slouched on a wall to the side, careless as a man leaning against a streetlight wolf-whistling at passing girls. Something moves him and he draws a notebook to his side and scribbles into it.

Above Bentley is a window that somebody's opened to let in a breeze. The air carries with it the sounds of chanting outside: "Let Willie go! Let Willie go! Let Willie go!" Hundreds of Negro protesters have gathered outside the courthouse. A small group have been allowed into the courtroom, and they're huddled in the back section marked off by rope.

In the section's front row sits Chet Freeman, looking clear-eyed and determined. He caught Shane's eye when he walked in and glared at him fiercely.

"Jeremiah," the judge says, "I asked you – "

"Yes, call the Robinson case."

"United States versus William Washington Robinson. Marshal, bring out the defendant."

The chant outside is growing louder. "Let Willie go! Let Willie go!"

The judge motions to the courtroom clerk. "I don't care how hot it gets in here, close that damn window."

A marshal leads Willie into the courtroom. Willie's hands are cuffed behind him and his ankles are shackled, he can only move by taking small hops. "Step it up, boy," the judge says.

Willie inches his way over to the defendant's table and then stands still, eyes closed, head down.

"Who's the boy's lawyer?" the judge asks.

"I am." Paulie Donovan hustles up the aisle, touching the benches on both sides for support. He gets to the table, drops a folder, bends to pick it up, nearly hits his head on the arm of a chair. He gathers himself. "Your honor, my client would be interested in entering a guilty plea in this case."

Willie doesn't move.

"Have you talked about it with the boy," the judge asks, "so you know that's what he wants to do?"

"Well, your honor, we've had general discussions – "

"No, Paulie. Have you specifically – "

"Could I take a moment to go in the back with my client? I think we can resolve this matter pretty quickly if I just take a few minutes."

"*Your honor.*" Jeremiah Faye has risen to his feet. "I think I can save Mr. Donovan some time here. There have been two developments that will affect the course of the case against Mr. Robinson."

"And what kind of developments are we talking about, Jeremiah?"

Faye rummages through papers on his table.

"I said – "

"Yes, of course." Faye walks behind Paulie and Willie and passes an envelope to the clerk. "I'm handing over indictments that were issued in secret late yesterday by the Municipal Court grand jury."

Faye saunters back to his table.

"These indictments," he goes on, "charge with the crime of perjury two individuals who provided false and misleading testimony under oath with respect to the Emily Rose murder and other matters."

Two individuals, Shane thinks. *He's charging me and who else?*

The Sarge's foot is tapping like a jackhammer.

The clerk takes the papers out of the envelope and glances at them, blank-faced.

The judge starts to lean over to claim the papers. "Oh hell," he says, "why don't you just save me some time, Jeremiah, and tell me who these two people are that you're charging."

"First," he says, "one Joseph Francis Barry, home address 1400 34th Street, NW, Washington, D.C."

The courtroom is so quiet that the only audible sound is Sarge's toe-tap.

"You mean, *Congressman* Joseph Barry?"

"Yes, your honor."

"And where is Mr. Barry?"

"I'm told that he's out of the jurisdiction today, engaged in a political campaign. But I've contacted his representatives and he'll be returning to the jurisdiction this afternoon to turn himself in and be booked and fingerprinted."

Barry must've thought he could charm the grand jury. He must've thought all he had to do was flash the grin and the sardonic humor and they'd fall at his feet just like everybody else does. But what did he lie about? And why would it matter?

The judge leans back in his black leather chair. "I have to hand it to you, Jeremiah. You certainly have a lot of nerve."

"The grand jury has the nerve. I'm just a servant of the people."

"So, who else did the grand jury have the nerve to charge with perjury here?"

Shane's watching the clerk go to a marshal and whisper to him. The marshal walks to the gallery, handcuffs jangling, and stops at the end of Shane's row. Just doing his job, blocking escape from the courtroom.

Faye speaks. "Yes, your honor. The other individual --"

"Stop, please! Stop!"

The court reporter is waving her hand. "I have to change my ribbon. Everyone wait one moment."

Shane closes his eyes. He's holding onto the seat beneath him with both hands, digging his nails into the wood.

The reporter fiddles with her machine.

Shane has his badge on his belt. He grips it with his right hand.

"Alright," the court reporter says, "go ahead. Mr. Faye, the last thing you said was– "

"I know what the last thing I said was. The other individual charged here with perjury is one Charles Patrick Moran, business address 300 Indiana Avenue, Northwest, Washington, D.C."

Shane looks to the aisle and sees the marshal leaning down to the Chief. "Sorry, sir, you have to come with me."

"I – what – I'm not –"

The marshal grasps Charlie Moran by the arm. "Please don't make this more difficult than it has to be."

How did Faye charge Moran?

He must've found the Negro girl in the pigtails, the one who ran up to me after I shot Willie. The girl who saw everything that happened before I got there. He got the Negro girl and he got to the bottom of the Chief's big lie.

The judge says, "Are there any other – are there –" He's having a hard time getting his words out. "Mr. Faye, are there any other grand jury indictments that you wish to inform me of in connection with this case?"

"No. I should only add that Chief Moran has been charged in two separate indictments. In the first, for perjury in the Emily Rose case. And in the second, for subornation of perjury in another case. With subornation of perjury meaning, encouraging others to lie --"

"I know what subornation means. In what case?"

"The case of the murder of Margaret Fitzwater, whose body was found two years ago in the lagoon near the Jefferson Memorial."

The grand jury took Shane's word over Moran's on the lagoon case. It's Shane's moment of vindication and he's too numb to savor it.

"But just to be clear," the judge presses. "There are no other indictments with respect to this case, the murder of Miss Rose?"

"No, there aren't."

Shane feels Bobby's arm around his shoulder, then looks over to the Sarge, who's gaping at the ceiling, smiling, with a tear rolling down his cheeks. Shane's foot is finally still. The only sound in the courtroom comes from Charlie Moran's lumbering frame as he's being hauled out of the room.

Then it hits him. *What about Willie Robinson?*

The judge says the words just as Shane thinks them. "So what are you doing with him, Jeremiah?"

"The police department's case against Mr. Robinson rested heavily on Chief Moran's testimony that the defendant confessed his guilt to him on the scene of his arrest. That testimony has been deemed false and perjurious.

The government has no choice but to drop the charge of murder against him at this time."

Silence. Then, from the roped-off area in the back, an explosion of exultant shouting.

The judge bangs his gavel three times. "Quiet back there! Quiet!"

He turns to Willie, who still hasn't raised his head. "You're free to go, boy, but the government here will still be looking into this case and if they get more evidence on you they'll have you back here so fast it'll make your head spin. And I understand there's a couple of other dead girls out there. So, I advise you to keep your head down and stay clean, boy."

Then he orders the marshal to release Willie out the back way.

Shane joins the masses surging towards open space. In a blur of smiles just one face stands out. It's a face he remembers.

Denton. No, Dalton. Quentin Dalton, the housing inspector who said he saw Willie with Emily on the Calvert Street Bridge.

Dalton's on the aisle, towards the back, and he yells at Shane. "What kind of police force do you guys run? I saw that boy with your dead girl with my own eyes. My own eyes!"

Shane is carried past him.

Dalton persists. "That boy's guilty as sin and you let him out." Then his shrill voice is engulfed by noise.

Outside the courthouse, the plaza is filled with revelers singing and hugging and jumping up and down. A few start chanting, "We want Willie," and everyone takes up the cry. Shane walks dully through the crowd. He comes up on Chet Freeman, embracing Willie's mother, who's decked out in church clothes. Chet hugs him and says, "Thank you for what you did for us." Shane starts to say, I didn't do shit for anybody, but holds his tongue.

Over to one side, someone's put together a makeshift stage out of loading crates. Five Negroes are rocking back and forth on it, singing a capella. In the front is a coffee-colored boy with a sly smile, liquid hips, and a pure, high voice.

Oh freedom, oh freedom
Oh freedom over me
And before I'd be a slave
I'd be buried in my grave
And go home to my Lord and be free

Shane wants to find out about this kid but all the Negroes in the crowd storm the stage and he's left with a white cop from Capitol Police. He takes a chance. "You know who this singer is? He's got a future."

The cop sneers. "I just heard tonight his name is Cook, from down South. Not to be disagreeable but it's all jungle shit to me."

Shane just walks away. There are times when you feel as if the world of ignorance is an ocean, and anything you might try to throw at it is just a stone that skips across the surface before it sinks beneath the waves.

The mob is swelling with new arrivals. Weaving his way through them, Shane sees Willie Robinson. He's trotting away from a cluster of stalking reporters, head down, frowning.

An old quote comes to Shane's mind: "There's no more joyful feeling than to be shot at without effect." Willie survived being shot at twice, once on the street and once in a courtroom. But from the looks of things he isn't feeling joyful. For that matter neither is Shane.

Bran Bentley was one of the reporters trying to keep up with Willie before he fell back. Shane pushes his way to him and shouts, "What happened to my father?" Bentley mouths 'I-can't-hear-you' and Shane guides him to an open area.

Bentley looks at the ground. Shane's never seen him stand mute.

Pop must've gone down.

"You Kinnocks," Bentley finally says. "You're like the cockroaches that'll survive a nuclear war."

"What do you mean?"

"The grand jury isn't charging your father. He's free as a bird. Somebody else took the fall."

"Somebody else?"

"A guy named Carlsberg got charged, he worked for your father for years. Loyal as they come, they say. Rumor is that Raymond ratted him out."

Raymond went down to the grand jury and threw Louis Carlsberg to the wolves to save himself.

Too much loyalty always comes to nothing.

Bentley's still talking. "Did you hear what I said?" He'd brought out his notebook. "I said, with Chief Moran stepping down, do you see there being any changes at your department?"

"You tell me. Who's going to step up?"

"Word is Calvin Rector's getting sworn in as Chief in half an hour. The only good news for you is that I hear your man Roncalli is moving up to be Assistant Chief."

To the extent he can think about the future, when the present and the past lie shredded behind him, Shane sees nothing good in it. "Doesn't matter who number two is, if number one is Rector. Nothing's gonna change. Just more busted homos, if that's possible."

A bead of sweat has appeared on Bentley's upper lip. "I need something more from you, Shane. I'm dying without a source. I'm going to be filing what everybody else is and I need more. And you owe me."

"What about Faye's big police corruption probe? How many cops went down for all the graft?"

"Precious few. Maybe Faye just figured your department is like a snake. Cut off the head and the rest doesn't matter, you get to start over."

Bentley has a few inches on Shane and bends over him, nose-to-nose, leaning him back. "I'm not mincing words. You promised me an exclusive on the Chief. Faye couldn't have indicted him for the lagoon case without your testimony. Now that he's been indicted it's an even bigger story."

"In due course, Bentley." Shane pushes back, gives himself space. "And what happened to Matt Barry and the warship thing?"

"He's free and clear, too."

Bentley pockets his notebook.

"Isn't it funny how things work," he says coldly. "Four men. Raymond, Matt, Joe, you. Two fathers and two sons, all under fire. And the one among you who had the brightest future ahead of him is the only one who's facing jail. A man could look at that and say it's not fucking fair."

He pivots and leaves.

Shane gives him no more thought. He wanders back towards the loading crate stage and the gospel group with coffee-colored Cook. They're all wearing tight purple suits and spats and the backups' wild movements are syncopated with a drill team's precision. The Cook boy sounds different now, low and throaty.

Somebody's knockin' at your door
Somebody's knockin' at your door
Oh sinner, why don't you answer?
Somebody's knockin' at your door

Shane knows he should disdain his father even more than he ever has – twisting the truth, betraying a constant friend, letting him suffer in sacrifice, and that's just the beginning – but he can't. In moments when they're faced with extinction the Irish retreat to their clan, even when it's fractious. The Kinnocks were under siege, and they survived, and that's as deep as he wants to go at the moment.

7

Someone grabs Shane by the shoulder and he spins around. It's the Sarge, and everything that happened in the courthouse is suddenly old news.

"You need to come with me," he says. "Something's going on."

He lowers his voice: "You need to see it while most everybody else is headed to Rector's swearing-in. While headquarters is mostly empty."

Sarge leads Shane by the elbow to the sidewalk and they walk at least a hundred yards before he lets go.

"A goon just fell in our lap, Shane. Says he knows Kaufman, says he knows you. We think he knows all about the Park case, how it happened."

Shane can still hear singing behind him. "Nothing's right about this, I can tell."

"This goon got roughed up good, is all I'll say. Now we've got to figure out what we're going to do with him. I need to have you take a look at him."

They pass a newsboy on the street. The boy has a Post special edition, tightly bound. He's working the twine with a penknife, waiting for the *snap*! that says he's got something ready to sell. Shane sees the word **EXCLUSIVE** and bends down to look over the boy's shoulder. There are grainy pictures of two figures, a man and a woman, topped by a bold banner headline.

JOE BARRY TRAPPED BY STAKEOUT PICS

The story had to come from Haynes Nickens, no one else. He said he'd never leak anything to the press. Now the 200 cubic feet of concrete that guards his secrets looks softer than oatmeal.

Sergeant Roncalli bears down on headquarters, Shane catches up. "I'm assuming that me being part of this, means I'm back on the case."

"Don't get ahead of yourself. I just need you on this right now."

"Where's your fair-haired boy Nickens?"

"He had Congress business to deal with. I don't know when the man sleeps. Look, I just need for you to see this guy we've got in custody."

They go to a room with a two-way glass window looking into another room with a table and four chairs. A man is seated at the table. Three men in cheap suits are standing over him.

Beckley, Ackerman and O'Dell-Gets-Fucked-Again.

"God Almighty," Shane says, "those guys. How did they make it into plainclothes?"

"They got transferred into Morals a few weeks ago and they've been helping out on the homo cases. Rector says it's given the three of them new energy. Quoting him exactly."

"Are they going to know that I'm watching them now?"

"Not if you don't go in there."

Roncalli flicks the transmit switch on an intercom next to the window. "Boys, give me a good look at him."

Beckley moves to the man and lifts his head off the table. The man squints towards the glass.

"Got it." Sarge shuts off the switch and nods to Shane. "Seen him before?"

"Yeah."

He's the blond-haired guy from the Neptune Room, the one who ogled Claire from the next booth over. The one that she saw following him into the bathroom. The same one, Shane now knows, who launched his head against a urinal and then tried to drown him in a toilet.

"Where do you know him from?"

"A lounge."

"You ever have any conversation with him?"

"It was hard for me to talk at the time because I was gurgling in piss water."

At another time, Shane might've had the urge to go into the room and take the man by the scruff of his neck and pound his head against the table until his face was mush, hold him by his feet and hang him out a window until he screamed for mercy. Tip him back and force water up his nose so hard that he'd not only think he was drowning, he'd actually want to drown.

Shane doesn't have the urge, but it doesn't matter. The man looks as if somebody did all that to him already.

He's shaking, barely conscious. His face is wet and bloody, his nose is spread across his face and he's missing teeth. His wavy blond hair is stringy and greasy. His dimpled chin is bloody from a gash. His piercing eyes are swollen half-shut.

Sarge goes to the intercom. "Boys, let him go for a minute. I'll tell you when to start questioning him again." He clicks off the intercom and slumps in his chair.

"So who is he, Sarge?"

"Guy named Jensen. Around two this morning Morals got called into the Roger Smith Hotel for a men's room scuffle. Apparently, this guy chose the wrong time to go in and pick a fight and a guard happened to walk in and caught him pummeling somebody. So the guard called for help and Morals happened to be right outside the building."

"And how'd this guy get to look like this?"

"It probably started when he came in the station, and somebody saw it was a men's room collar, and they drew the wrong conclusion and figured he was a perv."

"Did it have to be this bad?"

"No, but they say that tough guy here started fighting back. And in the middle of it all they started bracing him, and he gave up just enough about stuff he knew to make them think he knew more."

"About what?"

"About Jake Kaufman. This is big, Shane. We've never been able to snatch up anybody who's close to the man. So they turned up the heat and he started giving it all up."

"Don't tell me they just went off on their own on this."

"They didn't. At one point they called Rector and he told them to give the guy the full treatment, don't stop until he gives up everything."

"They could've killed the guy."

"Could've is would've, if I hadn't gotten called about it and told them to stop dealing with him until I got here."

"Are these guys going to tell Rector that you undermined his order?"

"Nah," the Sarge says grimly. "I think their knuckles were getting sore anyway."

Shane looks at Jensen. His head is rolling back and forth on the table and spittle is dripping from his open mouth. O'Dell is sitting cross-legged, drinking a glass of water and smoking a cigarette. Ackerman is leaning against the wall, reading the paper.

Roncalli gives Shane the brief.

Jensen was a lineman, got picked up by the Redskins out of college, but blew out his knee and then drifted. He has violent priors but never spent a day in the jail, "on account of he's got friends in high places."

He worked for Kaufman for years, and while he doesn't know anything about the money side of the operation he's admitted to being Kaufman's muscle, the stooge that was sent around to bang heads when necessary.

Early on in the interrogation, Roncalli says, all Jensen would own up to were a few random batterings, but later – "under more insistent questioning, so to speak" – he went further. "He gave himself up on a couple of stabbings, and then to the murder outside the Merry-Land club on New Year's Eve a few years back. Now he's pretty much to the point where I think he'd fess up to the Lindbergh baby kidnapping."

"Does he have Kaufman doing anything violent?"

"Up to now, not directly. But he says Kaufman knew about everything this guy was doing, before he did it. And this guy made a reference to the Park case. Maybe there's something to it, maybe Jensen here did something on Kaufman's orders. At least that's what our boys in there think."

"Our boys in there are fucking idiots."

"So consider the source. But I'm gonna let them talk to him a little longer to see if he gives it up."

"That'll be a waste of time."

Sarge hits the transmit button on the intercom. "Alright boys, start questioning him again. You got just 10 minutes." He hits the receive button and turns back to Shane. "Then I have to get you out of here. If Rector knew you were here – "

"I know."

Beckley takes the man by the hair on the back of his neck and pulls him until he's leaning back in his chair. "Hey beefcake, wake up. You started talking earlier about some Italians. Start flappin' your gums. You know, flap your gums."

Jensen starts moving his mouth slowly. "Italians. From Philadelphia."

"Philadelphia. You gotta do better than that. These guys're actually from over on 3rd Street, right? That's where all the dagos live. These guys you're talkin' about, they gotta be from there, right? You know, from 3rd Street, right?'"

"No, I said Philadelphia." Jensen is looking in Beckley's direction, but his eyes are trained on outer space. His arms are free, but he doesn't even try to move them, maybe he can't anymore. His tongue is probing the spaces where his teeth used to be.

"Don't backtalk me, beefcake. And if you say another word about Philadelphia, I'll plant your face on that table again, you hear me? On the table again. Hah."

Shane turns to the Sarge. "Jesus, all this guy is trying to say is that the Italians from Philadelphia were moving in on Kaufman. We need to hear more about that. But these guys are thugs with badges and they're too stupid to know how to handle this guy."

Roncalli nods. "There's only so much more we're gonna get before he drifts off or clams up. If we're going to get the whole story out of him, it's gotta be soon."

Smack!

Jensen's head swivels, Ackerman is next to him. Jensen didn't even flinch in self-defense. "I've got to get in there," Roncalli says.

"You can't, Sarge. Not after everything that happened before. You can't be a part of this interrogation."

Sarge jumps up and goes for the door. Shane elbows him. "I'll go. It doesn't matter if I'm part of this. And anything you can do in there to make it right, I can do too."

Roncalli tries to shove past him. Shane pushes him down to the floor and thinks, If it wasn't for his own good I could've never done that.

Jensen sees him coming through the door and goes bug-eyed.

"Get the fuck out of here," Shane says to the other three. "Get out of here, fast. And if you buck on me, an official is watching this whole thing."

He grips Jensen by the shoulders. "Stay with me," he says. "Stay with me." He takes the glass from the table and throws water in Jensen's face, then leans in. "Kaufman knew I was working the Rose case, right? And he sent you down to tail me, to rough me up to put me off his trail, right?"

Jensen nods. He mouths, *I'm sorry.*

Shane moves back. "Now before, you were talking about the Riccobenes, right?"

"No – no. I mean, yeah. Yes."

"The Riccobenes from Philadelphia, right?"

"Yeah – yes."

"They came down here and tried to move in on Kaufman's operation, right?"

"Yeah."

"Now, Kaufman had a girlfriend, right? Girl named Barbara, right?"

Jensen summons a smile at the memory of her.

"She was quite a honey, right?"

Jensen starts to lift his hands. He moves them in circles. He's trying to show her shape. His hands drop.

"And look – Jensen, don't fade on me. I'm thinking that the Riccobenes may've tried to scare Kaufman into giving them what they wanted. Am I right?"

Jensen swallows hard and nods.

"How'd it happen?"

"At a lounge. I was with Mr. Kaufman and her. She looked like a million dollars." Jensen pushes himself to sit up straight in the chair and for the first time he looks squarely at Shane. It's as if the mere vision of the girl rejuvenated him.

"And somebody from the Riccobene organization was in there?"

"Yeah. Sal Riccobene, the number two guy himself, he come all the way down. He – he musta tailed us to the lounge, and they talked, him and – and Mr. Kaufman. And things didn't go so good. He ended up – he ended up saying that if Mr. Kaufman didn't let him into the territory here, they'd start killing his people one-by- one. In fact, he said – he said, I'm staying down here long enough to make sure the job gets done right."

"The girlfriend was right there?"

"Nah, she was sitting a ways away, like always. She – she never got near those kind of talks."

"Was there any doubt in your mind about who the Riccobenes would kill first?"

"No, no doubt. Her. If they knew anything about Mr. Kaufman –" Jensen holds his side and grimaces, then hangs his head.

"It's okay, you're doing fine, go on."

"If they knew anything about Mr. Kaufman, they knew she's all he really cared about. And Mr. Kaufman knew that's who they meant."

"And what did he say to that?"

"He said, fuck you, you guinea cocksucker. Then he took the girlfriend and we left. He didn't think they had the nerve to come at him like that on his home turf."

Jensen coughs hard. He starts to shiver again. Shane takes off his suit jacket and drapes it over him. "So what happened next?"

"A week or so later, she wasn't around for a few days. Mr. Kaufman didn't think much of it at first. Then he got a box in the mail." Jensen's still shivering.

"What was it?"

"A cut-off finger. Her finger."

"How'd he know it was hers?"

"It still had a ring on it that he gave her."

"So, what did Jake have you do?"

Jensen stares at the table. He takes a long breath, and another. Both hands are trembling. "Nothing," he says.

"Come on, Jensen. You're almost there. Jake Kaufman wouldn't just sit back and take that. He had you go up to Philly. You went up there and took out one of theirs, right?"

"No."

"*Come on*, Jensen, you're this close."

"*No*. Mr. Kaufman did it himself. He told somebody about it afterwards and they told me."

"What?"

"He took the train by himself to the 30th Street Station. He called a meeting."

Jensen is breathing harder.

"And he killed three of theirs. All by himself. Got three of their top guys in the car they drove up in. Then he dumped the car with the bodies in the river up there."

"When I check this out," Shane asks, "how am I going to know it isn't all horseshit?"

"Check the police reports. Mr. Kaufman did it – he did it – he did it the way he knew how to do it."

"You mean, he cut out the eyes – "

"Yeah."

"And all that."

"Yeah."

That's why Kaufman never reported the girl as being missing. Because he'd already taken care of matters.

"But why," Shane asks, "didn't he ever have one of his lackeys pick up her stuff from the place on Washington Circle?"

"I think he held onto this crazy idea. Even with what he knew about the Riccobenes and the finger and all that. Like she might still be alive. Like she might still come back to him."

Jensen sags, his energy sapped. He coughs hard again and a red gob dribbles onto his shirt. His chest starts heaving, he bends over and vomits, all blood. He gets up, takes a few steps, topples face-first and starts convulsing. Shane rushes to him. "Did they club you on the back of your head?"

Jensen groans. "Over and over." He passes out.

Shane wheels around to the window, Sarge is already on the phone calling for an ambulance.

Five minutes later, two men in white coats come to the door and Shane rises to meet them.

Behind him, Jensen is curled up on the floor, with Shane's jacket as his blanket and his fedora as his pillow.

"You brought the wrong vehicle for this job," Shane says.

8

It's past nine, five hours after what happened, and Shane's following Jensen's litter out to the morgue wagon.

Cops from Internal Affairs came to headquarters. Beckley, Ackerman and O'Dell gave statements that tracked almost word-for-word: When they finished processing Jensen he somehow got hold of one of their service weapons, so they had to use force to disarm him and he kept coming at them, and they did what they had to do.

The coroner arrived late and worked slowly. In the end, he concluded that Jensen must've had a "pre-existing medical condition" and ruled the cause of his death "undetermined."

During the investigation, if it can be called that, Roncalli asked Shane what he thought should be done with the three cops. And Shane said, let 'em go, and the Sarge got angry at first and said, I think your time in the nuthouse must've made you soft. And Shane said, maybe it did but I spent Jensen's last minutes with him and I wasn't even supposed to be there, and you were right there watching me, so we don't have much incentive to see this thing go anywhere.

"And besides all that," Shane said, "you didn't know it, Sarge, but Beckley worked security on the side for Jake Kaufman. And for all we know, when Beckley heard Jensen start to put Kaufman in the middle of a murder he figured, I can get on the big boss's good side if I just eliminate this problem right here. Which would make this a premeditated murder on the department's watch."

Maybe that's giving Beckley too much credit, thinking he could put two and two together and find his way to four, but why take the chance?

Shane now looks down at the shrouded figure on the gurney and pats it around the shoulders. *Someday I'll make it right. Just not right now.*

As for Beckley, Ackerman and O'Dell, they're getting themselves some fat steaks at Blackie's and then they'll be back on the homo circuit by midnight.

He passes through the courthouse plaza, which is empty but for a few "Free Willie" signs scattered here and there. The good news for Willie is, he's free. The bad news for him is he's back on Glick's Court.

Well, at least he's home with his mom.

Shane passes the newsstand and sees a row of fresh special edition Posts with a fresh banner headline.

MATT BARRY COLLAPSES, IN COMA
Shock of Son's Charge Is Being Blamed

The Barrys and Kinnocks waged a long war with a lot of collateral casualties with no real winner. Now it's over.

Too much is happening. He doesn't buy the paper, doesn't even slow down, his head is too small to accommodate it all. He finds his car, in the space where he parked it that morning, in what seems like was a different decade.

He wants to talk with somebody and stops to call Bobby at a payphone but gets no answer. He tries Claire but she doesn't answer either. He starts to call his father but doesn't.

He hasn't eaten since last night and on a whim decides to try out the Calvert Café for dinner. As many times as he's been through the place on the case, he's never actually eaten there. He gets the meatloaf special with milk and takes his time with it. The place is filling up with a late crowd, but the waiter doesn't try to hustle him out.

Things have fallen into place. He now knows who killed Emily. All the questions have been answered, he can move on.

He starts to get up.

He settles back in his seat. He orders more meatloaf.

Somebody left the morning Post on the chair next to him and he checks out the movie listings. The fare's thin and he eyes something called "Washington Story" at the Palace.

I've got a Washington story for you.

He rises from the table and pays the check. Outside, he hears a squawking voice: his police radio.

Sarge has an update. The Philly P.D. confirmed that three Riccobene goons in a car washed up last April on the banks of the Delaware River, eyes gouged out and shoved in their mouths, pants pulled down around their ankles for good measure. The Philly PD will just take MPD's reports and close out their case. Nothing's going to happen to Kaufman because the only known witness against him just got beaten to death.

"Rector," the Sarge goes on, "is reading the reports on the Jensen interview right now. He's scheduled a press conference for tomorrow at noon, to close out the Rose case and say it was solved on his watch."

Sarge goes quiet for a second or two.

"It's all done with, Shane. Take tomorrow off, you've had a tough couple of days." He hangs up, like that.

****

Shane sits still for a few minutes. His mind strays to Joe Barry in late May, lounging in a mansion in tennis whites, plotting his Presidency with father in residence.

How quickly a man's past and his future can both be taken away from him.

He starts his car and heads for Georgetown.

Parking on 34th Street, it occurs to him that Barry might not even be home. *If he's back in town, he's probably with his father, assuming he still has a father to be with.* But coming closer to the house Shane sees that the black-poled lanterns that flank the entrance are lit, and he hears a Broadway soundtrack coming from a record player on the second-story patio.

Joe Barry answers the door wearing a satin bathrobe and carrying a champagne glass. He squints into the lantern glare. "Who is it?"

"I just came by to tell you I'm sorry about the way everything went for you today."

"Oh, Kinnock. Christ." Barry comes out on the front step. "I've got some people staying over, ostensibly to cheer me up." He pulls the door behind him, but loses his grip on it and with a long creak it eases back where it wants to go.

Barry's bristly hair is askew and his blue eyes are red-tinged.

"Joe, I heard you never drink."

"I never have, until tonight. Now I see what I've been missing." He's grasping the glass by its stem as delicately as a circus juggler balancing dinner plates on a stick.

"How's your father?"

"Stable, at least temporarily. I was at the hospital a while ago, but came home. There's nothing else I could do." Joe Barry isn't one to linger by a bedside unless the bed holds a nubile female.

Barry pats him on the shoulder and summons a wan version of the famous grin. "It was nice of you to come by," he says. "Let's stay in touch."

"Wait. About your charge."

"I've got to fight it, that's all. It's not the worst thing I've ever come up against." He starts to turn away.

"Dammit, Joe, listen to me. There's been a development in the case, a big one, and it could help you out a lot. But I need to know what the hell you said in that grand jury that got you indicted."

"The truth, the whole truth, and nothing but the truth, just like that son of a bitch Faye asked for." Barry rests his hand on his doorknob and starts to push it lightly.

"Joe, stop. Did you give him the same line of bullshit you gave me about Emily? Jesus, I tried to tell you, don't hold back."

Barry hesitates, then pulls the door shut with a click. He squares around. "Faye raked me over the coals and I gave it all up. How she was hired and what she did at the office and how we first got together and where and when and how often. I thought he was going to ask me how good she was in the sack, for Crissake. He covered everything else, even whether I still think about her."

"Which –"

"I do."

Shane presses. "Is there anything Faye asked more than once? Like he was staying on a particular point to trip you up?"

Barry stares at his glass as he swirls it and the champagne laps at the edge. "He kept hounding me about whether I was with her at any time on the day she was killed."

"Were you?"

"No. Hell, when all this first came up, I couldn't even say. Then I saw in the paper that you all decided she was killed on May 1st last year. And I figured out that I'd gone to the Nats game earlier that day, and then I went back to my office and worked late."

"How'd you figure out you were at the game that afternoon?"

"I had a pretty good memory of the game I saw. And I had someone on my staff check the old newspapers at the library."

"Can anybody say they were with you later on when you were back at your office?"

"No."

Barry draws closer and drops his voice further. "Jesus, Shane. Emily wanted to get together that night and I didn't want to. I had other things going on, okay, so I didn't see her. But in the grand jury Faye kept asking me about the restaurant where she and I always met. He kept going back to, was I sure I wasn't with her there that night, was I sure that I didn't pay the check, all these other questions about the check."

That's it. The FBI found Barry's fingerprint on Emily's receipt from the Calvert Café.

"Joe," Shane says, "what if Faye has solid evidence that you were with her at the restaurant that night?"

Barry shakes his head. "He can't, I wasn't at the restaurant. I wasn't with her that night."

"Faye thinks you were. Which would make you a suspect –"

"He didn't charge me with a murder."

"– or a witness. Which means that Faye can end up not charging anybody with the murder and he can still put this perjury charge on you, because you didn't help him find who did it. You could end up being the only mope who ever goes to the jail for anything having to do with this."

"It doesn't matter. I wasn't with her."

Shane's had enough. "Why are you lying about this?" He goes ahead and tells him about everything Jensen has said about why Emily was killed. "It was all over some stupid gangster shit, Joe. Everything'll come out soon, you can come clean about this and you won't be in any trouble."

Joe Barry clenches his jaw and glares at him. It's a righteous look.

Then again, the man looked pretty righteous back in May, when he was trying on tuxedos and denying up and down that Emily Rose was anything more to him than just another broad in his typing pool.

"You have a lawyer now, Joe?"

"Yeah, finally."

"Any lawyer worth his fee can make the whole thing go away just by telling Faye that you're willing to come in and say, yes, you were with her but no, you don't know what happened to her after you left her. And once Faye finds out that MPD is folding up its tent on the big show he's not going to want anything to do with your sideshow, after you say the magic words."

Barry tips back his champagne glass. "Except it's not the truth. And politically, I'm still fucked, whether or not Faye drops the case against me. All the photos are now out there, I can't even get my wife on the phone. I'm finished all around."

A few blocks away, a small round of fireworks go pop-pop-pop. Kids warming up for tomorrow's July 4th celebrations. There's another pop, and then silence.

Overhead, Shane hears the door to the second-floor patio open and close.

Barry says, "Your father's behind all this, he has to be."

"He's not. Faye may be a –"

"A prick."

"A prick, but he's his own man. And whatever my father is capable of doing, he didn't push you into bed with the girl, and he didn't put any lies in your mouth, either."

There's no point in talking with him anymore. "I've got to be going, Joe. I'll say some prayers for your father. And I mean that."

Shane walks towards his car, leaving Joe Barry on his front step with his empty champagne glass.

"Joey!" A woman's voice.

"Joey, who's down there with you? I can't see."

Shane stops and turns around.

Claire Montgomery is standing at the second-story patio railing, wearing a diaphanous nightgown.

She's shielding her eyes with one hand. "Joey, come up. Bran's getting impatient. He's mixed some Manhattans. We're all waiting for you."

Behind her is a blond wearing pajamas. Presumably Bran Bentley's date for the night, and definitely not his wife.

Claire pirouettes and a faint breeze tugs her gown against the body that just two nights ago shook passionately beneath Shane. Now she hovers high above him, blinded by a brighter light.

Nothing that he's seeing is really much of a surprise, when you go back through it all. Not that that makes matters much easier.

Then again, you can't miss what you never really had.

He lingers for a moment, taking in everything about her, knowing that he'll probably never see her again. And if he ever does, it'll be a small-town happenstance, like ex-lovers bumping into each other at the post office.

Joe Barry is still standing on his front step, glass-hand hanging slack, Adonis slumping in sleepwear.

Shane is as much the betrayer as the betrayed and he knows it. The universe, at least for a few moments, is in balance. Considering that just recently he felt so beleaguered as to try to immolate himself, that's more than enough recompense for any pain that he'll feel in the days to come.

He drives over to Wisconsin and eases up to Martin's. Through the window he can see the same hunchbacked bus boy waiting tables. A neon sign in the window flashes, "Ballantine, Ballantine, Ballantine." The TV high on the back wall is showing a prizefight from somewhere and a group of men is clustered beneath the flickering image of mayhem.

Shane drives off, distracted.

He's weighing Claire's deft evasions against Raymond's, and he's remembering the outright lies of his own past.

He's thinking about deception and whether it's ever entirely innocent.

He's still thinking about Joe Barry.

9

THE WASHINGTON POST
Friday, July 4, 1952

D.C. RELAXES ON NATION'S BIRTHDAY
But Protests May Mar Holiday Festivities
By a Staff Reporter

An array of parades, picnics, outings and commemorative speeches will mark another Fourth of July for Washington area residents.

The highlight event on the Washington Monument grounds is expected to draw a quarter-million people, but anyone who doesn't want to fight the crowds can see fireworks at other locations in the area, including the Carter Barron Amphitheatre in Rock Creek Park. Tonight's show will be introduced by Rep. Raymond Kinnock (D-N.Y.), Majority Leader of the House of Representatives.

Extra police officers will be on duty for the fireworks shows, but MPD officials report that resources will need to be diverted to the Second Precinct, where disturbances flared last night following the release and exoneration of Willie Robinson in the Emily Rose murder case. An additional round of outbreaks, protesting Robinson's May arrest for the murder and his treatment at D.C. Jail, are expected today. The police say they will be firmly dealt with.

****

Shane stumbles into Roncalli's office.

"We've got to get in and talk with Rector, right now."

The Sarge stares at him. "Jesus, I've seen this movie before. You can't help yourself, can you?"

He comes around his desk and puts his hand on Shane's shoulder. "You need more help, son."

"Don't start going off about how I should let God find me. I haven't had a drop."

He's spent all night driving, dead sober. First in loops around and through D.C., then across the bridge into Virginia, all the way out where the country roads start, past Annandale, past cow pastures made silver by the moon, then tracking back by a light rising in the sky to a city whose nighttime glimmer faded in daybreak.

"God, Shane. Did you sleep at all?"

"Has Rector met with the press yet?"

"No, but it's on in half an hour."

"We've got to stop him. There's no way this was a gang hit. He can't close this case out."

"Keep your voice down." Roncalli closes his office door. "You're on a short leash."

"I've had all night to think about it. It makes no sense. If the mob killed this girl, there's no way they would've done it in a public park, just down the hill from a major street, where she could scream and some nosy passerby could fuck everything up. They'd have found a way to snatch her up off a quiet road and gag her. They'd have thrown her in the trunk of a car, gotten her into a place they could completely control."

"Maybe they just botched the job."

"The Riccobenes are professionals. According to Jensen, they had days to plan this. They wouldn't have botched it like this."

"Maybe they killed her someplace else and just dumped her there."

"That doesn't make any sense either. You know as much about these things as I do. When the mob gets rid of a body they cut it up, or they bury it in fresh concrete, or they do what Kaufman did with the ginzos from Philly, just drop it in a river. They don't leave it in a park where somebody could come across it in a few hours with fingerprints and God knows what else still on it."

"She ended up getting buried in sand."

"Whoever dumped her didn't know that was going to happen. That was their lucky break."

"Maybe they dumped her in public because they wanted to make a statement to Kaufman."

"They were already making a statement to him. They sent her finger to him. Why make a public dump if you're sending the finger? Why send the finger if you're making a public dump?"

"So, I take it you think Jensen was lying when he gave us all this."

"The problem with beating the shit out of a guy is that he'll tell you pretty much anything if he thinks it'll keep him from getting beaten to shit even more."

"He was right about the Riccobenes getting killed."

"I have no doubt about that part. Kaufman thought the Riccobenes killed his girl and so he got his revenge."

"And doesn't that count for something?"

"You mean, if the evidence against the Riccobenes on the Rose murder was strong enough to convince Kaufman, it should be strong enough for us? Last time I checked, the police generally don't count mobster intuition as something establishing probable cause in a murder case."

They go at it like this for a while and it takes Shane back to how they used to argue over cases, night after night, on the graveyard shift not even six years ago, and how it always turned out alright. Shane, fresh from the academy, slightly deranged and altogether unrooted, fell into a squad led by a sergeant who had more than enough sons on his hands at home but took one more in on the job.

The Sarge circles back to the Riccobenes. "If they didn't kill the girl, how is it they got her finger to send to Kaufman? And how is it that Jensen's story about the finger matches up square with our inventory of the girl's bones? Remember the missing ring finger?"

"I remember." Shane settles against the edge of the Sarge's desk. "I don't know how. I just know Emily Rose didn't get killed by any gangster. The rest of it, I'm gonna figure out. Or, I should say, you are."

Roncalli walks to a mirror on his office walls, stares into it. "You're still crazy with this, aren't you?"

"I am, Sarge. Except now it's for all the right reasons."

Roncalli turns back to him: "There might be no holding Rector back from the press conference. And once that happens there'll be no going back." He leaves, muttering something to himself.

He comes back not five minutes later. "I bought us time."

"What'd you tell him?"

"First, I said you never meet the press on a holiday, nobody's paying attention. Wait a day and you get a banner headline. Second, everyone'll be watching you to see if you measure up to how your old boss Charlie Moran would've handled this. It's your maiden voyage and down deep you know you're not exactly FDR in the public speaking department."

"You busted his balls like that?"

"He is where he is. But he'll always be just what I've always known him to be. And he and I both know that."

"You're on borrowed time here."

"Like you. Like everybody everywhere."

Roncalli turns his chair to the wall. "You're back on this case," he says quietly. "You and Shiflett and me. And Nickens, of course."

"We need Nickens?"

"He's got a strange take on life and if you were to ever wake him out of a sound sleep in the middle of the night there's no telling what you'd hear come out of his mouth. But he's a genius."

"And how much will you tell Rector?"

"You let me worry about that. In the meantime, all hell is going to break loose again tonight. He's all bent out of shape over the ruckus in the Second, with all the protests going on. So he's going to have another sweep over there."

"And he's probably looking to put some shit on Robinson because it's got to be killing him that the boy got let go."

"Just get the word out to your boy to lay low," Sarge answers.

The Sarge is still facing the wall.

"It'll all be alright," Shane says. "I'm that guy again. The guy who broke the hooker. I'm that guy."

Sarge spins around. "*What*?"

"Remember? The Uline case, Negro girl raped by a white guy. I broke her and she testified."

Sarge just stares at him vacantly.

10

"Jesus fucking Christ."

Shane's never heard Sarge even say the word 'fucking,' now he's out with this.

"Jesus fucking Christ," he says again.

"So even after all this talking," he says, "we can't even agree on who our best target is. Shane, you think it's Joe Barry, or Matt Barry, or anybody named Barry, or some Barry flunky. Right?"

"Don't put words in my mouth. I just can't see why Joe's lying about being with her that night if he didn't have something to do with it."

"And you, Shiflett. You just know it's not the Negro."

"When we was with him I looked him right in his eyes and I didn't see a man who could do somethin' like this."

Roncalli groans, shakes his head. He's testy, distracted. He gets up from the table and his favorite swivel chair and goes to his office. A few seconds later the clamor of his beloved opera is resounding throughout the squad room. "It's by Handel," he says. "It's called Giulio Casare. To you mopes that's Julius Caesar."

He's shuffling through papers. The meager case file, last seen in Charlie Moran's custody. His attention is sporadic.

At one point he asks, out of nowhere, when do the Nats open at home every year, and Shane says, in mid-April. And Sarge says, definitely not on the first of the month, right, and Shane says, no, the President always comes out and it's a big deal so I know for sure. And the Sarge just nods.

Sarge doesn't even spare his man Nickens. He tells him that there's something in one of the reports that he has a question about, and when Nickens doesn't reply right away Sarge snaps, "We need to talk about it, you hear?"

The radio opera reaches peak force, a tenor agonizes in Italian. Sarge pauses for a moment, listening. Then: "You hear that? Christ, you don't have to know another language. You can hear it in his voice, he's talking about being betrayed."

He moves the Park case file to the side. He stands still for a moment, eyes closed, then turns to Nickens. "So what about you, Haynes," he says. "What are you thinking."

"Me? To be honest," Nickens answers, "I don't know why we're all here. This thing was solved yesterday."

He hasn't before deigned to lower himself into the discussion, preferring to devote his attentions to his pocket watch. Setting it and re-setting it, turning the stem and watching the hands move in counter-rotation.

Shane's had enough. "An hour and a half has gone by, Nickens, and this is your first contribution? Let's get serious here. You can't really tell me you think this was the work of a professional criminal organization."

Nickens winks, then winks again.

"First," he says, barely looking up from the watch, "nobody's said a word here about the girl's finger, and that by itself is solid corroboration for what Jensen told you. And second, Kinnock, look at the word you just used, criminal. How do we catch criminals? Because they do stupid things. Look at who we're talking about here. I know their type. I'm the only one here who's actually worked a mob case."

He's staked out their houses, their jobs, their wives, their girlfriends and their girlfriend's boyfriends. He's sat for days in the woods behind their vulgar houses in their gated cul-de-sacs, just waiting for just one dago to hand just one thing off to just one other dago. He's hauled their "guinea asses" in front of him in hearing rooms and grilled them for hours. "And one thing I've learned is they're not masterminds. I've seen how they'd shoot each other in front of their own mothers, how they'd dump a body in anything from a burlap sack to a phone booth to a public street. No offense intended to your family heritage, sergeant, but the worst of your breed is barely a step above a primate."

Nickens goes back to his watch, still winking.

The Sarge is flush and Shane thinks he may even go across the table at Nickens. But all he does is turn to Shane. "This thing is as wide open as it was the day we stumbled on this broad's bones. So somebody just tell me, is there anybody else we should be looking at?"

The intercom on the table buzzes. Sarge needs to see Chief Rector, right then. He leaves, breathing hard.

His question lingers. Is there anybody else?

Sure there is. Somebody who had a pretty good reason to resent Emily Rose, maybe even hate her so much that in a stray moment she'd want to see her dead.

Shane just can't bring himself to offer up Claire Montgomery to the Sarge as a murder suspect.

The Sarge comes back, looking calmer than before. "I think the picture just got a little clearer."

He starts towards his command post in his swivel chair but claims instead a standing position. The opera in his office has been muffled.

"Rector got a call from Park Police," Sarge says, "about a fresh case they'll want help on. It'll be coming over the wire..."

The old teletype machine in the corner clatters to life.

"... now."

The four stand over the machine as it spits out its story line-by-line.

U.S. Park Police reports that on 4 July 1952 at 1014 hours it responded to a call at Rock Creek Park south of Carter Barron Amphitheatre and located a Caucasian

```
female with no signs of life lying unconscious in grass
next to a walking path. The coroner, called to the scene,
concluded as follows. Time of death between 2000 and
2200 hours 3 July 1952. Cause of death strangulation.
Manner of death homicide.
```

The machine goes quiet, then jumps back to life.

```
Evidence of forcible sexual activity, post-mortem.
```

Bobby nudges Shane. "What does post-mortem --"

"He screwed her after she was dead."

```
Recovered from victim's purse, underneath body, was
U.S. currency, assorted jewelry and identification bearing
name FLORENCE COOPERMAN, age 25, employment status,
secretary with U.S. Bureau of Labor Statistics.
```

The machine goes silent. "Another dead girl in the Park," Shane says. "There's going to be mass hysteria. Plus, they have fireworks up at the amphitheatre tonight."

Sarge rips the teletype page from the machine and folds it in half. "Which is exactly why I'm going to tell Rector to keep this away from the press for a while. But it won't be long before they get wind of it."

"Did Park Police say if they have any leads?"

"Yeah," he replies, "apparently they did a quick canvas and found a guy who lives right near the amphitheatre. He was walking his dog around 9 and he noticed a girl, he'd never seen her before, she wasn't from the neighborhood."

"How do we know it was the dead girl?"

"The way he described her fit her to a T. He said she was standing near a man, seemed to be talking with him, and then she started towards the Park and the man was walking behind her."

"Any description?"

"He didn't get a great look, but he could say he was a young Negro."

"No height, weight, light, dark. Just, young Negro male. Which means it's pretty much open season on all the Negroes in town."

"No," the sergeant says, "it means it's open season on just one Negro, Willie Robinson. Rector's moving up his sweep and he's hitting Glick's Court hard at four o'clock. His exact words were, the coon's out less than a day and another one of our girls is already gone, let's go get him."

Shane feels a sharp pang. Bobby says, "It just can't be. Willie's too smart to go right out and do somethin' like that."

"I know how you both feel," the Sarge says, "but anyone has to admit this narrows our focus. Unless these things are unrelated."

"No," Shane murmurs. "Two young white women, both strangled, both dumped in the Park, both seen with a Negro before they got killed. If they're not related, nothing is. And he's escalating. It wasn't enough to kill this one, he had to defile her corpse too."

"Okay, let's assume the same guy did them both. So, what next?"

"Joe Barry's out of the picture. There's no reason for him to do this one, unless he's secretly the Jack the Ripper of Rock Creek Park. And if Joe's out, that means that anybody who's connected to him is out, too. And anybody connected to the Kaufmans or the Riccobenes. If Emily wasn't a mob hit, this one sure isn't."

Nickens, transfixed by his pocket watch, says nothing.

The sergeant unholsters his gun and checks it. "I haven't had to even think about bringing this out since the last sweep."

Shane stands up and starts to pace. "Rector says there's no other witnesses, just the dog walker?"

"So far."

"And where was this girl found again?"

"Colorado Avenue. About a hundred yards down from where Colorado and Blagden Terrace cross."

Nickens suddenly shows an interest. "Colorado. Blagden. You all talked with somebody who lives up there."

"Right," Shane says. "Dalton. Quentin Dalton. The housing inspector."

Nickens rouses himself to stand. His facial tic is gone. "We need to get over and talk to him. Right away."

He picks up his pocket watch and juggles it in the palm of his left hand. "I can go see him. I think I know – the essence of him. If I need help, sergeant, I'll call back here. We just have to make sure the rest of your department doesn't get wind of this because one of your imbeciles will tip off the press."

"You think Dalton might have seen something?"

"No. I think he might have *done* something."

It would be easy for Nickens to explain, so of course he doesn't, and the Sarge has to prompt him. "So how do you figure?"

Nickens shambles over to the Sarge's swivel chair and sinks into it, wiggling himself back and forth against the worn seat cushion. He has the stage, with a story about the killer that only Haynes Nickens can tell, in a voice that could sooth a wildcat into a deep sleep.

Quentin Dalton. Nickens has read the interviews with him, and everything he's read is converging.

Born and raised in the spawning ground for the Ku Klux Klan. Goes to war. Comes back stateside, hoping for something better than what he's seen before.

Instead he ends up a housing inspector in D.C., maybe because that's all he can get. Gets married, probably to somebody who reminds him of back home, and they have a few girls, but the wife leaves him and takes his girls and he spends all his working hours crawling through the city's shacks.

And one day our man Dalton walks near a park and sees a white girl talking to a Negro and then the next morning, according to him, he gets seized by the impulse to call the police about it, and the police don't do anything. Of course, it's a day later, but now he's on the record as Joe Citizen doing his duty.

Some time goes by, the girl he saw turns up dead, and our man Dalton goes around again to the police to talk about it, knowing that everybody's going to see him all over again as Joe Citizen doing his duty. Some more time goes by, and lo and behold another white girl gets killed in the very same park, and this one's found right down the street from his house.

"And gentlemen," said Nickens, voice rising, "who would believe it, but she was last seen talking with a Negro."

Sarge is squinting. "So you think all that proves just *what*?"

"Alright, sergeant. Let's break it down some more."

Imagine a boy growing up in a small town. And it's a segregated town, and his parents are traditional people, but he's happy with his life growing up there. He develops certain, say, attitudes.

And the boy becomes a man, and he reaches a certain age, and he has some experiences in life that should broaden him but they really don't. They just confirm over and over again all those suspicions he had about the people he grew to hate when he was a boy.

The hate he has in him has been buried so deep, buried by his past, maybe by his mother and father, maybe especially by his mother, that nothing can touch it.

And he starts seeing the races mix, and he doesn't like it, and everything he learned as a boy and learned all over again as a man comes hurtling towards him.

"I can't put it any plainer than this," Nickens says. "The man sees a good-looking white girl anywhere near a Negro and it drives him to violence. Do you see it now? He killed this girl, and he killed the Rose girl, and he probably killed others before that."

"So, the Negroes aren't doing it, they're –"

"They're just the reason it's being done."

"But Dalton holds down a job," Sarge says, "He works for the city."

"His *respectable* self works. His *disordered* self runs around and does bad things.

He's two different people."

Nickens rests his watch on the tabletop and puts a cupped hand over it.

"So how do you get all that from some write-ups of interviews with this guy?"

"I could say by reading between the lines but that wouldn't be true. I get it by just reading the lines. What did Dalton himself say? It really was her own fault. Remember, he said that?"

Nickens spins his watch with a sharp flick of his wrist. He's just playing now.

"Remember what else Dalton said. Looking like she did, he said, standing in front of the wrong kind of guy, something was going to go wrong. He said that, his words, not mine. Kinnock, you were right there. Did something go through you when he said that?"

"Yeah, I suppose – yeah."

"You thought there was something a little strange about him, right?"

"You could say that. And – yeah. Never mind."

"You were about to say something. Don't let me hold you back."

"I don't know what it means," Shane answers. "Just that I saw Dalton in court after Faye dropped the case against Robinson. And he was a lot hotter about it than I would have thought he'd be."

Nickens turns to the Sarge. "And these two murders happening the way they did, with all the details lining up. Do you really think it's all just coincidence?"

"If you put it that way," the sergeant says, "maybe not." He still looks apprehensive.

Nickens's spinning watch slows to a halt. "So that's enough reason to go talk to this Quentin Dalton."

For the first time since Shane laid eyes on the man, Haynes Nickens is smiling broadly.

"Go do it, then," Roncalli says. "Call me here if you need me to come up there. Shane, Shiflett, run up to the Second and snatch Robinson up. We've still got to act on the assumption he could've done this. Nobody's above suspicion now."

And if Rector's boys get to Robinson first, there's no telling what that boy might end up looking like.

*If we don't find him at home, we'll go everyplace else where we might
have a lead on him.*

*And if we still can't find him, we'll head to the Park and look for him
there.*

Nickens picks up his watch, puts it on its fob and stashes it in his vest.
"You can go ahead and try to find this Robinson boy," he says, "but it'll be
pointless. If he's got a place to go to that's far away from here, he's already
gone. Long gone."

11

"Them over there are cottonwoods, and them there are some black
walnuts. And just ahead, if you look close enough you'll see a whole mess
of other trees, them are your pignuts, your beeches, your sycamores,
everything."

Shane and Bobby are back in Rock Creek Park, purposefully going
about a fool's errand, and Bobby's lapsed into the role of park ranger.
Underfoot is the compacted residue of a hundred autumns and overhead,
in the twilight sky, the first faint glimmer of the implacable galaxy.

"It's all right here," Shane says to Bobby. "All here in this park, the
universe from top to bottom."

But he's talking to himself. Bobby's lingered behind, trailing an owl
hoot.

From headquarters they raced straight to Glick's Court and found it
lifeless. Word of the dead white girl in the Park no doubt had already spread,
in the way that murder news races through a city. All the alley regulars
were locked inside the shanties like beach town dwellers hunkered down
for a hurricane. Shane and Bobby went to Willie's house at number 16 and
banged on the door and from inside just heard a fretful silence.

"Willie, if you're in there, open the door," Shane cried out. "Open it
up for me now and nobody'll knock it down later. Please, open the door."

Finally, a voice from inside. "He ain't here. And he ain't gon' be here."

Shane believed it, and even if he didn't it wouldn't have mattered, he didn't have the stomach to barge in all over again and knock around black people over who knows what. From there they went to Reverend Williamson's church and found the doors locked, then to the Calvert Café and found a "Closed" sign hanging crooked in the window.

Now Shane and Bobby are working their way up from the zoo towards the amphitheatre, looking for a scared, blameless Negro who's short on traveling cash.

Or maybe, on the other hand, looking for a public menace who's seeking cover in the wild.

Shane thinks, I don't care what Nickens is saying about Dalton, this case is still wide open and nobody's in the clear.

Bobby catches up to him. Shane points overhead. "There's Venus. You can always tell it, brighter than anything else."

"I don't know nothin' about a bright sky," Bobby answers. He's gnawing on a tobacco chud and takes a spit to the side, barely missing Shane's feet.

They come to a thicket of bramble and long strands of rusted barbed wire and Shane rips his suit sidestepping through it all. Just past the bramble and the wire is a canopy of vines. "I've done this walk a buncha times before," Bobby says. "Everything sorta changes here." The ground drops into a ravine, the woods get denser, the last shard of sky disappears.

He leans against Shane. "The trees bein' thick like this, reminds me of back home. Guess everybody knows a dark place or two, right?"

"I suppose."

Shane catches his shoe on a root and tumbles down a small incline. His suit is already ruined. He doesn't even care now. He starts back the wrong way and Bobby hooks his arm and says, "Over here." A cacophony of cricket-chirp surrounds them.

They press on. Shane feels for his watch on his wrist but it's missing, maybe lost in his fall. "What the hell time is it?" he asks.

"Don't know. Hard to tell in here."

"Whose idea was this? There's no way we're going to find him in here, there's too much forest and just two of us. Let's just find an open space and get out."

Bobby doesn't answer.

A shrill shriek cuts through the heavy forest air, three times. "That's a fox," Bobby says. "Sounds like he's rabid."

Shane pulls a flashlight from his back pocket and trains it on the path. It lights up a dead dog lying off to the side, cut up.

"Christ," he says, "are there wolves in these woods?"

"Animals don't do nothin' like that. Human being did that."

Bobby hangs back.

Shane quickens his step.

He knows every damn bird whistle and tree stump and squirrel turd in here. It's like the geese call him up for permission before they fly south for the winter.

What the hell else does he know that he's not telling me?

And where the hell was he last night when I was trying to call him?

Shane starts running.

Behind him he hears, "Hold up!" Bobby's chasing him. Shane knows he's too big to be able to close the gap much but still speeds up. Shane runs, for a quarter-mile or a mile, for a minute or ten, until he sees a light glow on the right and he races towards it. He hears Bobby's voice from way behind. "Where're you goin'? Where should I go?" Shane slows and turns. "Make your way up to Carter Barron!" He hears Bobby yelling, "What?" but he doesn't turn back around, just goes back to tracking the light, which starts to flicker and dim but suddenly widens to a glare.

The cricket-din gives way to car horns and squealing streetcar brakes.

He emerges onto a street at least a mile from where he parked his car. He hails a cab. He's winded and sweaty, in a tattered, dirty suit, and the driver slows to get a good look at him and starts to pull away but Shane

badges him and he stops. Which is good for the driver, since Shane wouldn't
have thought twice about drawing down on him and dragging him by the
neck from his cab and just taking it.

Back at his squad car Shane calls for Sarge but doesn't get him, just
gets his message from the switchboard girl. "Get Shiflett," the message says,
"and haul it on up to where the girl was killed last night."

"That's it? Nothing else?"

The switchboard girl pops her gum. "The sergeant said he's with
Nickens, come quick, he needs help."

*Nickens got Dalton to cop to both killings and he and Sarge took him
to the second scene.*

Shane drives down to Blagden Terrace, parks close to Dalton's
address and trots towards the Park. From the amphitheatre a quarter-mile
away he can hear a faint, echoing voice on the gathering breeze. It's his
father, master of the evening's ceremonies, commanding a loudspeaker.
"Thank you (you, you!)," Raymond is saying. "For letting me come here
tonight (night, night!). On this great Fourth of July (July, July!)"

Shane enters the woods squinting. He sweeps his flashlight beam
across the wall of greenery before him and it lands on two figures in a
clearing a short walk away.

Haynes Nickens is sitting on a felled tree trunk. Next to him is a man
lying face-down.

Shane can see the man is wearing a dark uniform.

Nickens must've snatched Dalton right off of his housing inspector job.

Nickens is staring at the man, whispering to himself.

"Jesus, Haynes," Shane says, coming up, "did he buck on you? Are
you okay?"

The man's hands are behind his back. His hat is propped on the back
of his head, and blood is draining from somewhere beneath it.

Nickens looks up slowly. "Fine, Kinnock. Knew you'd be coming.
And Shiflett isn't too far behind, I imagine."

"He should be here in a few minutes."

"There's your man right there, Kinnock. Take a look." Nickens rises and takes a few steps back.

Shane bends down over the form, turns it over and shines his light on it.

It's the Sarge. He has a bullet hole in his forehead, his eyes are bulging, his teeth clamped down hard on his tongue. He's as dead as the fallen tree that's next to him.

Shane lurches backwards and slams into Nickens. His flashlight drops to the ground next to the Sarge's face. He gets on his hands and knees and vomits, choking.

"It's all right," Nickens says from behind him. "Get it all out."

Shane vomits again, then starts dry-heaving. "Where's Dalton?"

"Funny you should ask. I looked in on him a while ago. He's watching his TV by himself, just like last night. Hasn't left the house in a couple of days."

Shane feels the cold prod of a gun muzzle at the back of his head. He hears Nickens say, "Do you get it now?"

"I'm starting to," he says.

He wipes foul spit from his mouth. "That was you, wasn't it? That was you that you were talking about a few hours ago, as if it was Dalton. The boy growing up in the small town, seeing white women with Negroes and getting violent over it all. Jesus."

Looking sideways at the Sarge, he fights back tears. *Sarge was a man of God and this son of a bitch didn't even give him the chance to fold his hands before he killed him.* "So why'd you have to do that to him?"

"It was only a matter of time. And to a certain kind of man, nothing can ever come down to being just a matter of time."

"He'd figured it out, hadn't he?"

"He hadn't yet, but he was going to – don't look back at me, Kinnock. Keep your head down." Nickens gropes around under Shane's suit jacket with his left hand, yanks the service revolver from its holster, sticks it in his waistband.

"There was something in your report, wasn't there, Nickens."

"Don't turn around."

When do the Nats start playing?

They've never opened on the first of April, have they?

Shane closes his eyes and sees nothing but white. The blameless, unsullied white of the eyes of a dead man. And two lonely black dots, floating in a white sea.

"You backdated your report," Shane says. "You backdated your report, and the Sarge ended up noticing it, and he knew something was fishy. That was why he asked me about the Nats' opening day, right there in front of you. You remember, when he was talking about betrayal."

"Shut the fuck up. Excuse the language."

"No, wait," Shane rasps. "We know each other. All the woods around here, they changed you. Having to perch in them every day, just watching. They changed you just like that jungle on Guadalcanal changed me. So hear me out. You'd followed Barry and Emily around all the way up to the night of May 1, the night you killed her, and that's the night of the same day that you'd tracked Barry to the Nats game. And you'd notebooked it all, like the persnickety bastard that you are."

"Do we really have to go through all this?" For a moment, there's no anger in Nickens's voice. It's as if he's enjoying the recitation.

"And then a year went by and the girl's body was found. So, then you figured you'd better put all your surveillance notes into a report and stick it in a file, in case anybody asked. But you couldn't use the real date because it'd show you were following her the night she was killed, and people would think you'd know something. And you'd have to answer a lot of pesky questions."

Shane's still on all fours, talking to the darkness beneath him.

"So, you backdated the report," he says. "You just moved it back a month, to April 1. You're a busy guy, right? What was it you said when you were talking about Dalton? The respectable side and the disordered side. The respectable side, it had its hands full, what with the stakeouts and the hearings and God-knows-what-else going on. Then there's the disordered side, well, it's disorderly, right? And you –"

"He."

"What?"

"He. It's a word. Use it."

"Okay. He didn't take much time with this report. Let's face it, he got sloppy, and this is where he made his mistake. He didn't know the Nats weren't even playing for real yet on April 1. They hadn't even made their way up north from spring training yet, for Christ's sake."

"He could've gone back and checked."

"But that was way beneath the great Haynes Nickens, right? Nobody was going to be so picky and second-guess Haynes Nickens on something so small as a date in a report. Besides, he hadn't given baseball a moment's thought since, when, about five years ago. Which happens to be when they started letting Negroes in."

"Who?"

"Negroes."

"*Who*?" Nickens thrusts his gun harder into the back of Shane's head.

"Nigras." Shane swallows. "Niggers."

"Fine, fine. Only it wasn't a mistake. A certain kind of man never makes a mistake."

Shane raises his head slightly. Clouds are moving deliberately across the moonscape. Soon they'll throw a charcoal blanket across the city.

The wind is tossing around Raymond Kinnock's speech. It's starting to sound like a BBC wartime dispatch on short-wave. "Our history...we celebrate...great country of ours...dedication."

Nickens cocks the pistol and digs it harder into the nape of Shane's neck. It feels small, like a .22. Shane mumbles. "So how is he going to explain away two dead cops?"

Nickens laughs, though it comes out sounding more like a hack. "He's not going to have to explain anything because nobody'll be alive to say he was ever here. As for who'll end up being blamed – well, Kinnock, a certain kind of man always leaves himself with options. There's any number of places he can plant this gun."

Shane doesn't feel it against his neck anymore and glances back. "This gun," Nickens says, "it could end up in Dalton's house up the street. Mr. Lonelyhearts up there, pining away for the wife who left him. Spends every night by himself, not exactly an impressive alibi."

Nickens has loosened his grip on the gun and is running his left hand up and down the barrel and tapping his index finger on the sight. "Nobody could read your interview with the man and not be a little disturbed by it. 'She had it coming to her.' That's what he said, right? Once the gun turns up in his place, your people will see it as case closed."

Again, a hack from Nickens.

"No," he goes on, "he's not going to have to explain anything. And you know – this is beautiful – he could put the gun in Robinson's house. Let's see a nigger try to explain that away."

Shane looks back again. Nickens's grip on the gun is still soft and Shane thinks about going for it but doesn't. So, he stalls. "Somebody who looks like you – him – would have a tough time sneaking in and out of Glick's Court to plant anything."

"Or," Nickens goes on, unlistening, "this could just go down as another unsolved mystery in the Park. What was the phrase that was in the newspaper a few months ago. 'Sometimes strange things just happen in that place and there's no rhyme or reason to them.' He can sit back and do nothing, just watch your local keystone cops fall all over themselves trying to solve this. But whatever he ends up doing, you and the Sarge over there will be watching it all from the same place."

Nickens clutches the gun hard. "Now, turn around towards me, Kinnock. Turn around and sit down."

Shane complies, having no other options.

Nickens picks the flashlight off the ground and shines it in his face, then carefully guides the gun muzzle to the bridge of his nose.

"He likes it," Nickens says, "when he can see the life leave their eyes. A few seconds after the final act. The moment when all recognition passes, and he knows they're his. It's like bringing a woman to a climax."

Nickens moves the gun muzzle around Shane's forehead in small circles.

"You know, Kinnock, you should've seen the show your Rose girl put on after the neck bone broke. The arching back. The rough grunt. The longing stare."

The wind shifts and gusts. "Always remember," Raymond is saying, "our best days are still ahead of us (us, us!). The second half of the Twentieth Century is ours (ours, ours!). So on with the fireworks (works, works!)."

The last sound I'm going to hear on earth will be people cheering my father.

Nickens doesn't shoot. He keeps moving his gun in circles, looking for a place to land it.

Just get it over with.

A bird is trilling overhead. Nickens moves the gun back, just an inch or so, for just a moment.

"Nazca boobie."

"What?"

"The Nazca boobie," Shane says, louder. Nickens moves the gun back slightly. "That's the bird you told the Sarge about, right? I know that bird." *What do I know about the bird? What do I know?*

"You're not really stupid enough to think that's a boobie up there, are you?"

"Me? Hell, no. Of course not. The Nazca boobie flies off of – that island off South America. Floriana, right?"

Nickens drops the flashlight to his side. The wide, blinding strobe is now just a yellow oval on the ground.

"And," Shane stammers, "the thing I love about that bird is, it knows its place. Nickens, you and I know each other, we're two peas in a pod. And you know that I know, that's a bird that knows its place."

"You know about that bird?"

"Yeah, I went to a library and looked it up in an encyclopedia. Because it sounded so interesting." *I looked it up just yesterday because the Sarge said you kept talking about it, and the whole thing sounded fucking weird to me and now I know why.*

The first shell of a fusillade explodes overhead, and all of a sudden Nickens glows in the dark. His gun is poised and ready, but his eyes look blank. "The Nazca boobie, sure enough, it knows its place," he says. "You come into nature and everything's always the same, that's the most wonderous thing about it. The raccoons don't try to mate with the grackles. The bees don't try to pollinate off the dogwoods. And the Nazca boobie, God, if I could only see one, but there's none around here. The boobie, it always stays right there in the same four corners, the same area that's bounded by those tectonic plates a mile below the water. A mile below, imagine that. Somehow or another it knows its boundaries. Why can't everybody be like the fucking booby? Excuse the language."

There are some crack-crack-cracks and some oohs and ahs in the distance, and Shane's watching the .22 as its waves about in front of him, and he's thinking, next time a big one goes off, I'll go after him.

There's movement in the trees, some twigs snapping, a voice. "Shane?"

Nickens wheels around. Another round of firecrackers goes off. Shane can't hear anything else, but he can see gun-spark in front of him and then hears the voice cry out, "My God, my leg."

Three quick flashes above, three staccato bursts of light, give him the chance to see the figure fall. "It's Shiflett," he shouts at Nickens. "You just shot him, goddammit!" He springs to a crouch, but Nickens pushes him back. "He's beyond help, Kinnock. It's all just a matter of time for him, for you too. Just a matter of time."

"Fella," Nickens calls over to Bobby, "you're in the wrong place at the wrong time. Now sit up for me." He points his .22 at Shane. "Go over there and sit down next to your friend."

Pow! A misfired rocket heads wildly for the heavens. It half-explodes in the night void, still wanting to blossom into a golden, overarching palm tree, but it's lost the best part of itself and falls off limply.

There's a lull in the fireworks and Nickens fades to black. Shane bends down to Bobby, who's squirming in pain. He feels around in the dark for Bobby's legs and moves his fingers up and down the left leg: no reaction. He goes to the right leg and hits a soft, wet spot and Bobby screams out. He takes off his necktie and wraps it tight above the wound, which is gaping. *It's bleeding too fast. He's going to need help, real soon.*

He can tell that Nickens is standing motionless, as if he's heard something, and now Shane hears it too, coming from the edge of the Park. Hushed cadences, a giggle, the sounds of adolescent fumbling. "Sounds like a couple of teenagers rolling around up there," Shane whispers towards Nickens. "If I were you, I'd want to move deeper into the Park."

Anything to buy some time.

"Alright," Nickens says, "We're walking." The clouds part for a half-moon and Shane can see Nickens cocking his head, out of habit – a fresh scent is riding in the air – then he turns about, solemn. "You're a Frost man, aren't you, Kinnock? You'll like this, Frost man. Because the woods are lovely, you know, they're dark and they're deep. But I have promises to keep. Oh, do I ever have promises to keep."

Nickens puts both guns on his hips. There's a shine to his features. "But first," he hisses, "you have a job to do." He gestures towards the sergeant. "Move your friend into that ditch over there and cover him up with leaves. Pick up that flashlight and shove it in your back pocket. Then take Shiflett and follow me."

Shane rolls Roncalli over to the gully as if he's a bale of hay. He hears a gurgle inside the carcass. *This isn't you, Sarge. This isn't you.*

He slings Bobby's arms over his shoulders, pulls both of Bobby's hands against his chest, and starts to lumber ahead. He can feel Bobby's light steps behind his heavy steps and he calls back to him, "Can you walk some," he says, and Bobby says, "I'll try" but then he goes slack. When Shane says, "Bobby!" he gets no reply.

Shane can feel the back of his right pants leg getting wet: Bobby's blood, seeping slowly. A few feet behind Bobby is Nickens. "Hurry up. He wants you to hurry up."

Shane loses the grip on Bobby's right hand and he starts to drop. Shane's knees buckle but he's able to grab Bobby's hand and hoist him up again. He feels Bobby's wheeze against his back, it's steady and rhythmic, and he feels himself getting stronger, as if his lungs are being filled with the breath of two.

They're moving farther from the amphitheatre but they can still hear festive noise. More eruptions; a band playing "Yankee Doodle Dandy." Shane smells gunpowder, and hot cinders land in his hair. On the ground in front of him is a large, singed cardboard cylinder. *There's no way they should be firing these things towards the woods, but they are. They're firing them right towards us.*

Nickens shouts, "Move it!"

Shane answers, "Why did he kill her?" He doesn't shout.

"What?"

Shane moves straight ahead. "Why did he kill her?" Again, he doesn't shout. He wants Nickens next to him.

The path has widened. Shane hears quick footsteps behind him. Even Haynes Nickens needs to share his heroics with somebody.

Nickens is now on his left shoulder, bumping up against him as he struggles with Bobby. Nickens has both guns by his side. "He was watching her for a very long time," Nickens says.

"Longer than he was told to, right? A lot longer."

"She had a beautiful white dress she'd often wear. And another outfit with a cardinal-red jacket. So many nights, this lovely white girl, cavorting around with that nigger-lover Joe Barry."

From the amphitheatre: *A real-life nephew of my Uncle Sam, born on the Fourth of July …*

"So why – "

"It was hard enough when she was with that nigger-lover Barry. Then she had to meet up with a nigger. Right there, just a few feet from my Park."

The blasts overhead are getting so loud that Shane now has to raise his voice. "How'd that happen?"

"Barry stood her up. He was supposed to meet her at the café up there but he never showed. So, she left, and next thing you know she was outside the place, talking with one of them."

"What did you, what did he think when he saw her with one of them?"

"She was in that cardinal outfit. He looked at her, up there with the nigger, and it was like she was taunting him, like she was challenging him to do something, thinking he was weak, that he'd never amount to anything."

Bobby groans again but Shane can still feel his life-breath and surges forward. "So, he killed her," Shane says, "and he took her purse so it might look like a robbery. And then he cut off her finger. And he sent it to Jake Kauffman. Right, Nickens? Jake Kaufman."

Nickens stops short, then starts walking again, more slowly. "He'd followed her enough to know who she kept company with. He knew about her being with Kaufman."

"So, the finger went to Kaufman, and Kaufman took it from there."

Bobby is whimpering with every labored step Shane takes, and the fireworks above are in full force, but the mirth in Nickens's voice is still audible. "You know," he says, "right as it was all happening, as the girl was arching her back – "

"*Go on.*"

"– he heard somebody on the hill above, and he had to take the finger off the body fast." Nickens chortles and bends over. "It was easy, really. A man can cut through finger cartilage just like that. It's not as if it's the breastbone of a Doberman, for God's sake."

Bobby starts to convulse and Shane thinks he might be going into shock but then he settles down.

"So if Barry was never in the café, how did his fingerprint end up on the receipt?"

"It never did. Who was it that was trusted with everything, even the evidence? When a man has that kind of play, saying it so makes it so."

"Did you – he – go back to check on the girl's body later?" *Keep asking questions, buy more time.*

"Of course. By then it was buried in the sand pile."

"He was a lucky man."

"Luck is the residue of design."

"And so, he killed Emily, and he killed the girl last night. What about others from the Park. The Meslin girl, the lagoon girl. And the eight-year-old boy."

"You're starting to get on his nerves."

The path widens further, into an open field. Nickens strides in front of Shane, guns still by his side, and gazes at the light show in the sky as if it were all meant for him. "Bring Shiflett over here," he says to Shane. "Lie him down on his back and you sit down next to him. And give me the flashlight."

The grand finale is about to begin. Booming sound and dazzling light.

With a grunt Shane eases Bobby onto the ground, seeing his friend's ebbing lifeblood mix with the dirt underneath him.

Four robust bursts follow, one after the other, and four flares scream into the atmosphere.

For a couple of moments the woods are quiet, waiting for the tumult. Then, *thud!*

A gray speck trails behind the four flares. It's a dud, for sure. Shane says, "Look up there, Nickens. Those golden streamers and that poor gray speck just chasing. Chasing and watching, just like you always do. Chasing and watching, but it'll never catch up, as long as it tries."

Nickens stares at the sky. The four flares climb high but the gray speck stalls right overhead, and then it suddenly gets bigger and bigger and it lands with a crash not ten feet in front of them, and Nickens flinches.

Shane jumps over Bobby and lunges for Nickens and grabs both of his wrists and forces him backwards. Nickens hits the ground and his .22 flies out of his right hand and Shane wrests the other gun from him.

It's all over so fast that Shane can't take it all in. He has his service revolver against Nickens's temple and his knees on Nickens's chest and chaos reigns above and all around him.

Haynes Nickens is laughing.

"What do you find so funny?"

"You're going to try to take him in now, aren't you?"

Shane grabs him under the arms to lift him up, but Nickens goes limp. "He's not going anywhere."

Shane cocks the gun but Nickens is mocking him.

"You forget, Kinnock, your file is an open book. It must have been just like this for you on Guadalcanal. The night sky, shells overhead, a moral dilemma. An expedient choice you've had to live with for years, your whole life changed in a few minutes. You've never been the same. Here's your moral choice, all over again."

In Shane's mind he sees the Sarge gawking up at the leaf blanket resting on top of him.

"There's no choice here," he says.

"Oh, there's *always* a choice, especially here. You can drag your man in, get him off the streets, make sure he doesn't kill again, save lives and all that. But it'll take awhile, and he's not going to make it easy, and your friend over there will die, for sure. And if this sounds familiar, there's a reason. You craven fucking *fuck*, it's what you did before. All about numbers, all about how to save the most people. Do you want to live with that kind of decision all over again? Do you really want to leave your friend here to die, just so you can play hero and take your man in? Or do you want to just let your man go, you can even take the guns. Let him go, you'll never see him again, and you can be on your way with Shiflett there in five seconds, maybe even save him."

Shane eases off Nickens, who rises to sit, adjusts his bow tie, brushes himself off.

He says, "Look, Nickens, between you and me."

Nickens picks at a whirligig on his pants, flicks it off.

"Between you and me, Nickens." Shane takes him by his tie.

Nickens looks up.

Shane puts a bullet in his brain.

Shane waits. He sees the mouth go wide, the eyes start to go backwards.

"Between you and me, Nickens. I've got miles to go before I sleep. *Miles* to go before I sleep."

December 1952

"The rock is a God of faithfulness and without iniquity, righteous and just is he, perfect in all his works. Who can say to him, what have you done? He rules below and above, he brings death and he restores life, he brings down to the grave and he raises up from the grave."

The rabbi pauses to wipe the winter mist from his glasses. A cemetery worker steps up with an umbrella to hold over him.

The worker's too late. A sudden downpour is already drenching the rabbi.

He pockets his prayer book and goes on from memory.

"Please give us the kindness that we don't deserve. In the name of Isaac, who was found on the altar like a lamb, please grant our request."

A plain wooden coffin, indifferent to the hard rain, sits in a hole in the ground beneath a headstone. The worker with the umbrella stands ready to fill the hole when the time comes. The headstone bears two long strips of tape that cover an inscription.

Bobby's in his uniform, Shane's in his best Hecht's glen plaid suit, burn-hole now mended. Both of them are soaked to the bone. A cold wind blows the rain in their faces.

Down the hill a car is passing by, windows down, radio trumpeting a Christmas tune. It fades as the car rounds a bend.

The rabbi chants for a time in Hebrew.

Bobby's cane is slowly sinking into the wet ground. It slips and Shane catches his elbow. It's the first time Bobby's spent more than a half-hour outside since a six-month hospital stay.

"This'll all be over soon," Shane tells him.

The rabbi goes back to English for the benefit of Shane and Bobby, the only mourners there.

"May the great name be blessed forever and for all eternity. Blessed and praised, glorified, exalted and extolled. Honored, adored and lauded be the name of the holy one, blessed be he."

The rabbi looks at Shane and Bobby and nods. Shane nods back, silent.

The rabbi nods again, twice. Shane nods twice.

The rabbi mouths the word, "Amen," and Shane says, "Amen," and then Bobby says, "Amen."

"Gentlemen," the rabbi says, "please come forward and take a shovel."

Two hours ago, Shane helped to dig the hole for the coffin. A mound of dirt sits next to it. The mound is mostly mud now. He starts shoveling chunks of it onto the coffin. Bobby puts his cane to one side and joins in.

Plop. Plop. Plop.

To anyone who seeks finality, look for it in a ritual that celebrates the timeless.

The top of the coffin is now covered.

The rabbi goes to the large headstone and pulls away the pieces of tape, revealing the hand-carved engraving.

EMMA HADASSAH ROSENBLUM

December 3, 1927 -- May 1, 1951

The inscription nicely fills the gap between

ERIN SHEILA KINNOCK

November 16, 1917 -- October 15, 1940

and

SHANE FRANCIS KINNOCK

November 16, 1917 --

The rabbi works the balled-up tape in his fingers. He chants in Hebrew then goes back again to English. "May the all-merciful one shelter her with the blanket of his wings forever, and bind her soul in the bond of life. The Lord is her heritage. May she rest in her resting place in peace and let us say –"

"*Amen.*"

The harsh rain lightens to a soft crystal screen.

The rabbi comes over to Shane. He's still kneading the ball of tape in his hands. "I hope I've done the right thing here."

"Believe me, you have."

"We never do this. You know our tradition."

"I know it and as I told you before I respect it. Jews only being buried among other Jews. I wouldn't do this if it wasn't – appropriate."

"But her family isn't here today, none of them. Are you absolutely sure they approve of this?"

Shane has a vision of Leah at his bedside at St. E's.

When an Irishman proposes marriage the question he asks the girl isn't, will you marry me? It's, would you like to be buried with my people?

Buried with your people. That's good, remember that.

"Yes," Shane says, "they approve."

In a yellow grass patch, in what seems like another life, Shane came upon a white-yellow orb with a pulsing life force. Now it lies in repose.

The rabbi leaves, still worrying over the tape ball in his hand. The cemetery worker starts to fill up the hole in the ground, but Shane stops him. "Give us a minute here, okay?"

"Okay, boss."

Bobby says, "I guess everything's all together now, huh? More or less. Best as it could be."

"I guess it is, Bobby. I guess it is."

"How'd you ever get your father to go along with burying Emily here?"

"It was a contest of wills and I won."

Actually, it wasn't much of a contest.

In August, Raymond maneuvered Drew Pearson into exposing the connection between Joe Barry, Emily and Jake Kaufman. In the process he managed to kill Barry's Senate campaign for good. It would be his last triumph.

In November he managed to win reelection but just barely, and maybe not at all, since the vote count is still being contested in court. His party lost the House of Representatives, so he lost all his committee chairmanships and any hope to ever be Speaker. And Joe Barry's friends on the Hill exacted special revenge by moving him and all the photographs of him and his famous friends to three puny rooms that used to hold office supplies. With all of that, along with the rumors that Louis Carlsberg was about to roll over on him, Raymond faced too many battles to take on another one, and Shane knew it.

Any good son, faced with a flawed father, finds a way to surpass him.

Shane goes in his pocket and pulls out the Polaroid of Emily at the table with the revelers from her office. The picture has now faded to the point where only Emily's image is visible, and just barely. Shane holds Bobby by the arm and they walk over to the side of the grave. He drops the picture into the opening. It flutters and lands lightly on the mud-encased coffin.

They take the zigzag path to the cemetery gate. Shane eases his pace to hang next to Bobby. "Thanks for saving that picture when I was at the hospital."

Bobby stays quiet. When he speaks, his voice is rough. "I've been wantin' to find a way to say thanks to you."

"I owe you more than you could ever owe me. When you pulled me out of that car, you risked your life when you didn't have to. And as for me, when I saved your ass, I saved my own too."

The drizzle has stopped. Bobby clears his throat. "So you sure you're gonna be free and clear on what happened to Nickens?"

"Faye's not even putting it to the grand jury. He said to me, 'I may not have done what you did, but I can see why you did it.'"

Which are exactly the same words that Faye used about what Shane had to do to Bob Cushing on Guadalcanal.

Bobby stops and drops his cane. Shane moves to pick it up but Bobby waves him off, stands dead still for a moment, and then walks, Shane counts ten paces, then back ten more. He's wobbly at the end and Shane seizes the cane from the ground but Bobby waves him off again and turns.

"I'm not goin' back to policin', at least not right away."

Willie Robinson's plight made him a hero to Negroes across the country and he started receiving money from groups all around the South. "So," Bobby says, "him an' Reverend Williamson are puttin' together folks to go around down there and hold rallies, organize folks. An' I started thinkin', he's gonna need a bodyguard, so I asked him if I can do it once my leg heals up and he said yeah."

Shane lays both hands on Bobby's shoulders. "You're a constant surprise, my friend."

He looks down at Bobby's jacket lapel and points to the pin that the Sarge gave him, and Shane gave Bobby. "What you're going to be doing isn't going to be easy. Look at this pin and you'll know you're never alone down there."

Shane turns away so Bobby won't see his eyes.

They come to the main gate.

Bran Bentley is standing on the other side.

Shane tells Bobby, go ahead to the car, I'll catch up.

Brantley starts. "I heard you were doing this today."

"And who'd you hear that from?"

"People. And I wanted to pay my respects to her."

"Because you knew her."

"I did, a little." Bentley looks sheepish. Considering that he's a man who was born without the trait that produces guilt or shame, this is an event. "I knew she was a friend of Joe. Okay, girlfriend."

"And you never told me you knew her, had laid eyes on her, nothing."

" Joe Barry and I came to Washington a few years ago, and I landed in Georgetown, and he was one of the first people I met. A guy's allowed to have friends, right?"

"He's not allowed to help them out by holding back on a murder investigation."

"Who was it that put you onto Claire? Me, right? You ended up getting what you needed. Joe told me early on that he didn't have anything to do with Emily's murder and I believed him. And I was right."

"You betrayed my confidence. You told him what I was telling you about the case, off the record."

"No, never."

"So how come it was that when I talked to him, he seemed to know everything about what I was doing?"

"Because I told him some of what I was finding out about the case on my own. Newsflash here, your department is one big sieve. And, believe it or not, he really wanted to know whether any of you were getting close to finding out who killed her. Because, believe it or not, he cared about her."

There's more that Shane wants to say but he holds off. By now the cemetery worker has probably dumped half of the wet dirt into the open grave. In just a while a flat brown rectangle will mark the plot. Next spring fresh sod will sprout green and next fall it will brown, and by then the name **EMILY HADASSAH ROSENBLUM**, now so vividly etched in the stone, will have started to fade just ever so slightly. Down the street, in the distance, Bobby is leaning against a street sign, bent over to catch his breath, In a month or so, he'll be riding around trying to protect a man that every Dixie lunatic will want to lynch.

At this moment any grudge that Shane has against Bran Bentley or Joe Barry doesn't seem worth the energy it would take to hold onto it.

He shakes Bentley's hand. "Don't let me keep you," he says. "Go do what you came to do."

Bentley unlatches the gate. He stops. "Can I just ask you a question, something I'm curious about."

"Shoot."

"Wordless Willie, that whole thing about him not talking. Was it all a silent protest or was there something more?" Bentley slides a notebook out of his back pocket.

"Don't you ever stop working? No notebook."

Shane goes on to tell Bentley everything that Willie told Bobby and Bobby told Shane after it all was over. How most of Willie not talking, that was the protest, he went down that road from the very beginning. And he was way down that road when he figured out something else, that he had a truth inside him, and that he always promised his mama he'd tell the truth, every time he was asked, about anything, everything. And he knew if he told his truth, it would kill him. So on top of his not wanting to talk, there was a good reason not to.

"And what was his truth?"

"His truth was, he met up with Emily that night. She was in the café all by herself. And Willie could tell she was a gal who was dressed up for a date, and the date stood her up, and she started crying right there at the table. So his shift ended and he changed into his street clothes and then he saw her get up to leave."

"He followed her?"

"He felt bad for her and he wanted to talk to her, just to make her feel better, nothing else. And he went outside to see if she'd even talk to him on a public street. What with him being him, and her being her. And she stayed and talked with him. Because, you know –"

"Because she talked with everybody." For just a moment there's no cynical rasp in Bentley's voice.

"And Willie somehow came up with something to say that calmed her down. And she was ready to go home. Only by that time, there weren't many taxis going across the Calvert Street Bridge."

"And she damned sure wasn't going to get one with him standing there."

"So he went back to the café to call one for her, and when he came back out she was gone. And he never thought anything about it until after he got charged with killing her. And he knew that if he ever said he'd been with her that night it'd be the last nail in his coffin."

Bentley puts his notebook back in his jacket pocket. "There are some stories I'd never even try to write," he says. "Because I could never do them justice."

Shane starts walking towards his car, then stops. "All this time we thought she was killed over something that was close to her. Now we know it was over something that had nothing to do with her. Something that's always been bigger than all of us, maybe always will be."

"Listen," Bentley says, "let me pay my respects here. Then you and me, we'll go for a couple of drinks. They'll be on me."

Up ahead, by the street sign, Bobby waits. "I'll pass," Shane says to Bentley. "I've got to get Shiflett back home."

"But the day is young."

"And I have one more thing to do. On the case. Before I put it all to bed."

Shane sees the look on Bentley's face and thinks, he'd never understand.

****

A week ago winter's first frost slowed Rock Creek. A day ago winter's first thaw freed it up again. Now it dances near Shane's feet.

From his suit jacket pocket he takes out the shorthand diary that Emily kept in the name of Barbara Earnshaw. The first few pages, before the entries start, are given over to the sort of matters that would introduce a child's copybook. "Weights and Measures," "National Holidays," "The Proper Use of the Flag." And, "What the Stars Foretell." Shane recalls Emily's birthday – December 3 – and goes to "SAGITTARIUS (November 23 to December 21)":

They love liberty and freedom, and are very independent. They dislike a master and will allow no one to order or drive them about. In disposition they're frank, fearless, impulsive, outspoken, energetic, ambitious, sincere and quick to arrive at conclusions. They're sympathetic and loving, intuitive and prophetic. At times they're restless and high strung. In the professions or the political world they're generally aggressive, progressive, and aspiring. In these realms, the sky's the limit.

Emily underlined "very independent" and "will allow no one to order or drive them about." And she wrote two exclamation points in the margins.

The diary entries begin on January 4, 1950, a Wednesday. From that day on, every page is filled. The ink colors vary back and forth between black and blue, some days' events meriting bolder pen strokes than others. Only the occasional number is readable. "34th," "28-14," "7th".

Shane once intended to have it all translated. *What's in all that spaghetti writing? So many answers, to so many questions.* He never will. Everything else about the former Emma Hadassah Rosenblum has been exposed, let her have one small piece of privacy preserved.

Against the back cover of the diary, a newspaper clipping is pressed. Shane came across it in the diary a few weeks ago. He unfolds it and reads it again.

GIRL'S DEATH RULED SUICIDE
By a New York Times Staff Reporter

A 15-year-old girl was found dead in her room in her Brooklyn residence shortly after 1 p.m. yesterday. Police say her death was an apparent suicide by hanging. The girl was identified as Leah Rosenblum, a tenth grader at the Central Yeshiva High School for Girls. Her step parents, Mr. and Mrs. Jakob Siegel, found her body.

Miss Rosenblum is survived by the Siegels and an older sister, Emma. A private burial service is planned.

The clipping is two years old, dated November 12, 1950.

The Sarge always told him, Let God find you. Little did either of them know that the God who would finally find Shane would turn out to be a teenaged Jewish girl.

He takes the clipping, tears it in half and tosses it into the rushing creek. He gently tears out all the pages of the diary and tosses them in too, page after page of scribbled inscrutability.

He stands and watches as they bob gently southwards and eastwards, towards the great unknowable sea.

****

It's 2:45. School will be letting out in 10 minutes.

Shane crosses the Sousa bridge, bound for the city's southeastern edge. On his lap is a map that he glances at as he weaves through traffic. He rarely crosses this bridge, rarely comes over to this part of town, which is so sparsely populated that taxi drivers won't accept passengers who want to come over here from downtown because they know they won't get a return fare.

He takes a left when he should take a right, makes a U-turn, corrects his course and then promptly makes another wrong turn. *Fuck*, he says under his breath.

Finally, he pulls up to a school. He hears a bell ringing and a group of little girls wearing matching plaid uniforms and carrying bookbags rush out the front door, followed by a group of older boys in pressed white shirts and blue pants, with another group of girls behind them. Some boys and girls pile into cars parked at the entrance, others run to mothers who've been waiting on benches, smoking.

Shane parks his car next to the school playground. He walks between the swing-sets and the teeter-totters, past a baseball field, towards the school entrance. If he were paying more attention to it, he'd notice that the playground very much resembles another one across town, the one that once gave up its sandpiles to bury a dead girl with dignity.

But he's not seeing that. What he's seeing is, a mother walking up to a boy and hugging him.

He knows the mother. Her name is Maureen.

He knows the boy. His name is Buddy.

He's seeing the mother clearly. She looks almost the same as she did when he last saw her six years ago. Shorter hair, still so pretty.

He's seeing the boy, really a young man, shy away from the hug and shake his head. The boy's broad shouldered, he has the build of a ballplayer.

He's seeing a woman who never really had a chance to have a marriage.

He's seeing a boy who spent his childhood without a father.

He's seeing a blank space between the words in a holy book.

****

Acknowledgments

I would like to express here my immense gratitude to, not to mention my unreserved admiration for, four individuals without whose assistance, advice and encouragement this book wouldn't have been published, certainly not in its present form. It's no exaggeration to say that *Rock Creek* is the end result of years of effort. Each of these individuals was involved in a discreet phase of the project. All of them were fellow travelers with me on this journey, at different times. It is appropriate, then, for me to credit them in the chronological order of their collaborations with me.

Howard Yoon, of William Morris Endeavor, represented me in the publication of my first book, a non-fiction work entitled *Relentless Pursuit*. The concept for *Rock Creek* was born in 15 minutes during a lunch we had shortly after the release of *Relentless Pursuit*; Howard's particular genius lies in framing a good story. Over many, many months to come, through multiple drafts consuming reams of paper – and later their electronic equivalent – he devoted endless time, and (almost!) endless patience, to help me develop this work. His counsel, guidance and support were and are invaluable to me.

Jonas Goodman edited this manuscript in the incarnation that immediately preceded the one that is before the reader. As any author can attest, the editing process can be prolonged and frustrating. A friend of mine in the publishing industry once advised me, "If you don't hate your editor, they're not doing their job." Well, Jonas did his job, and we're great friends. The experience of being able to work with him was sublime. I only have two things in common with F. Scott Fitzgerald and Ernest Hemingway: I've now published more than one book, and I know what it's like to partner with an editor who has all the virtues of the legendary Maxwell Perkins.

Due in no small part to Jonas' reference, Paul Bresnick took on *Rock Creek* as its agent. The list of authors that Paul has either edited or represented reads like a "Who's Who" of modern American literature. I'm truly humbled just to be on the roster of his past and present clients. Much more than that, though, I thank him for his unstinting belief in the promise of *Rock Creek*, and the unerring sagacity of the advice he provided to me throughout this process.

Finally: my friend of 40 years, Jeffrey Londa. The journey that many if not most books take from writer's mind to reader's eye is an arduous one. This book's journey unexpectedly took it through a legal minefield that for a time threatened its very existence. The circumstances behind this unwelcome change of course are irrelevant here. What matters is that *Rock Creek* survived intact, thanks in no small part to the extraordinarily generous assistance I received from Jeff -- a lawyer, and a person, *par excellence.* We met while working on a case together many years ago, and the only saving grace of this unfortunate detour was that it gave me a chance to practice law with Jeff all over again.

Printed in the USA
CPSIA information can be obtained
at www.ICGtesting.com
CBHW071139140724
11573CB00006B/164